PATRIOTS

PATRIOTS

William Morris Endeavor Entertainment, LLC
1325 Avenue of the Americas
New York, New York 10019
Attn: Britton Schey

ISBN-13: 9781475141962
ISBN-10: 1475141963

PATRIOTS

a novel

by David Frum

For Linda Frum

Most loving of sisters,
Finest of senators,
Dearest of friends.

CHAPTER 1

I didn't get the job through merit, my girlfriend said. But then, I didn't get my girlfriend through merit either.

I got her the way I get everything.

"What's your name?" she shouted over the party noise.

"Walter."

"Walter what?"

"Walter Schotzke."

"Like the mustard?"

"Yes, that's right."

"Kind of funny to be named after a mustard."

"The mustard's named after me."

That's how it had started with my previous girlfriend, and the one before that, and the one before that. After a couple of months, though, visions of the glamorous life of the future Mrs. Walter Schotzke bumped up against actual life with Walter Schotzke.

"Walter, where are we going?"

"I'm going to play a little Xbox."

"No I mean *us* – where are we going?"

"You want to play Xbox too?"

Valerie never asked such questions. I don't remember exactly how she ended up living in my apartment. Or telling the cleaning lady what to do. Or becoming best friends with my grandmother. She just did it.

She was doing it again that morning.

"Hey," I said sleepily, "it's 6 AM!"

"Don't you like it?" Valerie murmured from beneath the covers. "Do you want me to stop?"

"I like it," I admitted. "But I'd like it better at nine."

Her tousled brown hair and big matching eyes emerged from below the sheets. "We have to be on the road by nine. It's your grandmother's birthday, we're expected for lunch."

Oh no. I protested: "I'm not going!"

"Don't be silly, of course we're going." The long straight nose pointed downward to its target. "Now shhh – we're going to start the day in a good mood."

Three hours later, and my old Range Rover was inching across the Whitestone Bridge on the way to Little Compton.

"I can't believe I'm doing this."

Valerie rested a calming hand on my forearm. In black slacks and beige silk blouse, she looked demure, even prim: not a hint of the seductress of three hours before. The long dark-brown hair that had bounced so wantonly before dawn was now tied into a sporty ponytail.

"Your grandmother is the only family you have."

"That's not my fault."

"She loves you."

"She loved my dad. Me – I remind her of my mother."

"Your dad was a great man."

"Fine. I know. Everybody says so. They don't add anything to his reputation by trashing my mom."

"Your grandmother doesn't trash your mom."

"She enjoys hearing others do it."

"Besides, she gives you all your money."

"She doesn't give me money. It's my money."

"Well she decides how much of it you can have, which is next to the same thing."

Three more hours, and we were pulling past bare late autumn trees into a suspiciously empty driveway.

"Where's everybody else?" I demanded.

Valerie opened the car door. The smell and sound of ocean poured into the cabin. "The other guests are joining for dinner. It's just us for lunch – your grandmother thought that would be nicer."

"It would be nicer to eat my lunch in the tiger cage at the zoo."

"That's not funny."

"I don't want to stay for dinner with her dismal friends. And I don't want to drive back to the city in the middle of the night."

"You don't have to drive back in the middle of the night, we're staying over. I packed your toiletries and a tie."

Valerie opened the back of the Range Rover. She extracted a small powder-blue suitcase and presented it to me to carry.

"Staying over? Where? Grandma never allows unmarried couples to stay over."

"Well, she and I talked about it, and she said she'd make an exception this one time. Hey - there she is. Happy birthday, Clara!" Valerie ran across the gravel and up the two verandah steps to kiss my grandmother's proffered cheek.

"It's wonderful to see you, Valerie. Hello, Walter."

"It's so good to see you too!" Valerie beckoned to me. "Come kiss your grandmother."

I did my duty.

Until you drew near enough to see the deep creases around her mouth, the polished black cane in my grandmother's hand was the only clue that the birthday she was celebrating lay on the further side of eighty. She stood straight and tall and slim; her white hair still full and thick.

I followed my grandmother and Valerie into the familiar front hall. When my grandparents bought the house in 1954, my grandmother had repainted bright white the old dark wood paneling. Between the panels, she had pasted lurid wallpapers:

white and lime; white and tangerine; white and watermelon. You could almost make a fruit salad out of her color choices.

Around the corner from the hall, on the way to the (raspberry mousse) guest bathroom, there glared a huge dark oil portrait: the founder of the family fortune.

The ancestral Schotzke had been short and round, black-haired and red-faced. Luckily for me, I had not inherited any of *that*. In late middle age, my great-great grandfather had married a pretty girl from the old country, with the result that his two sons and four daughters emerged significantly less short, less round, less black-haired and less red-faced than their progenitor. My grandmother had improved the family looks even more, and as for my mother – well, she stopped traffic, quite literally. In her last year of high school in New Jersey, she had skipped class to spend a day with friends in New York City. A motorist on Canal Street gawked at her minidress so hard that he smashed into the car in front of him. When the rear-ended driver jumped out of her car, the driver who had caused the accident just pointed at my mother. The rear-ended driver happened to work for one of the big New York modeling agencies. A star was born.

Valerie and I walked through the hall into my grandmother's sunroom. I'd spent a lot of summer afternoons playing on the lawn beyond those windows. My mother would be away filming one of her direct-to-cable movies. My father would be traveling in Europe or the Middle East. Between sessions at summer camp, I'd be deposited with two distracted old people.

Those empty summer days blur together in my memory now, but there's one I will never forget. It was after my parents' separation, but before my father's death. My grandfather was serving late afternoon drinks on the verandah to some business friends. I was indoors, lying on the sunroom floor, watching an ant crawl across the aquamarine carpet. One of the guests began to talk loud and to laugh in a way I did not like.

"I saw your ex-daughter-in-law's new movie last night," he boomed. "That girl may be crazy, but you gotta appreciate her body."

My grandfather's voice abruptly turned icy. "That's the mother of my grandson you're talking about, and don't you ever forget it."

The loud man started to apologize. Through the wall of the house, I heard my grandmother's voice, low and fierce. "I wish *she* wouldn't forget it."

Settled now in that same sunroom, my grandmother and Valerie exchanged pleasantries about the plans for the evening's party. At one o'clock, my grandmother's shuffling ancient houseman, Eduardo, opened the door to the Chinese red dining room.

We took seats. Eduardo passed a platter of grilled sole around the table. My grandmother served herself first, her one deviation from a lifetime's worship at the altar of Emily Post. She never trusted anybody to know what to do with the serving spoons unless she demonstrated. What she was demonstrating today was how to find the *Guinness Book of Records* smallest slice of sole ever imagined as a meal. Valerie served herself the runner-up. Eduardo presented the platter to me last. I reached for a piece, then a second, then a third. Valerie and my grandmother looked at me curiously. I dropped the third fillet to rejoin the rest of the school. The platter vanished into the kitchen. Next passed a dish of tiny boiled potatoes, then tinier roasted squash and miniaturized zucchini, then finally a great silver boat filled with butter sauce. My grandmother spooned out just enough to lubricate a contact lens. Valerie emulated her. I splashed sauce all around my plate.

After Eduardo poured white wine into our glasses, Valerie excused herself to retrieve something from her powder-blue suitcase. A moment later, she reappeared and placed a lavishly gift-wrapped box on the dining-room table.

"Oh Valerie, how thoughtful of you!" exclaimed my grandmother.

"Walter and I found it in London, when we stopped on our way back from South Africa last month. Your friend Mr. Henchley helped us." The paper rustled, the latch on the wooden box was popped, and my grandmother's ringed fingers extracted from the padded interior a statuette of a flirting couple: a big-titted girl in a too-tight dress with a come-get-me smile painted on her porcelain face and a young man who looked like he'd rather go get the pageboy at stage left.

My grandmother studied the nauseating object with genuine delight.

"It was made for King Louis of Bavaria. Mr. Henchley bought it at the Ratonne estate auction. He says it's very rare and important."

"It's beautiful," my grandmother agreed after a connoisseur's pause. I winced as I anticipated the invoice from Mr. Henchley. Valerie was fibbing about the "Walter and I" bit. On our first morning in London, as I slept off the business-class champagne, Valerie had slipped out to "meet friends." But my grandmother accepted the improbable story and smiled an unforced smile at me: "Your taste is improving."

The wine did not return.

After lunch, we returned to the sunroom. The carpet had faded over the years, but the orange cushions on the white wicker chairs glared as luridly as ever. Eduardo shut the doors upon us, and my grandmother proceeded direct to business.

"Walter, neither of us is getting any younger. You are 28. At your age, your father was already heading all of our overseas operations. You on the other hand have been let go from two different investment banks. The marketing job did not work out. The volunteer teaching program thought you should employ your talents elsewhere. The Peace Corps turned you down. You would not consider the military. I spoke to the people at General Brands, and while there will always be some kind of a job for a Schotzke, I'm not prepared to ask for that job until I feel more confident that you will meet your responsibilities. Frankly, I had almost run out of ideas."

I stared at the carpet in front of my feet. No ants today.

"But it's important that a young man with your advantages in life contribute something to society. After Valerie and I talked last week, I had one last thought. You remember Senator Hazen?"

My grandmother always spoke to me as if I could not be expected to remember anything other than the schedule of trust fund pay-out dates. Valerie sensed my reaction, because she caught my eye to look pleadingly at me. I bit back my words and nodded yes.

"Good. Senator Hazen used to do some of your grandfather's legal work before he entered politics. He was wonderful to us after … after we lost your father. He has an opening in his Senate office in Washington. Filing, answering the telephone, tasks even you cannot mishandle. I told him you would be delighted to accept. You'll meet people. It will pull you out of yourself. Perhaps you'll learn something about this country that has been so good to our family."

Another pleading look from Valerie, and I bit back my words again. Without waiting for me to speak, my grandmother asked Valerie: "Will you help Walter organize the move?"

Evidently calling a moving van fell into the category of tasks it was possible for me to mishandle.

"Of course!" Valerie answered.

Now at last there was a short pause, a chance for the accused to pronounce a few words to sway the court.

"Grandma, I don't think I really want to …"

My grandmother frowned, cut me off.

"If you don't want to, you have until next month to produce another idea for full-time, year-round work of some use to society. Otherwise, the distributions from the trust funds will stop until you inherit under your father's and grandfather's wills. And that does not happen until you turn thirty-five."

"It's a wonderful idea!" Valerie declared. She grasped my hand to turn me toward her. "Your friend Samir is in Washington, you always say nobody ever made you laugh like Samir. Charlie Feltrini – you like him! And Annie Hampton from your class at Brown, I read in your alumni magazine that she just got an economist's job at the Treasury Department ..."

She was reading the alumni magazine?

"Annie Hampton was my girlfriend in junior year."

"I know," she replied serenely. "Annie and I are Facebook friends."

Outmaneuvered, as usual. I tried again. "But Valerie, what about you? It's a long train ride." That came out sounding even more sarcastic than I had intended. Valerie only smiled lovingly. "I'll come with you. Don't worry, I'll find work." Still holding my hand, she finished, "Thank you, Clara. It's such a great chance for Walter. We both appreciate everything you do for us."

My grandmother smiled back at her. "Thank you, Valerie." The smile vanished as she turned to me. "You're welcome, Walter."

CHAPTER 2

Three days after my grandmother's birthday party, Valerie and I rode the train to Washington to tour apartments. She made her choice of home as decisively as she'd made her choice of me.

"It's perfect!" she announced of the fourth apartment on our list. "You can practically walk to work from here. The second bedroom is worth the money. We can turn into a TV room so you can play a video game without worrying that you're bothering me."

"There's a gym in the building," the agent added helpfully.

"That's fantastic!" said Valerie. "We can get you exercising more regularly."

I shot the agent a dirty look, but her back was already turned. "Come see the roof deck."

A few moments later, the three of us overlooked more domes and columns than the Caesars ever built. The agent's finger traced the skyline. "You can see the National Archives just over that building. There's the Washington Monument! And look – the Capitol!"

We signed the papers that afternoon and moved a week later. My New York apartment had been decorated with family hand-me-downs. Somehow, Valerie persuaded my grandmother to release a small moving and furnishing fund. I told her she could decorate the apartment any way she wanted. What she wanted was to live in an apartment that looked like a room from a W hotel, all white and beige.

Until the new furniture arrived, the only place to sit (other than my soon-to-be-discarded old bed) was a lurid red kilim sofa that my mother had bought to outfit my first prep school dorm room. Aside from a few photographs and postcards and a pair of gold cufflinks, that sofa was my only inheritance from my mother. Everything else had gone to settle her debts, except for a few pieces of jewelry somehow reclaimed by my father's estate and now safeguarded in a trust-fund safe.

In the echoing apartment still smelling of fresh paint, Valerie cooked an improvised dinner in the two pots that had survived her purge of my old junk. "Until I can find a job and start contributing to the rent, it seems the least I can do," Valerie said as she poured sautéed tomatoes and onions over brown linguini. "It's the easiest recipe in the book. I'll try something more ambitious tomorrow."

"Maybe I should learn too."

"Later. There's something else you have to study first."

She disappeared for a moment, then returned with a new-looking brushed-chrome tablet computer. She laid it on the insta-table in front of me.

"Valerie!"

"Don't worry, I didn't pay for it. There was a little money left over from your grandmother's furniture budget. But I did buy these."

She hunched over the tablet and touched the screen. "Subscriptions to the *Washington Guardian*, the *Wall Street Transcript* and the *New York Tribune*. I signed you up for the morning bulletins from SitRep.com and HillCall. I've also downloaded for you that new book about the war in Mexico that was reviewed in the *Tribune* last Sunday."

Valerie registered my lack of enthusiasm.

"I'm not trying to pile up homework for you. But it probably would be a good idea if you understood what happened in the election."

"I know what happened. The black guy lost."

"Maybe a more sophisticated answer?"

"The crippled guy won."

"Please – read."

"I do read!"

"Yes, but usually not until after you've failed the course. Remember that party at the Ambersons in March?"

"Was that the breast-cancer party or the famine-in-Africa party?"

"Don't be sarcastic. Anyway I got into conversation there with your old headmaster from Wellfleet."

"Jesus, Valerie, what are you, the Stasi? Can't a man have any secrets?"

"He said, 'If Walter had handed in more of his assignments, he'd have done much better at school.'"

"Wow, thanks."

"He meant it kindly. Now here's the chance to let the world to know what you can do. Make this chance count."

I collected the empty plates to put in the dishwasher

"Don't run away," she said as I stood up.

"My best trick."

CHAPTER 3

The office of Senator Philip B. Hazen, Constitutionalist of Rhode Island, was located in the middle – and least imposing – of a row of three Senate office building. The building to the left spread its neoclassical pillars across an entire city block. The building to the right gleamed bright white in its ultra-modernism. Hazen's budget-conscious Depression-vintage building was wedged almost apologetically in between.

I passed through a metal detector and took an elevator to the third floor. I emerged into a long clattering corridor and spotted the entry from a distance, framed by the flags of Rhode Island and the United States.

One of the office's three receptionists greeted me cordially.

"Welcome! Daphne isn't here yet. She asked me to show you around." Daphne was the name of the chief of staff, Daphne Peltzman. Still wearing my overcoat, I followed the receptionist out of the suite.

Teresa was the name of my guide. A recent graduate of a Catholic college back home in Rhode Island, she wore a small bright silver cross around her neck and a tight black turtleneck that showcased not only the cross but also the voluptuous body underneath. A little too plump for me, but she would definitely call somebody to Jesus.

At the end of the building tour, Teresa said, "Now let me show you the subway."

Yes, the Senate has its own subway. On foot, the trip from the remoter offices to the Senate chamber could easily take half an hour, even for a brisk walker – and "brisk" is not always the first word you'd apply to a U.S. senator.

We rode the elevator to a sub-basement and walked toward a pair of doors marked "subway." I was telling her about my trip to South Africa. An amazed look spread across her face.

"You were away for the election?"

She halted abruptly just before the doors. People stepped round her, muttering.

"October is the best month for seeing the animals. After that the brush gets too thick. Then we spent a few days in London on the way home."

"So you voted absentee?"

"Um, no – well, actually, I forgot."

Teresa wasn't amazed any more. She was offended. Her fingers tugged at the little cross in irritation.

"But look it didn't matter, right? General Pulaski won by a landslide! He didn't need one more vote from me. Anyway, I'm fairly sure my girlfriend is a Nationalist, so our votes would have canceled each other out."

I heard the sound of rubber wheels. Teresa walked fast away from me, her temper worse than ever, leading me toward a little platform on which stood three small, vaguely futuristic cars linked together atop a metal monorail. Teresa stepped into the last car without a look back. I hurried to catch up, entering the car just before the door whooshed close.

We were the only passengers, but she still lowered her voice. "This was the most important election of our lifetime. Our country was at stake, our freedom, our Constitution, our way of life, everything we believe in. We wouldn't have recognized this country after four more years of Monroe Williams! And you forgot." She shook her head in disgust.

The train raced quietly into a surprisingly bright tunnel.

"Is President Williams really so bad?" I asked. "He seems like a decent guy, trying to do his best."

"A decent guy!" Teresa was most definitely not cute when she was mad. "He sent goons to attack our rallies. His gangs shut down speakers on university campuses. His lawyers sent intimidating letters to our donors. My God, it was like living in a Third World dictatorship. It *would* be a Third World dictatorship if Williams had managed to steal the election. I'm sure he would have tried too, if it had not been such a landslide."

She simpered triumphantly. "But when it's not close, they can't steal it."

We pulled into the platform of the adjoining Senate office building, the oldest and grandest. A couple of staffers stood waiting. When the doors opened, they hopped into the car just ahead of ours.

"I don't see Williams as the kind of guy who'd employ thugs and goons," I said. "Image consultants maybe. Are you sure that that really happened?"

"If you're too" – she paused theatrically – "*busy* to vote, you are probably too *busy* to watch Patriot News. You probably get all your information from the comedy shows."

I allowed that this might be so.

"So, no wonder you have no idea what's going on."

The mood in our car of the little monorail sank toward the chilly as we rode the route to the Capitol and back. As we exited onto the platform we had started from, Teresa sneered at me. "I suppose you don't need to care. It's middle-class people who need the Constitutionalists to stand up for them against the spread-the-wealth crowd. You're rich, your family is famous, your accountants watch out for you. Nobody's looking out for me."

"Will Pulaski look out for you?"

"He'd better," she answered. We returned in silence to Hazen's suite, where Teresa deposited me in a medium-sized room claustrophobically crowded with padded cubicles, three facing each wall. Teresa pointed me to one of the six cubicles. On a small desktop there stood a not-new computer. A user name and password had been handwritten on a sticky note affixed to the monitor's upper rim.

"Wait here until Daphne can see you," said Teresa, her voice frozen cold. She huffed out to return to the front reception room.

The other cubicle dwellers gathered for quick handshakes. One lingered for a while longer than the others. I made a special effort to remember his name, Jack Campozzo.

Jack was a classic Rhode Island mutt: long Italian name, pointy Irish face, blond Polish hair. He would have measured five inches shorter than me in his stocking feet, but when he stood on his cocksureness, he reached just as tall.

I liked him right away and gave him a full description of my gaffe with Teresa. He laughed hard. "You're in the shit now! Teresa was like a Pulaski *maniac*. She thought President Williams was the anti-Christ: Stalin and Hitler and Malcolm X all rolled into one. She took three months leave without pay to canvass for Pulaski in Pennsylvania after the convention."

I said: "If she wore that sweater, I bet she won him some votes too."

"Careful, dude. No rude remarks where Teresa can hear. She's a virgin you know – okay a secondary virgin."

"What's that?"

He stepped close and raised his mouth to murmur into my ear. "It means that after three years of fucking everything in pants in Capitol Hill – every Constitutionalist, the girl has some standards – Teresa has returned to Holy Mother Church and pledged chastity until marriage."

"Seems kind of too late doesn't it?"

"Careful again, you sound like a heathen."

"What if I do?"

"Word of advice in that case: keep it to yourself. You'd be surprised how many people keep score of things like that. But hey, I've got a question for you."

"Go ahead."

His voice resumed a more normal volume.

"So we all know your story: the heroic dad killed in action, the movie-star mother and the tragic plane crash, the mustard millions. With a background like that, how come you're here and not in the fucking south of France – or the psych ward?"

"Don't speak too soon."

We took our seats, and I started to play around with the computer. Moments later, a clatter of announced the arrival of somebody important: Daphne.

I know we live in an age when professional women feel no need to deny their femininity. But - whoa! Daphne had come to work today in ultra-tight black jeans and knee-high boots. Her hands glittered with bright red nail polish; her white teeth gleamed through even brighter lipstick. The effect was the opposite of alluring. Every man in the room tensed with apprehension at her entrance, as if a very dangerous shark had slipped into the lagoon.

"Welcome, Walter. I hope everybody has helped you settle in?"

"Yes Ms. Peltzman, thank you."

She smiled a sharky smile, then began talking – almost purring – in an exotic, non-specific foreign accent. "You may call me Daphne; we're a team here. Now, Walter, here's something I need you to understand. Senator Hazen has won three terms in a Nationalist state for two reasons: because he's the only honest politician in Rhode Island and because we run the best constituency service operation in the Senate. Everybody in the state knows that if he or she has a problem with the U.S. government, Senator Hazen will fix it. Every problem starts as a piece of mail, so you are the first line of response. If you mess up, you lose the senator a vote, and probably a whole family's votes. There's a second chance for everything except losing mail. You lose mail, we lose you. Got it?"

She exited, and the room relaxed.

"Tough lady," I said to Jack.

"Oh, man, you have no idea."

Jack wheeled his chair around, hushed his voice, and then told me this story.

Hazen had decided he needed an on-staff expert on electrical grids. He found the person he wanted, a lifer in the Department of Energy. An offer of more money and more clout on Capitol Hill lured the lifer away from his secure civil service berth.

Not 48 hours after the lifer started work, Daphne began complaining that the new hire was an incompetent disappointment. She would send the new hire on the road, and then schedule him to brief the senator. When the new hire inevitably missed the appointment, Daphne would poor-mouth him for his irresponsibility. Daphne would call the new hire's phone, start screaming at "hello," then deny that the conversation had ever occurred. After six weeks, the man quit. He never did get back his civil-service job.

Jack glanced over his shoulder as he finished his story. Our four officemates continued hard at work. I asked in a low voice, "Why would Daphne do a terrible thing like that?"

Jack stood up suddenly. "Let's get a soda."

I followed Jack out the reception room and down a flight of stairs to a vending machine.

"It's awkward to keep whispering," he said in a more normal voice. He fed quarters into the machine. "Let me sport you, Mr. Mustard King." Two cans rolled out the bottom. We clinked in mock-toast.

"Senator Hazen," Johnny continued, "is the last of the New England moderate Constitutionalists. He got along with

President Williams, even sometimes cast a vote or two his way. That enraged all the other Constitutionalists. And it made Daphne very nervous."

"Why would Daphne care? And what's any of this got to do with the electrical guy?"

"Jobs are temporary, even chief of staff jobs. Networks are forever. Hazen is probably retiring when his term ends in four years. What happens to Daphne afterward? She wants to move downtown. But a lobbyist is only as valuable as her connections inside her party. If she is going to earn the big seven figures, she needs to prove that she is a 100 percent solid reliable Constitutionalist. Which is tough when you work for a so-called squish like Hazen. So when Hazen hired the electrical guy, Daphne panicked. She guessed that Hazen was thinking of working with the Williams administration on the president's smart grid project. Man, the Constitutionalist leadership in the House hated that project! They thought it was Washington run amok, big government interfering with state sovereignty, our constitutional liberties in jeopardy. Plus the local power companies are huge contributors to state Constitutionalist organizations. Daphne decided she had to shut down any possibility of Hazen cooperating with the president on the grid. And she needed to make sure that everybody *knew* she had shut it down."

"So she destroys a man's life?"

Jack shrugged and swigged his soda. "It's a tough town, as I won't be the last to tell you."

"Why does Hazen tolerate Daphne? She works for *him*, right?"

"The Hazen you see today isn't even the Hazen I saw when I started here 18 months ago. He lost his wife three years ago. He had a bout of stomach cancer last year. He's fading right in front of our eyes. Daphne makes his life go smoothly. He doesn't want to know the rest."

My new government-issue BlackBerry pinged.

"It's Daphne," I said. "She wants to see me in 15 minutes."

"That can't be good."

It took me fewer than 15 minutes to reach Daphne's door. Through the door reverberated the angry sounds of a ferocious one-sided argument:

"This is outrageous, Hannah, absolutely unacceptable. Just once – *just once! -* I wish you could think about a human being other than yourself. The answer is 'no.' I said, *NO!* Mummy is very busy, and I cannot possibly do it. And I don't care what you say Daddy said. If your father wants to tell me something, let him say it to me!" I heard a handset slam hard into its cradle.

I looked at my watch. I counted off the time to 15 full minutes, then waited 60 seconds more before I knocked.

"Come in."

The room was not designed to impress. A small window framed a view of a bleak interior courtyard. Inside: a long desk surmounted by an outdated computer monitor and a scuffed desktop phone. Facing the desk were two side-by-side televisions, both muted, one set to the Senate floor, the other to Patriot News.

"You wanted to see me?"

Daphne straightened herself in her high-tech office chair, the one new-looking item in the place. There was only one other chair in the room, alongside her desk. Too close. There was a battered blue couch along the wall. Too far. I stood in place.

"Yes," she said. "I spoke to Teresa this morning after your orientation tour. She told me something I could not believe. She told me that you had not voted in November's election."

It was not a question. But speaking of things not to be believed – had Teresa ratted me out on a personal conversation? I stammered a quickly concocted excuse.

"I was traveling …"

"I had an intern look it up, and you're not even registered to vote in Rhode Island."

"I've been living in New York."

"Or New York. Of course we checked that too."

"I'm not?" I faked my most convincing look of surprise.

Daphne's voice seethed with contempt. "You have never worked on a campaign. You have no consistent work history. As a student, you were twice put on academic probation. At Brown! As if going to Brown isn't academic probation all by itself!"

"I did graduate on time."

She fixed me with an accusing glare. "Have you processed any constituent mail today?"

"I am still familiarizing myself with the office organization."

"But you spent an hour exchanging dirty gossip with Jack Campozzo?"

Was this office full of spies?

"I'm sure it wasn't an hour."

"Honestly, if Jack's uncle weren't the mayor of Pawtucket, I'd have fired his ass long ago. On the other hand, at least he knows who the mayor of Pawtucket is. Do you?"

"No," I admitted.

"Mm," she said, half disgusted, half satisfied. "Can you name the governor of the state?"

"Give me a second, and I'll have the answer for you."

"The day I need you to tell me that answer is the day I fire my own ass."

She folded her hands on the desk. I could feel a lecture taking form. Might as well be seated. I took the side chair uninvited and pulled it to a safer distance. Daphne did not object. I suppose she had more urgent complaints. Her voice hissed again, "Can you tell me the names of some important

Constitutionalist politicians other than General Pulaski and Senator Hazen?"

"I think we're out of luck there too, sorry," I said with what I hoped was a winning smile.

No smile in reply. Instead Daphne said, "I know that the senator has a special connection to your family. When he asked me to find a role for you, I expected the usual preppy numbskull. But either you are spoofing me – or you are like some superstar preppy numbskull. If it were up to me, I'd put you on the next train back to New York. Lucky for you, your hiring is one of the few things in this office that wasn't up to me. If you continue to act as dumb as you sound, I promise you that your firing *will* be up to me. But I know the senator wants you to have your chance. So here's what I'm going to do."

She paused theatrically, like the boss in a gangster movie.

"I'm sending you to boot camp at the Constitutionalist Institute. It's ten days until Congress resumes and Senator Hazen returns from his trip to the Far East. I've spoken to my friend MacArthur Kohlberg. He's the vice president of the institute. He'll put together an educational program for you, based on the program for freshman members of Congress. Don't take that as a compliment, it's not meant as one. As ignorant as the typical new member is, at least they have done something with their lives."

Unlike you, she meant me to hear.

"You'll attend the program at the Constitutionalist Institute every working day for those next ten days. You'll what read they tell you to read, you'll do what they'll tell you to do. If you can learn something, good, we'll put you back on the mail. If not - well there are plenty of other preppy numbskulls who'd like a job on Capitol Hill. Clear?"

"Loud and clear."

The chief unmuted her TV. Time to leave. On Patriot News, a young blonde woman in a sleeveless dress was leading three ugly old men in a discussion of George Pulaski's military career. Was he our greatest soldier since Ulysses S. Grant?

I walked out of the office, and kept walking: out the building, down the street, headed home. You never get used to being a disappointment. I felt tears sting my eyes. I blinked and swallowed. My throat rasped. I passed a row of empty storefronts on E Street. The last storefront held a Starbucks. I entered to buy an ice tea. A sandwich too, why not? It was nearly lunch.

I sat down at a little table to check my office email. No messages.

At the next table, there sat a light-skinned black man at an antique-looking laptop. Maybe ten years older than me, wedding ring, hair beginning to turn grey. His Brooks Brothers blazer looked like it had seen a lot of wear. A broken eyeglass frame was held together at the temple with yellowed Scotch tape. At his elbow was the smallest container of iced tea Starbucks sold. All the ice had melted a long time ago. I glanced at his computer screen. He was scrolling through the listings on a job site.

He caught my glance. He shrugged, embarrassed. "They keep telling us things are getting better."

"And?"

"Nah. No bailout for me."

"Live near here?"

"I used to work over there," he said, pointing to a stone office building on the opposite side of the street. "We don't have internet at home any more, so I come down here a couple of times a week. It gets me out of the house. But it's six bucks here and back on the subway and another couple of bucks for the ice tea, so I can't make a habit of it."

"You've been here all day?"

Another shrug.

"That's OK with the management?"

"They're not so busy."

I contemplated my sandwich. I noticed he was contemplating it too. I felt a pang of embarrassment. I said, "I'm trying to lose weight. You want half?" The little plastic knife did a surprisingly good job slicing through the wrapper. I offered the larger slice.

He shook his head – no, no, he was fine. I pressed. He accepted.

The sandwich vanished in three bites.

CHAPTER 4

When I entered the apartment an hour later, I found an obstacle course of newly delivered boxes in the small entry. Crate & Barrel? No, not that one. Williams-Sonoma? Nope. Bed, Bath & Beyond. Keep looking. Ah, there it was: McPherson Liquor.

An hour later, I was pouring myself a second glass from a new bottle of Talisker when Valerie burst into the apartment toting a Whole Foods bag. She looked extra fine in a tight grey skirt and the same beige silk blouse she had worn to visit my grandmother. Valerie's code did not allow me to buy her clothes, so she had to make a few items stretch far. Her face was flushed and happy.

"I guess the job interview went well?"

"They made me an offer on the spot!" She hurled herself at me, and I folded my arms around her. "And guess what? I'll be earning more than the senator is paying you! So now you're my kept man!" She pulled away to kiss me on the cheek. "You'll have to do just what I say!"

"I do that already. But congratulations – although that skirt may deserve a lot of the credit."

"I don't think so. My boss is a woman. It's your grandmother who deserves the credit."

"My grandmother? How?" I dumped myself into the kilim sofa, still the only furniture in the living room. Valerie slid into my lap.

"Your grandmother persuaded the manager of the Newport Country Club to write a letter of recommendation for me, praising my excellence in event management."

"The club manager doesn't know you."

"Your grandmother vouched for me. Isn't that enough?"

She laughed at her own joke. "The company is called 'Perfect Party.' It's owned by a woman called Melanie Maurice, her husband is some big deal lobbyist. She has the cutest offices in Georgetown, right on top of the canal. There's a Washington Sport and Health three doors away, so if for any reason I miss my morning workout, I can exercise after work. By the way, did you do your treadmill today?"

"Tomorrow."

"Mm. Anyway, Melanie says, 'We're not the biggest event manager in Washington. But we are the best. And, of course, we are the most expensive.' So now when there's an event, you and I will never have to hear, 'Sorry, you're not on the list.'"

She levitated out of my lap, looked into the Whole Foods bag and grasped a package of turkey cutlets. She surveyed the boxes. "Good. The pans arrived. And here are my new knives! Give me 30 minutes for dinner. Did you get wine? We should celebrate."

I pointed to the liquor-store box. "I'm happy to celebrate *you*. I didn't do so well today."

The pleasure vanished from her face. "Tell me." I narrated while Valerie cooked.

"Daphne sort of has a point," she said after I finished. "If you work at the Gucci store, you wear Gucci. If you work for a Constitutionalist senator, you'd better vote the Constitutionalist ticket."

"I get that! But if I worked for Gucci, they wouldn't expect me to talk as if Versace threatened everything good and decent. They don't want you just to agree with them either. You have to super-agree – or else some spy will report you to the boss. It's like a police state. And now I've been sentenced to re-education camp."

"You're being overdramatic here. It's a team sport, so of course people expect you to stand by your team."

"Wait a minute. Aren't you a Nationalist?"

Valerie rinsed a pair of new-bought white plates and peeled the store stickers from their undersides.

"I'm a Walterist. I want Walter to succeed, so I want Walter to do what he needs to do in order to succeed. I know how hard you are working, but if you could try just a little harder ..."

"I got to the office at 8 AM today!"

"Yes, but a little *extra* effort it could mean so much. For you. For us." Valerie placed the second of the two plates on the table and reached for my hand. She clasped it between both of hers. My eyes drifted toward the gap in the silky blouse.

"I'll try."

"I know you will!"

She kissed me on the lips, gently first, then enticingly. I kissed back. My hand snaked around to stroke the tight skirt. She wriggled away.

"After."

"I can eat fast."

"I mean, after you do your treadmill."

CHAPTER 5

The next morning a little before 8:30 AM, I walked through the portico of the Constitutionalist Institute, an exact replica of the façade of James Madison's plantation house, Montpelier. Don't be impressed by my historical knowledge. I am only repeating what I read in a brochure while waiting in the lobby.

I did not wait long. "Mr. Schotzke?" The formal name startled me. The person addressing me was young, shockingly young. I suppose he had to be 22, but he looked 17 in his brand-new discount-store suit and his tightly knotted dark-red bowtie.

"I'm Walter." We shook hands.

"I'm Dr. Kohlberg's assistant. I can take you up to see Dr. Kohlberg now."

The bow-tied boy led me to a pair of glass doors and passed a card over the reader. He held one of the doors open for me, then showed me into an elevator and pressed the button for the seventh floor of eight floors. Affixed to the interior wall of the elevator was a brass-colored plaque stamped with the words:

THE CI MISSION
Building a free, secure, and prosperous America under God and the U.S. Constitution.

We emerged from the elevator into a hushed blue-carpeted hallway lined with large mahogany-colored wooden bookcases showcasing sober-looking volumes. The tips of their neo-Georgian peaks scraped the acoustic tiles of the hall's low ceiling.

"This is our executive floor," said Bowtie Boy. He pointed at the cases. "These are some of the famous books by CI scholars. Dr. Kohlberg's office is the second door from the end, right next to the office of our president, Dr. Gordon Munsinger."

I reviewed the nameplates on the doors as we walked past.

"Dr. Margaret Hastings"

"Dr. Francis Arnovilla"

"Dr. William Shelby"

"It must be handy to have so many doctors," I said, "if anyone gets sick."

Bowtie Boy did not appreciate the joke. "They are not medical doctors. Dr. Munsinger is a Ph.D. from the University of Aberdeen in Constitutionalist studies. Dr. Kohlberg is an honorary doctorate from Maxwell College."

"Maxwell College?" I'd never heard of it.

"It's a liberal arts college in Michigan that offers a full undergraduate program based on Constitutionalist principles. It's the only consistently Constitutionalist college in the whole country! I'm a graduate of Maxwell myself, just this past June."

"Congratulations," I said.

"Where did you go?" he asked.

"Brown."

He shook his head sympathetically. "That must have been tough. All those progressive professors!"

The plushly carpeted corridor opened into a kind of foyer in front of the offices of Kohlberg and Munsinger. Three young women, each as well-scrubbed as my young guide sat at four desks. A fourth desk evidently belonged to the guide himself. "Just a minute," he said, and rapped at a door trimmed in mahogany veneer.

"Come in!" boomed a deep voice. Bowtie Boy opened the door to reveal Kohlberg rising to meet us. A thick neck protruded from a white button-down shirt, adorned by a dark-red tie spun from some industrial fabric and stamped with multiple silhouette of a man in a Colonial pigtail: James Madison, as I correctly guessed. A round bald head jutted from Kohlberg's thick neck, the kind of baldness you see on the football coaches interviewed on ESPN, as if the hair had just drowned in the body's surging testosterone.

"Walter Schotzke!" Kohlberg boomed again, clutching my right hand with both of his meaty paws. I'm tall myself, but he loomed over me. His thick body looked to have been fed on a lifelong diet of steak and potatoes. "Glad to meet you! Damn glad! I still remember the day I heard the news of your mother's death. What a terrible thing. What a beautiful woman. Of course, I'm a huge admirer of your late father. We're honored to welcome a member of such a distinguished American family to the Constitutionalist Institute. We'll use your time well, I promise you."

Still gripping my hand, Kohlberg levered me like a wrestler into a thickly upholstered blue wing chair facing a picture window framing a postcard-perfect view of the Capitol dome. His big mahogany-colored desk stretched across the opposite side of the room, under a wall of shelves of awards, trophies, books and bright-red binders with years stamped on their spines: 1998, 1999, 2000, 2001 …. He ordered his assistant, "Get Walter a soda. What would you like?"

"Diet Coke, please."

I thanked Kohlberg for accepting me. He waved my thanks aside. "Educating rising national leaders is exactly what CI is here to do!"

"Daphne thinks I need a lot of educating."

"Daphne has very high standards. But I said to her on the phone, 'The Schotzke family are patriots. The Schotzke family are wealth-creators. So the Schotzke family are good Constitutionalists already, even if they don't know why. All we have to do is give Walter the *reasons* for what he already knows.'"

"If you put it like that, it doesn't seem so hard."

Bowtie Boy arrived with two tall soda glasses stamped with the same red-tinted head of James Madison as was stamped in white on Kohlberg's red tie – and (I now noticed) the bowtie too. Drinks delivered, the assistant backed respectfully out of the room.

"Tell me," demanded Kohlberg in a way that made clear his total confidence that I would answer correctly, "do you like paying taxes? Do you think the government makes good use of your money?"

Once a year I signed a tax return generated for me in Providence. The return filled more dozens of pages. I never bothered to read it. I just signed on the indicated lines, then forwarded it to the IRS in an envelope the accountants provided.

"I suppose not."

"Right! And do you think that if your family were allowed to keep more of their own money, you might start new businesses and create new jobs?"

If I had more money to spend, I'd go back to South Africa and spend the winter fishing off Cape Town. But that did not sound like the right thing to say, so I just nodded affirmatively.

"Right again! And do you agree that it's our Constitution that secures our freedom – that makes the United States the greatest nation on earth?"

"For sure."

Kohlberg slapped my knee with his big hand. Hard. "Just as I told Daphne! All the rest is filling in the footnotes. By the time you have finished here, you'll be able to qualify for your own doctorate in Constitutionalist studies. I've worked out a schedule for you" – he slipped me a piece of paper – "My assistant will email you a digital copy. We've divided your days into sessions with different experts. Your lunches too, right here in our own dining room. We have a terrific chef. Come to me any time you have a question. I mean, *any time.* I look forward to getting to know you a lot better. You and the whole Schotzke family."

I thanked him once more.

"We'll set you up with a password for our wifi system. And a desk and phone on the eighth floor. That's what we call our Founders' Floor – where you'll meet some of the greatest minds of our Constitutionalist philosophy. These are men who go back forty, fifty years in the Constitutionalist movement. They are national treasures, and they are all available to you anytime. Just rap on the door – and ask them anything. Don't be bashful," he chuckled, "that's why we pay them!"

He twisted to the side, toward a little table and hit a button on a phone, summoning his assistant to lead me out again.

We both stood. Another wrenching handshake, another big jovial smile. "Remember – *any time!*"

Thus my re-education began. I should say, "my education," for what education had I had before I started at CI, despite all those years of schooling? I'd lived my mental life in a blur. Random facts would stick to my memory, but they didn't connect to other facts.

I knew who had won the Civil War, and why the dinosaurs had gone extinct, and the difference between a stock and a bond. I could bluff my way through an art museum and pay a bar bill in Spanish, French, and Italian. The college course I'd liked best had been a junior year seminar in political philosophy: Machiavelli seemed to know what he was talking about. I still feel bad about doing such a half-assed job on the term paper.

But after that? Half a million dollars of tuition over the years, and I was as ignorant as a hillbilly. In all my life, I'd never sat down and read the Constitution from beginning to end. It never occurred to me that I could do it, or that I'd understand it if I did.

"Walter, tell me some of the rights protected by the Constitution." The question was posed by a CI legal specialist, a fierce middle-aged African-American with rapidly receding grey hair and a thick grey mustache. I was told that two decades ago he had headed an important federal agency.

"Freedom of speech, the right to privacy ..."

"Stop! Show me where it says 'right to privacy.'" He tossed me a small paperback copy of the Constitution with the Institute's logo stamped on the red cover.

I flipped forward, then backward. "I can't find it."

He snorted. "It isn't there. It comes from over here." He pulled a big book onto his desk and read aloud:

"The foregoing cases suggest that specific guarantees in the Bill of Rights have penumbras, formed by emanations from those guarantees that help give them life and substance. Various guarantees create zones of privacy."

"I don't think I understand that."

"Of course you don't understand it! It's gibberish. But that's our Supreme Court talking. The purpose of the Constitution is to enable the American people to govern themselves, to make their own decisions, including their own mistakes. Personally, I think it's stupid to tell adult Americans they cannot smoke marijuana if they want to. The Constitution doesn't tell us what the answer is – it tells us how we must decide together."

I didn't like everybody I met. One day I made the mistake of wondering aloud, "Was it fair that some people had so much when others had so little?"

I had actually directed the thought to the pretty economist named was tutoring me at a long table in the CI library on the difference between the deficit and the debt. She was maybe 40, maybe 50, but still as slender as a girl and with just the faintest air of seductiveness on the tips of her long fingers and in the corners of her smiling mouth. Her name was Celestine, and her accent was as French as her name.

Unfortunately, my question was overheard by a CI scholar standing behind a bookcase full of old government reports. The eavesdropper barged uninvited into my conversation with the French economist: a small whirligig of baldheaded, dandruff-flecked non-stop talk.

"Are you Walter Schotzke? I can't believe you'd ask that question!"

The ferocious little man dropped into a chair on the other side of me. He did not pause for breath.

"Okay," he commenced, his eyes glittering intensely behind smudged metal-rimmed eyeglasses, "let's say they decide, 'Hey – we'll be *fair*.'" "Fair" was pronounced with sneer quotes. "We'll take from those who have, like you, and give to the people who work less hard or don't work at all."

"Actually, I wouldn't say I do work very hard."

The former eavesdropper ignored the comment.

"Maybe they'll say, 'Let's tax the top 1 percent or 2 percent and use the money to benefit everybody else.' That's the morality that led to the Holocaust! They'll say, 'We're not targeting everybody, just a small percentage. What are you worried about? It's not you. It's not you. It's them.' And arguing that it's OK to loot some group because it's them, or kill some group because it's them and because it's a small number, that has no place in a democratic society that treats people equally."

Celestine looked pained.

"Walter and I have an appointment on the Founders Floor." She rose to her feet and motioned to me. I followed – but so did the argumentative little bald man, talking at the back of my head all the way to the elevator. He was still talking as the doors closed.

She smiled fetchingly. "His heart is in the right place, but sometimes he gets carried away."

"I'll say." As the talk drifted away from economics, my tutor's French accent became more noticeable.

The elevator doors opened. Through a jumble of mostly empty cubicles, I saw my own workspace, ornamented only with the coat I had dropped on the chair three hours before.

"It's strange," I said. "Everybody talks about the Founders Floor, but nobody ever seems to go there. When I sit at my desk up here, I feel like I'm in a ghost town. At like 9 o'clock, a few of the scholars wander into their rooms and close the doors. At 5 o'clock, they wander out again. In between, you barely see a soul up here."

"No?" she asked. I liked her smile, the first sympathetic smile I'd seen inside these walls.

"No."

"Well, why don't we look around then?"

The Founders' Floor was laid out on a very similar plan to the executive floor below, minus the mock Colonial finishings. The doors lacked mahogany veneer, but the names on the doors were blazoned with the same heavy brass plates as on the executive floor below.

"Many of our founding scholars are semi-retired," she said, "so that may explain the quiet. But they still attend CI events and eat in the lunchroom and mentor our younger people. They are such a tremendous inspiration to all Constitutionalists. Just to read these names is to walk into history."

She pointed to the nameplate nearest the elevator.

"Marcus Hanson. Back in the 1960s, he revolutionized the way we think about antitrust and competition. Do you know, they used to punish companies for selling their products too cheaply or producing a product that was too good? Dr. Hanson argued that we should protect the consumer, not unsuccessful competitors. You have him in large part to thank whenever you buy a better and cheaper product at a lower price."

We stepped deeper into the silent corridors.

"Irving Minkstein. He and his late wife Gloria showed that the Great Depression could have been just an ordinary recession, if it had not been aggravated by a collapse in the money supply. You don't need a big public works program to pull an economy out of a deep recession – just a central bank committed to recovery. We could use one now.

"Julius Wendell. He proved that the most important thing you could do to reduce crime was to hold the hardest-case criminals in prison longer. We call him the man who saved New York City."

I nodded appreciatively. "Thank him for me."

"Oh look," she said. "Vladimir Starkovich is here today!" She rapped on the door, then pushed it open without waiting. "Vladimir?" We caught side of a tall white-haired man hastily stubbing out a cigarette – apparently in an ashtray secreted inside the open drawer of a big wooden desk. The room smelt strongly of smoke. "Vladimir," said my tutor with the same winsome smile. "You have no need to keep secrets from me!"

We stepped into a room where every inch of the wall was covered with bookcase, and every inch of bookcase was filled with books: books upright and sidewise, books stacked atop books, more books on the top of the bookcase, and then pillars of books rising like stalagmites three and four feet from the floor. Beside them were stacks of file folders filled with papers, stacks of paper as high as the piles of books. The books and the papers hemmed the work area, two wooden filing cabinets on either side of the big wooden desk – filing cabinets that hung a little open, and that always *would* hang a little open because they were jammed with too much paper to close shut.

A couple of the books propped open a jimmied window, beside with a little air filtration unit struggled to purify the room of illicit smoke.

"The rules are very strict," said the old man with a shy smile of his own. He had been handsome once. He was handsome still, despite the wrinkled skin and yellow teeth and the ashes on the tweed suit. "We used to be allowed to smoke in our own rooms, but then they stopped the filtration system. The superintendent is a fellow Russian, he helped me improvise a filter of my own. I like to smoke while I read. And it's so quiet up here, I don't think I'm disturbing anybody."

"May we sit for a moment? This is a guest of CI, Walter Schotzke. He's joined the staff of Senator Hazen. We are immersing him in a crash course in Constitutionalist thought."

"Of course," said the old man, rising to his feet and walking around the desk to move files off seats and onto the floor to make room for my tutor and me. "Fortunately, I have exactly two visitor chairs."

"Vladimir has written the definitive history of the Russian revolution. You read it at university?"

I shook my head.

"Ah, American higher education," my tutor said archly.

"Thank you," said Vladimir gravely returning to his own chair and pushing far enough back from the desk to gain a clear view of Celestine's knees, which he visibly appreciated. "But it's not quite definitive yet. There's still the third volume to finish."

"Yes naturally, but I thought the third volume was nearly finished? Forgive me, I don't keep up with the foreign policy side of CI."

"It was far advanced," Victor said. "Now there are … difficulties." He glanced at me, then back at my tutor. *Not in front of our guests.*

She ignored the signal. "Dr. Kohlberg told me, 'Answer all of Walter's questions.'"

Victor did not seem impressed by Celestine's confident reassurances. Then my tutor clasped both her hands to her left knee and asked, "Victor, may I share one of your cigarettes?"

The ice cracked. Delightedly, he pulled his desk drawer, extracted the pack, and proffered it. My tutor tilted her head to accept a light. They both tilted back together to exhale the smoke. Relaxed, relieved, Victor reached some kind of inner decision and narrated his story:

"I had a talk with Mac Kohlberg about two months ago. He came up here to see me, which was generous of him. He had many compliments for my work. He said he had always been my strongest advocate here when others questioned why CI should be supporting research not directly part of our mission. He told me that I was welcome to continue to use the office. CI would keep my wife and me on the health plan. But he said that with a new presidential administration expected, there were going to be many new calls on CI's resources. 'I think we can cross Soviet communism off our list of worries,' he said. So he was going to have to zero out my research support. And my travel grants. And my salary. 'You've had a good run Victor,' he said, 'but we can't provide income support forever for the study of ancient history.'"

"That's impossible!" protested Celestine. "At the annual dinner, Dr. Munsinger made you stand up in front of the whole room! He praised your work as one of the greatest intellectual achievements of the Constitutionalist movement! Does Dr. Munsinger know?"

Victor shrugged. "In the old Russia, they'd say after a Cossack rampage, 'if only the czar knew.' But the Cossacks work for the czar. The czar knows."

"But you could finish the third volume anyway?" my tutor insisted, still visibly shocked. "You must have savings, a pension, Social Security?"

"Yes," said Victor, "I am not in any financial difficulty. But I can't afford to pay my own way to the archives in Moscow. I certainly can't afford the bribes for the archivists. Anyway, I'm not so young, I can't do all the reading myself any more. I'd need assistants, and I can't afford them either.

"But it's not just the money. I've always relied on Mac and Gordon. If they tell me that my work isn't needed any more, maybe they are right. The two finished volumes are my achievement. I've left my unfinished draft for the third and my research notes to Yale University, where I did my Ph.D. Perhaps they will be useful to a younger man. Or woman," he corrected himself. "Or perhaps not. I was angry for a little time. But I'm at peace now. We work to serve the movement, do we not? And if our work no longer serves the movement, then our work must stop."

That sounded sensible to me, but for some reason it only seemed to upset Celestine even more. "I didn't know," she said softly and stubbed out her cigarette. She rose, I rose, and Vladimir rose. He walked us to his battered door. He extended a hand. "Truly a pleasure," he said. "Please come visit me again."

I shook the hand. Celestine kissed Victor on the cheek instead. Her lips lingered a full beat longer than I expected.

"You need to appreciate," she said softly as we stepped inside the elevator to the busier floors below, "how much CI has contributed to scholarship. Obviously we make mistakes from time to time. But on balance? We have contributed so much!"

CHAPTER 6

Please join us at 11 AM in the Arhaus Family auditorium for a short presentation by Col. Patrick Cleland, deputy chief of transition for President-elect Pulaski. Seating will be limited, no admission without RSVP.

The email was waiting for me on my last morning of boot-camp. I added my name to the list. I arrived at the auditorium 15 minutes early – and still found nearly all 200 seats already claimed.

I ended up in a seat at the very back, wedged beside Mac Kohlberg's personal assistant, the Bowtie Boy of my first day at CI. I asked him what he thought of the new president. He looked glum.

"None of us wanted Pulaski," he said. "He was our best hope to get rid of Monroe Williams. Everybody said we had to nominate him. But they can't make us like it."

As the clock touched 11:02, the lights dimmed and the room hushed. Mac Kohlberg and two guests entered from stage left, marching toward a row of four big black leather swivel chairs. The guests wore the dark suit and black shoe uniform of political Washington, but they stood straighter and looked fitter. One was a middle-aged, medium-height white man, his face all smooth planes and sharp angles under shaved, half-receded hair. The other, a black man maybe a decade younger, had the height and bulk of a former Mr. Universe. From atop the imposing body glared an unsmiling mouth and displeased eyes.

A lapel microphone magnified Kohlberg's already loud voice. "The Constitutionalist Institute is proud and pleased to welcome today Patrick Cleland and Jamal Harris, from the Pulaski transition team."

The gathered CI staffers burst into solid applause that lasted almost half a minute. When the applause subsided, Kohlberg chuckled heartily in the direction of the guests.

"Well, Pat, if we don't get past these opening formalities, we'll never get to the meaty part of the conversation. Let me start the ball rolling. We all agree, General Pulaski is a true American hero. But candidly and among friends, there's still a lot of uncertainty about his domestic policy agenda. Can you share some of your thoughts about how you intend to work with Constitutionalists in the country and here in Washington?"

Cleland spoke in a clear voice with just the faintest trace of the border South. Kentucky, probably.

"Mac, thank you for this warm welcome. In case any of you don't know my background, I served on General Pulaski's staff in Mexico. I was tour director during the election campaign, and now I am deputy-director of the transition team. My colleague, Major Harris, commanded an infantry company in the Battle of Chihuahua, where he won the Silver Star. He chairs the transition team's domestic policy council."

More sustained applause. Kohlberg waved the room quiet again, and Cleland continued in the same clear voice.

"All of us in the incoming Pulaski administration look forward to working closely with CI to advance an agenda of fiscal responsibility, deficit reduction, and shared sacrifice. We will be presenting plans early to reduce government borrowing. Every idea is on the table. Even more urgently, we will be working to achieve a successful outcome in Mexico that enables us to reduce our troop presence south of the border. Beyond that, why don't I just take your questions?"

"We look forward to working with you too," Kohlberg replied enthusiastically. "OK, let's open the floor!"

A dozen hands shot up at once. Kohlberg nodded to a face in the front row, a white-haired man in a tweed jacket, who spoke with the assurance of one who had seen many presidential transition teams come and go.

"Mac, I've got a question for Colonel Cleland. Like everybody in this room, I appreciate General Pulaski's service to our country. Saving us from Monroe Williams is his finest service of all. But guys, some of your early personnel choices make us nervous. Since the election, General Pulaski has not met even once with any of our CI economists. Yet he found time for a three-hour meeting with Manny Kaplan from Princeton, who makes fun of CI all the time in his blog."

The room rustled, as if to boo Kaplan in absentia, then collected itself.

The questioner talked on. "The head of our CI Job Bank reports that he can barely get your transition team on the phone. Can you reassure us that you'll keep faith with the people who elected you?"

Five minutes ago, I'd have said that Major Harris could not possibly have looked less pleased to be sitting in this room. I was wrong. Harris' face now descended to some new sub-basement of displeasure. If Cleland shared that feeling, however, he did not betray it.

"I'll call the director of the CI Job Bank myself the moment I get back to the office. I'll make sure he has my cell number too. We are a Constitutionalist administration, and that's the way we'll staff up."

The room clapped happily.

Cleland continued placatingly, "The president-elect has already announced his intention to appoint Tony Monckton as Secretary of the Treasury. That's an appointment that should please everybody in this room."

Another ripple of applause.

"As to this Manny Kaplan story – look, we're stuck in the worst economic crisis in a generation here at home. In Mexico, we're bogged down in the longest counter-insurgency operation in the country's history. Almost a trillion dollars! And the Mexican government no more stable today than on the day we intervened. We *have* to take some bold actions. My job is to ensure that all perspectives on these difficult problems get a fair hearing, including of course," he added gravely, "the perspective of the Constitutionalist Institute."

The applause for that answer seemed a little thinner.

Another questioner was recognized, a petite woman in a cherry red suit. "I am the director of development here at CI. It's my job to keep in close contact with our donors. A lot of them are your donors too."

The room gave a light laugh at her joke.

"Our donors are so proud and glad to see General Pulaski leading the cavalry to the rescue! But they are concerned too. The general does not have a long background with this party. He doesn't always seem …" she groped for words, "… familiar with a lot of our core principles. Maybe there's a language issue – if you could deliver a message in a way that makes Constitutionalists feel more comfortable?"

Cleland cocked his head in thought. He glanced away from the fundraiser's face, as if searching for the correct words in the far upper corner of the room. Then he fixed a cheerful look back upon her.

"President-elect Pulaski is a Constitutionalist. A committed Constitutionalist. You can reassure your donors on that score!"

For a moment, it seemed that Pulaski had won back the room. Then – uh oh.

"Still, we have to remember that George Pulaski is president of the whole United States. He wants to get big things done. A lot of Nationalists also voted for George Pulaski. We can't forget about them!"

The applause ceased, and instead a soft, unhappy murmur spread through the auditorium.

A small bald head burst upward. I knew that head. It belonged to the angry little eavesdropper who had followed me to the elevator the other day. "You *should* forget about them! General Pulaski would not have won the presidency without the Constitutionalist movement behind him!"

Cleland paused to weigh his words. A mistake. The pause left the little bald man's words hanging in the air long enough to goad Major Harris into erupting. And I do mean erupt: The guy was not only about the size of a volcano, but almost as heated.

"The Constitutionalist Party would not have won this election without George Pulaski at the head! You needed Pulaski much more than he needed you! Maybe Monroe Williams was not a successful president. But I had a chance to talk about him when he decorated me, and he is a brilliant and good man. Look at that field of losers you collected to run against him. What do you think would have happened if you'd nominated that phony Governor Tremain? That dope Senator Bingham? Never mind, *Esther Minden*?"

Harris pronounced with a sneer the name of the former swimsuit model turned governor who had briefly led the Constitutionalist polls. His sneer backfired. Somebody in the back of the room shouted, "Yes!" to Minden's name.

Cleland clutched Harris at the elbow, as if groping for some kind of pause switch. No success.

"President Williams offered to dump his own vice president from the Nationalist ticket to make room for General Pulaski as his running mate. He decided to accept the Constitutionalist draft instead – *his* choice."

The murmuring was growing louder and angrier. Cleland, still gripping Harris's arm, tried to interrupt his over-sized colleague. "Major Harris is only saying ..."

But Harris had worked up too much momentum to stop now. He lectured the room, "General Pulaski was going to lead the American people whether you supported him or not. So he's not going to take orders from anybody!"

At last, Cleland somehow silenced the big infantry commander.

"What Major Harris meant to say is that we're rolling up our sleeves to work with *all* our friends, especially our good friends here at CI."

Too late.

Mac Kohlberg pivoted his swivel chair to face Cleland directly. He mimicked the colonel's fake conviviality. "Colonel Cleland, I appreciate your very candid answer. We want to work with you too. And yes, we are your friends. We agree that you should work with Nationalists when you can do so consistent with principle." He repeated the three last words for emphasis. "Consistent. With. Principle. Let me add some friendly advice: the party system exists for a reason. You can't govern by taking a little from Column A and a little from Column B. You'll find yourself absolutely alone."

The room erupted in applause – applause for Kohlberg, not Pulaski.

Cleland countered in the same false friendly tone. "President-elect Pulaski is polling at 76 percent, I checked the overnights before I left the office. He's the most popular new president in half a century. I don't think he's in any danger of finding himself alone."

The bald eavesdropper bobbed up again to shout from his seat. "We're not impressed by one week's polls. Williams used to be hailed as the Messiah, now he's a has-been. If Pulaski walks away from the Constitutionalist party, he'll be a one-termer too."

Cleland's head whipped around. The friendliness vanished from his voice as he spoke to the spot in the darkened room where the angry little bald man's eyeglasses reflected.

"You think you can threaten this president? Try it. But before you do – you spend five hours on your back in a Mexican desert with two shattered legs, and your chopper burning, and all your crew dead, and the coyotes sniffing. If you survive that experience, you'll find … you don't intimidate so easily."

Kohlberg interrupted again. He had not lost *his* temper. "Pat, as I said, we all want to be supportive of the Pulaski administration. You are not alone, I promise you. And we all look forward to two very successful terms of the closest cooperation between this institute and your administration. In fact, perhaps I can interest you in reviewing Paul Mantua's resume as a potential press secretary for the Pulaski administration? You see for yourself that he won't yield an inch to the lame-stream media!"

That joke wrung one last laugh from the room, a thin smile from Cleland – and no reaction at all from Jamal Harris.

The Pulaski team glanced at their watches. Time to go. The two officers shook hands with Kohlberg and marched out. We all followed, milling and chattering in the small lobby in front of the auditorium. Mac Kohlberg saw me, walked over, and clasped a big arm around my shoulders.

"So Walter, what did you think?"

"I guess they don't teach tact at West Point."

"Nope. But those guys had better learn soon."

CHAPTER 7

Boot camp over, I was sitting in the chief of staff's office looking at a very unusual sight: a friendly smile on the carnivorous features of Daphne Peltzman.

"Mac Kohlberg tells me that you did very well at the Constitutionalist Institute."

"He did?"

"Yes, it surprised me too." She consulted her BlackBerry. "He wrote me to say, 'There's more to Walter than you might think.'"

"Um, thanks."

A puff of perfume wafted over the desk that divided her from me. "Of course you have a long way to go. But I will help you."

"Thank you again."

"First, though, I need you to help me. You saw at the Institute what we've all been worrying about. There is a trouble coming between General Pulaski and the Constitutionalist movement."

"Yeah. Wow. It got super-tense, super fast."

"You have to understand," said Daphne, picking up a pencil and twirling it between her long bright-red fingernails. "The general is a very ... self-confident ... man. Because Senator Hazen was such an early supporter, I had the opportunity to spend time with the general on the campaign trail. He thinks he is bigger than our movement. He thinks he can claim our support, then discard us after the election. We were counting on Iggy to keep him on the straight and narrow, but I'm hearing that Iggy is being excluded more and more from Pulaski's inner circle."

Even I knew who "Iggy" was: Ignatius Hernandez, the political guru who masterminded the "draft Pulaski" campaign that won the Constitutionalist nomination and then the presidency.

"The defeat of Monroe Williams has thrown the Nationalists into utter disarray. They're blaming each other, pointing fingers, and madly kissing up to Pulaski. That gives our new president a lot of freedom to maneuver. A very dangerous freedom. So we're headed into some turbulent waters. It's very important that Senator Hazen be on the right side of what's coming." The pencil spun again and again around the bright red fingernails.

"Which is the right side?"

Daphne's smile faded. I hadn't learned as much she'd hoped.

"The party's side, Walter – always."

"But if Senator Hazen is such a committed supporter of the president's …" My voice dwindled under the glare of Daphne's displeasure. As I fell silent, she recovered her smile. The pencil twirled again.

"If Senator Hazen follows the president, he'll find himself utterly isolated. Think what that will mean for the people who trust the senator – here in Washington, and here in this office. Think what it will mean for you. We'll all lose our futures. Unfortunately, the more these facts are explained to the senator, the more recalcitrant he becomes. He won't listen. At least he won't listen to me."

Hey, was she suggesting … ?

"I think he might listen to somebody else, however. You know Senator Hazen deeply respected your grandfather? He sometimes says he owes his career to him."

Yes. That *was* what she was suggesting.

"Daphne, I haven't seen the senator since I was a boy. He has no reason to care what I think about anything. Nobody cares what I think about anything!"

Daphne's voice slowed, as if talking to a laggard student.

"Your grandmother still generously supports the senator's campaigns. He might care what your grandmother thinks. And I suppose she might listen to you?"

Daphne supposed wrong, but I was not going to be the one to disabuse her. I lowered my head in a way that might be interpreted as a nod, if you wanted to. Daphne smiled appreciatively, the laggard student had grasped the lesson at last. Daphne's voice sparkled with good cheer again.

"This is probably the senator's last term. But you and I and everybody in this office, we're here for the long haul. We need friends. You need them. I need them."

"I understand."

"Good. Then we're agreed. We'll talk more."

Not an hour later, my phone rang. Without a hello or introduction, a woman's voice asked, "Walter Schotzke?"

"Yes."

"Hold please, I have Frederick Catesby on the line."

I was obviously supposed to know who Federick Catesby was – and why I should have to wait to speak with him. A pause, then a strangely squeaky voice: "Walter? Freddy Catesby here."

"What can I do for you, Mr. Catesby?"

"The question of the day, Walter, is what can I do for *you*? Our mutual friend, your boss, Daphne Peltzman, tells me that you are a brilliant young man – yes, she really did. And since I'm a brilliant old man, you and I must meet. You're not busy tomorrow for lunch, Daphne tells me. I'm a member of both the Farragut and the Sheridan club. The food is better at the Sheridan. One o'clock, meet me in the lobby. Good bye!"

CHAPTER 8

The day that Daphne recruited me as a co-conspirator was the same day as Valerie's first big party event: the opening of a new lounge.

The Ali Baba bar occupied a long stretch of glassed street front on Pennsylvania Avenue, a dozen long blocks northwest from the Capitol. The sun had already set when I exited the office a few minutes past six. The December wind blew cold flecks of snow into my face as I walked downhill.

Bouncers stood importantly around the door in dark suits and Secret Service earpieces. I gave my name to a haughty young man holding a clipboard and walked inside, into a wall of people and noise.

The crowd looked different from any I'd yet met in Washington: their clothes more flamboyant, their hair sleeked with "product." The slits of the women's skirts showed wide glimpses of thigh, necklaces gleamed in the open collars of men's shirts.

Who were these people? I'd spent almost three weeks living in a village barely one-mile square, surrounded by people who either received a government paycheck or directly serviced those who did. But spreading out beyond the village was a big city, bustling with people who cut hair and sold dresses, who managed restaurants and caught footballs. And here they all were. They were not exactly glamorous. But after all these days of being surrounded by gray and blue suits, at least they were something different.

I pushed deeper into the bar. I pushed too hard, because I lurched directly into a woman holding a bright pink drink.

Half the liquid sloshed onto the floor. "Excuse me," I apologized. "Let me get you another one."

She turned her face directly on me: an older face, illuminated by striking blue eyes. The dress more elegant than the attention-grabbing outfits nearer the door; the body inside the dress … thought-provoking. She assessed me for another minute. Her three friends watched her watch me. Girls' night out.

"No," she smiled flirtatiously. "Let me get *you* one."

I don't pretend to be a super-reliable guy. I might have said yes. But before I could say anything, Valerie had materialized beside me. "Look who's here," she said and pulled me away.

I shrugged my shoulders at my new friend. She reached out a hand to shake goodbye. Our fingers touched. A card was slipped inside my palm. She lofted her half-empty cocktail glass in a farewell salute.

"Who was that?" Valerie asked, as light and sweet as cappuccino froth.

"I don't know. I tripped over her and spilled her drink. I was trying to apologize."

"I guess she accepted. But come on. Samir is over here."

Samir? Samir! I would never have dared call Samir my best friend. He was just the friend I liked best. We'd lived in the same suite freshman year, had hung with the same groups for the next three years. Well I hung. Samir always led. He was a great athlete, a ladies man with an unequaled won-lost record. Everybody always deferred to Samir. Samir's appeal to the coach saved me from being cut from the squash team at Christmas of freshman year. I heard the story later from the coach. "Samir said if I cut you, I'd have to cut him too."

When I asked Samir, he laughed it off. "Coach is so melodramatic. What I actually said was that if they cut you, they could forget about your family renovating the courts."

It was not so easy for Samir to save me when I was put on academic probation in junior year. He knocked on my door one day, leading a beautiful graduate student. "Hey Walter, this is Lydia. She's going to coach you through finals, help you with all your papers, make sure you get through this term with flying colors."

"Wow, thank you."

Lydia smiled – but at Samir, not at me. "Samir's promised that we're going to Europe together this summer if I can save you from being thrown out of Brown. You're not going to disappoint me, right?"

When I think of Samir, I always think of him laughing and of me laughing with him. I remember a visit to New York, just after we'd finished college. We were drinking at the Bonobo Bar in Tribeca. Samir had arrived alone, but had somehow collected three beautiful girls – and then serenaded them with an obscene impromptu parody of "My Favorite Things" from The Sound of Music.

"Marzipan pigs that belonged to King Tut – these are some things that I shove up my butt!"

I still laugh when I think about it now. Samir worked for a private equity firm for his first couple years out of college. He thrived, as he always did, gained mentors. Then – just when he was poised to be promoted, he quit the firm. He moved to Iowa to volunteer on the Monroe Williams presidential campaign. For four months, he shared a motel room with three other volunteers, visited old age homes and churches, selling "hope" and "change." A year later, Samir was writing speeches for the president of the United States. He wrote about the financial crisis, about healthcare reform, about immigration, about war and peace – and of course, our children's future. And after four years in the White House, it was Samir who wrote President Williams' election-night concession speech.

I'd seen Samir a few times during the past four years: once at a summer weekend house party in Chappaquiddick, again at a wedding in New York, most recently at our fifth class reunion in Providence. But too many other people now claimed his attention for him to waste much time on me.

I'd assumed that with the administration winding down, he might have more time to see me. But every attempt went unreturned. Leave it to Valerie to solve the problem: send Samir a VIP invitation to a splashy party (Samir did love a party), then assign a pretty assistant to wait by the door to pounce the moment Samir gave his name (Samir never said no to a pretty girl). The assistant had dragged Samir to the very back of the room, underneath a giant pressboard genie and lamp, where she had gathered a little posse of her friends for Samir's benefit. I could see them through the throng, laughing merrily. Samir stood as tall and lean as ever, exuding importance and confidence in a once-expensive suit that revealed five years of hard wear.

Valerie walked a dozen rapid paces ahead of me. This opening was her first big event, but Valerie didn't know what it means to be nervous. She nodded commandingly at the wait-staff as we pushed our way through the throng. A cocktail girl in a harem costume carried a tray of mauve-colored cocktails under her chiffoned breasts. I plucked a cocktail from as close up to Princess Jasmine's cleavage as I could reach. It tasted like cough syrup.

Valerie swooped upon Samir, grabbed Samir's arm, and pulled him tight to her body to prevent escape.

"You see," she said to Samir rapidly, "I told you I had somebody you would want to see!"

"Samir! You bastard!" I called. "I called you when I knew I was moving here. I called you when I arrived. I called when I rented my apartment. I called you just this past weekend. I know you are busy with the transition, but the job search can't consume 24 hours a day, can it?" I extended a hand, but Samir couldn't take it – not with Valerie on one arm, and a tumbler of whisky in the other. No stupid purple drink for Samir.

Samir looked surprised to see me, and not in a good way.

"Hello Walter," he said curtly. I was so happy to see him that the unwelcoming tone didn't immediately register on me.

"Well, now that I've found you, come have some dinner with Valerie and me."

"Sorry, but I have a date later tonight." He was talking over my shoulder now.

"Well let us join you then – I always liked your girlfriends."

"I don't think that would be a good idea."

"Then lunch? Tomorrow? No wait, not tomorrow. The day after tomorrow? Or any day? Maybe the day after the inauguration? You have to be free then!"

"No, sorry." Samir's eyes moved further and further into the remote distance.

My BlackBerry buzzed. I ignored it.

"You can't?"

"No."

The intern and her girlfriends shots worried looks at each other. "See ya, Valerie," they chimed. "Nice to meet you, Samir!" And off they vanished in a chattering gaggle.

Valerie laid a gentle restraining hand on my forearm. "Isn't this a crazy city? Walter has been so busy too, there's never a chance to see the people we really want to see ..."

"As in ... ever?"

"No."

I was too wounded to be angry. I stepped closer to him, until I was almost shouting in his ear. "Did I do something wrong? You know me, you know I'm semi-autistic, I'll never figure it out for myself. Tell me."

Valerie interrupted again, coaxingly: "Samir is only saying ..."

"Tell me!"

My angry outburst pulled his attention back from over-my-shoulder land, but he spoke as coolly as ever. "We're on different teams now."

"I'm not on any team!" I took a big gulp from my horrible drink and choked a little. Valerie discreetly removed it from my hand, and deposited it on a ledge near one of the cartoon thieves.

"Everybody's on a team, whether they know it or not," Samir replied. "Congratulations, your team is riding high these days. My team? We're in the shit. Someday maybe I'll be a good sport about it. Right now, I can't. That was a fucking ugly campaign your team ran against mine, and I take it personally."

"Samir, I had nothing to do with any of that – obviously." Valerie squeezed my elbow. I realized I was shouting.

"No, you didn't. You didn't call me a Nazi fascist socialist. You didn't say I was planning to send your disabled nephew to a death panel. You didn't accuse me of wanting to foist Sharia law on the United States." He tinkled the ice in his whisky with a hard little smile to himself. "Well I'm innocent on the Sharia count at least."

He raised his eyes again. "But other people did do all those things – and they are the people you work with. I want no part of it. Or them. Or anybody connected to them. You hang your hat at the Constitutionalist Institute for the Study of Lying Crap. Oh yes, I know all about it. You may say that Senator Hazen is not the usual Constitutionalist wing-nut. But your new friend Daphne Peltzman will ensure that when it counts, your grand statesmanly Senator Hazen is lined up with Senator Joliette and Senator Bingham and Patriot News. You'll be lined up with them too, you'll see."

"What is this, the Bloods and Crips?" I was raving furiously now. "You can't be my friend any more because somebody neither of us ever met said something you didn't like in an election campaign? That's crazy!"

"You've shown up in the middle of the story," he said. "That's fine, I suppose we all do. But you need to learn what happened before you decided to grace the nation's politics with your attention. *Then* you tell me what's crazy and what isn't crazy. We're not just two college pals who happen to work for Coke and Pepsi. We're on opposite sides of a wall, we're officers in armies at war. And it wasn't me that decided it was a war either. I believed in 'hope and change,' 'what unites us is more important than what divides us,' 'we live in the United States, not the blue states and the red states.' All bullshit, but I believed it. I don't believe it now. The Constitutionalists decided it was war, they fought like it was a war, and they won. We didn't take it seriously enough, we believed in the system and played by the old rules. We lost. Well I've learned my lesson. I'm not playing this game by those rules any more. You got a TV network to tell lies about me? I'll get a TV network to tell lies about you. You raise special-interest money? I'll raise special-interest money. I'll fight for what I believe just as ruthlessly as your side did. And I only drink with those who fight alongside."

He place his tumbler on the ledge beside my discarded purple cocktail. He had not taken a sip.

"Well, fuck you too then," I answered.

Not even that provoked a rise in him.

"You're a good guy, more or less. But you're not big enough or tough enough or just give-a-damn-enough to change your team. So they'll change you. Probably started already. Pleasure to meet you, Valerie – Walter's a lucky man. G'night." He stepped away, subsumed into the crowd like the genie returning to the lamp.

I've had a lot of bad news in my life. I don't usually have a lot of emotion left in me. But what little there was – it got a decent workout that night in the Ali Baba bar.

CHAPTER 9

The Sheridan Club occupied an old mansion in the exuberant style of the Monaco Casino, built a hundred years ago by a robber baron to please his socially ambitious wife. The wife kept the house after a divorce, and brought it with her when she remarried a famous American diplomat of the 1930s. I knew the story because the famous diplomat was an uncle of my grandmother's – and (according to family history) flamboyantly gay.

As I sat on a marble bench beside the tinkling indoor fountain waiting for Frederick Catesby, I thought, *That's a good thing about being gay. If you do get married, you can really keep your eye on the ball.*

I was hungry. My stomach had adjusted to the early mealtimes of Washington: lunch at noon, dinner at 6:30. Lunch at one would have been tough enough if Catesby had arrived on time. He was very late. Twenty-five minutes past the hour, a vintage Porsche 911 roared up the circular drive to the front door. The driver stepped out, tossed his keys to the doorman, pulled off a pair of tan leather driving gloves, shoved them into the pocket of a short tweed overcoat, and stepped inside to shake my hand.

Whatever I'd been expecting, this wasn't it.

Freddy Catesby was a small, lithe man. He wore the most expensive clothes I ever saw before or since on a male inhabitant of the nation's capital: hand-tailored charcoal suit, shoes cobbled to order for his dainty feet, blue-and-yellow Turnbull & Asser shirt and carefully contrasted blue-and-yellow necktie. It must have demanded all his willpower to resist the temptation to add a pocket square.

The squeaky voice quavered with enthusiasm.

"Walter, Walter, good to see you, Walter. Come in, come in. Have you ever been inside? It's not as lavish as the Gotham, my New York club. But it has more a feeling of belonging, it's more a real gentleman's club. I'm also a member of the Reform Club in London. It strained my conservative convictions to join, but the Reform is the only other club that has this same feeling that there's more to the membership than who can afford the dues. We have to see about making you a member here. I've reserved a window table."

The window offered the grey light of a Washington winter day and sliced-off view of the Estonian embassy across the street. Catesby unfurled his napkin with a snap, laid it in his lap, and immersed himself in a thick vinyl bound wine list.

"I always have wine at lunch. I live by my friend Saki's rule: I buy the wine, I do the talking."

He beckoned to a waiter.

"The 2005 Beycheville, please. I'll take the veal chop, it's the best thing here. What'll you have?"

"The veal chop sounds great."

Catesby scribbled out the food order on a little pad, then settled confidentially into his powder blue armchair.

"So you are probably wondering: Why has Freddy Catesby invited me to lunch? Freddy Catesby, the founder of the *Constitutional Review*, Patriot News guest host, and bestselling author! Freddy Catesby: who has known US presidents, who has entertained a British prime minister in his home, and who - people say - once dated the Princess of Wales. And it's this same Freddy Catesby who is taking me out to lunch. Why? It's the most natural question in the world! It's exactly what I'd be wondering if I were sitting in your chair."

The waiter filled Catesby's wine glass, then looked questioningly at me. What the hell. I nodded yes.

"To understand why I invited you, you have to understand me. I'm not only the founder of *Constitutional Review*, although I'm proud of my role in launching the magazine. You know that Time magazine called us the most influential political magazine in the country on our tenth anniversary? I'll put you on the list for our thirtieth anniversary dinner next month as my guest, I'll put you at my table. No, no, don't thank me - it's my pleasure.

"All those things I've accomplished, all the awards and accolades – they mean nothing to me. I live for my principles, not for recognition. What I care about is fighting the *Kultursmog*. You know I coined the term?"

I'd never heard the term, but I gave no sign. The waiter presented a tray of rolls. Catesby pointed at one, and ripped it roughly in half as soon as it touched his plate. I declined. In Valerie's book, wine at lunch was a serious dereliction, but bread was a capital offense. Catesby dropped one half of his roll on a bread plate, then used the other half like a conductor's baton, waving in rhythm with his words.

"New people arrive in Washington, and the first thing they think about is how to get invited to cocktail parties in Georgetown and Chevy Chase. They ingratiate themselves with the Nationalists instead of supporting their own. Opportunists! Have you ever heard of that jackass Sheraton Feldman? No? Good. He's dead now. He was an art critic for the *Washington Guardian*, back when the *Guardian* dominated media in this town. Sheraton one day decided he'd become a Constitutionalist. Oh, we were all so excited. Here was this great media personality, joining our side. That was a big, big deal in those days.

"Then the *Guardian* offered me a column. I accepted – not for my own sake, but because the platform represented a huge advance for our movement. This man Feldman appeared on a television show, and the host asked, 'Why'd the *Guardian* hire Catesby?' Feldman answered, 'Bad taste.'

"Can you imagine? Feldman called me the next day to apologize. He said he was only joking. He said he had huge respect for me and my work. He said his tongue had slipped. I told him, 'I don't care what you say about me, I have no ego. I'm just sad that you would divide the movement.'"

Catesby took a savage bite out of the half-roll in his hand.

"You see, the important thing is for Constitutionalists to work together, to build each other up, not criticize or diminish each other. You should help me, and I will help you. I'll promote you and I'll support you. And of course you'll want to do the same for me."

"Thank you, Mr. Catesby."

"Call me Freddy, please."

Catesby drained his glass of wine and motioned the waiter for a refill.

The food arrived. Kind of disappointing after the buildup: the chop rather dry, dolloped with a too-sweet mushroom sauce that ran into a creamy puddle from the scalloped potatoes. But Freddy seemed satisfied, and his knife lunged into his chop with gusto.

"That's why it's so disheartening to watch our new president at work," he said as he sliced. "He is splitting this party down the middle. Says he wants to move beyond partisanship, build a national coalition behind him. No more principles, just salute the great leader. That sounds like fascism as far as I'm concerned. Progressive fascism."

He motioned the waiter to refill his glass again.

"Most people think George Pulaski is a hero," I ventured.

"That's because of all the Strange New Respect Pulaski is getting from the media. The Nationals lost the election. Now the Nationalists and the media – but I repeat myself – now the Nationalists want to steal the guy we elected and make him *their* president."

"Senator Hazen thinks Pulaski is a hero."

"That's why you are such an important person, Walter! If we could bring Hazen back onside – as a reliable Constitutionalist senator – we'd change everything. We could repeal the Nationalist healthcare law. We could pass the flat tax reform. We could see some real budget cutting. And the people who *brought* Hazen onside – they'd get the credit. There would be nothing they couldn't ask for." He cast me a meaningful look.

The waiter topped up my half-empty glass, then emptied the remainder of the bottle into Catesby's.

"I want you to meet our board of directors. I want your input: How can we take the fight to the enemy? I've been pressing Patriot News to launch a regular weekly program featuring our writers. I could host it, it would be a great way for me to support and promote our young talent. Of course, all these things require resources …."

Ah. Here we go. Catesby ordered a cognac for himself. I requested a coffee, then settled in to listen patiently to the fundraising spiel. I'm good at that.

At last the check arrived. Catesby signed with a flourish, then rose, a little unsteadily on his feet. We reclaimed Catesby's coat from the cloakroom; then walked together to the front door. The doorman saluted him, and Catesby reached a hand into his breast pocket. A look of bafflement spread across his face. He whispered in my ear,

"I seem to have left my wallet at the office. Can you give the doorman $20 to thank him for watching my car? Be careful, the rules here say, 'No tipping.' But they also say, 'No parking on the circular drive'!"

I paid the requested tip. We stepped outside together into the grey afternoon. The doorman held open the door of the Porsche. Catesby slid into the driver's seat, waved cheerfully, and called out, "You'll be hearing from me!"

CHAPTER 10

As usual, Teresa glared balefully at me when I arrived at the office Monday morning. But the two other receptionists mustered pleasant hellos. One of them, a pleasant perm-haired Providence lady who strewed her desk with Lucite framed photographs of her cats, said, "Daphne wants to see you straightaway."

I poked my head into Daphne's office, and she beckoned me in. "I've reassigned you. I'm pulling you off mail duty. You'll have more of a personal assistant role: a body man. You'll accompany the senator to his meetings, serve his personal needs."

That sounded like more work than I'd signed up for. "Are you sure the senator would want that?" I asked, looking for an exit from the situation.

"He needs the help. You'll move your work area too – you'll sit at Kimberly's desk in the senator's vestibule."

As I think I mentioned, the senator's private office had two entries.

One, the more formal, faced the little hallway onto which Daphne's own door opened.

But there was another entrance as well, which opened directly onto the building's main exterior corridor. From the corridor, this discreet secondary entrance to the senator's sanctum looked like it might lead to a utility closet. Unlock the handle from the corridor, and you'd enter a little vestibule containing one small desk shoved against the wall to your left hand side. Beyond that: the senator himself.

That vestibule desk had belonged to the senator's scheduler, the just-mentioned Kimberly. Daphne led me over to take a look.

"So long as Kimberly sat here," she said, "every scheduling decision turned into a conference call. So I'm giving Kimberly your old desk, and putting you here instead."

At that moment, the secondary door opened, and in entered the senator himself, looking very old and very worn. As he surveyed the unexpected crowd in his vestibule, the stooped frame straightened and a look of annoyance flashed across his face. Suddenly you could see in the face of the white-haired old man the face of the tough scholarship boy from South Providence.

"Hello Senator," cooed Daphne. "Welcome back, sir! I hope the flight was not too demanding." Hazen had just returned from a two-week congressional delegation to the Far East during the post-election recess.

"Where the hell is Kimberly?"

"Well sir, while you were away, I've developed some options so that we can do a better job of supporting you. We've had some unacceptable mix-ups lately. Remember the miscommunication that sent you and Senator Hamill to each other's donor appreciation events before the recess? I thought we'd do better if Kimberly worked directly alongside political and media staff – and then if we got you a personal assistant who could ensure you get where you need to be."

"Him?" demanded the senator, jerking a thumb at me.

"Sir, this is Walter Schotzke, you remember you asked me to find a role for him?"

His expression changed from scowl to sunshine.

"Why didn't you say it was Walter from the start?"

He grasped my hand with both of his. "How wonderful to see you, when did I see you last, let me think? Ten years ago?"

"Longer than that sir, I'm afraid."

"Well don't remind me. I know it's been kind of a bumpy ride for you since then, but I'm delighted you've joined our team. Now look, I need some time to get settled, but I'll buzz you shortly, and we'll have a talk."

Daphne moved to enter with the senator. He raised a hand to hold her at bay. "Just a few minutes to myself."

Daphne mobilized a little smile. "Of course."

I spent the next couple of hours on Facebook debating "Which is the best single malt?" About 10:30 AM, my desk phone rang.

"Walter, will you run down to the cafeteria, get me a glass of buttermilk and some arrowroot biscuits please?"

The senator had been saved from stomach cancer, but the chemo and surgery had wrecked his digestion. Over the next weeks, I'd become very, very familiar with his joke that the recovery had condemned him to "the diet of a three-year-old."

Fifteen minutes later, I was standing at the senator's sideboard, pouring the thick liquid into a glass stamped with the Great Seal of the United States. I spread the biscuits upon a similarly decorated small plate. I unfolded a purloined white cloth atop the senator's leather blotter and placed plate and glass on the senator's desk. Eduardo could not have done better.

The senator looked downward at the place setting, then up at me, visibly pleased. He motioned me to sit in one of the visitor chairs opposite.

What a room!

High windows looked westward out Constitution Avenue toward the Washington Monument. A large antique map of Narragansett Bay dominated the wall behind the senator's desk. On the opposite wall (the wall pierced by the doorway to my vestibule), hung an old oil portrait of Roger Williams, the founder of the Rhode Island colony. In the center of the room were arranged a couch, a coffee table, and two comfortable armchairs. Just behind the couch, there stood a wooden case, the sort of case in which a library would display an ancient manuscript.

Later, the senator would guide me through the contents of the case: an ancient edition of Roger Williams' book on Indian languages; state bonds to finance the Revolutionary war; scrimshaw carved by whalers; a cap and the belt buckles that had belonged to a private soldier from Rhode Island's Civil War second infantry regiment; the senator's father's Jewish prayer shawl; a pocket watch engraved for presentation to Oliver Wendell Holmes; a fountain pen that had belonged to Chaim Weizmann; a handwritten letter to Hazen from one of his senatorial predecessors, thanking Hazen for his hard work on the campaign of 1976.

Affixed to the wall perforated by the door toward Daphne's office were four tall dark-wooden cases, jammed with law books, books about Rhode Island, histories of the Senate, biographies of presidents, a history of Brown University. Three linear feet of novels in German occupied the lowest shelf of the remotest case.

This, I thought, was the room of a man who knew where he came from. Where did I come from? I remembered once having dinner with an aunt of a previous girlfriend, a prim schoolteacher type, who informed me, "You come from money, Walter." She was right too. I was born in Brussels, attended eight different schools in Britain and the United States, then Brown (the only college that would have me). I had spent my summers all over the world: camps, other people's houses and yachts, Europe, New York. Money was my hometown.

"So I hear nothing good about you for a decade or more," said the senator good-humoredly. "Now Daphne can't praise you enough. She's not an easy person to impress, as you probably have discovered. I'm very glad if you have found your footing here. I am greatly indebted to your family."

"Paid in full, sir."

He didn't laugh, but he made a small noise in his throat and bared a mouthful of yellowed but healthy-looking teeth.

"I'm serious. Your grandfather trusted me to negotiate the merger with General Brands. Not many men in a situation like that would give the chance to their regular lawyer. I got your family a very good deal from GB – a *very* good deal – but for me, it was the chance of a lifetime. That chance let me do politics, and ultimately brought me here."

He dipped a biscuit in the milk and chewed purposefully.

"And your father, what an amazing man your father was."

Another bite of biscuit.

"It must be a lot to live up to."

"Well sir … I don't know what to say to that. I suppose my grandmother would say that I am not living up to it very well."

"I don't know. Maybe you're just getting revved up. Some people start faster than others that's all."

The senator leaned into the desk. "Did you know I was at the ceremony at Langley to honor your father? The Distinguished Intelligence Cross: It's the Congressional Medal of Honor for spies."

"I don't know who was there, other than my grandparents. Mom wasn't invited, and so she didn't allow me to go either. I've never even seen the citation."

"The citation is still secret. Parts of the Middle East network your father built are probably still operating. But the information your father brought out of the Gulf saved hundreds of American lives. He was not just a great businessman, he was a true American hero."

"My grandmother still has boxes full of the *Business Week* with him on the cover."

"Your father deserved that cover. Almost all the company's growth in the 1980s and 1990s came from your father's work in Europe, Asia and the Middle East."

"When I met the CEO of General Brands," I said, "he told me that GB bought the Schotzke company as much to get my dad as to get the mustard."

The senator nodded. He'd heard that too I supposed. He thought for a moment, and then added. "But running a company and a clandestine intelligence-gathering operation at the same time? That would demand a lot from a man. I suppose that explains some of the troubles at home."

Now it was my turn to think of what to say. But what? In almost all of my memories of my dad, he was saying goodbye. Somehow I could never remember the hellos. I can still see that last wave as my dad stepped into the back of the limo after his last visit to my school, already talking on his cell phone. He'd driven me down to London for a birthday lunch at Simpsons-on-the-Strand. It's not a subject I usually like to talk about. But for some reason I couldn't quite explain, I liked talking to Hazen.

"It wasn't just the divorce," I began. "It was what happened after. Everything was already finalized between my parents when dad was kidnapped. My mom had been unhappy in the marriage for a long time. She'd moved to London, she was onto her new life. She didn't see why she should go into hiding because her ex-husband had been grabbed by some Islamo-crazies. But my grandmother – oh God, you'd think Mom had planned the kidnapping herself. Even now, if I ever mention my mother's name …"

"Yes, I can imagine." His eyes showed sympathy.

"And then after Dad was killed, Mom got wilder and wilder. It was like the whole world was scowling at her, not just Grandma. Here's this American hero murdered. While he was being tortured, his ex-wife is being photographed in clubs dancing with pop stars. Of course, Mom didn't have any idea of what the terrorists were doing to dad. My grandparents blamed her anyway. They blamed me too."

"You?"

"I was in one of the paparazzi photographs, the one on that Silicon Valley guy's yacht, with my mother in the bikini."

"I remember the picture. Your mother was an amazingly beautiful woman. Maybe she should have stayed in Hollywood. Things might have been better for her."

"Hard to see how they could have been worse. All those pictures from yachts and nightclubs and ski slopes, they never come with a disclaimer that she had no idea of what was happening to Dad. Everybody told her he was fine, that the company was negotiating a ransom, that he was sure to be released. She didn't know the truth!"

But that wasn't quite true either, was it? She had to have known something – not the whole truth, maybe, but something. And it was not just Dad she was done with. It was me too. If she didn't arrive late on visiting days, she was leaving early, if she didn't forget altogether. I was that kid at the school whose mother was never there on the prize days - not that I ever won a prize. And then she was gone too, as vanished as the smell of her perfume, not even a body to bury.

All this I didn't say to Senator Hazen, who was still nodding compassionately. "No," he agreed. "How could she have known?"

"After that, Mom went into overdrive. You know the whole story: the big lawsuit over the will, the drugs, the plane crash."

"That idiot. Bad enough he got himself killed. But to take your mother with him! How old were you?"

"Thirteen."

Six weeks later, I'd been expelled from my English school. My grandparents found a new place to park me, then another, and then another after that. Charlie Feltrini was the only friend I made in all those miserable years. Charlie – and whoever was selling me my marijuana that semester.

"I wish-" Hazen was speaking again. "Well, I don't know what I wish. But I'm sorry."

I rose to put away the glass and plate. "Thank you." I meant it. "I truly appreciate this opportunity. I'll try not to mess up." I meant that too.

CHAPTER 11

Freddy Catesby made good on his lunchtime promise. When I arrived home that evening, Valerie handed me a fat package of envelopes wrapped around envelopes: an invitation to the thirtieth anniversary gala of the *Constitutional Review*: January 13, black tie. Tissue paper encased a small RSVP card. A thick line of royal blue ink slashed through the requested donation of $1,000 per person, $10,000 per table. "I hope you & a friend will come as my guests. FWJC."

Valerie was impressed. "I've seen wedding invitations less elaborate."

"That's because the weddings were less expensive."

"Well, he hasn't saved you any money by inviting you for free. We're going to have to buy you a tuxedo."

"Can't I rent one?"

"Are you trying to make me mad? No, you can't rent one. Someday you're going to explain to me why it's OK to spend tens of thousands of dollars on a South African safari, and some kind of crime against decency to buy a new suit every now and then."

"That was my birthday money! Anyway, I thought you liked the safari."

"I'd like you in a new suit."

I finally caught up with Charlie Feltrini. He was volunteering at Pulaski transition headquarters in Arlington, but he had time for a lunch break. A half-dozen panhandlers rushed me as I emerged from the subway station. I brushed past them and then found the tiny sushi restaurant Charlie had mentioned, a few steps below sidewalk level in a shabby-looking office building. More than half the storefronts were boarded up.

Charlie arrived only a minute or two after me. Except for an extra couple of inches of height and a slight thickening of the torso, he looked exactly the same as when we met at our last-chance prep school. The same badly brushed sandy hair. The same bulbous nose. The same big grin as he chuckled at his own private jokes. We squeezed ourselves into a small Formica-topped table between Japanese-speaking diners on either side of us.

"I've missed you, man," I said.

"Me too," said Charlie, in the brisk manner of a once-close friend who has over the years become a lot more important than you. "I feel awful it's taken this long for us to get together. Suzie scolds me every day. 'Walter and Valerie have come to town, just give me a day we can have them to dinner.' But even the days that look totally calm turn into total train wrecks. It's awful for Suzie. The baby's due in February. She says she's going to be a single mother by presidential appointment."

"Have you *got* an appointment?"

"Not yet, not yet. That's the other thing. It's like being an actor or something. Every day, somebody gets the call: You're going to State; you're going to Treasury. The stack of available jobs keeps dwindling. I still haven't heard anything."

Charlie picked up the stubby pencil atop the table and began to fill out the order card. "Anything you dislike? I have to warn you, the food here is ultra-authentic."

"I'll eat anything, except monkey. But how is it that you've been left waiting for a job? You're super-smart, super-dedicated."

"Thanks. But I'm a civilian, and that's a huge issue with this crowd. If you weren't with Pulaski in Mexico, he'll never trust you. Never mind trust. They just plain don't *like* civilians. They blame us for everything that's gone wrong these past ten years, and they don't distinguish between Nationalists and Constitutionalists. Even guys who joined the 'Draft Pulaski' campaign in New Hampshire and South Carolina … I mean they're getting positions. Sort of. Office of Personnel Management, Department of Labor, crap like that. But the big jobs? Ex-military almost every time. At this point, I'd almost *accept* Office of Personnel Management."

I tried to cheer him up. "Did I tell you I saw you on BBC when I was in South Africa? You were great."

He flushed with enjoyment of the compliment. The first plate of fish arrived. Despite my big talk about eating everything and anything, I avoided the items with tentacles. The others were delicious.

"Look, I can't complain," Charlie said resignedly. "I'm inside the transition building. I know people, good people, who can't get in the front door. But still, today is another day of not being hired."

"You can always return to teaching."

"Have a heart. Anyway, you know there's not a university in America that's hiring these days."

Charlie's chopsticks picked up one of the tentacled items and plopped it in his mouth.

"Do you ever think of Mr. Hepburn?"

"Only every time I enter a classroom." Charlie pursed his lips to do an amazing imitation of our Wellfleet math teacher. *"Mr. Feltrini, you and Mr. Schotzke are not only the two worst-behaved boys in the class – you are the two worst-behaved boys in all my years of teaching here at Wellfleet Academy."*

"Poor bastard. We did give him a hard time."

"Yes, yes we did – still, we turned out OK, I think."

"You did. Jury's out on me."

Back at the office an hour later, my BlackBerry rang. It was Charlie. He sounded more relieved than happy. Very relieved. "Got the tap. NSC Director for Humanitarian Affairs. I was hoping for western hemisphere, but I'm not complaining. No presidential commission, so I can't take you to lunch in the mess. The ex-military guys all got their special assistantships right away, but I'm promised mine in six months if I prove myself. Meaning – if I keep my bosses happy. Which I will."

"Congratulations, I'm happy for you."

"You know what I did even before I called you? I tracked down the town where Mr. Hepburn retired. I sent him a box of those fancy cigars he liked, the ones he used to smoke to celebrate when the students left for Christmas and summer vacation. He must have hated teaching as much as I do. So I figure, I owe him."

CHAPTER 12

Senator Hazen's life proceeded by strict routine. Since it was my job to accompany him wherever he went, my life now proceeded by strict routine too. That required some adjustment. By nature, I'm a guy who can't remember when it's time to go to the bathroom.

I met the senator every weekday morning at 7 AM at his apartment overlooking the Naval Memorial on Pennsylvania Avenue. By then, he would be sitting at his breakfast table, showered and shaved and dressed, except for his necktie and suit jacket.

The senator ate the same breakfast every day: a soft-boiled egg, wheat toast, tea, and a cheerful colorful array of capsules and tablets, all served on beautiful china dishes, the same pattern (he would later tell me) used by Marie Antoinette for her breakfast.

A portrait of the senator's wife as a young mother hung on the wall of the dining room. The painter presented the late Mrs. Hazen as a pretty petite dark-haired woman in a light summer dress. A baby sat on her lap, a toddler tugged impatiently at her hand, and an older girl of maybe six peeked out mischievously from behind her mother's wicker chair.

Now those three children had children of their own. Silver-framed images of the extended family filled the apartment, frozen in time at the moment of Mrs. Hazen's death. The senator had apparently not moved or changed or added or removed an item in the apartment in three years. I'd later discover that this newborn grandchild was now walking; that freckled 11-year-old was now a troubled teenager. The wall-to-wall deep blue carpeting was sun-faded in large squares near the windows. The silk on the yellow chairs and sofas had frayed at the arm-rests. Later in the winter, the senator would invite Valerie and me to a bachelor dinner. Valerie chirped, "I know somebody who can match this fabric perfectly and reupholster the chairs beautifully!" The senator shook his head sadly. "They'll see me through."

The senator was tended by an older couple who had migrated decades ago from South America. They lived in a small apartment he had bought them on a lower floor of the same building. They arrived at the apartment even earlier than I did, to cook and serve the senator's breakfast.

The first day I arrived for breakfast, I was asked what I would like. I pointed to the senator's plate: "The same will be fine."

That's exactly what I got, minus only the capsules and tablets. I was never asked again.

Breakfast and the newspapers were assigned half an hour of total silence. At precisely 7:30, the senator would rise from the table and return to his bedroom. A few minutes later, he'd emerge fully dressed, tie immaculately knotted, shoes always polished but never glossy. He told me once that he relaxed by lining up every pair he owned and shining them all.

Shortly before we exited the apartment, he'd pronounce his first words of the day, other than the absent-minded good morning with which he would greet me half an hour when I entered: "What's the weather like today?"

Depending upon my answer, the senator would assemble some combination of coat, hat, scarf and / or umbrella. Then we would stride out for the senator's morning walk.

The walk, too, always proceeded by the same route: out the front door of the senator's apartment building, through the middle of the Naval Memorial straight toward the National

Archives, past the little collection of vagrants in sleeping bags on the corner of Constitution and Fifteenth, then south to the Washington Monument. There we reversed our course, walking back toward Capitol Hill and the senator's office building. From home to office, the walk took 50 minutes. Valerie approved the routine. "It's not what I'd call exercise, but it's better than nothing."

"I'm not doing 'nothing.' I did my treadmill on Sunday!"

On our walks, the senator told me stories of my father and grandfather. He smilingly inquired how things were going with Valerie. He explained the strange rules and customs of the Senate and the grinding boredom of much of the institution's work. He named the senators he liked, the senators he respected, and the senators he trusted. (Three quite different categories it turned out.) He talked about his qualms about the Mexico commitment – and about how he didn't see any way out.

Rhode Island is a Nationalist state, yet Hazen had won three state-wide elections. He explained how he had done it.

"I have a lot of friends. I take care of everybody in the state who needs help: trouble with Medicare, a small business loan, an immigration problem. Every high school class that visits Washington gets the presidential box at the Kennedy Center and meets with the Secretary of State. Plus I have $12 million in my campaign treasury. That should scare off any troublemakers."

Of course, that $12 million didn't just materialize. Senator Hazen worked hard for his money. At 5:30 every evening, as most of us were getting ready to call the day quits, his day would rev into higher gear: receptions with lobbyists or industry associations, often two back-to-back. Donors claimed three of his five weekday lunchtimes. I'd accompany him to the first event, but he'd humanely order me away from the second. "Go home for dinner, I'll be fine."

He booked an hour of telephone time every day to talk to individual donors, usually in the car on the way to events. He returned to Rhode Island every weekend to work the voters. He dialed for more dollars as he was driven by the in-state staff from weddings to funerals, from christenings to bar mitzvahs.

One morning, after a day in which he'd been scheduled for *three* evening receptions, he allowed himself a little grumbling. I tried to cheer him. "Well at least all this fundraising keeps you close to the people."

The senator snorted from under his grey fedora. "I'm very close to the people who own private planes."

"People who own private plane are people too."

"Yes, and God bless them. But Walter remember – half the working people of this country earn less than $45,000 a year."

"You pay *me* less than $45,000."

"More than you deserve," he said with a gentle smile.

"At least you keep in contact with business leaders, heads of corporations, the people who make our economy go," I suggested.

"I like businessmen. My father was a businessman. My clients were businessmen. Your father and grandfather were businessmen – and great businessmen too. But you know who else is a businessman? The man who now owns my father's old store. An immigrant from Peru, he sells rotisserie chicken, very tasty, I'll take you the next time we're in Providence together. Who listens to people like him? Who cares about him?"

"So long as the Constitutionalists are in charge, we try at least to keep their taxes low. Isn't that something?" I repeated my lines like an apt pupil.

"Yes, that is something. I'm proud of it. But it's nothing like the full concierge service we provide the people who can write a campaign check."

An oncoming walker recognized the senator, stuck out his hand. The senator shook, without breaking stride.

"Your donors are the people who pay this country's taxes," I said. "When you have five percent of the people paying half the taxes – and half the people paying no taxes – maybe it's no surprise that Congress pays more attention to the taxpayers than the non-taxpayers?"

Hazen turned a quizzical look upon me.

"Where'd you hear that?"

"From my Tax Facts session at CI."

He shook his head.

"That 'fact' is a fact only if you don't count payroll taxes. Or excise taxes such as those on gasoline or alcohol. Or the share of the corporate income tax included in the price of all goods and services. Or highway tolls. Or the tariffs we place on the cheap glassware and running shoes poor people buy. Not to mention state and local sales taxes and property taxes. And never mind that the reason that poorer people are paying so much less federal personal income tax today than, say, ten years ago is that the economy has collapsed and they don't have jobs."

"Sorry, I didn't mean to provoke you,"

"You don't provoke me, but my good friends at CI sometimes test my patience. They call themselves a think tank, but it seems lately their real business is to manufacture and distribute pseudo-facts and pretend-information."

For a man who claimed not to be provoked, the senator was scowling very fiercely.

"But you gotta admit: It's the rich who pay the taxes."

"It's the rich who have the money! A much bigger share than they used to, too. I wouldn't even object to that, so much, if they didn't feel so sorry for themselves."

I changed the subject:

"You must be doing something right, you keep winning elections."

"There are 800,000 people eligible to vote in the state of Rhode Island, more or less. My last election, I got 247,612 votes. I won because my opponent did even worse."

"Oh yeah, the crazy 'I am not a witch' lady.'"

"Right. She didn't break 80,000. But even the first time I ran – a tough race, against a good Nationalist candidate – the two of us together got only a little over 400,000 votes. Half the state decided it didn't care. And really, why should they care? I'll listen to the chicken roaster if I happen to stop by his store. But I'd never call him on the phone, never mind twice in a month, the way I call my good friends at the U.S. Chamber of Commerce."

"You sound like a radical, sir."

The senator just laughed. "I'm no radical. I play the game according to the rules. You can't expect me always to like it. Ah, here we are. Good morning, Officer Boskin!" The senator passed to the left of the metal detector, leaving me to join the line.

CHAPTER 13

My first Christmas with Valerie's family had not been a success, and I was not eager to repeat the experience. Don't get me wrong. I had liked the McNaughtons. It was the reverse that had been the problem.

The McNaughtons lived just outside of Johnstown, Pennsylvania. Valerie's dad headed the county's legal department, chaired the local public transit authority, and taught at the local campus of the University of Pittsburgh. Valerie's mother – well what didn't she do? She ran the volunteer committee for the city library system, raised money for the struggling local symphony, and tutored failing high school students.

Valerie's older brother was an engineer at Johnstown's new wind turbine factory and an enthusiast for green energy as the salvation of the town. The next brother was a captain in the army just returned from South Korea. Both were married; the elder already had two children.

The McNaughtons were all athletic; all tall and good-looking. Girls like Valerie get their genetics from somewhere, after all. And every last one of the McNaughtons disapproved of me.

The family owned a large wooden house badly in need of a coat of paint. I'd been shown to a guest room in the basement paneled in some kind of vinyl stamped to look (not very much) like knotty pine. I had the luxury of my own bathroom, the only private bathroom in the whole house: a small gurgling toilet and a shower about 18 inches square.

Valerie's mother asked me how I liked my room. I answered approvingly, but apparently not approvingly enough.

The next test came on Christmas Eve. By long tradition, the family spent the evening volunteering at the local Lutheran nursing home. This test I recognized. I packed all the enthusiasm I could into my answer. "Yes, I'd love to join, that sounds wonderful!" I failed to convince – especially after Valerie found me in the TV room, watching *It's a Wonderful Life* with half a dozen of the geezers when everybody else was washing up after the holiday meal.

The final test came on Christmas day. I went to church for the first time in I can't remember how long. I tried to join the hymns, tried to listen to the sermon. I stood on the steps in the cold as the family chatted happily with the minister. I spent the frigid early afternoon pretending to enjoy tobogganing down snowy hills with Valerie's niece and nephew. I ate the Christmas dinner, choking down the canned cranberry sauce.

After dinner, I submitted to a searching interrogation by Valerie's mother about my life plans, as Valerie's father played piano with the grandchildren and pretended not to listen. I kept trying to escape by asking, "Why don't I help Valerie and the boys with the washing up?" And Valerie's mother just as often thwarted me by answering, "That's for family, you're a *guest*." The word "guest" had never sounded less hospitable.

When I was finally excused for the evening, Valerie whispered to me, "I'm going to sit up with my mom for a little. My folks will be asleep by ten, I'll come down to you after that."

In the uncomfortable basement room, I made an interesting discovery. If I sat on the toilet, I could hear through the papered bathroom ceiling about half the conversation in the upstairs parlor. Half was more than enough.

The conversation went something like this:

"Valerie, I know money is very enticing. But I'd think you'd want more than that in a serious relationship. I'd think you'd want someone who shared the values we raised you with, somebody on your intellectual level ..."

"Walter's not stupid!"

"I didn't say he was."

"Do you really think the only reason I'm interested in Walter is his money?" I was pleased to hear that she sounded very offended.

"He is a nice-looking boy, I'll admit that. But Valerie you have everything you need to make your own way in the world – and to find a man worthy of you. It's tempting to look for a short cut. But the short cut can lead to a very hard road."

"Mamma, if you can't have faith in Walter, have faith in me. He's got more promise than you think. You'll see."

"And what about *your* promise? From the time you were a little girl, your father and I always said you could run the world."

"I'm lucky to have a job running the parties for the people who run the world."

"Does he love you?"

"He needs me."

"Do you love him?"

There was a pause before Valerie answered – and suddenly I didn't want to listen to any more. I got off the toilet at that point and climbed under the thin scratchy coverlet. When Valerie tip-toed downstairs half an hour later, I pretended to be asleep.

After that first experience, I opted against return visits to the McNaughtons. Valerie had accepted my excuses when she planned her spring and summer visits home. But as Christmas ominously rolled around again, she pressed harder.

"I can't."

"Why not – did your grandmother invite you down to Barbados?"

"Very funny, I'd only ruin her bridge foursome. No, I've just started a new job, I don't think it would be responsible for me to leave town."

Valerie's eyes widened in unfeigned amazement.

"Sorry, I thought I was talking to Walter Schotzke." Her voice turned teasing. "I know you don't like my mom's canned cranberry sauce. But it just seems rude not to come see my parents. It's our most special time of year."

The little gears in my brain whirred. "Daphne knows that I don't have family of my own. So she's asked me to spell off the people who want extended holiday time."

That sounded plausible, but still some bell of feminine suspicion tinkled in Valerie's ear. "What's going on in your office that's so important? I thought Senator Hazen was spending the holiday in Palm Beach?"

"He is," I improvised. "That's why we can get by with a skeleton staff. But we need somebody – and it looks like it's going to have to be me. Daphne will stay too, but she can't take responsibility for everything all by herself."

Valerie conceded the point, but not even my gift of a pair of Louboutin shoes she had coveted quite dispelled Valerie's irritation with me for shirking the visit.

I arrived at our skeletally staffed office a few minutes before nine on the morning of Christmas Eve. The whole building was ghostly quiet. One good thing: Teresa had wrangled a long holiday, so for once I could enter the suite without encountering her unpleasant face.

I sat at my desk and started to read a new book about the Mexican insurgency that Valerie had recommended I download. An hour passed, then two. Then the phone on my desk buzzed. Daphne. "I want to talk to you."

I poked my head through Daphne's door. As always, the first set was fixed to Patriot News. But with Congress recessed, her second television set was set to ProgTV rather than the Senate channel. A panel of TV pundits was savagely attacking the incompetence of the Williams re-election team, painfully recapitulating the worst moments of the previous four years.

"Hi," I said to claim Daphne's attention.

"Have a seat."

I sat.

"I'm very pleased with your work," she said. No - she almost purred. She could not have surprised me more if she had hit me in the face with a wet fish. In fact, a wet fish would have been a lot less surprising. "Thank you," I managed to say. Then: "I don't know that I'm doing anything much."

"Let me be the judge of that. The senator likes you. He trusts you. And those are very important accomplishments."

"Really?" I felt my face turning pink. I didn't know what to say. Nobody had ever complimented my work before.

"I want to share something with you," she said, leaning forward confidentially. Outside the window with the bad view, snow was beginning to fall, fluffy and flakey.

"We're getting more worrisome signals from the new Pulaski team. Iggy Hernandez is trying to steer them in the right direction. But the word is that Iggy is only succeeding in alienating himself from the president-elect. If Iggy is cast out, there won't be many Constitutionalist voices that will be able to reach the president. Except Senator Hazen's voice. The president will listen to Senator Hazen. And now the senator is listening to you. The senator will be a very important player. And that means *you* will be an important player."

Was she kidding me? Maybe yes, maybe no. Then I remembered a line I'd read in one of those "power lessons" Valerie was always forwarding me: *Insincere flattery is more flattering than sincere flattery.*

"So it's very important," Daphne continued, "that you play intelligently. I'll share all the information that comes to me. But if you're to have the benefit of the best counsel I can give you, you must share everything the senator tells you." The smile that accompanied those words went beyond cordial. It was downright friendly. Any friendlier – and I feared she would tear off the latex face covering, reveal the lizard head beneath, and eat me.

"I hear you."

"Good. You may take the rest of the day off. We won't need you until after Christmas. See you Thursday."

I headed home. Two and a half unsupervised days. Total freedom. But freedom to do what? The snow was falling thicker. This was not a day to go anywhere. The book on Mexico provided a few hours interest. Facebook an hour more. As the sun set, I poured myself a Talisker. Then another. I began to feel lonely.

I didn't dare call Valerie. If she knew I was free, she'd summon me to Pennsylvania. Charlie wouldn't want to hear from me on Christmas Eve. Jack had left for Rhode Island. I sure didn't feel like hanging out with random drunks at the Capitol Hill bars.

Then I remembered something: a card in a suit pocket. Yes, it was still there, from the night at the Ali Baba bar. The name read: Sylvia Tescher, Executive Vice President, Patriot News. The card listed an office line, an email address, and – bingo – a mobile phone number. Probably she had Christmas plans. But she was single, and she had seemed friendly. Valerie was always after me to "network." Surely a meeting with a Patriot News VP could count as "networking"?

"Hello, is that Sylvia?"

"Yes, this is Sylvia. Who is this?"

"We met at the opening of the Ali Baba bar a couple of weeks ago. I spilled your drink. You offered to get me another one. I didn't have time to accept then. But I thought maybe the offer remained good. My name's Walter."

She waited so long to answer that I thought the call had been dropped. "You took your time calling."

"I'm new in town, I've been getting settled."

"And that pretty girl who took such a proprietary interest in you – is she helping you settle?"

"Oh … she's left me."

"She didn't seem the leaving type."

"She's left me alone for Christmas."

"I see."

"And I thought – you might have been left alone for Christmas too."

"That's not a very complimentary thought."

Ouch, clumsy. "I didn't mean it that way. I meant, a lot of people get stuck in Washington working over the holidays – in case the nation is attacked by space aliens or something."

Sylvia saw right through that one too.

"I don't know that I want to spend Christmas with a strange man, especially not one who waits two weeks to call, and then only because his girlfriend has gone out of town."

I'd never been a pickup artist. Usually the girl had done all the work. But it was going to be embarrassing to retreat now. And- and well you can't spend a month on Capitol Hill without learning to push a little.

"At the bar you didn't seem to mind I had a girlfriend."

"At the bar I was drunk."

"So let's get drunk together. It's the holiday! Isn't that what people are supposed to do? Beats getting drunk alone."

Did I say that? There wasn't anybody else here, so yes I guess it had to be me. There was a moment of silence, and then – success.

"OK, fine. Tell me again what your name was?"

"Walter." I almost added "Schotzke." Then I decided to hold that detail back. I thought of Valerie in Johnstown surrounded by the family that did not approve of me. This one time, let me see how far I get on my own propulsion. "How about a glass of champagne at the Four Seasons bar?"

Sylvia laughed a sarcastic laugh. "How about posting an announcement on Facebook? No, meet me at the bar at the Essex. Nine o'clock. It will be just us and the waiters."

I had to look up the Essex: a hotel bar way beyond Dupont Circle that had been popular back in the 1980s. I arrived a few minutes before nine. Inside, the Essex bar was all pine paneling, nautical prints, and visiting grandparents returning from Christmas Eve dinners.

I ordered a bottle of champagne, waited to uncork it till Sylvia arrived. Nine passed. 9:15. 9:30. 9:40.

At three-quarters past the hour, Sylvia slipped in. Whatever I was expecting, this was not it. No sexy dress tonight. Pants. Sweater. Flat shoes. Not much makeup. But the body was still interestingly full where it should be and slim everywhere else. The eyes still blazed bright blue. And with less makeup, she actually looked fresher somehow.

I stood to greet her. "I ordered the champagne."

"I don't like champagne. I'll have a martini."

We sat in the furthest corner of the bar. It was very nearly as empty as promised.

"I brought you a little present." I held out a small gift-wrapped box: an expensive new perfume for which Valerie had managed a launch party at the Tyson's Galleria.

"I've turned down guys who offered to fly me to Aruba."

"In that case, this shouldn't compromise you."

She shoved the box into her handbag without another glance.

She proceeded to drink three martinis. I drank three-quarters of the bottle of champagne, and then followed with a martini of my own.

By then, we were having a pretty good time. I was making her laugh with stories of my more psychopathic prep-school teachers. We'd exchanged brief, highly edited autobiographies. Sylvia – who held her liquor a lot better than me – edited much more deftly. She teased out most of my story, but my fuddled brain gleaned barely more about her than when I had known when we sat down: she was alone and she was available.

"You're a nice boy," she said. "Nicer than I expected."

"You sound like a schoolteacher when you talk that way."

"I feel like your schoolteacher. How old are you anyway?"

"Twenty-eight."

"Oh, God help me."

"Lady and gentleman," announced the blue-jacketed Filipino bartender, "I must close in ten minutes."

I lurched to my feet. "I'll take you home. Where do you live?" At least that's what I tried to say. The room was whizzing pretty fast around my head, and the words must have sounded garbled to her.

"You're in no condition to go anywhere. Let me see if I can get you a room."

She vanished. I rested my head against the banquette, hoping to stop the rotation of the world. Sometime later – A minute? An hour? – she rematerialized with a room key.

"You're in luck."

I banged my knee hard against a couple of the little bar tables as I reached for the key. She steadied me and took my arm. "I'd better take you."

She led me to the elevator, walked me down a corridor, and unlocked a dark dull room. She pulled my sweater over my head and unbuttoned my shirt. I felt her hand on my bare chest – and I reached for her. She eluded me, but she kept unbuttoning.

And then, suddenly, we were on the bed, thrashing and tumbling, my loafers kicked off, my pants tangled about my legs. Sylvia was very different from Valerie in bed: very single-minded, very focused on what she wanted. Beyond that ... well I don't remember very much.

I woke up early to see Sylvia wrapped in a sheet, picking her clothes off the floor. I got out of bed to help, but she waved me back.

"I need to clean myself up. Then I need to figure out what stupid thing I've just done."

Still wrapped in the sheet, she padded barefoot to the bathroom to shower. My BlackBerry buzzed just as the water started.

"Merry Christmas, my love!" It was Valerie.

"Hey sweet face, merry Christmas to you," I said softly.

"Is everything OK? Did I call too early?"

"Ah – yeah a little – I'm not feeling too well – actually I'm headed out for breakfast – can I call you when I'm back in the apartment?"

"You're headed out for breakfast at 7:30 on Christmas morning?"

"Ah – see – I had a couple of whiskies last night on an empty stomach. I fell asleep very early and didn't eat any dinner. So I woke up early and starving."

"Poor boy! But who on earth is open at this hour?"

"The Mayflower hotel, they're always open."

"Okay. Call me back when you've finished breakfast."

I thrust the phone under the sheets as Sylvia stepped out of the bathroom, a towel wrapped around her head, a hotel bathrobe around her body. "Your girlfriend checking up on you?" she said.

I couldn't continue fictionalizing. "Yes."

"We'd both better get moving then," she said. "I've thought it over. I'm not sorry. I hope you aren't. Keep my card. Just in case we're both alone over the next holiday."

I dressed rapidly, bolted for the elevator. As I reached the lobby, I realized I was desperately thirsty and very hungover. I stopped into the hotel restaurant. It was just opening. I asked for a cup of coffee in a to-go cup. That took a few minutes of rattling in the kitchen. I waited, resting my back on the wall.

The elevator pinged. Out stepped a voluptuous blonde, no make-up, hair pulled back, clutching a raincoat over crumpled clothes. I recognized the face: It belonged to one of the sexpot reporters on Patriot News. She rushed past me, then past the forlorn woman camping atop the hotel grate. We're awfully far from Capitol Hill, I thought. Why would Patriot News billet its reporters all the way up here?

I turned for a rear view as the sexpot disappeared into the drizzle: very nice, even better than the front. I turned back and – whomp – nearly crashed into a big man's body, moving almost as fast as the already vanished blonde. It was Mac Kohlberg. Our eyes locked. He looked terrified at the sight of me. I had an inspiration. Before he could react to me, I said, "Dr. Kohlberg, please don't tell anyone you saw me. I'm not here, OK?" His face melted into relief. "Of course Walter, of course. You have my word." Then he too stepped out the door.

CHAPTER 14

I probably would have felt guiltier about the Sylvia episode if I'd had a better time. Or else if I had not suspected that Valerie had spent the holidays hearing her parents dump on me. Instead, the whole encounter faded from my mind as soon as my knee recovered from the damage I'd done in the hotel bar.

Valerie returned home the day after Christmas to hurl herself into the work of New Year's party planning. I spent New Year's eve playing poker with Jack Campozzo and his friends. I lost $150.

Congress returned from recess on the second of January for a short lame-duck session: two and a half weeks of work and maneuvering before the swearing in of the new president. The gains and losses on the table in *that* game would be tallied in the hundreds of billions.

"I had a call last night from Iggy Hernandez," Senator Hazen said to me as we strode out of his apartment building on the morning of the third day of January.

"Yes?" The cold bit me in the face. Washington winters are supposed to be mild, but the weather sites described this as the coldest January since 1984. My skin tightened. Hazen seemed unbothered. We stepped around the little clutch of vagrants at Eighth and Constitution.

"Iggy said the president-elect will not support the re-enactment of the tax cuts that lapsed at the end of last year."

There was a time when I would have had no idea of what the senator was talking about. But I had learned a lot over the past six weeks.

A dozen years before, a Constitutionalist Congress and president had passed a big tax cut. To comply with some complex budgeting rule, the tax cut expired after a decade. President Williams had been bullied into renewing the tax cut for an additional two years, but he had balked at a second renewal. However, the big Constitutionalist victory this past November had seemed to guarantee a rapid renewal. The tax cut, back-dated to December 31, would be re-enacted by the Constitutionalists in Congress and signed by President Pulaski as soon as he took office.

Or so everybody had expected and assumed. After all, the demand for the renewal of the tax cuts had united Constitutionalist donors from Marina del Rey to Bar Harbor. General Pulaski had never explicitly endorsed the demand. But he had never opposed it. He had allowed it to be written into the party platform. Speaker after speaker had agitated for it at the Constitutionalist convention in Las Vegas. Constitutionalist National Committee advertising had blasted Monroe Williams for opposing it. Pulaski had smiled and waved at a hundred campaign events as the people introducing him uncorked their most fiery oratory on the subject. If Constitutionalists had so much as suspected that Pulaski harbored the least reservation about renewal, they never, *ever* would have nominated him for the presidency.

So that was quite the bombshell the senator was calmly revealing to me.

"The party will not like it," I said wonderingly. The Washington Monument loomed clear and bright through the cold January air.

"According to Iggy, the president-elect says the budget must be balanced first."

"I can see his point of view."

"According to Iggy, the president said it would be indecent to cut taxes on the rich while cutting government programs for the middle-class and the poor."

"He said 'indecent'?"

"Allegedly. Nothing Iggy says can be taken as true until it has been independently verified."

"What happened then?"

"Well, Iggy says they had an intense confrontation. Iggy accused Pulaski of betraying the people who elected him. That offended Pulaski who said – and again this is all according to Iggy – 'I was elected president of the United States, not president of the Yellowstone Club. I'm here to serve the whole country, not your rich pals.'"

"Ouch."

"Ouch for Iggy." We turned off Constitution Avenue into the Mall. "Iggy says that the president ended the conversation by asking him to serve as Secretary of the Interior."

"That's impressive! You can criticize the president to his face and still get a cabinet job."

Hazen turned to eye me. "You don't get it. Iggy wanted to be White House chief of staff. Or something like it. Interior? Dealing with public lands? And Indian tribes? In a building next door to the Office of Personnel Management? Iggy? Ha! General Pulaski might as well have appointed Iggy ambassador to Kazakhstan."

"Will he accept?" The wind howled into our faces as we looped the Monument.

"Iggy will accept the job," he said finally. "He won't accept the situation. Pulaski is working on the old theory that it's better to keep somebody like Iggy inside the tent pissing out. But he doesn't know Iggy. Iggy is perfectly capable of pissing inside the tent."

"So what happens?"

"We have a test of strength."

"That's not much of a contest: a war hero president vs. some political operator?" My breath emerged in little frosty puffs.

"You'd think. But you'd think wrong. Constitutionalism isn't a 'what.' It's a 'who.' Constitutionalism is an informal central committee of maybe 20 people. They decide the party line and define who is a true constitutionalist and who is not. A sitting president has a lot of leverage over them. But the central committee trusts Iggy in a way they will never trust a retired military man with ideas of his own."

The wind abated. The sun was warming the air. I hadn't yet got used to the Washington climate's ability to rise or drop ten degrees in an hour. But I was enjoying the improvement.

"Do you really think that Iggy can win?"

"I think" – he hesitated, then smiled craftily – "I think it's going to be a fine day after all."

CHAPTER 15

Constitutional Review threw itself a lavish party. Valerie and I picked up our seating cards in the wide hall just outside the big dining room on the hotel's lower level, jostled and crushed by the throng of other guests.

I recognized almost nobody, except for the occasional face I had seen on TV. But who was this rich looking man walking beside his much younger, razor-thin wife? A lobbyist? A CEO who'd jetted from out of town? A K Street super-lawyer? A big advertiser? Sometimes Washington feels like a village, sometimes it feels like a world.

A few steps further into the melee, and we saw Freddy Catesby shaking hands at the end of an improvised receiving line. Freddy welcomed us with delight. He made a special fuss over Valerie. In her heels, she stood three inches taller than him. That seemed to bother Freddy not at all, probably because it brought his eyes closer to the point at which the neckline of her black dress plunged toward the skin.

After a few moments of hungry attention, Catesby disenthralled himself from Valerie's chest to greet his other arriving guests – including, at last, the grandest attraction of them all. "Iggy!" Catesby shouted as the famous face drew near.

Iggy it was, his white hair clipped round an olive-skinned bald head, little glasses stretched over alert brown eyes. Eyes that warned: being on the bad side of Ignatius Hernandez would be a very uncomfortable location.

Iggy's "good evening" was cordial enough, delivered with just the faintest trace of a Cuban accent, the exile's stamp on his American passport.

Valerie and I lingered in the vicinity long enough for Catesby to remember that he had left us stranded, hemmed in between the backs of people all furiously networking with each other. In no other city on earth would a woman who looked like Valerie, wearing a dress like her dress, have gone ignored in a roomful of men. But in the opening days of a new administration, with jobs being distributed after four years of waiting, the men were far more concerned to be noticed themselves.

Catesby, however, was more susceptible. He reached back into the churning human scrum to grab Valerie's hand and pull her forward. I followed. "Iggy, allow me to present my young friend Walter Schotzke – of the famous mustard family. You remember his magnificent father and the sad story about his mother? Walter now works for Senator Hazen. And this is his friend, the lovely Valerie McNaughton."

As Catesby burbled his details, Hernandez's eyes flickered with calculating interest. I could feel his precise mind assigning my details to a location inside some inner data-retrieval system.

Catesby reoriented Valerie and me toward a big, soft, doughy man plodding determinedly toward Iggy. "This is Bill Mihailovich, editor of the *Wall Street Transcript*. Bill, please meet Walter Schotzke and Valerie McNaughton." Valerie extended her hand. Mihailovich looked her dead in the eyes – and then declined to shake or even say hello. He cut us dead at a distance of 24 inches. We'd flunked some test of worthwhileness before we even opened our mouths. I shot Valerie an outraged look. *What an asshole.*

She shrugged. *It's a city full of them.*

"You know Mac and Grace Kohlberg, of course?" Beside Mac stood a thick-set woman in her mid-50s, wearing a bright silver cross over a department-store prom dress in an unflattering dark red. Her untinted grey hair was cut in a no-fuss bob around a cheerful, matronly face.

I almost jumped out of my skin, but Mac showed not a flicker of discomfort, just the familiar hearty greeting. "Of course I know Walter, Freddy, he was my star pupil! Valerie, a pleasure to meet you." Mac turned an expert's appraising eye upon Valerie, starting at the ankles, appreciating every curve. Suddenly he felt his wife's appraising eyes upon him and cut short his examination. "Hey, Walter, if you really want to understand Constitutionalism, you have to listen to Grace – she's been in the movement and at CI even longer than I have." He gracefully stepped away, skillfully extricating himself and abandoning his wife to be amused by Valerie and me.

Mrs. Kohlberg nodded emphatically. If she had seen anything, she said nothing. "I've been at CI 33 years, can you believe it? My first job after I married Mac was at the old Constitutionalist Institute building. We fit all of CI into an old row house! We were a real guerilla insurgency in those days, only eight of us. I answered phones, ran the mailroom, and processed our tax returns too. No talk radio in those days, no Patriot News, no cable at all. No Internet or email or texting. Not even fax! We did all our communicating with our supporters by mail, if you can believe it."

"Sounds like pioneer days," I suggested.

"Now you're making fun of me. But we did have one thing: commitment. And another: trust. The idea that we could support a president – and that he'd turn around and betray us like this ...."

Mac Kohlberg deftly inserted himself into Mihailovich's and Iggy's tight conversation, but over the four intervening feet of crowd sound he somehow still heard his wife's too-candid comments. He turned over his shoulder to caution her. "You're not starting the impeachment proceedings already?"

Mrs. Kohlberg ignored the warning, and Mac Kohlberg resumed his conversation, as if he had long ago resigned himself to his wife's indiscretion.

"This Pulaski is not even inaugurated yet," she said, directing the remark at her husband's broad back – he had already "and already he's nearly as bad as Williams. Just wait till he's in office, the treacherous ingrate. I see right through that uniform of his. Pulaski owes Iggy everything, and now he's dumping him over the side."

A waiter offered canapés. Mushrooms stuffed with bacon. I reached, - felt Valerie's death gaze - and dropped my hand. Mrs. Kohlberg helped herself to two of the caloric mushroom caps "I said all this during the nomination campaign. I warned everybody. But Iggy had all these graphs and charts and focus groups to prove that only Pulaski could beat Williams. And you should have heard everyone gush. *Don't worry! Pulaski is recruiting all our friends. He's taking advice from Tony Monckton.* Sheeple."

Somebody bumped the tumbler of Diet Coke in Mrs. Kohlberg's pudgy fist, sloshing a little onto the carpet below. It was going to take more than spilled soda to shut her up now. "But it's no good having the right principles if you won't do the work! I appreciate Tony Monckton too, but he is so lazy! And between you and me – kind of a sycophant. All those years at the Chamber of Commerce saying 'yessir' to every CEO in America. Monckton supported all the bailouts! Every single one!"

The canapé tray returned: some kind of spring roll. Mrs. Kohlberg took one and dipped it deep into the sticky orange sauce.

"Anyway it's Pulaski's people, not Monckton, who are choosing all the key economic appointments. Monckton will jet off to those international conferences he loves. The sellouts will run the store. And now they are saying that Pulaski will balance Monckton with a Nationalist at Justice! Can you believe that! There goes any hope of ever investigating any of the Monroe Williams people – or that greedy wife of his!"

Valerie spoke up in faint challenge: "Maybe that would be a good thing? Maybe the country is ready to move on?"

Mrs. Kohlberg's tumbler was bumped again, but fortunately for the carpet, the glass by now held only a little watery fluid. "Well of course Pulaski wants to move on! He's got scandals of his own, or so I hear. Our friend General Meyer has an interesting theory about the shooting down of Pulaski's helicopter. General Meyer says that Pulaski was doing business all along with the Chihuahua cartel. Pulaski was leading the raid to serve notice that he'd personally destroy anybody who did not pay him. But his own aides tipped off the cartel! So the insurgents knew Pulaski was coming, and that's how they shot him down."

Bad luck for Grace Kohlberg. The waiters were sounding the chimes for dinner. Her husband and Bill Mihailovich had turned to retrieve her just in time to hear her expound her conspiracy theory. Mac Kohlberg winced in embarrassment. Mihailovich interceded with grave ponderousness. "Dick Meyer says a lot of outrageous things. You should not be repeating them. Pulaski was not my first choice either. But we're going to work hard to keep him on a solid Constitutionalist path."

"Bill's right," agreed Kohlberg. "Grace, you should be more careful what you say."

"Well, you should be more careful about picking our party's nominees!" retorted Mrs. Kohlberg.

The doors to the hotel dining room were flung open. Clutching her table assignment card in hand, Mrs. Kohlberg strode forward. Most of the guests stayed in place a little longer, extending the gossiping and networking until the last possible moment. The dinner chimes rung louder and louder.

Waiters began to move amongst the chattering groups corralling guests. "Dinner please, you must take your seats."

Catesby took Valerie's arm to escort her to dinner. I moved to follow, but I was restrained by Mac Kohlberg's big hand.

"You're an interesting guy, Walter. You keep your head down, but you've impressed a lot of people: Daphne Peltzman, Freddy, a lot of people."

"Everybody likes mustard."

"Yeah well there's that. That doesn't hurt. Especially not with Catesby. But maybe there's more. I think there might be more. I'd like to find out."

"Thank you." His grip on my arm prevented me from obeying the exasperated wait-staff's orders to move along.

"So here's the thing: There are a lot of opportunities for somebody like you. The Institute can really help. The party can really help. I think I can help."

The waiters had won their battle against the crowd at last. Most of the guests had by now been shepherded past us. Kohlberg and I huddled almost alone in the outer hall. He continued, "What makes Washington work are the little deals. You see it again and again. One guy gets into trouble – bang he's dead. Another guy? All sorts of people step forward to say, 'Let's give him another chance, I can vouch for him.' The thing that kills guy number one bounces off guy number two. We all need those kinds of friends. Even guys with trust funds."

A waiter stood beside us, and struck a chime only three feet from my ear.

"Go away," Kohlberg growled at him, and the slight brown man retreated.

I wanted to hear more. "So how do I make friends like that?"

"You invest in them. You make deposits now. Then if you need it, you can make withdrawals later."

"Like what kind of withdrawals?"

"Well let me just pull an example out of the air. Daphne is hoping you can help her realign Senator Hazen away from Pulaski, back with the rest of the party. I don't know if that's possible, but your family launched Hazen's career, maybe there's some lever you can pull. Or not. But if you do succeed, do you think Daphne intends to share the credit?"

"She's been very nice to me recently."

Kohlberg looked at me like I'd just won first prize in the stupidest man in town contest.

"Of course she's nice to you! She's messed up, and everybody knows it. If Senator Hazen follows Pulaski away from the party, Daphne's going to have to take that phony accent of hers and apply for a job as receptionist at the Turkish embassy or whatever the hell language it is that she pretends to speak. There won't be another job in this city for her, not on our side anyway. She's desperate and you're her last hope. But if you get the job done – do you think she'll remember any of that? Man, you'll be lucky if she doesn't drive you to the woods, put a bullet in your head and bury your body to get rid of the evidence."

"Yeah, that would be her style."

"But suppose you had more friends than she did." He was leaning close enough to me that I could smell the Scotch on his breath. "And suppose Hazen did do the right thing. They'd make sure that the credit went to you, not Daphne. You'd be a huge hero. Huge. And then ... a lot of opportunities would open."

The sound of scraping chairs bounced out of the dining room into the hall. Kohlberg again extended that over-sized hand. I shook.

CHAPTER 16

Catesby's seated Valerie beside him at the more desirable of the two big tables booked for *Constitutional Review* editors and guests. Untroubled by girl-boy-girl rules, Catesby placed Hernandez on his other side. I was left to sit at the lesser of the two tables, with some advertisers, a couple of magazine staffers, and Grace Kohlberg. I took a chair as far as possible from Grace.

The room had been lavishly decorated in CR's house colors, red and black: red and black bunting on the dais, red and black ribbons on the chairs, red and black centerpieces atop the red and black tablecloths. A huge *Constitutional Review* banner stretched behind the podium for the benefit of photographers and video cameras.

As the room subsided, Catesby broke away from Valerie and Hernandez to walk toward the podium. He tapped the microphone for attention. I reviewed the elegantly printed program, flipping past the pages of thanks to the evening's sponsors: banks, defense contractors, pharmaceutical companies. At last I reached the menu. A lot of adjectives in French, but it amounted to the inevitable Washington hotel banquet menu: green salad topped with sliced radish and shredded carrot; beef tenderloin accompanied by out-of-season asparagus; chocolate mousse for dessert. I tested the glass of white wine in front of me. Ugh. I tested the red. Worse.

Catesby opened by reminiscing about the early days of the magazine, telling jokes, complimenting important people, thanking everybody for coming.

Then he glanced down at a sheaf of notes and launched into an oration.

"Just four years ago, people were talking about the death of Constitutionalism. Somebody even wrote a book about it … Well ladies and gentleman, we're back! In fact – we've never gone away!"

The audience applauded lustily.

"I wish to toast our new president-elect. We've waited four years to say these words with pride. Ladies and gentlemen, a toast to the president of the United States, George Pulaski! May he remain debonair, true to his ideas and ideals – and always stalwart against the out-of-touch elites of Washington!"

The room rose to its feet, raising glasses, murmuring "The president!"

The room jumped to its feet again, cheering, stomping and whistling until my ears ached. I glanced toward Valerie. Her attention was fixed on Catesby. I stealthily reached for the basket of rolls – and suddenly saw Sylvia Tescher across the room, presiding over a table of her own.

Boing! Panic! What if she saw me? What if she approached me? What if Valerie remembered Sylvia's face from the Ali Baba club?!

Sylvia's head rotated turned toward mine – and did not stop. Her eyes passed over my face as if she had never seen it before in her life. Whew. Safe. But also, ouch, kind of insulting. Not even a wink?

The first course hit the table: the salad, still chilly from the big hotel refrigerator.

I turned to introduce myself to my neighbor on my left, but he was already up and out of his seat, hovering deferentially over a diner at the next table over. My neighbor was not alone. A lengthening line of people snaked in front of that same diner, waiting their turn to pay respects.

There seemed nothing very impressive about the seated man receiving all these attentions: medium height, spongy body, a bland forgettable, unsmiling face not improved by his battered tuxedo.

"Who the hell is that?" I wondered to the woman at my right, as she resumed her seat after her own excursion to pay her respects.

"That's Elmer Larsen," she answered.

"Who's Elmer Larsen?" I asked as softly as I could.

"How long have you lived in Washington?" she asked incredulously.

"Not quite two months."

"That's long enough to know about Elmer. Elmer is brilliant, he's the man to see, the whole movement is run out of Elmer's office."

"What does he do?"

"That's hard to describe. He runs his own group, Americans for Entrepreneurship. He's on everybody's board of directors, ours too. He's a fantastic fundraiser. If Constitutionalism had a General Secretary, it would be Elmer. Tell you what, when it gets quieter, I'll introduce you to him. By the way, who are you?"

I introduced myself and collected her details in return.

She was the publisher of the *Constitutional Review*, a professional-looking middle-aged woman whose face showed the strain of financing Freddy's lifestyle.

Salad now disposed of, Catesby returned to the podium. The line in front of Elmer regretfully dissolved.

"Ladies and gentlemen," Catesby opened, "Nobody who owns a television set needs an introduction to my friend Ignatius Hernandez, the crafty strategist who outfoxed the whole Nationalist party. Iggy, we are behind you every step of the way. Come on up and delight us for a few minutes."

Hernandez stepped forward, clasped Catesby's hand, and then jokingly clasped both of his own hands over his head like a championship boxer. The tuxedoed dignitaries laughed and clapped. Somebody started a chant: "IG-gee. IG-gee. IG-gee." The whole room took it up, and the cheers lasted and lasted.

Hernandez smilingly calmed the room. "Friends! – Friends! Ladies and gentlemen."

He saluted Catesby as Castesby scuttled back to his seat. "Freddy, CR doesn't look a day over 29." More laughter.

Then Hernandez grew serious. "Friends, we Constitutionalists scored a great victory in November. We could not have won that victory without the leadership of General Pulaski, and I'm proud to have supported this great American hero. Now our president must govern in a time of challenge. We want him to be the best president he can be.

"The best *Constitutionalist* president he can be," Hernandez added with heavy emphasis. "I'll be proud to help our new president anywhere he asks me to serve. This movement and this magazine can serve the president best by speaking up strongly for our principles. When we mess up – you tell us. If we stray from the right path – correct us. No more bailouts! No more compromises! And no new taxes!"

Passionate applause. In the thunder, my publisher friend leaned toward Elmer. "Elmer, let me introduce Walter Schotzke. He's a special guest tonight of Freddy's."

Elmer looked at me – and what a look! Two bleary eyes that stared, then suddenly blinked rapid-fire, then went wide open again. A mouth that didn't smile. A face that barely registered other people's existence, not mine, not anybody else's.

"Schotzke? Like the mustard?"

"That's me."

"How much of the company does your family still own?"

I'd learn over the coming months that Elmer either had never learned – or else did not accept – the ordinary rules about how people talked to each other. But at that moment I was so surprised that I couldn't think of anything to do other than answer the question.

"We sold out to General Brands in 1985." That answer did not impress, and on an impulse I added, "But we're major shareholders in GB."

Elmer absorbed that information, as the waiters returned to clear the ruins of the first course.

"What brings you to Washington?"

"I've started work for Senator Hazen."

Elmer stared harder. "Hazen is a traitor." Was he joking? There was no sign.

The publisher spoke up for me. "Walter is a protégé of Daphne Peltzman's. He's working hard to pull Hazen back to the party. His family has great influence with Hazen."

Another hard stare from Elmer. Then: "Call this number if you ever want to talk." He passed me a card and turned away to shake hands with the reassembling greeting line.

I was left to talk to the publisher. "That was weird."

"That's Elmer. But say, Walter," (and here a little gleam came into her eye), "how much pull do you have with General Brands?"

Uh oh. What was the right answer?

"Me personally? Not so very much. The stock is all voted by trustees."

"Would you or anybody in your family be able to set up a meeting with General Brands?"

Think, think.

"Yes, probably."

"That's wonderful. I'll follow up with you on that. But it looked for a minute there that you wanted to ask me something?"

"Well here's the thing I don't get: Catesby and Hernandez go up to that podium to praise Pulaski and everybody cheers. But over cocktails everybody trashes Pulaski."

The publisher nodded sagely at me. "The people who bought tables here tonight – lobbyists, advertisers, friends of the magazine – want to know that we're close to the administration, that we have clout. So we want to sound supportive. And let's face it, most of our readers are still so grateful to see the back of President Williams that they'll cheer almost anything Pulaski says or does."

I nodded, hoping I sounded as sage. "Plus of course they have to speak nicely about Pulaski, what with their great pal Hernandez lined up behind the president."

The publisher snorted at me. "What makes you say that?"

Now I felt stupid. "Um – isn't that what he just said?"

"That's not what he said! Just the opposite!"

"Wait – what?"

"Iggy is telling the president, 'I can turn up the heat on you anytime I want. You'd better keep me happy, so that I can keep all these crazy Constitutionalists happy. Or else it's going to be a bloodbath.'"

"Oh. And I thought you guys would be happy that you'd just won this epic victory."

"We've had victories before. Victory after victory. What have we got to show for it? We keep being sold out. I'm the publisher of CR, I have to keep the lights on. So, yes, I'm glad we can publish a big gala inaugural edition, stuffed with ads from aerospace companies and healthcare conglomerates. But speaking as a Constitutionalist just personally – if Pulaski doesn't keep the faith, I say, tear his heart out."

Suddenly the publisher didn't seem like such an agreeable lady any more. So what the hell, I spoke my mind.

"You're going to tear the heart out of General Pulaski?" I remembered what Colonel Cleland had said at the Constitutionalist Institute. "The most popular new president in half a century? Excuse the expression, but – you and what army?"

She inclined her head to indicate the lengthening line again snaking its way toward Elmer's chair. "The army is being built right now."

CHAPTER 17

Inauguration Monday: sunny, balmy, fifty degrees, a freakish change from the past weeks of unusual cold. Despite the gentle weather, this inauguration did not attract the huge crowds that had cheered President Williams four years before. With unemployment over nine percent and gas at $6 a gallon, Americans did not travel unless they had a very good reason. Better to stay home and watch on TV. Unless of course the TV had been repossessed.

I was one of those TV-watchers. Senator Hazen had made clear he didn't need me to escort him. Anyway there would not be room. When I proposed to arrange car and driver, he waved irritably, "Waste of fuel. The forecasters predict a beautiful day, I'll walk."

I slept till eleven on Inauguration morning, the longest sleep I'd had in weeks. I had nothing to do until evening.

Hazen had donated to us his two ultra-VIP tickets to the Florida state inaugural ball in the Air and Space museum. As the (adopted) home state of the new president, the Florida ball was the hot ticket. Hazen himself planned to stop briefly by the New England ball at the Hyatt, then home to bed.

Valerie had left the apartment at seven to get to the office to supervise the final details on the half-dozen parties she was overseeing. The plan was that we'd connect at seven at the dinner GB was hosting for newly elected Constitutionalist senators, then proceed to the Florida ball.

I fixed myself a turkey sandwich. It was getting close to noon: show-time. Pulaski (still *General* Pulaski for a few more seconds) glided forward in his wheelchair to take the oath.

Mrs. Pulaski stood beside and above him, regal, her black hair just touched with gray, a statue of the stoicism of the military wife. Was she proud to reach this zenith of ambition? Was she disappointed that her hope for a quiet post-retirement life of her own had been snatched away? None of the billion people watching would read an answer in her unmoving face.

Then President Pulaski propelled his chair toward the cameras to deliver his inaugural address.

Monroe Williams had aged visibly over his four years in office. President Pulaski seemed to have decided to get the aging over with all at once. At sixty-two, his hair had already receded from the front half of his head. What remained was grey and limp. Before his wounding, he had been lean and fit. Now he was thin to the point of gauntness. But his eyes were piercing. His voice was strong. His cheeks and chin pointed forward like a war chieftain's.

"My fellow Americans," he sang out in a voice of command. "It's the custom of our nation that a new president begin his term with a declaration of his intentions. I will do so only very briefly, because our nation has had enough of good intentions. America wants results, and my administration will be judged by the results we deliver.

"For more than a dozen years, under three different presidents of two great parties, our political system has delivered disappointing results to the voters who elect us. Now we are sunk in a prolonged economic depression. We are mired in an equally prolonged war in Mexico, the longest war in our nation's history, and one seemingly no closer to success today than on the day we first intervened to support the Mexican government against violent drug lords."

Wow, I thought. *That's certainly a downer.*

"I pledge to you to restore our prosperity and to end the war. In the days ahead, I will be laying detailed proposals before the Congress to achieve both these great goals.

"I am not the first president to make such promises. The American people have heard them before. The men who spoke these promises spoke in good faith. But they were defeated by the poisonous and paralyzing partisanship of our political system.

"The American people cannot endure another such defeat. We must transcend the rancor and suspicion that has made our government useless to our people. We must overcome the habits and practices that have brought us to our present trouble.

"I am under no illusion about the difficulty ahead. It will take much more than calls for goodwill and cooperation to change the way our government works. We have heard such calls before, and they have achieved nothing. Success will require a new approach. And what is required – I will do.

"We have a saying in the military: 'Failure is not an option.' But sadly, that saying is untrue. Failure is always an option. It's an option our government has chosen too often in the recent past. You voted in November for a different option. And that is the option for which we must work together – regardless of pressure from special interests, regardless of past positions, regardless of party."

At those last words, the camera pulled away from the new president's face, and the sun glittered on the metal of his chair.

I wandered into the kitchen to ransack the refrigerator. I found a forgotten slice of plum tart from the local bakery. It wasn't too stale. I brewed some coffee and settled into the couch to watch the panels on Patriot News and ProgTV.

The ProgTV people seemed to like the address a lot better than the Patriot News crew. It was just as Daphne had predicted. The Nationalists had begun to claim Pulaski as their own. One panelist on Patriot News complained, "This Constitutionalist landslide has rescued the country from Nationalist socialism and fascism. You think that President Pulaski could maybe say a positive word or two about what has been accomplished here."

The moderator asked, "But what about Pulaski's comment about 'poisonous partisanship' – do you think he's trying to distance himself from the Constitutionalist party?"

A very pretty woman spoke up. "The Nationalists have shown poisonous partisanship, and I'm glad President Pulaski has called them out." Hey wait a minute, I recognized her: Mac Kohlberg's girlfriend.

After a half hour of TV chat, I clicked off. I did a half-hearted workout on the treadmill in the basement gym. Afterward, I read some of the new book about the Mexican war that Valerie had downloaded for me. After that, I answered some email. Then I got bored. I searched out Sylvia's Facebook page. I thought about sending a friend request. No, better not.

At 5 o'clock, I started preparing my new tuxedo for its second wearing in almost as many weeks. For company as I dressed, I turned on the *Mark Dunn Show*.

Dunn had erupted out of nowhere at the beginning of the Williams presidency to become a huge cable TV star. Up in New York, he was regarded as a shock-jock joke, a muppet-voiced paranoid crazy person who ranted and raved about secret messages printed on the back of the new hundred-dollar bill. Here in Washington, he terrified holy hell out of out everybody. Jack Campozzo called him, "Shiva, the destroyer of worlds."

For four years Dunn had blamed President Williams for everything from crop failures to the way kids today wore their pants. What would he do for ratings in the Pulaski era?

The show opened with almost aggressively cheesy graphics, homage to Dunn's theme that the country had been running steadily downhill since Captain Kangaroo went off the air. Dunn dressed like an old-fashioned math teacher: checked shirt, knit tie, horn rim glasses under a grey crewcut that accorded very badly with his round fleshy face. But his voice – that was the magic. It exuded sincerity, concern, kindliness. By repute he was the only Constitutionalist broadcaster whose audience ever exceeded 20 percent female.

As the show started, Dunn was leaning on a metal desk. "Three months ago, this country witnessed the greatest upsurge of constitutional values in our history. Millions of Americans – people like you – went to their polling places to vote out a regime that had trashed their freedoms. Benjamin Franklin had promised us a republic if we could keep it – and we've kept it."

Dunn walked toward a blackboard, possibly the last blackboard still in use in North America. He selected a piece of chalk from the little ledge beneath the board, tossed it into the air and deftly caught it.

"The question ahead: Will President Pulaski govern as a Constitutionalist? For our sakes and for his, let's hope so."

I tied my black tie and elevatored to the street.

CHAPTER 18

Valerie had worried for days over the right gown for the Inaugural ball. She had finally found something she liked. I'd been strictly forbidden an advance viewing.

Valerie shimmered into the General Brands dinner in a long silver metallic sheath, her thick dark hair swept up, a black jet necklace around her throat. For warmth she wore some kind of white fur wrap she had found months ago at a second-hand store in New York. The wrap looked a little scraggly close up, but from any distance Valerie seemed an image out of the golden age of Hollywood. I was very embarrassed to have to escort her into and out of a broken-down D.C. taxi jalopy.

I was not the only one to like the dress. Minutes after we entered the Air and Space Museum, we were standing beside the display of moon rocks reconnoitering the situation. A drunken partygoer came stumbling up to her – an older guy, heavy, wearing $5,000 worth of ugly, oversized wristwatch.

"Are you a wife" – he couldn't get his tongue working properly, the word emerged as "waaf" – "or are you a prostitute?"

You never know what's going to upset Valerie and what will make her laugh. This time, she laughed. "Why can't I be both?"

I put a hand on his chest. "Friend, maybe we should see about getting you a taxi."

He got belligerent. "Who the hell are you? You're no friend of mine."

Valerie whispered something in his ear, and he grew calm, very formal. "I apologize to you, sir. Good night." And off he slunk.

"What did you say?"

"I told him you had hired me for the whole weekend. He's a Constitutionalist. He respects contracts."

"Very funny." I surveyed the crowd. "But do you think we maybe have come to the wrong place?"

At that moment we were passed by man wearing a mullet haircut and a bright red tie studded with little lights that switched on and off at two-second intervals.

"Looks that way," said Valerie. "Somehow I imagined an inaugural ball would be … less gross."

"Maybe it will be better in the VIP room?" I glanced down at the secondary ticket atop my general admission pass.

"Maybe," said Valerie, not very hopefully.

The VIP "room" turned out to be an exhibition space that opened off the museum's main hall. The big placard advertising the show was now trimmed with red-white-and-blue bunting: *ANIMALS IN SPACE!* The placard was illustrated with a black-and-white photograph of a crew-cut astronaut wearing a monkey around his neck.

As we showed our passes to the guard at the rope line, I was knocked aside by a short man with a white comb-over, charging forward double-quick into the VIP space. He must have had his pass bar-coded onto the shoulder of his antique tuxedo, for he did not break or even slow his stride. The guard caught me as I stumbled.

"Who the hell was that?"

A nervous young man just behind me the line overheard and answered, "That was Marvin Spivak. You know: the Constitutionalist guy on the Point-Counterpoint show on ProgTV."

"What a jerk. Is he blind?"

"I think he assumed you were going to get out of his way."

Inside the VIP room, the bowties at least didn't flash. On the other hand, neither was anybody going to be inspired by the scene to sing, "I could have danced all night."

Nobody was dancing here, despite the efforts of a five-member band belting out hits from the 1980s. Men in tuxedos and women in bright jewel-tone dresses crowded in thickets of intense conversation. The faces I didn't recognize from TV still somehow conveyed an expectation that I should. Waiters moved in between the thickets, maneuvering trays of wine and champagne. I tried the champagne. Boring. I switched to the wine. Bleh. Back to the champagne.

Unless I felt like walking up to a justice of the Supreme Court, and receiving a second dose of the Bill Mihailovich treatment, there was nobody for us to talk to.

"God this is grisly," I said to Valerie. "Do you think it was like this when the Romans inaugurated a new emperor?"

"It's no worse than that horrible *Constitutionalist Review* dinner. The endless speeches, people leaving their tables between courses in search of somebody more important to talk to. Then at the end of the evening, the women lunged at the centerpieces, and the fastest pair of hands took the flowers home!" Valerie shuddered at the memory.

Cutting abruptly through the noise, I heard a congenially familiar sound: the squeaky voice of Freddy Catesby.

"Hello Walter, good evening Valerie. Let me introduce you to somebody. This is Lou Rogers. The most courageous man on radio! But Lou now faces a big problem. What's he going to talk about now that he's chased Williams out of town?"

Rogers was a squat, bald-headed man who sported a scratchy-looking gray goatee. His tuxedo had been bought at least 25 pounds ago. His gut bulged against the jacket, his fat short legs crushed his ankles. He looked deeply discontented with something. The tuxedo maybe. Possibly tonight's party. Or perhaps the nullity of human existence.

Rogers snarled, "Don't worry, I'll have lots to talk about. I expect nothing good from this man Pulaski. And I still think we would have done better to stick by our principles and go with Esther Minden. Or Senator Bingham. Or even Governor Tremain, despite his being a two-faced weasel."

"You don't seem in a mood to celebrate," said Valerie.

"I celebrated the defeat of Williams on election night, the way I like to celebrate: at home, in my bunker, with my dogs. I don't see anything to celebrate tonight. If Freddy weren't my good friend, I'd never have jammed myself into this monkey suit to drive into this horrible city. And if Freddy were a better friend, he wouldn't have asked me." Rogers twisted his mouth into an expression that I think was a smile. The effort squeezed his left eye shut in a horrible squint.

"Speaking of home," I murmured to Valerie, "why don't we get out of here?"

"Yes I've had all the glamour I can stand," she whispered back. "I feel like an idiot that I spent a week shopping for this dress. I should have gone to Macy's and picked the first damn thing I saw off the rack."

We excused ourselves to Catesby and Rogers, then fought our way through the wall of VIPs. Then out through the throngs in the big hall, until finally – escape.

The weather had executed one of those Washington about-faces. The balmy day had turned into a bitterly cold night. Valerie's heels precluded a walk home. Of course there were no taxicabs. Instead, a long line of limousines waited at the curb for the Florida high-rollers inside the museum.

I walked along the shining hoods until I came to a shabby town car at the tail of the queue. A freelancer. I held a $50 bill in front of the car's side window. The driver lowered the glass.

"My girlfriend didn't bring a coat. We live just on the other side of the Mall – you'll be back in ten minutes." The driver lowered the glass another three inches and snatched the bill.

I opened the rear door, slid Valerie into the back seat, and tumbled after her. The disreputable limo somehow restored her good spirits.

"Hey," she said, "why don't we take this car to the Hotel Monaco and have a drink in the bar? Maybe we can retrieve the night. I can walk home from there, even in these shoes."

I stroked the line of her dress. "I know a way to retrieve the night."

She smacked my hand. "You'll get that too. But I want my party first."

Ten minutes later, we were walking through the lurid reds and purple of the Monaco's lobby. If Dr Seuss designed furniture, he'd have designed just these bizarre twisted chairs and up-tilted couches. We aimed for the door to the hotel bar. To one side of the door, I spotted Colonel Cleland, his back to the room, his shoulders hunched to his ears as if to hide his face, talking intently into a mobile phone.

The bar was jammed, but I managed to shove my way through and collect a passion-fruit Cosmopolitan for Valerie, a Talisker for me. I wrestled my way back out to the lobby, where Valerie had found us a lone absurd armchair. We wedged ourselves in together.

We had a good view of Cleland, still talking intently. Valerie followed my stare. "Friend of yours?"

"Hardly. That's Colonel Cleland. I saw him talk at the Constitutionalist Institute, not that he'd remember. He was just named deputy chief of staff at the White House. Important guy, one of the Pulaski inner circle."

"By the look of it, he's not having a good time tonight, either."

"No. He's probably signed up for four years of not having a good time." We both sipped our drinks and were quiet together. After a time, I asked:

"Valerie, do you like it here?"

"You mean, here as in this hotel? Or here as in Washington?"

"Washington."

She considered the question for a moment.

"Yes, I do like it here. I like sitting on our building's roof garden when it's not too freezing cold and looking out over the domes and monuments. I like my work. I like our life together here. And I like what it's doing for you."

I liked the feel of her thigh through the silk against my trouser leg. I wrapped my arm around her and squeezed her waist.

"What's it doing for me?"

"You're working hard at something. You're thinking about things. You have responsibilities. And people are respecting you."

"When they're not snubbing me at parties."

"Just you wait, they'll be sucking up to you soon enough."

"They'll be sucking up to my mustard money."

"Yes, OK, that too. What's wrong with that? Everybody's got something. You've got mustard. The issue is, what do you do with your advantages? You used to do – forgive me – dick-all. Now you are doing something. So I'm happy."

"But what about the ugly parts? What about Daphne plotting with me against Hazen? What about my friend Samir refusing to talk to me ever again because I took a job with a senator with a 'C' instead of an 'N' after his name?"

Valerie nestled herself into my lap. "Samir's just a crybaby. I doubt he got bent out of shape about all those sad Constitutionalist losers when his team won four years ago."

"Samir wasn't complaining about losing. He was complaining about how we played the game."

"Oh, please. If he'd won, he'd think the game was played just fine."

I couldn't argue with that. I couldn't usually argue with Valerie. That beautiful head held a better brain than mine.

"As far as I'm concerned," she said, "politics is mostly noise, money, and ego. Just like everything else. There's no point getting worked up about it. And maybe that's the way it should be. Maybe it's the people who talk about principles who are the really scary ones."

She brushed her lips against my cheek, then slipped up and out of my lap. "Let go home." The wind smacked us as we stepped out of the hotel, and she huddled against me in her wrap as we walked past the panhandlers on E Street. The long lines of traffic-jammed limousines filled the air with hot exhaust, red light, and angry honks.

CHAPTER 19

My tongue felt thick from the preceding night's drinks when the alarm buzzed Tuesday morning, the first full day of a new administration. I lay in the sheets for ten extra minutes, then bolted upright in panic: I was going to be late. I hurled myself into the shower, dressed rapidly. I was in the elevator when I realized that my socks didn't match. Too late to turn back.

I raced toward Pennsylvania Avenue and Senator Hazen's apartment. Even before I entered, I knew something was wrong. I could hear the muffled voice of the television through the door. I grabbed at my BlackBerry to read my email, but the door was already being opened for me, and I walked toward the sound.

Hazen was sitting in an armchair watching the news, his breakfast cooling on the dining room table. I did not need to stand very long alongside him to catch the gist.

"What some are calling the worst battlefield defeat for US forces since the Korean War ... night-time ambush ... 47 bodies recovered ... up to 100 more missing in action, possibly taken prisoner ..."

I sat down myself to scroll down through my Black-Berry. Nobody seemed to have a very clear idea of what had happened beyond the basics. Insurgents had ambushed US troops as they rolled through a mountain defile in Durango state last night. Fighting had continued past midnight. A relief column supported by attack helicopters arrived a little past dawn. By then the insurgents and any US survivors were long gone.

I walked over to Hazen and touched him on the shoulder. "Senator, you probably want to get to the office early this morning. Should I call the car?"

He didn't hear me at first. His eyes were fixed upon the TV. He seemed to be trying to squeeze more information out of the box by force of will. I was surprised to see that he was watching BBC, not Patriot News.

I carried his plate to the table beside his chair. "I have a feeling today will be a long day. It won't do you any good to miss breakfast." He took a piece of toast without speaking.

Some retired military man was now giving his opinion.

"It is unprecedented for insurgents to attack such a large U.S. force … Raises disturbing question how insurgents obtained access to night-fighting technology … No the Americans would not have exhausted their ammunition, a force that size would carry enough firepower to sustain even a very heavy firefight well into the daylight hours …"

On my own initiative, I canceled the walk. I telephoned the senator's driver, Mehtab, and asked if he could come early to the apartment. "Yez, Mizter Walter," Mehtab replied stoically.

In the back of the car, the senator flipped through the newspapers without interest. They were already obsolete. As we entered the office suite, Teresa rose to greet us. She told the senator that a team from the Pentagon and the NSC would be arriving at 8:30 to brief as many senators as could assemble in time in the old Senate chamber. (Not the one you see on C-Span. The one down the hall, the chamber the Southern senators had filed out of just before the Civil War.) No cameras. She turned a malignant glare at me. No aides.

I walked the senator over to the old chamber. Lingering outside, I called Charlie to ask if he knew anything more than what was being said on TV.

"Walter are you out of your fucking mind calling me on my mobile on a day like today?"

"I couldn't get through on your landline."

"Duh. Look, I'll talk to you later, maybe tonight if I can. I have to keep this line clear in case anybody needs me."

"Charlie, you can hang up if your call waiting goes. I'll owe you the biggest favor you can name, but just tell me – what's the real story here? They have pulled the entire Senate into some secret session. Jack says they didn't do that even for Pearl Harbor."

"Geez, Walter, I don' t have time for this."

"You don't have time to tell me you don't have time."

"All right, damn it, just headlines. The insurgents took prisoners, we don't know how many, but a lot. That's really bad. The troops surrendered before exhausting their ammunition. That's worse. And here's the worst news of all: We've recovered the body of officer in command of the column, a colonel named Kapil Mali. He was killed by a bullet to the back of the head. An American bullet. Fired at close range."

"Fuck."

"You need to improve your vocabulary. Now bye."

Hazen emerged from the chamber, his mouth fixed and grim, in no mood to talk. But everybody else in town was talking like crazy. Everybody knew somebody who knew something – or at least, knew somebody who knew somebody who knew something. Everybody was gathering fragments of information or rumor or invention, and out of all those sworn-to-secrecy fragments, rumors began to cohere, then to spread.

Somebody had communicated the column's route to the insurgents. The column had been infiltrated. There were Mexican-American soldiers in the column. The Mexican-Americans had turned their guns on the other American soldiers, surprised them, forced them to surrender. Our army had been betrayed from within.

That news could not be kept quiet for very long. And of all unlikely places, it was a Los Angles-based Spanish-language breakfast chat show that broke the scoop.

Not even 15 minutes after the senators emerged from their briefing, a woman on the breakfast show erupted in an enraged tirade against those who would question the patriotism of Mexican-American soldiers. She repeated all the rumors, line by lurid line, and then condemned them as an insult and a slur. Nobody ever did discover how this guest heard the news.

The breakfast broadcaster proceeded to hurl an allegation of her own. She charged that senior Anglo officers in the US army had been corrupted by drug money. She said they had fabricated evidence against Mexican-American soldiers to conceal their own guilt, with help from the Russian mafia and Israeli intelligence. She urged the show's listeners to email or call their representatives in Congress to demand an investigation.

That happened at 7:40 AM Pacific time. By 11 AM Washington time, the servers in both House and Senate had crashed under the weight of indignant emails.

CHAPTER 20

That morning computer fail was only the appetizer course. As we moved past the noon hour, the English-language media joined the battle.

Senator Hazen was called to an emergency afternoon meeting of the Constitutionalist Senate caucus at 2 PM. His walk to the meeting was consumed by a furious call from the archbishop of Providence, denouncing the insult to his Mexican-American parishioners. I waited in the hall outside the conference room, surfing the Web and sending texts begging for news.

When we returned, Daphne briefed Hazen.

"The volume of calls was intense, but the tone of the calls not as bad as could have been feared. The English-language media have been very restrained, even the right-wing talkers. I understand that senior military officials called the big radio hosts and urged them to avoid speculation or accusation before all the facts were known. But some pretty wild things are being said on the blogs, and some of the more out-there shows are repeating them. And then there's Mark Dunn. He could say anything."

Hazen frowned at the mention of Dunn's name. Maybe he watched more cable than I knew. And maybe it was with Mark Dunn in mind that the White House sent an email blast a few minutes after four o'clock, announcing that President Pulaski would hold his first press conference that evening at eight.

Wow, were we exhausted by the end of the day. Yet nobody wanted to leave. At 6 PM, Daphne sent an intern to pick up a stack of pizzas to sustain the staff until the president spoke. I texted Valerie not to expect me for dinner.

Valerie didn't reply to my text. Instead, only a few minutes after the pizzas arrived, Valerie stuck her head through the entry of the suite. "Hey, everybody, I figured you guys might need a drink." She toted two big paper shopping bags. The bags clinked with the sound of glass. From them, Valerie produced three bottles of Johnnie Walker.

Daphne was staggered. "How in the world did you bring alcohol into the building?"

Valerie smiled conspiratorially. "I brought a fourth bottle for the guards. I figured they'd need a drink today too."

Daphne shook her head amazed. "I'm glad you never decided to become a terrorist."

Valerie extracted two tubes of plastic tumblers from her bag and arranged the Scotch bottles on the receptionist's desk. A delighted Jack Compozzo raced down the hall for ice. We had ourselves a staff cocktail party as we waited for the president. Even Teresa thawed.

The noise grew lively enough to pull Hazen out of his sanctuary. He accepted a tumbler from Valerie's hand and nodded a toast at her.

Then we all gathered in the suite's conference room to watch the press conference. Daphne swooped upon the chair beside the big swivel armchair reserved for the senator. All through the next hour, she would lean in toward him to murmur her views in a low voice inaudible to anyone else.

At eight exactly, the cameras showed the president's wheelchair moving down the red carpet to the East Room. The president arranged himself at the low podium. "Good evening. I'll open with a brief prepared statement."

The roomful of reporters arrayed in incongruous gold-backed ballroom chairs waited expectantly.

The president pulled a folded sheet of paper out of the pocket of his charcoal grey suit. During the campaign he had made a lot of jokes about President Williams always needing a teleprompter. So now President Pulaski was stuck with paper and ink.

He unfolded a pair of reading glasses. The voice of command rang out, a voice used to being heard without dissent or disobedience.

"Approximately 48 hours ago, an American mechanized infantry column was ambushed by insurgents in Durango state. US forces fought well, but the insurgents had caught them in a very unfavorable tactical situation and US casualties were heavy. At least 37 soldiers were killed in an hour of fierce fighting, including the column's commanding officer, Colonel Kapil Mali. I knew Colonel Mali personally, and I can attest that he was a courageous and effective officer. I send my condolences to Colonel Mali's family, and I know that every American joins me in mourning the loss of life."

Reporters tapped feverishly at laptops.

"Facing certain defeat, the surviving soldiers laid down their arms. We can confirm that 88 Americans have been captured by the insurgents. We have opened a line of communication to the insurgents, and we have received information that the prisoners are being appropriately treated. Seventeen of the prisoners have suffered wounds, and they are receiving medical care."

The president removed his glasses. What he had to say now, he did not need to read.

"There is much about this incident that remains uncertain, and I would urge all Americans not to heed rumors and speculation in advance of the facts. But there is one particular rumor that does need to be addressed."

He glared a parade-ground glare at the room, as if he were holding each and every one of the reporters personally responsible.

"About one in eight of the men and women in the military service of the United States trace their ancestry to Mexico. These brave men and women have served with honor and distinction. One of the last things I did before resigning my command to run for president was to endorse a citation for Specialist Frank Ramirez, who died of wounds sustained while laying down covering fire in a battle on the outskirts of Chihuahua. Specialist Ramirez was posthumously awarded the Congressional Medal of Honor."

The chin jutted forward, as if the president were daring the press to question Ramirez's patriotism.

"And as a field commander in Mexico, I could not have done my job without the superb work of Mexican-American intelligence and law-enforcement officers who helped us penetrate the insurgent organizations, often at extreme personal risk. I remember the case of DEA agent Veronica Estrada. Captured by insurgents, she was tortured and abused for hours before she finally died. Agent Estrada had been brought to this country illegally as a girl of five. When she applied to the DEA a decade ago, she wrote" - here he pulled his printed paper notes to eye level – "'I broke the law of the land once in my life – but I pledge to honor and enforce the law for every remaining day that God gives me to serve my one and only country.'"

A more experienced politician might have left the words to linger in the air a little longer. Pulaski curtly returned to business, dropping the paper back to his knee and resuming his clipped military tone.

"Inescapably, with any large group, you will find individuals who engage in negative behavior. You will find service members of every race, religion, national origin, gender, and sexual orientation sometimes derelict in their duty. But as Americans, we believe in judging people as individuals: the wrongdoers as well as the heroes. All right – questions. Let's start with Felicia Miranda, Globovision. Go ahead."

The cameras pulled away to reveal a startlingly attractive woman, tall and auburn-haired in a form-fitting black suit. Felicia Miranda looked about as Latina as the Queen of Norway, but tonight she carried herself as the tribune of her people, if tribunes began their careers as lingerie models.

"Mr. President, you have cautioned us against speculation and rumor. Yet your remarks today strongly indicate that more is known about this incident than you have stated. In particular, the tone of your statement suggests that you believe that individual soldiers in the column did betray their duty – and that these wrongdoers were Hispanic or Mexican-American. Can you be any more specific about what exactly happened and who was responsible?"

You got to hand it to Pulaski. His eyes didn't wander to any of the places where my eyes would have wandered if Felicia Miranda had been breathing fire six feet away from me. He looked unflinchingly into her ears, returning her fire with his own icy cool.

"Felicia, I have shared all the factual information that I have. As we learn more, we will share that too. But I cannot pretend not to have heard the ugly rumors. And let's remember, please, which media source was the first to put those rumors into circulation. This country has suffered a terrible loss. I think we should be mourning together, not manipulating emotions for ratings."

The room pulsed. Reporters like accusing other people of wrongdoing, not being accused themselves. The president disregarded the evident annoyance and signaled for another question.

About 40 minutes into the hour, the president called on a reporter from one of the old TV networks, the kind where the news programs were supported by ads for motorized scooters and hearing aids. If the reporter's geriatric audience was watching tonight, they were about to get a jolt.

"Mr. President, a few minutes ago, while we were talking here, the right-wing website Dirigible.com posted a photograph of what it claims is the body of Colonel Mali, apparently taken after the body was retrieved from the battlefield. If the photograph is authentic, it suggests that Colonel Mali was not killed in an exchange of fire, but at close range to the back of the head. Can you confirm or deny the accuracy of this claim? If true, how do you interpret this fact?"

The room buzzed with suppressed shock. Abruptly, every reporter's head dived down toward his or her Black-Berry or laptop. Our conference room buzzed too. Daphne whispered into Hazen's ear. A look of pain crossed his face, and his pen twisted in his hand. He nodded "yes" – he had known.

The Dirigible.com site took a long time to load. Whatever traffic it was built for, it was not built for the traffic it was getting now. But suddenly there it was, and there was the gruesome photo.

On the television screen, President Pulaski did not so much as blink. But he did pause noticeably before answering, "I've seen a lot of battlefield wounds. The origin of a wound cannot be reliably ascertained from a photograph. I am awaiting final medical reports. Typically, as you know, out of respect for the feelings of families we do not disclose the details of fatal wounds. But if the details are of public significance, we will brief the press as soon as we have confirmed information. One more thing: I know that media practices have changed a great deal in recent years. But I would hope that we'd all still have the respect not to post images of an American soldier's final remains on the Internet."

The president now called on chuckling, roly-poly Jim Fenwick, the new White House reporter for Patriot News. Fenwick was famously dim and lazy, a big spongy contrast to the grimly adversarial correspondent whom Patriot News had assigned to cover the Williams White House. But Pulaski's expectations of a softball question were disappointed.

"Mr. President," said Fenwick, and this time he was not chuckling. "Just yes or no: Was Colonel Mali killed by enemy action?"

Pulaski's eyes flashed with rage. "As I said, I intend to wait for all the facts before commenting. That's how we do things in my White House."

Daphne shuddered. "Not good, not a good answer." She said it loud enough for all of us to hear.

Fenwick did not wait to be invited to follow up. "Mr. President, are you saying you don't know? Or that you won't tell us?"

The look of pain crossed Hazen's face once more.

Pulaski visibly seethed. "I want the facts as much as your news organization, Jim, but the facts don't always arrive in time for that same day's broadcast. I have time for one more question."

Actually, there were eight minutes left in the hour. Pulaski had decided to run out the clock. He signaled a reporter in the very back corner, a nervous young man who spoke weak English. The TV subtitle identified him as being with the *Beijing Times*. "Mr. President, do you have any comment on the recent fluctuations in the renminbi-dollar exchange rate?" Pulaski smiled, relaxed, and launched into a long disquisition on monetary policy.

All eyes in our office turned to Hazen. He lifted a hand to the back of his head, then patted his skull lightly before speaking, an odd tic of his, as if he were trying to set the ketchup flowing out of a slow-moving bottle. "Look everybody," Hazen said, "obviously there's more to this story. We'll know more soon. And obviously General Pulaski has had better nights. But he's our president, we support him, and I'm glad he has stood up against speculations that single out any group of Americans." He turned to me. "Walter, call the car please. I'm very tired."

CHAPTER 21

Hazen's staff were still gathered around the television sets when I returned from walking the senator to his car. Jim Fenwick was filling the screen on Patriot News. "I smell a cover up," he announced breathlessly, his big moment arrived at last.

Valerie supervised the tidying of discarded tumblers and the recycling of the empty pizza boxes. She sealed and bagged the unfinished whisky. We said our goodnights and exited the building. Another balmy day had turned into another very cold night.

A thin-faced panhandler stepped forward to meet us. "Could you spare some change for something to eat?"

Valerie impulsively handed the panhandler a half-emptied bottle of Johnnie Walker. He looked embarrassed. "That's very nice of you," he said away, refusing the bottle. He sounded like an educated man. "But I really am hungry." Now Valerie was embarrassed. I offered a $10 bill. The panhandler clasped it eagerly.

While we were walking home, somebody at Patriot News must have sent round a memo: Be careful, go slow. On the next morning's talk show, there was no more "cover up" talk. One guest after another agreed that the president had "underperformed." They worried that a "politically correct" military was ignoring "loyalty problems." Beyond that, they did not go. Not yet.

Hazen did not look well when I arrived for the next morning's walk. I asked if maybe today he would prefer to omit his exercise. He insisted he could manage, but he spoke little.

When I asked about the previous night's unfortunate press conference, he said only "I'm afraid this country has absorbed all the bad news it can handle."

The country was going to have to handle more. A few minutes before 11 AM, the senator was sitting behind his desk at a hearing of the Banking Committee. I was waiting for him in a small adjacent staff room with a half dozen other Senate aides. Suddenly one of them nudged me.

"Take a look!"

He extended a tablet computer opened to the Dirigble.com home page.

Over a photo of a pockmarked, dark-skinned young man in army camouflage, Dirigible splayed the headline: "Face of a Traitor?" The accompanying story alleged that this man, Sergeant Tommy Montoya, was believed by military intelligence to have pulled the trigger on Colonel Mali.

I skimmed the details. Born a U.S. citizen in 1987. Parents had entered illegally in the 1980s, benefited from the 1986 amnesty, and settled in El Paso. One of Montoya's uncles had emerged as an important figure in the Durango drug cartels. Another uncle was a senior insurgent military commander. Montoya's phone records showed calls to numbers associated with the insurgency in the weeks before the Durango ambush. Four weeks before the attack, intelligence officers had apparently recommended that Montoya be reassigned to another theater of operations. That recommendation had somehow been disregarded.

I tiptoed into the hearing room. I approached Hazen from behind and tapped him on the shoulder. "You'll want to read this." I handed him my own BlackBerry, opened to Dirigible. com. Hazen donned his reading glasses, squinted at the little screen, and scowled. He handed the device back to me and returned his attention to the witness before the committee. I withdrew into the little staff room to wait for the hearing to end.

Which it finally did at 12:45. Hazen's schedule had him committed to a "power hour" fundraiser at party headquarters at 1 PM. I asked whether he still wanted to proceed with that plan. He nodded.

Party headquarters was located on the opposite side of Capitol Hill, on a slope below the House office buildings. Hazen telephoned Daphne from the car to hear more about the Montoya story. I could hear her voice from the earpiece. "It's rumored that the White House internal polls show a steep overnight drop in the president's approval ratings." Hazen seemed unsurprised.

"I warned Colonel Cleland in the caucus meeting yesterday," he said, "not to withhold information. Unnecessary secrecy only inflames paranoia. But nobody in the White House inner circle has ever been elected to anything. They are obsessed with 'operational security,' as they call it. They've got even me half-convinced that maybe they do have something to hide."

Hazen then placed a call on Banking Committee business that lasted until we pulled in front of the party headquarters building. As he stepped out of the car, he asked, "By the way, did you have time to pick up that gift I asked you for yesterday?"

"Yes, I found it. There's a kitchen-supply store at Pentagon City. But sir, why are you giving Senator Joliette a set of steak knives?"

"Inside joke."

At headquarters, we were directed to an office with a desk and telephone. A party employee had the call list. Down the long hall, a half-dozen similar rooms had been outfitted for other senators. I walked downstairs to the lunchroom to pick up sandwiches for the senator and myself. I deposited his at his elbow: turkey, no butter or mayo, on whole wheat. I unwrapped my steak sandwich at a small table just outside the calling room.

As I was chewing my last bite, the elevator door opened and out stepped Elmer Larsen. He blinked at me, surprised to see me in his field of vision. "Hello Elmer," I called out.

He blinked again. "You work for?" The question dwindled away uncertainly. I decided not to aid his memory. He'd called my boss a traitor. Even in Washington, that's strong language.

"Who are you looking for?"

"Senator Joliette."

"He's in the second last room. Say, Elmer, maybe you know the answer to this: Why would Senator Hazen give Senator Joliette a box of steak knives?"

Elmer frowned, still straining to identify me. "It's a joke from an old movie. The best salesman gets a Cadillac. The second best gets a box of steak knives. God damn Hazen, he thinks he's a fundraising genius because he sits on the Banking Committee. The banks are the other team anyway. Hedge funds, private equity – the people who didn't get the bailout dollars, those are our guys."

Elmer cast a look down the hall. Senator Joliette was still in the thick of a call of his own. Just to keep the conversation going, I asked, "So what do you make of the news from Mexico?"

More blinks. As if he were thinking, *Who the hell are you? How long will Joliette's call take? Is it less of a waste of time to return in ten minutes or to wait here and tolerate your questions?*

He decided on the latter.

"The news from Mexico has been awful for a long time. The insurgents are fighting for the right to do business. They've got a product. They want to sell it. Legalize the drugs, allow refugees in this country the right to work, withdraw our troops. Let the Mexican government solve its own problems. If the insurgents win – well they're businessmen, we can deal with them. Which is more than I can say for General Pulaski." The answer sounded rehearsed, as if delivered many times before.

Senator Joliette now emerged from his office: a tall, bulky man with a thick head of white hair and thicker cornpone accent. "*AYL*-mer – glad to see you!"

"Thank you, Senator, I was just talking to …" Elmer indicated me. He'd mistaken me for a Joliette aide.

Hazen emerged now too, gift-wrapped box of knives in hand. Joliette knew the movie and laughed at the joke. "I'll join you in a minute Elmer, I just want to visit a moment with my good friend, Senator Hazen. This is bad business in Mexico, isn't it, Phil?"

"Yes," answered Hazen, "very bad."

Joliette placed a hand on Hazen's stooped shoulder. "You and I have disagreed on a lot. But we have been Constitutionalists together for a very long time. For George Pulaski, the Constitutionalist party is just a vehicle to take him where he wants to go. Who knows where that is? If we lifelong Constitutionalists wish to make our voices heard, we have to speak together just this one time."

Hazen looked quizzically at Joliette. "So now I'm included in the Constitutionalist family?"

Joliette now wrapped his arm all the way around Hazen's stooped body. "I never excluded you, Phil, no matter how much we disagreed in the past. You know that not a dime from my Victory Fund went to any of your primary challengers, not ever. I've always said you were the only Constitutionalist who could hold Rhode Island – and that the day you retire is the day we lose your seat. Hell, you've got so much money in your war chest, you don't *need* to be here making fundraising calls. You are donating your time to the party, to serve all the rest of us. Everybody on the senatorial committee knows it, and we're all appreciative."

Hazen looked even more quizzical. *Why are you flattering me?*

Joliette squeezed Hazen closer.

"This is a very uncertain time, and we have a very uncertain president. A united party can help steer this presidency in the right direction. But if Pulaski gets the idea that he can put together his own personal coalition in Congress, he may be tempted to wander off in some unpredictable directions."

Hazen's look faded from quizzical to serious. "Dick, I supported Pulaski because I thought this country needed a strong presidency after the Williams years. I worked damn hard to elect him. So did you, as I recall – at least once Pulaski had won the nomination, anyway. Now you want me to join a mutiny against him?"

Elmer was blinking faster than ever. He didn't seem the type to have a personal conversation in front of. Yet the two senators took no notice. On the other hand, Hazen was not saying anything indiscreet, and Joliette probably trusted Elmer to keep the secret. What was I thinking? Elmer had probably written Joliette's script.

Joliette's smile spread wider and wider. You could see he thought himself quite the charmer.

"It's not a mutiny," Joliette chortled cheerfully. "We are strengthening the presidency, just as you say. Pulaski is mishandling this Mexico business. He's so determined that nobody think any Hispanic soldier is a traitor that he's going to convince the country that every Hispanic soldier is a traitor. You've fought intolerance your whole career. Now this president is undoing your work out of pure ten-thumbed clumsiness. And he's so damn sure of himself he won't listen to anybody who wants to help him. Except he might listen to *you*. So I'm appealing to you. You're in the minority in the caucus on almost everything? Well, this time you'll be the leader. We'll all follow you. We'll all do whatever you say. Anything you want from the caucus, you just say what it is, it'll be unanimous. Move the U.S. Naval Academy to Newport? It's done!"

Hazen laughed; he couldn't help it. "Dick, what do you want me to tell the president? He's the commander-in-chief. Congress can't run a war."

"I agree! Mexico is just a symptom of the problem. I have my eye on the next thing: the deficit reduction plan. We can't even get meetings with the president's people. They are holed up in the Executive Office Building like it's a war room. We keep hearing these ugly rumors about what they have in mind – and I'm hoping you can talk reason into them."

"If I did, what would I say?"

"You would say: We have a Constitutionalist majority in both houses of Congress, and the president has to work with us. We won't roll over for him. And if he tries to roll us, we'll bite. Hard."

Hazen pondered. "Let me think about that. Thanks for the candor, Dick. And while you're doing your dog training lessons," here he jerked a thumb toward Elmer, "you'd better call him to heel."

"Ah, Ayl-mer's no trouble."

"Not to my face he's not. But I am about to turn my back."

I'm sorry you feel that way, Senator," Elmer replied coolly. "I've always been direct about our disagreements."

"Mmph," said Hazen through tight lips.

Back in the car I said, "May I ask what that was about?"

"Joliette and Elmer have good ears," said Hazen – then fished some papers from his open briefcase and plunged into his reading.

CHAPTER 22

"I gotta say, I never heard President Williams speak up for undocumented Americans the way President Pulaski did tonight." – Panelist, ProgTV, January 21, 10:06 PM.

"That letter from Agent Estrada brought tears to my eyes." – Panelist, ProgTV, January 21, 10:09 PM.

Somebody needs to start a mymanpulaski hashtag @williamsfanboy January 21, 10:11 pm.

.@williamsfanboy +1! @DownWithDunn January 21, 10:12 PM.

Beginning to like our nu prez #mymanpulaski @MalcolmandMartin January 21, 10:14 PM.

Voted for Williams, but Pulaski reading Estrada letter was way gutsy

#mymanpulaski @nationalistgurl January 21, 10:14 PM.

"FOR MANY NATIONALISTS, A STRANGE NEW RESPECT FOR PRESIDENT PULASKI." – Headline, *The New York Transcript*, January 22.

"Do you think that there's a chance that President Pulaski can lead us beyond what he's called the 'poisonous partisanship' of the past two presidencies?" – Host question, *Morning Edition*, National Public Radio, January 22, 7:14 AM.

"I loved Monroe Williams, but not even his best friends would have called him an effective executive. I'm wondering if Pulaski may turn out to be the president we've been waiting for." – "Mo" Brampton, host ProgTV's "Mornings with Mo," January 22, 7:37 AM.

"Will Constitutionalists Turn on President Pulaski?" Headline on Center for National Progress blog site, January 22.

CHAPTER 23

Bzzz. Bzzz. The BlackBerry on my nightstand was sounding every 20 seconds. I grabbed it, looked at the time. 3 AM? What?

I fumbled to read the small screen. Emails from Daphne, from Charlie, from Jack, from a dozen other people. They all said the same thing: "Have you seen this?" – with a link to a URL for the *Wall Street Transcript.*

I pulled on the red leather slippers Valerie had given me for Christmas and padded out to my laptop to read more comfortably.

The link led to an op-ed titled, "The Army's Loyalty Problem."

I scanned it. It was too dense for me, full of opinion survey statistics, but I got the gist. Montoya was not just one bad apple. The army was riddled with soldiers and officers it could not trust. The army did not like to admit the truth – and that was a big part of the problem, going all the way up to the very top.

I checked the byline: Vernon Mallory, president of something called the Center for Military Readiness in Santa Monica. I'd never heard of Mallory, but he seemed to know his stuff. There were certainly a lot of facts and figures in his article. Hazen read the *Wall Street Transcript* on paper every morning, but I printed out the item for him, just in case. Then back to bed.

When I arrived at the apartment, the senator had already digested the Mallory article. "Who is this Mallory person?" he asked. For once I looked every inch the well-prepared aide, thanks to an early morning email from Daphne. She had sent me a link to a profile of Mallory and a clutch of press releases under the urgent subject line, "WE NEED TO BE ON THE RIGHT SIDE OF THIS!"

I informed the senator, "Vernon Mallory is a former RAND analyst now running his own shop, funded by some Constitutionalist donors in California. You'll have a chance to see him today. He's already in Washington. He'll testify before the House Armed Forces committee in the morning, then he's a guest over the whole hour on Mark Dunn this afternoon."

Hazen stared at me. "Well, somebody's done quite a media rollout here. I wonder who."

On our walk, Hazen placed a call to the White House to ask what they knew about the Mallory article. They had been completely blindsided. They had never heard of Mallory, and had been given no advance word about his testimony. Now they were scrambling to prepare some kind of response. Were they pissed that the House had scheduled this testimony without alerting them? Oh yes, they were pissed.

I caught some of the testimony on C-Span. Mallory made a great witness. Surprisingly youthful, just past forty, he was tall and starkly thin. Face: not handsome, but serious and confidence-inspiring. His thinning black hair was cropped close to his head, above a fashion-forward Left Coast black suit and fashion-forward black metallic eyeglasses.

Mallory got the tone of his testimony exactly right, too. Nobody could be more distressed than he was by the disturbing information he had discovered. But (as he kept repeating): "You don't like it and I don't like it, but the data says what the data says."

Mallory delivered an even more impressive performance on the *Mark Dunn Show* that evening. The high-styled Mallory looked bizarrely out of place in Dunn's defiantly retro-style set, like a Hollywood agent sitting in a high-school math class. But

Dunn and Mallory got along famously from the very first seconds of the show.

Mallory picked up a kind of remote control and swiveled in his chair. The camera followed his eyes to a large screen in a corner of the set – the modern cousin of the blackboard at center stage. Mallory clicked a button, and the screen filled with numbers. Every time he cited one of the numbers, it expanded to fill the whole screen.

"Here's a survey we conducted about a month before the Durango incident," Mallory explained, as comfortable on TV as if in his bathtub. "We asked different groups of Americans whether they were highly confident, confident, only somewhat confident or not confident about the reliability of Mexican-American soldiers fighting a war on Mexican territory. Among Anglo Americans, only 12 percent expressed high confidence, and only another 33 percent described themselves as confident."

Dunn removed his drugstore eyeglasses and chewed on the tip of one of the earpieces.

"Are Americans right or wrong to be concerned?"

"They're right," said Mallory. "Even a few disloyal elements within a unit can compromise that unit's effectiveness, including its survivability."

"So we have a major problem?"

"We have a serious problem. We have to address it – seriously."

Daphne materialized in my doorway, jerking my head away from the streaming video on my laptop. "Have you spoken to the senator about Mallory yet?"

"Not yet."

"I'm counting on you to keep Hazen on the right side of this issue. I know he won't like it. But our email is running 11 to one in favor of Mallory. He's been invited to speak to the Constitutionalist Senate caucus tomorrow. The party is following him – and Hazen has to follow too."

"Why don't you tell him?"

"I have told him. He was not receptive to me. He said that Mallory smelled phony. He called the whole thing an indirect attack on the president by reactionaries in the party."

"You think he's wrong about any of that?"

Daphne grabbed the edge of my desk, shoved her face angrily toward mine. "Yes, he's wrong! Of course, he's wrong! And we have to find a way to guide him back in the right direction. You have to do it. That was our agreement."

Those had been her instructions, anyway, and from Daphne's point of view, her instructions were every bit as binding as any agreement. She stomped out of the vestibule with one last parting command: "Get it done."

The *Mark Dunn* show was nearly over. The camera had closed upon Dunn alone on the set. It was time for the concluding editorial. Dunn walked around to the front of his metal desk, sat upon it, and threw a leg over the edge.

"America, I don't want anyone to jump to any conclusion about any individual based on what you've heard tonight. But we cannot ignore Dr. Mallory's evidence either. I implore our president: We need a more detailed investigation. You've heard tonight the voice of the man to lead that investigation. Give Dr. Mallory the tools, and let him do the job. Good night, America."

In the reception area, the phones began to ring.

CHAPTER 24

"It's total bullshit."

That was Charlie Feltrini, on the phone the next after-noon. "DoD crunched every available number over the past 36 hours. Nobody can replicate anything like Mallory's research. Where he did his own surveys, he arrived at results completely different from anything done by anybody else. Where he used public information, he interpreted it in the most perverse way. I don't want to call the guy a liar, but ..."

"Better not, Charlie. He's the hero of Patriot News – and if the decision were up to Congress, he'd be the next Secretary of Defense."

"OK, I won't call him a liar. I'll call him ... the Music Man." Charlie burst into a little tune. "*You've got trouble, right here in River City* – and of course now he wants to sell us something."

"We're hearing that the House is preparing an emergency defense earmark of $12 million for Mallory's Center."

"Twelve million? To do the fuck what?"

"To develop tests to screen out disloyal soldiers."

Charlie sighed. "Twelve million is my request for sewage treatment at the Oaxaca refugee camps."

"Maybe they won't take it from you."

"Everybody always takes it from me. Bye, Walter."

I clicked on the TV. For once they weren't talking about Mallory or Mexico. There was some commotion in the bond market in Tokyo. Not my problem! Click.

Over the next ten days, Vernon Mallory became a familiar face on the evening lineup of Patriot News, always received with the utmost respect. A Nationalist website had posted a big article debunking Mallory's research. If Mallory had ever returned to Capitol Hill to testify, it might have gone harder with him, at least from the Nationalist members. He never did return.

As for the Constitutionalists, they dismissed the debunking article with a sneer – assuming they ever heard of it in the first place.

If Mallory had vaulted to become world-famous on Patriot News, Montoya was world famous, period. Turn on the car radio, and somebody was raging against him. Switch to FM, and a smoother voice was setting him in context. On cable they debated him, on the old networks they did human-interest stories about his background, and on daytime TV they interviewed women Hispanic officers about the challenges of combining military service with bicultural motherhood.

Hazen had read the debunking article on the Nationalist website, of course. He had read the classified DoD paper on which the debunking article was based, too. He had spent hours on the phone and in his office with Pentagon briefers. Now he could not even bear to hear Mallory's name mentioned. Whenever anyone referred to Mallory, Hazen would mutter, "*Vashmutzer.*"

I asked Jack if he understood what Hazen meant. "I grew up in Warwick. I practically speak Yiddish. It's an especially nasty word for 'slanderer.'"

There was not much Hazen could do about Mallory. Anyway, by now Hazen was consumed with another problem. The bond market commotion was spreading through East Asia. I did not remotely understand it. Sometimes the price of US Treasury bonds went down and that was bad; and sometimes the price went up, and that was bad too. Hazen lapsed into troubled silence on our walks together. And was I imagining it, or was the senator moving slower?

CHAPTER 25

"Remember," said Valerie on the first day of February, "you promised to hold tomorrow night free to take Dana and Brad to dinner. I've reserved at Alessandro's."

I had of course completely forgotten, but I also of course didn't admit it. Besides – Alessandro's? That was good news.

The noisy bar at Alessandro's was the place where Redskins cheerleaders, K Street cuties, aspiring trophy wives, and Ukrainian escorts displayed their talents to an appreciative audience. Valerie disliked the place; normally I could go only on nights she was working late. Now she was actually proposing the venue? Was an evening at Alessandro's my consolation prize for enduring Dana and Brad? If so, I certainly deserved it. Not so much for enduring Dana, I didn't mind her. But an evening with Brad? God damn!

Dana was more than just a friend of Valerie's. The two girls had met at summer camp a decade ago, attended Penn State together, moved together to New York, and stayed best friends ever since. I met Dana at the same party at which I first met Valerie. Actually I met Dana first, earlier in the evening. But she immediately made it clear that she was already spoken for.

Which was no loss, since Dana was very much not my type. Only a year out of college, you could see the woman Dana was meant to be: the attractive mother of three, loading the kids into the hybrid SUV after tennis practice, blond hair clipped back, legs still looking great, always believing her husband's stories about how he'd spent his time on his visit to Hong Kong. Dana was always the nice one, Valerie the hot one.

By some inescapable law of nature, it was the nice one who ended up with the bigger jerk.

I'd never taken to Brad. A big hearty lacrosse player two years older and an inch taller than me, Brad had proceeded straight to Wall Street from Cornell. The first time I met Brad, I was between jobs. Something of a repeat condition for me, I admit.

Valerie had asked Dana to ask her successful boyfriend to instruct me on how to make something of myself. Brad took me to a cigar bar, unwrapped a pair of Cuban Cohibas purchased in London, and imparted his wisdom.

"It's all salesmanship. Every Wall Street firm has its rocket scientists, but it's not the rocket scientists who make the big bucks. The bucks go to the guys who believe in themselves, believe in their product – and who can persuade others to believe too."

Two strong fingers thumped me in the chest.

"Your product is ... Walter! If you don't believe in Walter, who else will?"

Valerie and I pulled in front of Alessandro's a little before eight. A crowd of valets surrounded a yellow Lamborghini parked in front of the restaurant entrance.

The maitre d' led us to a table in the front corner. Valerie pointed me to the chair facing the bar. "You have to sit right there so you can see everything. Check out that girl over there," she said, pointing to a triumph of the plastic surgeon's art.

I cocked my head at her like a confused spaniel. What was going on here?

We opened our menus.

"You're going to have a tough time tonight," Valerie said with a smile. "They have both the breaded fried veal chop *and* the lobster linguine on the specials."

Most definitely suspicious – Valerie recommending something breaded and fried?

Brad and Dana suddenly loomed over us. With a little squeal of joy, Valerie jumped up and hugged her friend. Brad pumped my hand. Ouch. Valerie placed Brad opposite me, still enthusing. I plunged my head into the wine list. Valerie tapped my elbow. "Order some wine. Red." I beckoned a waiter. I pointed to an item on the list, the second cheapest. Valerie's eye followed my finger. She shook her head, "no." I raised my finger three dozen lines. Valerie nodded "yes." As Brad enjoyed two rapid big gulps, my heart sank as I tallied the cost of a three-bottle meal.

Appetizers were ordered, eaten, and removed. The noise in the restaurant was rising to jet engine levels. It was hard to hear even across the table. Valerie had to lean forward to be sure of being heard by everyone. "I want you to talk to Brad about opportunities in Washington."

I looked at Brad incredulously, then back to Valerie. "You mean … job opportunities?"

Valerie nodded.

"But Valerie – Brad wouldn't ..."

Brad leaned forward, full of his familiar golf-club confidence. "I know what you mean. I recognize that public service involves sacrifice. But this country is at a crossroads. I think I have something to contribute."

"Sure, sure." I thought: *Yeah, there's something you could contribute all right. You could teach a course on how to be an asshole.* But I didn't say that. I said, "You'd better brace yourself for the scale of the sacrifice. Most of the jobs here pay less than your firm pays first-year MBAs."

Brad magnanimously waved my qualms away. "I left the firm a year ago. I've been doing private equity placements, consulting, strategic counseling. I know the pay scales are different in Washington. As I said, I'm looking to contribute. Down the road, maybe that leads to some new opportunities. If so, great. But that's not the priority. The priority is to deploy my skill set to support the success of the new administration."

I took a calming sip of the expensive wine. "I hardly know what to tell you. I barely know my way around town myself."

Valerie laid a reproving hand on my arm. "They can't have filled all the slots at Treasury yet. And the SEC is always hiring."

WTF? Since when was Valerie an expert on federal personnel?

"The key thing," Valerie continued, "is to have the right sponsor. Brad has a lot of ability. But connections matter too. Especially with the economy so bad and so many people competing for slots."

Oh. *Ohhh*. Click.

"Like what kind of sponsor?"

Dana glanced at Valerie. Valerie looked sweetly at me. "We were thinking that maybe if Daphne placed the call to the president's personnel people – just so that they read Brad's resume carefully?"

I scrutinized Brad's salesman-smiling face. Not so tan as the last time I'd seen him. An expensive wristwatch still decorated his wrist, but the cuffs of his bespoke shirt were beginning to fray.

Washington had crawled with guys like Brad during the weeks of presidential transition: former Masters of the Universe riding the Acela to kiss up to guys they had snubbed at the class reunion. Unfortunately for him, Brad was submitting his application dangerously late.

"I don't know that I can call that kind of a favor," I said in a low voice.

"Of course you can," cooed Valerie. "Daphne needs you. There's no need to bring Senator Hazen directly into it … Daphne's say-so will get things moving, you'll see."

A thought occurred to me. I whispered, "Have you and Daphne already discussed this?"

Valerie's face suddenly went all vague. "I don't think …
well maybe just a little … the night of the press conference. I
didn't mention any names or anything. I'm leaving all of that
completely to you."

Check and mate. The only thing left was to surrender
gracefully. As Brad poured himself the last of the second bottle
of wine, I said, "Can you email me your resume tonight? I'll
talk to Daphne first thing in the morning."

Then, I thought, *What the hell, let's have some fun.* I ordered
the inevitable third bottle. I clasped my hands together on the
tabletop, leaned my head self-importantly into the center of
the table, and commenced a lecture. "Brad, let me offer a few
pointers on how to make the right impression here in Washington …"

At the curb, we helped Brad and Dana into a cab. Valerie
clutched my upper arm with two hands.

"Thank you. I know you didn't want to do that. But they
need it. And I appreciate it." Then she leaned into me, and gave
my ear a little lick. "Which one did you like best?"

"I don't know what you are talking about."

"The Asian girl with the boobs? No, not your style. The
black girl in the tight jeans, the one all over that football player?
Closer, but no. I'm going to bet it was that girl at the left side of
the bar. The dark brunette in the white blouse? With the East
European accent?

"No, not at all …"

Valerie's voice dropped to a whisper. "Pretend I'm her.
You've picked me up at the bar tonight. I am looking for a rich
American to help me get my green card. *I'll do anything.*"

Female friendship is a beautiful thing.

CHAPTER 26

I woke up late Sunday morning. Valerie had left a note: "Gone for a jog, TRY do your treadmill before I get back."

I did start the treadmill. As I was jogging, a text arrived on my BlackBerry.

Free for lunch tomorrow? 12:15? White House mess?

The message came from Charlie Feltrini. I tapped: "U bn promoted? Thought no mess prvlgs 4 u."

The answer whizzed back. *Host is Nia Robinson, dep assistant for Leg'ive affairs. Confirm u can come, then call me when u r free for bkgd briefing.*

I would have called then and there, but Valerie had just entered the basement gym. She surveyed the digital record of my exercise. "Not bad. Let's kick it up a little." She hovered over the electronic display to ensure I met expectations.

I called Charlie after I'd showered and dressed.

"Hey, what's up?"

"I dunno exactly, but Nia is very eager to meet you. She somehow discovered that I knew you, so she asked me to arrange a lunch. I'll join you to break the ice."

"Who is Nia?"

"Are you joking me?"

"When you talk to me, always assume you're talking to the dumbest guy in Washington."

"But you read SitRep, right? They did a big profile of her last week."

"I get the SitRep Morning Score on my BlackBerry, but I don't always have time to click all the links."

"Well Nia's a rising star. She reports to Armand Bragg. He's the top legislative affairs guy at the White House. You must know him, he's responsible for the care and feeding of Senator Hazen."

"I've heard his name mentioned."

"Armand's a huge disappointment. Nia's carrying the whole load. And like I said, for some reason I don't understand, she wants to meet you. So you'd better come, and you'd better not spill anything on yourself – make me look good."

I'll admit: I was not too cool for the White House.

To visit the Capitol, you pass through a metal detector at any one of dozens of entry points. Once admitted to any of the House or Senate office buildings, you can wander through the underground tunnels to any of the others. The Capitol police will stop you if you try to enter the House or Senate chamber while actually in session, but otherwise have fun! You paid for it!

Not the White House. My email specified that the gate at which I was to enter the complex: the Seventeenth Street gate of the Executive Office Building, a block away. They would need my date of birth in advance, driver's license, Social Security number. Be sure to bring photo ID. Arrive 30 minutes before appointment time.

I did as instructed. Valerie fussed over my clothes that morning. "Your first visit. It won't be the last. But see if you can take a picture when nobody's looking!"

I arrived at the huge grey granite pile of the Executive Office Building at 11:45. A long line of visitors slowly moved forward to a reception desk. When I finally reached the head of the line, a guard checked my identification, confirmed my appointment, and presented me with a badge to wear around my neck. He asked me to stand aside. I would not be allowed to proceed through the metal detectors until Charlie came to claim me.

"What, no colon exam?" I asked when Charlie materialized.

"This way, funnyman. It's faster if we go through the basement, but let's take the scenic route."

We stepped up a broad flight of stairs into a huge echoing
corridor, the main axis of the EOB. Ceilings lofted high above
us. Long dizzying rows of doors seemed to stretch forward and
back along hallways wide enough for a chariot race.

I followed Charlie around two turned corners, to a vast
heavy wooden door inset with glass. He pushed it open, and
we stood outside again, at the top of another mighty granite
stair – and looking straight ahead at the most famous building
in the world, shining white. Not a picture. Real.

"So there it is: the prize that cost the Constitutionalist
party a billion dollars to snatch back from Monroe Williams.
Smaller than you expected, isn't it?"

I didn't know what to say. The granite steps led down to a
street lined with front-in parking. The top and bottom of the
street were sealed with ornamental wrought-iron gates. Charlie said that the street had been closed as a temporary wartime
measure in 1942. It had of course remained closed ever since
as a parking lot for senior staff.

"Once I get my commission," Charlie said, "I'll be able to
park over there." He indicated a curving asphalt drive just outside the wrought-iron gates.

We walked across the street toward a long blue awning
protruding from the side of the West Wing. It looked exactly
like something you'd see leading from the golf carts to the pro
shop at a mid-priced golf club.

Stop me if I'm telling you something you've heard before,
but the West Wing is not literally part of the White House.
It's an oblong attached to the White House by a colonnade.
A symmetrical colonnade leads to the less famous and much
larger East Wing, where (as Charlie explained) the military

attaches have their offices, as does the First Lady's staff. In this militarized administration, people were already joking that the East Wing was the new West Wing.

We walked under the awning, toward a very ordinary door with a very ordinary metal handle, stepped down three steps, and passed a desk guarded by a security officer.

"We're one floor below the Oval Office, the Roosevelt Room, and the Cabinet Room," Charlie explained.

I gawked. Blue carpets, white walls, low ceilings. Charlie nodded toward a recessed doorway. "That's the way to the Situation Room."

We took turned right into another very narrow corridor and descended a couple of steps to a small waiting area. At the end of this narrow short passage stood a little podium at which awaited the head steward of the Mess in a blue jacket with gold braid epaulets, grandly holding in his hand a clipboard listing his lunchtime reservations. Behind him, a huge bowl filled with – were those M&Ms? For anybody to reach in and grab? I could see a little plastic scoop protruding from the bowl, but still: for the lunchroom of the staff of the leader of the nation, the untended candy basin seemed rather epidemiologically risky.

We sat upon a little couch to wait. At 12:15 exactly, Nia stepped in front of us: a tall, slender, African-American woman in a sober navy blue pantsuit, her hair cut very close to her elegant head I'd estimate she was closer to her 35th birthday than her 40th. Charlie snapped to his feet like an ambitious lieutenant caught napping by the colonel. She gave his shoulder a friendly tap. *At ease, soldier.*

Nia shook my hand and thanked me for coming. We followed her past the head steward into a dining room about the same size as the living room of my apartment.

The unwindowed dining room held one large table, and maybe half a dozen two-tops and four-tops covered with white table linens. The deep blue walls were decorated with nauti-caul gee-gaws: old barometers, antique prints of bygone war-ships. Charlie had told me that the dining room was run by the navy. If so, the admirals were working overtime to remind General Pulaski's staff of the existence of Uncle Sam's Canoe Club. Charlie cautiously motioned his head toward the long wall of the dining room. Always the tour guide, he whispered, "The senior staff eat on the other side."

"So how is my dear friend Senator Hazen doing these days?" asked Nia, as we settled into the uncomfortable wooden dining chairs. She was about the most formal person I had ever met.

"He's doing fine," I replied. "He's got a lot of worries. But who doesn't? How long have you known the senator?"

"About ten years. My first job on the Hill was answering phones for Senator Timkiss. He was the last Constitutionalist senator from Connecticut, a moderate like Hazen, so we were always getting calls from Hazen's offices. Then I moved to the Banking Committee staff, and I saw a lot of Hazen there. He's such a wonderful man."

"I'm enjoying working for him."

"And from everything I hear, he's really taken a liking to you."

I scrutinized her face. No, she wasn't flattering me. She was simply describing the lay of the land, a landscape she knew a lot better than me.

"That's very nice of you to say," I answered, "but I can't believe that somebody with all your responsibilities has the time to track anonymous Hill mice."

Charlie nervously crinkled the wrapper of a package of oys-ter crackers. The noise somehow summoned a waiter. Charlie whispered into my ear, "Order the crab cakes." Nia requested a bowl of soup and an iced tea.

"Tracking which of their staffers our US senators have confidence in *is* one of my most important responsibilities," said Nia.

The food arrived. Nia broke off a corner of a cracker, dropped it into her soup. A steward refilled my glass of ice tea.

"Walter, may I speak confidentially to you?"

"Of course."

"I wouldn't speak so frankly if Charlie had not assured me that you could be absolutely trusted." She nodded at Charlie, who crinkled his wrapper more nervously than ever. Another tea refill was poured.

"I know," she continued, "that you are new to Washington. You are still finding your way. And you are probably feeling a little uncomfortable talking about your boss with somebody outside your chain of command."

I nodded.

"You are thinking: Why doesn't Nia talk to Hazen directly? Or at least to Daphne Peltzman?"

I nodded yes again. More wrapper-crinkling from Charlie.

"The trouble is that there are a lot of things I want Senator Hazen to *know* that it's not proper for me to *tell*. He might feel that I was trying to influence him, when I was only trying to inform him."

I didn't quite grasp that, but I let it pass.

"I need a relationship with somebody where I can say, 'Here is something your senator might want to consider.' I'm not lobbying him – not yet! I'm just sharing news that might be helpful to him."

Nia came to the main point. "The financial picture is getting very bad, very fast. The administration may soon have to take some painful decisions much earlier than we'd wish. We'll need all the backing we can get in Congress. Senator Hazen was one of the president's first, most important, and most valued supporters. We'll need to rely on him more heavily than ever."

Nia's spoon dipped into the soup. She delicately caught a fragment of soup-soaked cracker and transported the mix toward her perfect white teeth.

What was I supposed to say to any of this? "Nia, I carry Senator Hazen's briefcase for him. He does not ask me for advice on which way to vote."

Another faint smile. I guess Nia Robinson did not need me to analyze the sources of Senator Hazen's decision-making.

"I know very well Senator Hazen's independence of mind. But when you plunge into a crisis, keeping channels of communication open can become urgently important – and also surprisingly difficult. Especially if senators have people in their offices who wish to shut those channels down."

Ah.

"But I report to Daphne Peltzman."

"Oh," she replied, unflustered. "I thought you worked for Senator Hazen." *Shoosh.* Another big refill of my iced tea.

"Walter, here's the reason for this lunch. You are independent, more independent than most people in this town can afford to be. Senator Hazen likes you, and to be frank, you owe him. All I'm asking you for is this: I want to be able to count on you for direct access to the senator when the president needs it. Unscreened. Unmediated. I'm not asking for anything that the senator himself would not ask you for, if only he understood how big a problem he had on his hands inside his own office. I have a feeling you know exactly what I'm talking about."

Charlie had been right about the crab cakes, but I wish he had warned me against the ice tea. Suddenly, I had very badly to go to the bathroom. Nia reached into her purse and extracted a card. She scribbled ten digits on the back.

"Here's my mobile number. Please make sure the senator has it – and please be careful with it otherwise. May I have yours?"

I presented her with my Senate card.

"I have to leave now for my next meeting," she said efficiently. "But please have some dessert on my tab. Thank you for coming. We'll talk again."

Another handshake, then I could escape to the john. I returned to ask Charlie his dessert recommendation, but he had to return to his desk too. He escorted me out of the complex. Lunch had not lasted even 45 minutes.

CHAPTER 27

Today was my day to be popular. On the taxi ride back to the office from the White House, my BlackBerry rang, and out squeaked the voice of Freddy Catesby.

"Hi, Freddy."

"I've got an invitation for you. I don't care what else you are doing Thursday night, cancel it and come to this instead."

Lamont P. Forrest, one of Washington's richest Constitutionalists, was giving an important dinner for members of the new administration at his house in McLean.

"Walter, I have secured you an invitation to this Lucullan repast. I don't ask for thanks. It will suffice to name your first child after me. But I insist you attend, and I will accept no excuses."

"I'll attend Freddy, thank you."

"With the delicious Valerie?"

"She wouldn't miss it."

I got that right! It turned out that Valerie's company was organizing the dinner. Valerie gained extra connectedness points at work for being invited to one of her own affairs as a guest.

On the appointed night, we drove over the bridge, out Chain Bridge Road, and pulled off that mansion-lined route just past the Saudi ambassador's compound. We drove toward the river, then up a long driveway to an array of awaiting valet parkers.

Now let me stipulate: The Schotzkes have no standing to complain about vulgar display. My grandfather and my father knew how to spend money. My mother knew even more. If and when I come into my inheritance, I have a few spending ideas of my own.

But the Forrest house? Ridiculous even by Schotzke standards. From the street it looked like a medium-ostentatious Beverly Hills mansion: a bizarre jumble of two-storey Corinthian columns, sloping grey mansard roof, white doors, and pink brick.

But step inside, help yourself to a glass of champagne from a waiter, then walk toward the wall of glass at the back of the marble-floored reception room, and suddenly the house opened into crazy grandiosity. A triple-height living room had been extended out the back, cantilevered from the high cliff out over the Potomac River. Through the high wall of glass, you stared over the rocky Potomac rapids to the opposite cliff of the Maryland shore. If the front of the house was Aaron Spelling, the backside was pure Dr. Evil.

Valerie and I turned left into a grand drawing room, paneled in some kind of polished light wood. Freddy Catesby was standing beside a prosperous-looking couple I correctly guessed as our hosts. Catesby was dressed even more nattily than usual: tailored double-breasted blue suit, white shirt, red-and-white dotted bowtie, hand-made brown shoes.

Lamont Forrest, a short, plump man in his sixties, beamed self-satisfaction, and why not? Beside him stood a tall, lustrous brunette in her late thirties, the big-breasted mother of his second family. All around him gleamed the eye-catching rewards of what a man could buy with $300 million of proceeds from a "liquidity event."

From her work planning this party, Valerie had gathered the details of the liquidity event and the career that had led up to it. Forrest had served in the Alabama state legislature on the Nationalist side back in the 1970s. He'd served a term in the U.S. Congress, where he spotted his business opportunity. He quit politics and entered the nursing home business. As he got richer – and as state Medicaid authorities kept issuing citations of his nursing homes – his politics shifted. He became a generous supporter of Constitutionalist causes, giving not only to candidates but also to the Constitutionalist Institute and *Constitutional Review.*

Forrest had beautifully timed the sale of his business. The check was cashed six months before the financial crash and the Williams administration's crackdown on nursing home standards. With his liquid wealth, he had divorced the first Mrs. Forrest, remarried, and moved to Washington.

The second Mrs. Forrest was dressed tonight in a tight brown suede skirt, opened-toed pumps, and a shimmering bronze silk blouse opened to offer revealing views of the assets she had brought to the marriage. Her Alabama accent was all lilting and melting. It made you think of warm nights and giggles behind the bushes at the country club.

"Shall we make a minute to talk with Walter?" Catesby murmured to Forrest.

"After dinner. Let's welcome the other guests first."

The welcoming was not a small matter. Including the Forrests, 36 of us filed into the dining room on the other side of the grand entry. The decoration of the dining room was done in bold plutocrat style: wide stripes of green, gold, and cream.

Valerie's party planning company had matched the rented tables, chairs, and elaborate floral centerpieces to the opulent wall colors.

The guest list sparkled as brightly as the vermeil electric candlestick sconces. Ignatius Hernandez had come. Bill Mihailovich of the *Wall Street Transcript* had taken the train down from New York. Senator Joliette warmly shook my hand, and his shy wife was equally nice to Valerie.

Forrest himself introduced me to the president of the Constitutionalist Institute, Gordon Munsinger, a portly man in aviator glasses who scrutinized me very carefully. I felt I knew him after walking past his closed door so many times. I thanked him for the excellent education I'd received at CI.

"I hope we turned you into a sound Constitutionalist?" Munsinger asked gravely.

"Yessir."

"I hope that does not cause you trouble with Senator Hazen?" he added with heavy humor.

There was no good answer to that, so I just laughed.

I met a correspondent at one of the old-line networks in the days when they dominated national media, now a regular on Patriot News, where he ceaselessly and bitterly denounced the dying institution in which he had gained his fame.

I spotted a justice of the Supreme Court talking to a uniformed general. Beside them stood somebody I did recognize: Ramdam Sessnip, a Patriot News regular.

Catesby introduced me to a woman who had worked as the manager of Governor Tremain's losing campaign for the Constitutionalist presidential nomination, and then to a stooped elderly man who had served as Attorney General in a Constitutionalist administration three decades ago.

From the current administration, the Forrests had attracted two more star attractions: Treasury Secretary Tony Monckton, a tall, sharp-featured man, gray-haired and gray-faced, accompanied by an equally drab wife; and Colonel Cleland, who arrived solo. Little excited circles formed around each man. Hernandez and Mihailovich had disappeared together deeper into the house.

The invitation had said 7 o'clock for cocktails, 8 o'clock for dinner. A few minutes before 8 o'clock, the headwaiter admitted one last guest: Vernon Mallory.

Valerie's firm had arranged a fine dinner: lobster meat en croute, roast veal in sauce, good wines. The crisis had ruined many once-rich people. However, if you had preserved your money, or most of it, you felt richer than ever.

We sat at tables of six. Valerie and I shared our table with Catesby; the grouchy radio host I'd met at the Inaugural ball, Lou Rogers; and the former Tremain campaign manager and her husband.

Forrest had placed his wife at a table of her own with Vernon Mallory and Iggy Hernandez. He had reserved Cleland and the Moncktons for himself.

Despite Catesby's best efforts, ours was not a very enjoyable table. The former Tremain campaign manager wanted to speak only to Rogers. She launched into a promotion of her candidates for the next political cycle, like a procuress displaying her inventory to a jaded customer.

"You have to meet this incredible woman I'm running for attorney general in California: smart, tough, ultra-Constitutionalist! My client in Florida faces a Nationalist challenger backed the teachers' unions! By the way, your listeners might be fascinated by the Brazilian congressional elections. I'm advising the Brazilian Democrats – no, no," she said anticipating a negative reaction, "in Brazil the Democrats are the right-of-center party!"

So this is what a consultant is reduced to if her presidential candidate does not win. Rogers showed no sympathy.

"I wanted Esther Minden," he said brusquely, rooting with two hands through the bread basket. "I would have settled for Tremain. But you bungled the Tremain campaign. Pulaski won. Now we have to live with him and his bullshit about moving beyond political labels. Which is code for selling out to the Nationalists, if you ask me."

He found a roll that pleased him and ripped it apart. He threw the pieces in his mouth and talked as he chewed. "I think your political instincts are garbage, and I think your candidates are probably garbage too. And I don't care if you represent that all-Rio samba dancing champion."

The former campaign manager laughed with mock delight. "That's why we love your show. You are always so hilariously outrageous."

"I say what I think," Rogers answered as he prospected for a second roll. "Why is that hilarious?"

His excavations were arrested by the arrival of the first course. Rogers slashed at the elaborately presented dish, tearing away the pastry wrapping, spearing the lobster meat. He ate like an act of war.

The former campaign manager's husband, a retired newspaper editor with great grey tufts of hair sprouting in his ears like beach grasses, meanwhile commenced a long meandering anecdote about the election of 1984. I don't think he intended to change the subject; he had not heard one word of Rogers's exchange with his wife, nor one word of anything else said that evening either.

Rogers glanced at my place card as the waiters removed the soiled appetizer plates. Obviously, he did not remember meeting me on Inaugural night. "You're one of those trust-fund kids who comes to Washington in between college and daddy's business, aren't you?"

I pondered this. "Yes, I suppose I am."

"What did you do to defeat Monroe Williams?"

"Not much."

"I worked my ass off. I was on the radio three hours a night, every weeknight. I was the first to warn what he was going to do to our Constitution. I was the first to call Williams a Marxist. Then all these backbenchers imitate me – and everybody forgets who they got their ideas from. See that Indian guy over there?"

He pointed to Ramdam Sessnip.

"Look at him simpering to Forrest tonight. I made his book a bestseller! You didn't read it? Jesus, where do they find you punks? *The Crimes of Monroe Williams*. But now that he's on Patriot News, Ramdam just waves to me across the room. See, I'm not refined enough for this crowd. I tell it like it is. Now I'm telling them that Pulaski is no good. They don't want to hear it. They want to tell their friends" (and here Rogers veered into some imaginary high-society accent, as if rich people still talked like Katherine Hepburn in the *The Philadelphia Story*) "'Do you know Colonel Cleland? Gruff at first, but so *chaahr*-ming when you get to know him. He's spending the weekend with us in our St. Michael's house.'"

I leaned around a wine-pouring waiter to ask, "So how did you decide that President Pulaski is such bad news?"

"He didn't come on my show during the campaign," said Rogers, mopping the bottom of his plate with another roll. "He banished my friend Iggy to the Interior Department. He's filled up his White House with military henchmen, spineless Constitutionalists and Nationalist crossovers. I can smell a sell-out the way a dog can smell another dogs' piss. Not that I mind. It's good for business."

"What's good for business?"

"The sell-out. Monroe Williams was the greatest thing ever to happen to talk radio. Galvanized our audience. Winning this election has put them to sleep. Now I can wake them up again." He hoisted his glass of Coke, rattled the ice cubes, and for the first time all evening, he smiled.

As the waiters removed the last of the gold-rimmed plates that had presented our main course, Forrest rose to his feet to propose his own toast, in the latest of the evening's succession of costly wines.

"Friends!" Forrest called the room to attention in his folksy Alabama accent. "Friends! I think we all will want to toast the beautiful Crystal, who planned this wonderful evening."

The room murmured in agreement. "To Crystal!" Mrs. Forrest happily nodded her appreciation.

"If Crystal Forrest isn't the premier hostess in Washington," Forrest continued. " I can't think who is. At least – the premier hostess on the *pro-American* side of our politics."

The room laughed at this sally – except (I noticed) for Patrick Cleland, who looked as if he had been having an uncomfortable evening.

"We all will also wish to toast our friends who have accepted positions of trust and honor in this new Constitutionalist administration: my old friend Tony Monckton and his lovely wife Sherry; my new friend Colonel Patrick Cleland; and, of course, the great Iggy Hernandez. We look to you to uphold our Constitution and to repeal the attacks on our liberty by the Monroe Williams administration."

Applause. Cleland tapped his palms silently together.

I thought Forrest had finished, but no. He was only just settling into his speech, his face beaming admiration of his own words.

"Colonel Cleland – Patrick - I have to warn you: Tonight you are dining among the hardest-shelled Constitutionalists, the true believers of the true believers. Some of us weren't so sure when Iggy began organizing the winning Pulaski campaign. My friend Holly Milmott," here he indicated my tablemate, the former campaign manager, "supported Governor Tremain."

Applause for the former campaign manager fluttered through the dining room.

"My friend Sam Basmajian and many others had hoped that Esther Minden might run."

At the name of Basmajian, the elderly former attorney general nodded acknowledgment.

"I know my friend Lou Rogers preferred Esther Minden too." Rogers executed an ungainly half-rise from the table on his stubby legs and waved to the room, extracting his own round of applause.

"But, Colonel Cleland, let me say: Once General Pulaski emerged as the best hope of this party, every one of us in this room rallied whole-heartedly to his cause. Some of us donated very generously to his campaign."

A few people clapped at this, but Forrest modestly waved them to silence.

"No, no, it was my duty, my duty to my country and to the Constitution. I am grateful that the Lord provided me with the means to do it."

That remark elicited more applause, which Forrest again smilingly silenced.

"But I do think my efforts have earned me the right to offer this toast, a toast I have been waiting more than four years to deliver: Ladies and gentlemen, the president of the United States."

The room clapped fervently. This time even Cleland joined in.

Was Forrest finished? No, he was not. "Crystal, much as we delighted in that delicious dinner – I don't think any of us can have forgotten that while we were enjoying the charm of your hospitality, 88 of our fellow-Americans are being held in captivity by enemies of our nation. Perhaps some are guilty of wrongdoing or disloyalty. Perhaps some have forfeited the proud title of 'American.' All things will come to light. For now, we hold them all in remembrance."

This time there was no applause, instead a self-consciously solemn bowing of heads.

"To help us understand the situation of our captive soldiers, I have requested Dr. Vernon Mallory to say a few words over dessert. I am thrilled to tell you that he has graciously assented."

Forrest now turned to face Mallory, at his seat on the other side of the large room beside Mrs. Forrest.

"Vernon, knowing you were to speak tonight, and that you had promised to speak with the utmost candor in this confidential setting, I gave a special order to our catering company. Adapting the words of our first general-president, George Washington, I told the caterers, 'Let none but Americans serve dinner tonight!"

At those words, the servers fanned out from the kitchen to place dessert plates and pour sweet wine. I noticed for the first time: The servers were all black, not an Hispanic or Filipino face amongst them. Valerie caught my eye, intuited what I'd noticed, and whispered, 'You have no idea how hard that was!'

The dessert looked great: a kind of meringue confection with little raspberries, garlanded with crispy brown spun sugar and a tiny chocolate wafer.

Mallory rose from his place, frowning contemplatively. The waiters poured sweet wine into small glasses.

"Lamont, Crystal, I thank you for your amazing generosity and public spirit. It's been the privilege of my life to meet so many friends committed to the defense of our country and our Constitution. Now I worry, is it too late?"

In reverent attention, forks ceased scraping plates.

"We confront something for which we have as a nation very little preparation: not an exterior threat, but an enemy within."

I saw Cleland abruptly stiffen.

"Colonel Mali's column was ambushed because it was betrayed. In the firefight, soldiers in American uniform turned their guns on soldiers in American uniform. Our higher-ups have information that Mali was not the only American soldier killed by a US-issued bullet. Montoya did not act alone."

The room gasped at this revelation. Cleland shook his head and visibly mouthed the words, "Not true."

"We do not know how many of the soldiers in the column belonged to Montoya's conspiracy" continued Mallory. "We do not know how many of the surrendered soldiers are prisoners – or collaborators."

Cleland's face flushed red. The flush started at the tips of his ears, then suffused over his neck, cheeks, and up to the high hairline of his shaved skull, as if his head were catching fire.

"We do not know how wide the conspiracy ramifies. But the data clearly shows that our country is divided, 70-30: 70 percent loyal American, 30 percent alien and unreliable. That division has been reproduced inside our armed forces in this time of war. Yet our military commanders won't face the facts. That failure extends all the way up to the very highest levels-"

Cleland could not stand it any longer. He jumped to his feet and, without shouting, made his voice heard through the whole room. "That is simply not true! You are exaggerating one man's crime into a slur against the whole U.S. Army!"

Mallory turned a surprised expression to the colonel. "With all due respect, sir, I am only reporting what the data says. If the Army does not like it, the Army's problem is with the data, not with me."

"Dr. Mallory," (the word "doctor" was pronounced with heavy sarcasm), "the Army has repeatedly double-checked your so-called data since you began to offer it. It's worthless."

Forrest interrupted the two quarreling men, his face distorted by embarrassment, uncertainty, and unhappiness. Patriot News and the newly elected Constitutionalist administration were the two lodestars of Forrest's mental life. It had obviously never occurred to him that they might pull in different directions.

"Colonel Cleland, please don't take offense!" Forrest interjected. "Dr. Mallory please explain to Colonel Cleland! We're all on the same team here! Dr. Mallory is not criticizing President Pulaski or anybody on his team. He's only criticizing political correctness in the media!"

Cleland clenched and unclenched his teeth. I suppose he was not used to being told what to do or think, at least not by pot-bellied civilians, no matter how wealthy.

His head still flushed, Cleland spoke with forced calm. "I do take offense, Lamont. This is a trumped-up political accusation. I've been looking into this matter ever since Mallory made his TV debut spouting his nonsense. Your expert is a fraud."

Cleland turned to address Mallory directly. Mallory gazed bemusedly on him, as if to say, *I expected this, but you can't touch me.* "You have fewer secrets than you think, Dr. Mallory." The word "doctor" was again pronounced with heavy sarcasm. "I know who stands behind you, and they are no more interested in 'military readiness' than in - for example - the workings of the Interior Department."

Cleland's head snapped back to face Forrest. "That's all I have to say. Excuse me, but I won't sit here and listen as this flim-flam artist insults better men than him, including the better man I work for and who you toasted a few minutes ago."

Cleland now turned to Crystal Forrest. He raised two fingers to his forehead in mock-salute. In a voice now only slightly tinged by sarcasm, he made his adieu. "Thanks for the lovely dinner, Crystal. When we next make contact with our prisoners, I'll tell them you and Lamont remembered them over the veal."

He pivoted to the Treasury Secretary. "Tony, you coming with me?" Both Moncktons reluctantly and awkwardly rose to follow.

Cleland directed himself to Hernandez next and demanded mockingly, "Iggy? What about you?"

Hernandez held up his dessert fork, his face void of any expression. "I think I'll finish Crystal's excellent dessert, Patrick."

The two men locked eyes for a minute. Then Cleland marched out of the room. The Moncktons hastened after him, miming a distressed, "Goodbye – thank you – we'll call" to the Forrests.

Cleland's departure reverberated for a few shocked minutes. Were guests imagining how it would read in Gawker or FishbowlDC? Was somebody tweeting the incident even as it occurred? I glanced at Rogers. His face radiated ecstatic excitement. Then, without even a look down, he smashed his dessert with the back of a table spoon. The spoon shoveled into the creamy mess and Rogers gulped down a great wobbly bite.

Mallory held his tongue until the front door had closed behind Cleland and the Moncktons. Then he shook his head sorrowfully and, with a glance toward an approving Forrest, resumed his intended remarks.

Hernandez pushed his fork into the meringue and speared a dainty bite, his face absorbed in thought.

CHAPTER 28

The rest of Mallory's after-dinner talk was received with respectful attention. He finished with a defiant promise that he would not be silenced, no matter what pressures were brought to bear.

Forrest finished off the formal portion of the evening with one more of his little speeches. Then Valerie's carefully selected waiters returned to pour coffee and offer port and liqueurs. Soon the clock showed 10 PM. On a Washington weeknight, 10 o'clock blows the whistle on the social round.

Guests rose, marveled their appreciation of the wonderful evening, deplored the unfortunate confrontation, and bid the Forrests good night. Mallory clasped hands with Lamont and kissed Crystal. He wished he could stay longer, but he had an early morning taping on Patriot News. Hernandez departed next, still brooding. Catesby approached my table, rested a hand on my arm, and said in an undertone, "Don't leave before me."

I nodded. Valerie and I lingered among the last guests. As the numbers dwindled to a final few, Crystal offered Valerie a tour of the mansion.

Forrest beckoned to Catesby and me to follow him into his library. One bookcase was filled with leather-bound antique volumes, another with new books, their spines all stamped with smiling photographs of Constitutionalist politicians and celebrities.

Forrest and Catesby settled themselves into red leather armchairs. I chose the corner of a sofa thickly upholstered in some kind of bronze plush. A few moments later, Munsinger and Senator Joliette entered the room, and each took a chair for himself.

Liqueur and coffee were offered. I accepted a small glass of Hennessy XO. Nice. The staff softly closed the doors behind them. Forrest offered cigars. I was tempted. Then I imagined Valerie's reaction when she smelled cigar smoke on my breath. I withdrew my hand.

Catesby opened the talk:

"You all know my young friend Walter Schotzke. Walter's family has a long history and deep relationship with Senator Hazen. And we all know how important the senator's leadership will be in the weeks ahead."

"Walter and I have met before," said Senator Joliette extending a hand, as if at our first meeting he had not treated me like a piece of the furniture. In an undertone he added, "I was a great admirer of your father's." Then he addressed the whole group. "I'm very worried. I've never seen an administration insulate itself so fast from the people who elected them."

Forrest contradicted Joliette. "I had a long talk with Tony Monckton tonight. He's working very hard to keep the administration on principle and on message. Every new president has some little differences with some of his supporters. But Tony assures me that the president has been listening very carefully to the advice I've been sending him. I think maybe there's a risk of losing the big story here. We need to keep our eye on the fight with the Nationalists."

"Tony said the president has been listening to you?" Joliette asked incredulously.

"That's not an exact quote. But something to that effect."

"And what did Iggy say?"

Forrest shifted uncomfortably. "Well, of course Iggy has to be very circumspect. He's the most powerful man in the administration, and ..."

Joliette's patience with Forrest finally cracked. His voice abruptly rose. "Iggy has been been frozen out!" Then, just as abruptly, Joliette caught himself. Maybe he remembered he was speaking to $300 million. His voice lowered and softened again. "Look at how that man Cleland interrupted your party tonight! In all my years in politics, I've never seen anybody behave like that. Nobody sober anyway."

Forrest frowned at the unpleasant reminder. Yes, the offense to him could not easily be overlooked. He spoke now with reduced self-certainty. "What precisely are you worried about, Dick?"

"If I knew what to worry about, I would not feel so worried."

"Let me tell you what I'm worried about," said Gordon Munsinger. He puffed a smoke ring. " I've had some long talks with Tony myself. The president is obsessed with the budget deficit. He thinks the financial markets are going into crisis, and that he must act fast. Even if it means doing business with the Mexican insurgency. Even if it means raising taxes."

Forrest looked aghast. "Raise taxes? Iggy promised me he'd never do that!"

Joliette tapped Forrest's arm pityingly. "That was before Iggy's freeze-out. Now there's only way to stabilize the situation. The Constitutionalists in Congress must unite and hold firm. Which brings us to our young friend here."

Eyes rotated toward me. I looked back and forth at these four powerful men. I felt overwhelming stage fright. I had no idea what to say or do.

"Guys – gentlemen – I just carry Senator Hazen's briefcase."

The room received the remark like a grand joke. "Nobody's asking you to do anything superhuman," said Joliette. "Or inappropriate. Or even outside your job description."

The smoke was getting uncomfortably thick. Joliette began to explain himself very delicately, putting one word after the next as carefully as a man crossing a stream on slippery rocks places his feet.

"Unfortunately, over the past few years, there has grown up an … estrangement … between your boss and some of the newer Constitutionalists. Senator Hazen represents an older tendency in our party, less … I'll say less 'confrontational' than some of our newer members. Some angry words have been directed toward him. Phil is not a man to complain, but he wouldn't be human if he did not feel a little resentment."

I knew that to be true.

"Phil has always been there for our party when we really and truly needed him. But who decides what that time is? It's indispensable to maintain some way for his fellow Constitutionalists to reach Phil when the crisis comes – keep his mind open, prevent him from committing himself in the wrong way for the wrong reasons."

"As Daphne should have done," growled Munsinger.

Joliette waved a calming hand. "Water under the bridge. The important thing is, this is exactly what Phil would wish."

Now Catesby chimed in. "And whoever can do it – that person would overnight become a movement hero."

Geez. First Nia, now this. If they wanted to talk to Hazen, what prevented them from just picking up the phone? I asked, "Even supposing I had these magical powers, what difference would it make? You keep telling me how isolated Hazen is. So who cares what he thinks?"

The men in the room glanced at each other. Joliette took it on himself to answer me.

"Hazen's isolated here in Washington. But out in the country, a lot of Constitutionalists think he remains still a leader of the party. And some of those who know the truth still think Phil *should* be a leader. If Hazen aligned with the president against our leaders in Congress, the media would say, 'The

Constitutionalists are divided.' That division would give the president an opening for mischief.

"But if Hazen aligns with *us*, everything would be different. Without Hazen, the president would never dare proceed with whatever scheme he's got in mind. We're not trying to win a fight. We're trying to prevent a fight. For that, we need Hazen. Which means, we need somebody to talk reason into Hazen."

As Joliette finished, Forrest offered to pour me another brandy. I shook my head and got to my feet. The smoke had thickened oppressively.

"Like I said, I just carry the man's briefcase."

Catesby grinned. "Don't underestimate yourself."

When I emerged together from the library, I saw Valerie and Crystal were standing and chatting in the foyer, the tour over. Valerie said, "There's a guest who needs a ride home. He lives near us."

"Sure," I said. "Who?"

Valerie nodded to an old man dozing in one of the foyer chairs: the former Attorney General, Sam Basmajian.

CHAPTER 29

Crystal Forrest gently roused the old man. Confused and sleepy, Basmajian struggled to his feet as waiters produced his coat, scarf, and hat. The Forrests' walk and driveway shone with treacherous patches of ice. I offered him my arm. Basmajian preferred to take Valerie's instead.

She settled the old man's thin figure into the front seat of the Range Rover. The temperature had dropped deep below freezing, and the meatlocker cold had penetrated the leather seats. Basmajian shivered. Valerie raced back to the house, emerging minutes later with a soft blanket. "I remembered it from one of the guest bedrooms. Crystal said I can return it tomorrow when I come to supervise the loading of the rentals."

The old man sighed happily as Valerie wrapped him up, leaving only his arms free. He clasped her arm in appreciation. Then the arm trailed away, down her back. Valerie pretended not to notice. I opened the rear door for her, then walked round to drive the old lecher home.

Women are funny. The wrong hand on the ass infuriates them. The right hand delights them. You can never predict which hand is which. At least I can't. Valerie had warmed to Basmajian, and now she leaned forward from the back seat to chat.

"How long have you lived in Washington?"

"Since 1983," Basmajian wheezed. His mind had outlasted his lungs. "I moved here from California to take a job as deputy White House counsel. I was named AG in 1987, when my predecessor resigned in the Pilkington scandal." He paused to catch his breath again. "That was before your time, you probably weren't even born." Valerie confirmed that he was right. "Both my sons live in the area. My dear wife is buried in Silver Spring. Washington is home for me now."

You must have seen a lot of changes here over the years," Valerie offered, raising her voice to be heard by old ears.

"A few, but fewer than you might think." Another pause to inhale. "The city's better governed than it used to be. New buildings go up all the time, the suburbs spread further than they used to. The members of Congress all go home on the weekends nowadays, and I can't remember the last time I saw a senator drunk in public.

"But otherwise? The rules of the game are always changing, but the game itself somehow always stays the same."

Basmajian had dictated an unfamiliar address to my GPS, ending in SW, not the usual NW. I was following a strange route back into the city via the treacherously unmarked George Washington Parkway.

"Do you ever get cynical about the game?" I asked.

"There was a time I did." He wheezed again. "The Pilkington scandal brought to light some bad practices. I got kind of disillusioned with some of my friends in the Constitutionalist movement. I thought we'd come to Washington to change the way this city did business. Instead, it changed us, or anyway a lot of us."

Suddenly a burst of energy came into the old man, his flow of speech accelerated, and his voice gained timbre.

"But you know what? My Nationalist friends, they say exactly the same thing. Maybe you remember Jane Barnett? No? Jane was a flaming Nationalist from the Bay Area. She was always leading demonstrations on my front lawn when I was Attorney General, demanding more action on housing for the poor.

"Anyway, the next thing I know she's being hired as a consultant to federal housing agencies. Soon she's serving on boards of directors. She ended up as vice president of Fannie Mae. She collected $27 million in compensation, then retired just before the whole thing went bust. Twenty-seven million! The way inflation's eating away my pension, I may end up camping on *her* lawn!"

That surprised me. "You didn't return to private practice?"

"No," he said, slowing down again. "I wanted to teach. I helped organize a national association of Constitutionalist law students and professors. For a time, I ran the legal studies program at the Constitutionalist Institute. I said Washington can change you, and it can. Whether it *does* or not, that's up to you."

We crossed into the city. The freeway deposited us into a disorienting neighborhood: all highways and anonymous apartment blocks, a part of town I'd never seen.

Basmajian noticed my confusion and smiled. "Welcome to the middle class, young man."

I thought that was uncalled for. "I don't exactly live on Park Avenue."

Basmajian wheezed again, his energy exhausted. "No? Well I won't be here to see the end of *your* story." A big inhale of breath. "I'll tell you something I tell everybody who asks me about Washington. Young people imagine that everyone arrives here full of burning idealism – then get somehow seduced into corruption. And yes, that happens. But most of the time, the temptations do not seek you. You have to seek them. Jane Barnett was nobody's victim. She was a victimizer. Remember that, the next time somebody tries to explain to you how the system made them what they are. There are no systems. Just people."

We pulled up in front of Basmajian's brick high-rise. I exited the car to open the passenger door for him. Valerie rushed out too and extended her arm to help him to the front door of his building – completely unnecessary, since this path had no ice at all. Yet Basmajian accepted. As they neared the front, he released his hold on her arm to let his hand fall for another grope. She pulled gently away from him, but in the doorway, she leaned forward to kiss him on the cheek.

On the way home, Valerie said, "What a lovely man. Kind of inspiring too, don't you think?"

"It would be interesting to know what Mrs. Basmajian had to say about that."

Valerie giggled. "What can you mean?"

"I mean, maybe when Basmajian talked about resisting the temptation for big bucks, it was because that particular temptation didn't tempt him. Maybe he chased babes, not bucks."

"True. He definitely showed some life in that department." I could see her smiling softly in the glow of the dashboard. "Still, couldn't you wait five minutes after your passenger got out of the car before insulting him?

"I didn't realize you two had grown so close."

Valerie turned a stare upon me. "Are you … jealous?" She put a little lilt into the last word.

"Should I be?"

"You *are* jealous!" She breathed the words with satisfaction.

CHAPTER 30

What to tell Senator Hazen about the Forrests' dinner? I had to say something, but I also had to be careful. Charlie Feltrini once told me a warning story about a scheming staffer on the NSC. One of the man's plots was accidentally exposed. Months later, another plot came to light. Both times the man had plausible excuses. Nevertheless, after the second incident, the National Security Adviser banished the man to the Tajikistan embassy. "But boss, I'm innocent," the staffer protested.

"Yes. True. Only, you've been innocent too goddamn many times."

I had not done anything wrong. But maybe the senator would wonder why had these men felt free to discuss their plans with me? Had I somehow signaled to them a potential for disloyalty?

But to hold back was also dangerous. What if he heard about these discussions from somebody else, as he very well might?

On our walk on the morning after the dinner, I began hesitantly as we rounded the Washington Monument. "Senator, I have had some very strange experiences lately …"

"Yes?"

I narrated the headlines. Lunch with Nia. Dinner at the Forrests. The meeting afterward.

Hazen absorbed the information. Then he said, "You did exactly the right thing. When you're in situations like that, I don't need you to defend me. I need you to listen attentively, learn everything you can. If you have to play along a little to learn more, play along. I won't be offended. I don't worry you will try to manipulate me. You could not succeed if you tried. As others have learned."

He put questions to me, extracting information. Did I mention that he'd been a very good lawyer? As we neared the office, he pressed one last query. "I want you to search your memory. Other than the contacts you have already mentioned, has anybody from the White House or any other senator's office reached out to you in any way? Don't worry if the contact seems trivial or irrelevant. But anything?"

I thought about the call Daphne had placed to the White House personnel office on Brad's behalf. I had not thought very hard about whether Hazen would approve or not. Probably I should have asked him. Probably he would be annoyed by it if I did mention it. Anyway, that did not come under the heading of the White House reaching out *to me*.

Besides, what were the odds of anything coming of it? Thousands of hungry Constitutionalists were begging for administration jobs. Not even the U.S. government could be so dopey as to employ Brad.

"No, sir, that's everything."

CHAPTER 31

I'll be the first to admit that I'm not a completely satisfactory boyfriend. However, I do a very good Valentine's Day, if I say so myself. The key is to launch early.

On the fatal day, I woke extra early. I dressed for work, then steamed a caffe latte for Valerie and shaved some chocolate sprinkles onto the foam. As soon as the coffee was frothed, I hit the iPod. Our bedroom room filled with Pachelbel's Canon. Valerie opened her eyes. "Hey, Happy Valentine's Day," I said planting a kiss. "This is a down payment. I've got a reservation at the Tabard Inn at 7:30 tonight." Valerie stretched like a sun-warmed cat. Mission accomplished.

As I put on my overcoat I heard Valerie's mobile phone ring. Through the bedroom wall I heard first a short pause then an ecstatic female scream. "What? *Really?!* Oh Dana – oh that's wonderful – oh I'm so happy for you – so happy!"

Long pause.

"No, no, don't thank us. The credit goes all to Brad, he's so talented."

Another pause.

"Really? They really said that? Well, then, I'm glad. And if we did anything, any little thing, we were delighted to do it. Truly. Walter was delighted too. He'll be so thrilled when I tell him. Of course he likes Brad! And he loves you, always has. You know Walter, he doesn't show things the way other people do."

Pause.

"Oh, yes, for sure. Of course you must. Absolutely. No, no, Walter won't mind, he'd be the first to insist you do it."

That did not sound like a conversation on which I could safely shut the door behind me. I waited for the burbles to end, then inserted my head back into the bedroom and asked as cheerfully as I could,

"Was that Dana? She had some good news?"

Valerie looked very pleased with herself.

"Wonderful news. Brad proposed! Brad had promised to marry her just as soon as he found a more settled position, and now he has, thanks to you and Daphne. That was such a good deed!"

I did not literally stagger. My feet and knees stayed motionless. But I was staggering on the inside. I told myself: Don't panic. Maybe it's not as bad as it sounds. Better get the full dimensions of the disaster.

"What's the position?"

"Brad got a call the day before yesterday from the chief administrator of NASA. The head of the agency called him directly! She said they have a senior executive slot open to work on space commercialization. It's not a Wall Street salary, obviously. But Brad says it's such an exciting field, with lots of potential, and it's exactly the opportunity he's been looking for. Dana is so grateful to you.

So much for the nation's hopes of commercializing space. At least NASA does not count as the White House, so I could arguably justify having omitted to mention Brad's case to Senator Hazen.

"I'm happy for Dana," I allowed, "but remember, Brad said he had sent resumes all over town. I'm sure he got the job on his own merits."

Valerie shot a quizzical look at me. She knew what I thought of Brad's merits.

"When did you get so modest? There's no doubt about who deserves the credit. Half an hour after the NASA administrator called, Brad got a call from the White House. From a woman named Nia. She said she was a friend of yours. She congratulated Brad on the job and said, 'Please tell Walter and Daphne to let me know if there's anything else I can ever do for them.' It's just as I predicted. You are becoming a very important man!" She stretched herself seductively. "Come kiss me before you go to work."

So the Brad situation was *just* as bad as it sounded, probably worse. I had to think. But first I stepped forward for the kiss as ordered. Valerie pressed herself against me in a way she knew I liked.

"Mmm," she murmured in a disappointed tone. "I suppose you are becoming too important for the likes of me."

"I'll be enthusiastic by tonight, I promise," I replied glumly. "I'm just worrying about a tough assignment Hazen gave me. I'll get it figured it out somehow."

I kissed the top of her head and stepped toward the door. What I'd heard already was so bad that the final menace had nearly slipped my mind.

"One more thing. You said something toward the end of the call. You said that there was something Walter wouldn't mind? What was that?"

Valerie lifted the latte to her lips with two hands, turning her eyes up at me flirtatiously, bending her legs to lift up the blanket and show a little more thigh below the long t-shirt she had slept in.

She cooed sweetly, "I've decided what I want for my Valentine's Day present."

Not ... it couldn't be ... she wasn't expecting ... the same thing Dana had just got?

"I want you to agree to this without complaining." She was looking directly and seriously at me. My heart went into full palpitations.

"NASA has asked Brad to start work in the first week in March. They need to find a place to live right away. So Dana wants to come stay with us this weekend while she apartment-hunts."

Relief! Then the awfulness of the request hit, hard.

"Aw, come on! I got them a job for God's sake. I don't want them staying here. I can't believe you said yes to that!"

"It's just Dana, and just for a couple of days. They have to be so careful about money, and a hotel is just one more expense. Please say yes. I promise I won't let any more dirty old men grope my ass."

I sighed, unable to reply.

"I'll super owe you," she said, smiling and touching a pink tongue to her white teeth.

I was so screwed. Nor was I going to win this argument. Might as well get the benefits of being a nice guy. "You're a good friend, Valerie."

She laughed a pleased little laugh. "I'll be much more than a good friend to you tonight, mister. Meet here or at the Tabard?"

"The Tabard," I mumbled.

I walked south toward the senator's apartment in a mood of worry and anger. Even assuming Hazen didn't learn how Brad got his job - even if I could persuade him I'd misunderstood his question - even in the *best case scenario*, Dana would be showing up to stay in the second bedroom sometime tomorrow. The big TV would be out of bounds all weekend. And what if Dana needed more than three days to locate an apartment? What if they had not found a place before Brad started work? They could be staying with us for weeks!

All kinds of other grim possibilities took form in my mind. Sunday night dinners with Brad and Dana. Tennis with Brad and Dana. Brad and Dana bringing over the new baby. Horrible. Why couldn't I put my foot down? I never won these kinds of fights, never, ever.

"Something bothering you?" asked the senator as we exited his building. I guess my misery was showing.

"Girl trouble, sir."

The senator perked up. He loved coaching his staffers on their romance difficulties, with all the authority of his 41 years of happy marriage.

"Did you mess up Valentine's Day? I completely sympathize!" He chuckled complacently as he warmed to his advice. "I always loved celebrating anniversaries and my wife's birthday, but how I *hated* that holiday. It's a conspiracy by the florists, in my opinion. Yet women can't help caring about it, even when they know better. You take my advice, send a big bouquet to Valerie's office where all her friends can see. She'll forgive you."

"That's a very good idea, sir." I couldn't raise my eyes from the sidewalk.

He nodded, gratified to have his expertise ratified, but he noticed I still looked worried. He considered for a moment and then asked,

"Perhaps you're worrying today whether Valerie's love is over-influenced by mustard?"

I couldn't help laughing. "That thought has sometimes occurred to me."

"Take an old man's advice. It's the wrong question. That girl is devoted to you. If the mustard money helped you catch her, then be grateful for your mustard money. The important thing is to be decisive. If Valerie is not what you want, then break it off, although I personally would say you would be a damn fool. But if she is what you want, then don't leave her dangling. She'll love you better 20 years from now if you spare her anxiety today. Why, I asked Mrs. Hazen to marry me only three months after the first day met her ..."

He launched into a reminiscence we had all heard quite a few times before.

I fretted and brooded. Should I interrupt and confess what Daphne and I had done for Brad? But the senator was enjoying talking. Probably I was blowing everything out of proportion. Let it pass.

We arrived at the office. I settled the senator at his desk and fetched his biscuits and buttermilk. He had a little office time before I had to deliver him to a meeting with visiting bank CEOs at the Capitol Hyatt at 11 AM. I opened my email and – salvation.

Hey Walter, sorry to send this to your office email, but somebody seems to have unsubscribed you from the Facebook group for Alex and Brooklin's wedding.

That would be me.

So we haven't heard back from you about your invitation to Alex and Brooklin's Jack-and-Jill celebration this coming Saturday night. As you'd expect with Alex and Brooklin, everything about this wedding is untraditional! Instead of the usual bachelor/bachelorette party, they are inviting our entire Brown class to a fundraiser for West African asylum seekers at New York's Orchard Street Tenement Museum. We'll have authentic West African performance artists, music, and food, and testimonials from asylum seekers and other undocumented persons. We're asking for a minimum gift of $300 – but of course we'll accept more.

The actual wedding will be in Conakry, Guinea, so for most of us, this will be our only chance to toast Alex and Brooklin.

See you Saturday!

Becca Mather.

PS – We are hoping for an especially generous gift from you!

Normally, I'd have chewed my own arm off rather than have any further contact with Alex Millstein and Brooklin Putnam – or as they'd be jointly known post-wedding, Alex and Brooklin Putstein. But for a man looking for a reason, any reason, to get out of town, this invitation was a God-send.

At dinner, I presented Valerie with a pair of pearl earrings she had lingered over in a jeweler's display window a few weeks before. She accepted them rapturously. Between the gift and the good news from Dana, Valerie's mood that night was happy and frolicsome. Her good mood lasted into the next morning. Time to put my plan into action.

I waited until she was on the other side of the bathroom door – less risk of her reading a clue in my face.

"Hey, babe, I've been thinking about your weekend plan with Dana. I'm only going to be underfoot. Maybe it would be better if I go out of town, leave you two alone to apartment hunt without having to worry about entertaining me. I was invited to a stupid Jack-and-Jill party for two classmates of mine, Alex Millstein and Brooklin Putnam. I hadn't intended to go, but if Dana is spending the weekend here …"

Valerie stepped out of the bathroom, a towel wrapped around her wet hair, the rest of her wrapped in a bathrobe.

"Getting out of Dodge?"

"Uh, no, but …"

"I'm teasing! I don't mind. Actually it would be a kind of a relief. One less thing for me to worry about this weekend. Will you stay at the Brown Club?"

"Yeah, that's the best deal."

"And maybe stop by Skip Waltham's poker night?"

"Well –"

She kissed me. "Go. Have fun."

CHAPTER 32

So how terrible was the Millstein-Putnam party? So terrible I can hardly describe it. And West African food? Disgusting! I paid my $300 at the door. I played stupid when Becca worked on me for more. Then the speeches started. *Taxi!*

But where to go? I'd emailed Skip Waltham the day before, only to hear that the poker night had dissolved. Skip's wife had had a baby, and he was on call for the 2 AM feeding.

I stopped at my old haunt, the Bonobo bar, for a drink. Depressing to drink alone. Too early to go to bed. Too cold to walk.

My BlackBerry rang.. "Hello," said a familiar female voice. Wait a minute. "Hey?"

"Yes, cautious boy, it's Sylvia."

This I wasn't ready for. "Uh, hi. Did you have, um, a good Valentine's Day?"

"You have an unbelievable talent for saying the wrong things. Mine was miserable. How was yours?"

"Okay, I guess. How'd you find me?"

"There aren't so many guys named 'Walter' who work for Senator Philip Hazen of Rhode Island. See, I'm not totally reckless. At least I Google *after* I fuck. You left out all the interesting bits of your life story when we had drinks on Christmas Eve."

"It's not that interesting." I tossed back the last of my Talisker and signaled the bartender for a check.

"Where are you? It sounds noisy."

"In a bar. In New York City."

"*Really*? That's a coincidence. So am I. Are you alone? Where are you staying?"

"The Brown club. We share a building with Cornell ..."

I signed the credit slip, trying to calculate both the tip and what Sylvia was up to at the same time.

"Am I making you nervous?"

"No, no," I replied insincerely, stepping out into the empty street.

"You didn't answer me. Are you alone?"

"Yes."

"Then come see me. I've got a suite at the St. Regis. All to myself. We'll have a glass of champagne."

"You don't like champagne."

"I'm broadening my horizons."

A taxi magically appeared. I weighed my options. Get drunk by myself at the Brown club? Read an improving book? Or else – well, what the hell.

Some might wonder: Walter, how could you even think of seeing Sylvia again? You slip up once, okay, it happens. But a second time?

Let me put it this way. My favorite meal on earth is a rib-eye steak medium-rare with French fries and creamed spinach. Suppose, though, that some doctor said, "Walter, we've solved the heart attack problem. Go ahead. Place your order now, rib-eye and fries for dinner forever starting next Tuesday." Sometime before next Tuesday, I'd want to slip out for one last plate of Peking Duck.

I'd been brooding over Senator Hazen's lecture about Valerie. Everything he said was right. Even so, I guess I wasn't quite ready to start my lifetime rib-eye diet yet.

So about 10 PM on Saturday night, I was crossing the opulent lobby of the St. Regis. My father liked to stay here, and I'd often crossed the lobby as a boy. But time had changed the place, and not just by planting a big red flag overtop the building and changing its name to the Jingjiang St. Regis since its purchase by a Chinese hotel chain.

Twenty years ago, the St. Regis had been a very nice hotel. "Nice" meaning it was a place where you might see a successful doctor from Kansas City staying with his wife and kids. Now a room for the night cost almost as much as that doctor could expect to earn in a week. The lobby was crowded with the world's new rich: Chinese and Russians and Brazilians. The only Americans in sight worked behind the desk. The desk staff wore black unisex jackets inspired by the Mao suits of the 1970s. They greeted me with a servility inculcated by a decade of economic depression.

"Ms. Tescher? Yes, sir, my pleasure, sir. I'll alert her immediately, sir. May I offer you anything while you wait, sir? Whom should I say is here to meet her, sir? She says please come directly up, sir. I'll have one of our hostesses show you the way, sir."

A young Latina hostess presented herself. She wore her black Mao jacket atop a miniskirt that revealed a nice pair of legs. I got the strong feeling that if I called room service here, I could order her, or another just like her, and that the reaction would be: "My pleasure, sir!"

The hostess directed me to the elevator, pressed the up button for me, stepped inside, and pressed the floor number. She rode up all the way.

A security measure? Maybe, but even though I'm not in what Valerie would consider good shape, I doubt that this little sylph would have been able to prevent me from wreaking mischief on the hotel guests. The hostess turned away before I knocked on Sylvia's door. So no, not security – just another of the small luxuries for the St. Regis class generated by the new cheap labor economy.

Sylvia opened the room door a few inches. The pale face looked even more care-worn than when I'd seen her last, but her blue eyes shone unnervingly bright. Tears? Drugs?

When she tugged at my arm through the partly opened door, I assumed she wanted me to embrace her. But as soon as I crossed the threshold I realized my mistake. Once she had me inside the room, she stepped back from me.

"God, you're an awful dresser," she said as she looked me up and down. "Where the hell did you get that tie?"

"J. Press."

"Figures."

I admired the hotel suite: pale tangerine walls framing windows with floor-to-ceiling views of Fifth Avenue, chairs and couches around a white marble fireplace. The gilt-handled doors to the bedroom had been thrown open to reveal the luxuriously cushioned bed on which Sylvia had been lying until a minute ago. Somehow it didn't seem Sylvia's natural habitat.

"It's only the contrast with your beautiful hotel room that makes me look bad."

She pursed her lips. "Take me out for dinner. I've been holed up in this hotel by myself for 48 hours. I'm sick of room service."

"At this hour?"

"God, Walter, we're not in D.C. Anyway I'm not very hungry, I'd like a couple of martinis. I don't care what they serve after that."

Come to think of it, I *was* hungry. All I'd had to eat since arriving in the city were a couple of the less revolting-looking African canapés.

"There's a great Chinese restaurant on West 64th that should be open late," I suggested.

Sylvia had already vanished behind the now-closed bedroom doors to dress.

CHAPTER 33

The after-dinner entertainment with Sylvia compared very poorly to Valentine's night with Valerie.

Sylvia seemed not even to feel the two martinis or the bottle of Riesling we shared with the food. After dinner, we had walked back to the St. Regis through the whipping February wind so that Sylvia could smoke a couple of cigarettes along the way.

In bed, Sylvia was as business-like as ever. Valerie liked to play, liked to see me enjoying myself. Sylvia did not play. Sylvia wanted something. She took it and then collapsed on me. I decided I was done with Peking duck.

I woke up late the next morning, past 10 AM. No sign of Sylvia. She must have stepped out for a smoke. I picked up the phone to order some coffee. A voice on the other end greeted me, "Good morning Mr. O'Grady."

It took a few muzzy seconds for the lightbulb to flicker on. O'Grady? Michael O'Grady? Michael O'Grady was the creator and president of Patriot News. So that's how Sylvia afforded this hotel suite.

I ordered a caffe latte, plus a second cup in case Sylvia returned, and what the hell, an omelet too. I checked my Black-Berry. It showed a text from Valerie. "Hope u didn't lose too much money at poker. Assume u r sleeping off Skip's whisky. Touring apts today from 9 am onward, call when u r awake."

I felt too guilty to talk on the phone right away. I texted back. "Just woke up. Feel like crap. Will call @ 12. No money lost, don't worry."

Sylvia returned just as I was tucking into breakfast at a table in the suite's living room. In jeans, boots, and tweed jacket, her hair pulled into a ponytail, she looked more like the corporate wife back home in New Canaan or Rye than like the mistress in the hotel suite. She surveyed the scene: the elaborate setting of the breakfast table and me wearing a St Regis bathrobe and St Regis slippers. "You've made yourself at home."

I didn't quite like the way she said that.

"Coffee?"

"I've had mine."

"Would you like to go to the Central Park Zoo this afternoon?" I asked her, buttering some toast. I felt like a walk and the rainforest pavilion would be warm.

"For God's sake, we're not on a first date. No, what I'd like to do is take this" – here she picked up an envelope on a side table, slit it open, and removed a black American Express card – "and buy myself something expensive at Bergdorf's. Then later I want to go to some trendy club and have loud sex with you in the bathroom. Make a real spectacle of myself."

"Discretion to the winds? You were so careful at Christmas. But what about *my* reputation?"

That did make her laugh.

"Your reputation as what?"

I shrugged and took a forkful of omelet.

"Do you mind if I skip the Bergdorf's part?"

"Who invited you?"

So I had a free day in New York. I showered and dressed. I called Valerie's favorite florist to order a big bouquet delivered to the apartment that afternoon. I dictated a note. "Won't do this again. You are the best. Walter."

I walked up Fifth Avenue toward the park. Last night's wind had abated, so the day was cold but bearable. The windows of the shops near the St. Regis were placarded with signs announcing big markdowns. I entered the park and walked toward the zoo. It had been my mother's favorite outing with me when I was small. If I stared at the penguins until I lost all conscious thought, I could almost feel her standing beside me.

At the zoo exit, I gave a dollar to a street artist who was strumming a guitar with frigid fingers and singing a funny little song with the chorus, "Don't let your boys grow up to be bankers."

At noon I called Valerie. She couldn't talk. "We've just walked into a promising apartment, can I call you tonight?"

I said tonight would be fine.

Sylvia had been joking about the public sex bit, thank goodness, but not about Bergdorf's. She returned to the room about five o'clock, her face flushed with winter, clutching three shopping bags in each hand. "Good hunting?" I asked.

"Yes," she said. "I bought something for you, too." She extended a bag from the Bergdorf men's store.

"I'm not sure I can accept this," I said, trying to apply my x-ray vision through the tissue paper wrapping the contents.

If I'm going to have to look at you through dinner, you're going to have to wear a less ugly shirt and tie. "I paid for it myself, if that's what you're worried about. Besides, I don't think I've been completely nice to you."

She put the bag in my hand, closed my fist around the handle.

"You have a funny idea of not being nice."

"You know what I mean."

I reached inside the bag, laid out the shirt and tie on the cream-colored sofa. The shirt was indeed very handsome, a shimmering blue, matched with a sumptuous maroon necktie. Valerie would like them.

I took Sylvia to the Post House for dinner. She drank only a single martini this time. I ordered the ribeye, with creamed spinach and French fries. Sylvia had a lobster salad. We shared a bottle of California zinfandel. The name of the wine seemed appropriate: "Porque No?"

"Would I be out of line to ask you about Mr. O'Grady?" I asked as the first of the wine gurgled out.

She considered. "Probably. But go ahead."

"Let me guess. He didn't show up for Valentine's Day?"

"No." She said this calmly, almost meditatively. "I wasn't upset about that. I know he has a family."

"Then why were you at the hotel?"

"This whole plan was his idea, not mine. I hate Valentine's Day. What single woman doesn't? But he asked me to come up to the city!"

She was sounding less calm now. "He said he'd take his wife out to lunch on Valentine's Day. He told me that he'd chartered a jet to fly her and the kids to ski over the long weekend. They have a big place in Montana."

She took a big gulp of her wine. Some of it stained her lips. "So I took the train after work, checked into the hotel, and waited. And waited and waited and waited." Sylvia was trying to say this in her usual what-the-fuck-do-I-care way, but her voice had begun to waver.

"I waited for him all day Friday. I fell asleep in the room. When I woke up Saturday morning, a messenger delivered me an envelope with the credit card and a note. *Sorry I couldn't make it. Buy yourself something nice.*"

Food arrived. The waiter started to ask, "Everything going all right for you folks?" Then he caught the look on Sylvia's face, closed his mouth and backed away – but not before he heard the first bit of Sylvia obliviously announcing:

"I'm not going to get all prim here. I know what I am. I'm a mistress, a girlfriend, a piece on the side. He takes me on trips, buys me expensive presents. But I'm not a kept woman. I earn my living. I pay my rent. He knows that! He's never just *given me money*. 'Buy yourself something nice!'" She repeated the phrase with some disgust. "Like some Russian gangster's whore!" Her voice was rising, the people at the next table - and the table next to that – glanced our way, then retracted their eyes.

"I thought you got yourself arrested if you used somebody else's credit card to go on a shopping spree," I said, almost in a whisper, hoping she'd follow my example.

"Maybe at the Gap, not at Bergdorf's. Of course," she smiled at her own joke, "the real mistresses have their own cards."

"Do you and Michael work closely together?"

She didn't like question. "No! Not at all! I'm in advertising and marketing, I report to the chief operating officer, who reports to O'Grady. I started at Patriot News years before O'Grady took up with me."

She slouched over the table, her face looked worn again. "There's nothing special at Patriot News about being one of Michael O'Grady's women. He's banged a lot of us, dozens probably. As for the on-air blondies, if he's missed any of them, it's a filing error."

I refilled Sylvia's wineglass. She had taken two bites out of her salad.

"What kind of a guy is he?"

"Don't be dumb. What kind of a guy tells a woman to buy herself something nice?"

"Any redeeming features?"

"He's a great visionary of the television industry."

"Interesting that you don't say, 'Deep down, he's a fundamentally decent guy.'"

"A fundamentally decent guy could never have invented Patriot News."

The waiter returned to clear the plates. He glanced questioningly at Sylvia's nearly intact meal. She waved it away.

"Would you like me to box that—" She cut him off with another wave, and he retreated again.

"I watch Patriot News," I said. "Yeah, it's kind of sensational, and maybe it's not the most accurate news in the world, but I don't see what's so indecent about it."

"Why do you think people watch Patriot News?"

"Because the info-babes are so hot?"

"Yes, that helps. Maybe on the way home we can make a betting pool on which one O'Grady will choose to replace me. But our prime-time lineup is full of ugly old men, and they do even better."

"I'd take you over any of the info-babes any day," I said, not very truthfully. "But go ahead, tell me. Why?"

"You must have seen that ad we run for carbo-monoxide detectors?"

She imitated an announcer's gravely voice. "'There's an invisible killer lurking inside your home.'" She giggled at her audacity. For a second her humor seemed good-natured. Then the bitterness returned. "That's what we tell them every moment of the day, in every story and commercial. They are surrounded by danger. The enemy is everywhere: cunning, ruthless, merciless. The authorities? At best, pitiful and incompetent, but more often, corrupt and duplicitous. Now we are testing a new plot line. That's all this Vernon Mallory business is, the latest twist on our basic story. This time we're telling the viewers that the danger has even penetrated the U.S. Army! The viewers can trust nobody and nothing - except Patriot News of course."

She signaled the waiter and asked for a double Armagnac. My head was beginning to swim, but I matched her order: a double Armagnac for me as well. Through the booze, I tried a little joke. "You make Patriot News sound like pro wrestling."

She smiled, but did not laugh. "Yeah, but in our business, people actually get hurt. And at least the pro wrestling audience knows the show is a fake. Our audience doesn't. Our audience is so old, they remember when there was this thing called 'the news.'" She dropped into another imitation of a grave announcer's voice. "'And that's the way it is.'"

She took a long sip of the Armagnac.

"But Michael O'Grady doesn't believe in '*That's the way it is*.' He doesn't believe it's his job to report reality. He believes it's his job to make reality."

"You're saying that most CEOs think they are God, but Michael O'Grady actually is God?"

"Walter, you are really quite a good-looking boy. You don't have to try to be funny too. It doesn't work for you."

She called for a second double Armagnac. I switched to coffee.

"When Michael and I first got together, he took me to one of those billionaires' retreats in Aspen. I *did* think he was God in those days. I worshiped him fervently enough. Not any more. Probably that's why he's tired of me."

She shook her head. To clear the booze? Regretting the good old days? Or blaming herself? *I can't believe how stupid I was!*

"Anyway Michael spoke on a panel about the future of news media. An executive from one of the old networks just raged at him. 'Your news is all fear-mongering fiction!' You know what Michael answered?"

"I'm all ears."

"He said, 'It's not fiction. It's myth. And this myth happens to be true.'"

Now I knew I'd had too much to drink. "What the hell does that mean?"

This time she did laugh. "You're right – that doesn't make any sense, does it?"

I paid the bill. We exited the restaurant to walk down Madison Avenue so Sylvia could smoke. At least Sylvia walked. I stumbled.

The night cold cleared my head a little. I noticed that New York did a much better job than Washington of excluding panhandlers from the high-rent districts. As the alcohol fog lifted, I remembered a question that had been bothering me:

"Sylvia, can you help me understand something? Why is Patriot News giving President Pulaski such a tough time?"

She took a long drag from her cigarette.

"I mean" – I groped for what I did mean – "you spend four years clubbing President Williams over the head. You tell your viewers that the republic will collapse if President Williams is not thrown out. Then the Constitutionalists win a huge, historic victory. And what happens?"

For a second I could not remember what I wanted to say next. Oh yeah:

"Three months later, and you've gone to war against President Pulaski. Why? It doesn't make sense!"

"What am I, your tutor? I'm bored with this."

"Please?"

We were crossing 61st Street, where some enterprising street person had somehow eluded the cops and built himself a little bed in front of a store displaying a pair of massive Victorian silver candelabra in its window.

Sylvia stepped around him, lit a second cigarette, inhaled, exhaled, and then answered wearily:

"As far as Michael is concerned, Patriot News does not work for the Constitutionalist party. The Constitutionalist party works for Patriot News. The fight to defeat a Nationalist president made for great TV. Defending a Constitutionalist president? The worst. We tried that last time, and our ratings suffered. So Michael will go the opposite way. He'll savage Pulaski night after night. Will Michael win? He usually does, but who knows? And anyway, Michael doesn't really care. Michael wouldn't have cared if Williams had won the election. In fact he'd probably have preferred that. Michael isn't fighting for Constitutionalist principle, whatever that means. He's fighting for box office."

We arrived at the St. Regis. I walked her into the lobby and touched her shoulder. "I think I'd better say goodnight here."

The weariness suddenly disappeared from Sylvia. "You're not coming up?"

"Better not."

I leaned over to kiss her cheek. She pulled herself away, and I lurched past her.

"You're serious!" The words had begun as a question, but they ended as an accusation, her voice shifting from surprise, to disgust, to indignation. The Mao jackets at the reception desk glanced our way. I smiled and waved. Nothing to see here, just a lovers' tiff.

"It's better this way."

"Better for you," she said bitterly.

"Better for you too." I reached again for her shoulder. She flinched, but she did not push me away. "You'd be the first to say I'm not a very smart boy. You don't want me in your life."

She'd recomposed her what-the-fuck-do-I-care face. "You're my favorite kind of coward, the high-minded kind."

I pretended to take it as a compliment. "Good night, Sylvia. Thank you for the shirt and tie. Really. I'll stop by tomorrow to pick up the rest of my stuff."

I turned to go.

"You pathetic asshole!" she suddenly shouted at the back of my head. "Who are you going to call the next time your girlfriend goes out of town?"

That whipped around the Mao jackets. I kept walking. If there was some clever answer, I'm not the guy to think of it. As I crashed onto the bed at the Brown club, I got an email from Valerie on my BlackBerry: "I think we've found an apartment for Dana and Brad. We're working on the paperwork now. How late will you be up?"

I tapped back: "Only about 60 more seconds. I'll take an early train tomorrow, be home by one."

Her reply arrived instantly. "Coast will be clear by then, promise."

When I entered the apartment mid-day Monday, Valerie threw her arms around my neck. "I loved the flowers – and the note!" Then she surveyed me. "Bad boy, you look like you've been drunk for three days straight."

"Pretty much."

"How do you feel?"

"Not sick exactly, but not so good either."

She bustled into the kitchen to steam a caffe latte for me. I collapsed on the living room sofa. "It's nice to be home."

CHAPTER 34

"Quit calling it the State of the Union," sighed Jack Campozzo.

"Right, right," I answered. "Sorry, I keep forgetting."

"President Williams delivered the State of the Union back in January."

"You can see why I get confused. That wasn't a speech. It was just a long email."

"The Constitution only says the president has to report on the state of the union. It does not say he has to stand up in Congress and read it. He can deliver the report by semaphore if he wants. By the end, President Williams had no stomach to face Congress in person. He sent his last report in writing."

"The way things are going," I said, "I don't know how much longer President Pulaski will care to meet Congress in person either."

"If you could keep the negative thoughts to a minimum for the next few hours, it would be appreciated by all."

The White House legislative affairs team had been working the Hill hard in advance of the non-State of the non-Union non-Address. Hazen had spent many hours on the phone, including two calls with the president himself. As the economic news had darkened in the past ten days, the intensity of the lobbying had accelerated. The dollar had dropped against every major traded currency. The *Wall Street Transcript* had only yesterday published a "light" feature about a busload of Chinese tourists being deposited in front of the Wilshire Boulevard Barney's and buying almost everything in stock.

Word was spreading that the White House was upgrading the economic section of the speech, preparing to announce tough measures ahead. Why else would the president have invited six key potential senatorial allies to lunch so close to the delivery of his first major televised address? Atop the list, of course, was Senator Hazen. I was to go with him – which is why Jack had expressed caution about my disrespectful attitude.

The senator had a committee hearing from 10 o'clock to 1 o'clock that day. Attendance was sparse in the high-ceilinged wood-paneled room, and the committee's biggest bore – Senator Plimpton from Oregon – was droning on even more more boringly than usual from his beige swivel seat on the other slope of the long semi-circular senatorial desk.

At 11:20, I slipped into the committee room as quietly as I could and touched Hazen's shoulder. "Time to go sir." I escorted him out the side exit from the dais to the corridor and the senators' elevator. The car waited for us on First Street. I helped Hazen into the back seat, then jumped into the front seat beside the driver.

"Let's roll!"

Seventeen minutes later, we arrived at the Southeast Gate of the White House complex and popped the car trunk. Uniformed Secret Service and bomb-sniffing dogs inspected us. A long mirror was passed underneath the car body. A guard returned the senator's identification to me through the passenger-side window, and we slowly drove toward the elliptical South Front of the White House.

The last time I'd visited, I had no sense of arriving at the building at all. I had passed through a confusing jumble of narrow, low-ceilinged corridors and windowless rooms, eaten lunch in a basement, then exited the way I'd entered. This time we were taking the grand entrance.

The grandeur seemed, however, not much to impress the reception team. Bored White House ushers in striped waist-coasts stepped listlessly forward to open car doors, with all the alacrity of postal workers at tax-return filing time.

We entered directly into a large oval ground floor room. The walls were painted with murals of American landscapes. A huge intricate oval carpet spead over the floor; yellow, uphol-stered Colonial-style arm chairs were arrayed along the curving wall.

Nia Robinson and a passel of eager young assistants were waiting to greet us.

"Senator Hazen!" she called with delight, taking his spotted old hand in both of hers.

"Hello, Nia, my dear, how are you?" the senator said, lighting up with pleasure.

I suddenly felt the ground dropping away beneath my feet. Would Nia make any reference to Brad's hiring?

Fortunately, before Nia could say any more, the other senators began to arrive. She had time only to nod a greeting to me.

I had studied in advance the names, faces, and bios of the other senators expected the lunch.

First to enter: young Paul Yamashugi of Hawaii, son of a former governor of the state, and notoriously the most ambitious of the Senate freshmen. The green eyes that Yamagushi had inherited from his beauty-queen mother darted about the reception room, broadcasting one all-consuming thought: *Why don't I live here?*

A slight, nervous, thickly hair-sprayed woman in her late fifies emerged from the same car as Yamashugi. This was Senator Honey Matthews, nicknamed "70-vote" Matthews because of the simple rule she had followed to survive as a Nationalist in Constitutionalist North Carolina: She would not vote for any measure that could not gain at least 70 votes. Nia greeted those two senators with almost as much enthusiasm as she'd apportioned to Senator Hazen. Almost, but not quite.

Another car pulled up, and out stepped the huge bulk of Mississippi's Humphrey Gaskell. Something was wrong with Gaskell's right hip. He lurched into the White House, inadequately supported by a black rubber cane. Hazen often quoted Gaskell's aphorism: "Those who support my campaigns generously will have my undivided attention. Those who support my campaigns less generously will still have my attention. And those who oppose me – they'll get good government."

Next Sally Friedkin from Maine smiled her way into the room. Short, and plump, she had begun her career as a nurse. She rose to head her state's nurses' union and then run for office on the slogan, "She cares for us." The validity of that slogan depended on the meaning of the word "us." Here in Washington, Friedkin was notorious as one of the most abusive and demeaning bosses on Capitol Hill. Yet she never lacked for applicants for positions on her staff, because her ruthless advocacy of her state's interests had opened a swift-moving conveyer belt from her office to some of the most lucrative lobbying jobs on K Street.

Following Friedkin came the enormously tall and magnificently white-haired Douglas Rasmussen from Minnesota. Newly elected to a fifth term, Rasmussen had managed by natural dignity, hard work, and astute talent-spotting to more than compensate for his own slow-moving wits.

By now it was five minutes past noon, only ten minutes to the lunch. We were still missing – who? Of course, who else? Ricky Jimenez of Florida, who charged into the room chattering on a cell phone. He stepped over the threshold, shouted "Nia!" then tossed the phone to his bodyman, who nimbly caught it. Everyone else had shaken Nia's hand. Jimenez grabbed her, turning his head up to reach her cheek. He stood at least three inches shorter than Nia, but he pulsed with a salesman's energy and grinned with a lecher's leer: *So Miss Robinson, how badly do you want my vote on the Intermodal Transport bill?*

This month, however, the lecher's question could be reversed on him. In December, the Justice Department had opened a securities fraud investigation into one of Jimenez's most important supporters. Now Nia could ask in reply: *So Senator Jimenez, how badly do* you *want us to take a sympathetic view of the legal problems of Osman Bazlan?*

Yes, I could see why these six had been invited to meet the president. But, rationale aside, what a crew! This was the Senate's swing bloc? Hazen aside, if I were a president who had to depend on these people to support my plans, I think I'd get new plans.

With the whole group assembled, Nia led us out across a red-carpeted hall to a grand stairway, and up to the first floor – onto the long corridor so familiar from TV; along the paintings on the wall of presidents living and dead; past the big central staircase leading up to the family quarters.

Jack had mocked me when I'd said something about feeling history. He said, "You know they gutted the White House in the 1940s right? What you'll see today is a reconstruction, except for the mantelpieces, there's nothing in the building older the World War II. It's all in your head."

Okay, maybe – but that's always true isn't it? Except for what's in your head, what are the Pyramids? Just big piles of rock.

We were led down the long red-carpeted corridor of the mansion, the corridor the president himself walks on his way to press conferences in the East Room. We followed the corridor into a huge white-paneled dining room ornamented by a portrait of Lincoln over the fireplace. Nia led us through that big dining room around a corner into a smaller dining room, this one painted bright yellow, the floor covered by a carpet even more brightly yellow.

I feel a little churlish saying this, but if it weren't so thrilling to be standing there, I'm not sure I'd describe the room as very attractive – except for the mysterious ghostly portrait of a bygone First Lady all in white directly atop the fireplace. That was cool.

Nia addressed the whole group. "The president will join us in another five minutes. Senators, I thought you might want to introduce your aides to the president. After that, Angelica here will lead staff to lunch in the Executive Office cafeteria. Staff, please be finished in time to convene here to meet your senators at 1:45, when our lunch is scheduled to end."

Then through the door rolled President Pulaski in a blue suit, a photographer clicking every moment.

Weeks later, we'd receive in the mail a photograph of the president shaking my hand. My eyes were closed, I'd forgotten to brush the hair at the back of my head, and my suit was very badly wrinkled. Valerie framed it and placed it on a table in our little entry area, beside a picture we already had of the two of us with Senator Hazen. "It's not a very good picture," she conceded. "But five years from now, we'll have enough to panel the front hall. In the meantime, it'll remind you to look in the mirror before you leave the apartment."

CHAPTER 35

The other staffers and I followed Angelica out of the White House, across West Executive Avenue, and into the basement of the granite Executive Office building. I chased a dreary turkey sandwich with a thin cup of coffee. Then all of us staffers returned to the ground floor oval room to await our senators.

When Hazen materialized, the look on his face could only be described as "stricken." I helped him into the car, then piled in after him. As we pulled slowly out of the driveway, he said miserably, "I think I just heard the worst idea I've heard in all my time in Washington."

"I bet it took somebody very smart to think of it."

That got a smile.

"Can you say what it is?" I pressed.

"Not yet. I gave my word to keep it a close hold. But it'll leak soon enough. And if it doesn't – well the whole world will know the day after the president's joint session address."

The dark metal gates at the bottom of the elliptical drive slowly opened to allow us exit, then closed behind us.

"Was the president asking for your support?"

"That was his agenda, yes. I spent almost all my time arguing against the idea. By the end, I was practically pleading."

"What about the other senators? Did they agree with you?"

Hazen snorted. "There's something in the water in that building," he said, jerking a thumb back in the direction of the White House. "Strong people – professional politicians – U.S. senators – just go all gooey. They won't say no. They'll say, 'That's a bold plan Mr President.' And a new president like

Pulaski, he thinks that's a compliment! Of course they'll desert him when the shooting starts."

"May I ask what position you will take? Have you decided?" The moment I asked the question, I regretted it. If he answered, I'd have to decide whether to share the answer with Daphne. Lucky for me, he did not answer.

"Not yet. I want to support the president, I truly do. The nation cannot afford another failed administration. But he's showing himself so reckless and stubborn!"

Hazen considered for a minute and then asked, "Do you have my schedule at hand?"

I showed him the calendar on my BlackBerry. He studied it briefly.

"There's nothing here Daphne can't shift. Mehtab," he said to the driver, "would you take me back to my apartment? I need a few hours alone." He began tapping the back of his head, the familiar gesture of Hazen-in-thought.

CHAPTER 36

Contrary to Hazen's expectations, the brainwave discussed at the White House lunch did not leak.

But don't credit the trustworthiness of US senators and their staffers for keeping the secret. It was simply overwhelmed by another sensational development in the Durango hostage drama: the release of the Pentagon's report into the killing of Colonel Mali.

Officials at the Department of Defense had interviewed the released prisoners. They had scrutinized the ballistic evidence. They concluded:

1) Montoya had killed Mali.

2) Montoya had acted alone.

3) Montoya was motivated by a personal grudge against Mali.

4) DoD utterly rejected allegations of a broader loyalty problem among Mexican-American troops.

If the Pentagon imagined that this report would quell the conspiracy theories, boy, did they get it wrong.

Hazen's entire office tuned into Mark Dunn at 5 o'clock. Dunn had invited Vernon Mallory onto the show for the full hour to debunk the Pentagon's report. Which Mallory did – brutally.

Mallory pointed out that the Pentagon report had accepted uncorroborated testimony from Montoya's parents that they were estranged from their dangerous relatives still inside Mexico.

The report had dismissed the calls to suspicious mobile phone numbers as dialing errors. If the third and seventh numbers in the sequences were transposed, they yielded the phone number of an ex-girlfriend of Montoya's. Mallory sarcastically rebutted, "I can imagine Montoya making that mistake once. But six times?"

As for the evidence that Montoya acted alone: "The Pentagon cannot possibly know that. They are relying on evidence from interviews – and disregarding data that does not fit."

Mallory concluded: "They do not want to know the truth. But only the truth can set us free – and defend our country's freedom."

Dunn seized on the phrase, "Truth is freedom." He repeated it half a dozen times before the end of his show. That night he spread the new catchphrase across the top of the MarkDunn. com website. The next morning, Dirigible.com reported that a Constitutionalist activist in San Antonio, Texas, was organizing a national "Truth is Freedom" convoy of tractor-trailers. The truckers would drive from San Antonio to Washington, park themselves in front of the Capitol, and demand a purge of disloyal soldiers from the armed forces.

CHAPTER 37

February 26: The day of the president's address to the joint session of Congress. Hazen had left the office early to rest for the long night ahead. Mehtab and I picked him up at his apartment at 7:30 in the evening. We drove him to the Capitol in time to arrive in the House chamber just before 8 o'clock.

I walked Hazen into the House cloakroom, so huge compared to the cozy Senate equivalent. Aides were supposed to scurry away immediately after depositing their principals, but Hazen clutched my elbow. "Come meet the vice president."

"Isn't he kind of busy right now?"

"Not too busy for me."

Hazen pushed and led me toward a big powerful bald-headed man standing near the big doors that would open into the House chamber. Garth Pappas had been a star receiver for Texas A&M in the early 1980s. He'd parlayed fame into business success, first as a car dealer, then as a sub-prime mortgage lender. He'd sold out of that doomed business in good time, then campaigned and won election to the Texas Senate. From the state Senate, Pappas vaulted to the governorship. Re-elected in the same year as Monroe Williams won the presidency, he should have been a leading candidate for the Constitutionalist nomination for president. Somehow it never happened.

Many had speculated why. Did he have embarrassing financial secrets to conceal? Had the famously outspoken Mrs. Pappas rebelled? Did he lack the necessary "fire in the belly"?

The answer (as Hazen explained on one of our walks) was much more devious. Iggy Hernandez had struck a deal with

Pappas. Why fight a probably losing fight? If Pappas would mobilize his Texas donors to fund Iggy's Draft Pulaski movement, Iggy would deliver the vice presidency to Pappas. Only Pappas did not seem to be enjoying his reward very much.

"Hello, Senator," Pappas said glumly.

"Good evening, Mr. Vice President," Hazen said with surprising formality. "May I present my aide, Walter Schotzke? I hope you'll remember his name; he is amounting to something."

I flushed at the unexpected compliment.

"Schotzke? Like the mustard?"

Hazen nodded.

The vice president grasped my hand and turned on a 50,000-volt smile. "Good to meet you Walter. Of course I know all about your father. What a man! And what a tragedy about your poor mother – I was so shocked by that terrible accident. Well, if Senator Hazen recommends you, you must be some hell of a guy. I'll keep my eye out for you."

Who wouldn't like that?

An aide whispered in the vice president's ear, and the 50,000 volts subsided. The vice president said to Hazen, "We have to file out in 20 minutes."

"Yes. I just wanted to ask you. Was there any progress today persuading the president to reconsider his plan?"

"No, unfortunately. We got it out of the speech at least, but it took a morning of arguing. That's why the final text was so late."

As Pappas spoke, my BlackBerry buzzed. The advance text of the speech had just been released. "I've got it now sir," I said to Hazen. "Would you like to read it?"

"At this point, I might as well listen with fresh ears," he said. He returned to the vice president. "You've explained all the implications to the president's team? Colonel Cleland too?"

The look of concern on the vice president's face darkened. "Phil, I wouldn't say this to a lot of people. I probably shouldn't say it even to you. But this president doesn't listen to my explanations. What would I know? I'm just a dumb-jock mortgage broker from Lubbock, Texas."

Hazen smiled sympathetically. "He won't listen to mine either."

"Will you jump off the bridge with him?" asked the vice president sardonically.

Hazen answered, "Will you?"

"Aren't I constitutionally obliged?"

"That's not so clear."

"It's clear that you are a free agent. What will you do?"

Hazen shrugged. "I don't know yet."

"He really respects you, Phil. He doesn't respect many people – not many civilians anyway – but he respects you. I bet he wishes he'd given you my job. Right now, I kind of wish it myself."

The aide whispered in the vice president's ear again, and the big false smile returned to the big domed head. He shouted to the waiting throng of senators: "Three minutes to show time, people!"

And then it *was* show time. The vice president and the senators filed into the House chamber to take their assigned seats. Most of the aides filed out through an opposite door. A few of us stayed behind in the House cloakroom. Nobody objected, so we grabbed comfortable chairs and settled in front of a couple of the room's television sets. With a three-second lag between reality and broadcast, I heard a booming voice from the other side of the heavy doors: "The president of the United States!"

CHAPTER 38

"I speak to you in an hour of crisis," the president intoned. Then he itemized the country's problems:

Five years of halting recovery from the economic crisis had trapped millions in protracted unemployment. The budget seemed stuck in permanent deficit, accumulating huge debt. We were fighting a long war in Mexico with rising casualties – and now with with American prisoners in insurgent hands. Refugee flows from the war in Mexico had surrounded cities in the Southwest with shantytown slums, creating difficult environmental problems, especially water.

The president promised action to address these problems and to end the conflict in Mexico.

He promised to balance the budget while creating new jobs programs. He promised tax reform to lighten the load on middle-class families. He said the time had come to reduce spending on wars and invest more in roads and schools.

To my ears, it sounded fine: sober, realistic, and determined. Which just shows how little I know.

A few minutes before noon the day after the speech, the White House released a short bland communiqué announcing the appointment of 11 replacements to fill vacancies on the Deficit Reduction Commission bequeathed by the Williams administration.

I hadn't paid much attention to the communiqué when it showed up in my email. I get a lot of junk from the White House press office. This news seemed boring even by government standards. Wrong again.

Within ten minutes of the release of the communiqué, my Twitter feed was buzzing with rage. I didn't get it. Why was this news so exciting?

I scrolled through the tweets as I sat in a cavernous underground hotel ballroom waiting for Senator Hazen to finish a lunchtime speech. I could receive only two bars of signal, too weak to click through to the links. The little chirrups alone did not provide enough information to understand the commotion.

So as we rode the escalator up to the street afterward, I interrogated Hazen: "Why is everybody on Twitter yelling about the president appointing a few new commissioners to some defunct commission? That hardly seems a big deal."

Hazen's face sagged. "So they went ahead?"

I showed him the communiqué. He shook his head. "The print's too small." I read it aloud, and his face sagged deeper.

Back at the office, I picked up the phone to Freddy Catesby.

"It's Walter. Forgive me if I sound stupid, but may I ask –"

I did not have time to finish the question.

"It's a coup."

"A coup? Like with tanks around the presidential palace?"

Catesby was not amused by my levity. "You can make a coup with paper too."

"How?"

"This Deficit Reduction Commission was a typical piece of Williams *schlamperei*. Williams left it behind him like an undefused bomb. The commission has potentially enormous powers. If 14 of the 18 members agree on a proposal, that proposal goes straight to Congress for a vote within 30 days: no amendments in the House, no filibuster in the Senate. Straight to the top of the national agenda for an up-or-down vote. If the votes do not happen within the 30 days, the pay of all congressional staffers is suspended until the votes do happen. The original draft would have stopped the pay of members of Congress, but that would be unconstitutional."

"They're going to stop my pay?"

"That's what I like about you, Walter, you are always focused on the big picture. The point is, this commission is empowered to bypass all the usual budgeting processes. It can raise taxes, it can cut spending, it can do just about anything."

I still didn't get it. "But that was true yesterday too. Nobody cared about the commission then. So how is this a big deal now?"

"Because yesterday the commission represented the two political parties. Today it represents only the president."

"I'm looking over the names here, they seem pretty impressive. Former budget commissioners from California, New Jersey and Georgia. The president of the American Accounting Association. Hank Roszek, who turned around Amalgamated Motors …"

"And how many of them are solid Constitutionalists?"

"I don't know."

"That's the point Walter. You don't know. I don't know either, although I can guess: zero. But the president knows. The original 18 commissioners were appointed half and half, Nationalist and Constitutionalist. They had to be confirmed by the Senate, as is right and proper.

"But for some reason nobody knows, the law contained a loophole. If commissioners leave the commission, the president can appoint a replacement on his own. As I said, typical Williams *schlamperei*. And to 'leave' doesn't just mean die or resign. Any commissioner who misses three consecutive meetings is deemed to have quit."

Catesby was gradually working himself into a rage. His voice was growing higher and squeakier.

"So the president has all these vacancies to fill! Just so long as he preserves the nine-to-nine balance between Nationalists and people who say they are Constitutionalists. But get this: They don't have to be real Constitutionalists! The head of the NAACP was on the Commission as a Nationalist. He got angry at Williams over something and re-registered as a Constitutionalist. Now the president is saying the NAACP boss can stay on the Commission and count against the Constitutionalist total!"

"I thought you championed minority outreach, Freddy?"

"Hardee-har-har. But here's the real point. I'll bet you that a budget plan has already been concocted. The deal's done, I'm sure of it! I'll bet you that the president has the co-chairs in his pocket already. That's 13. And the NAACP guy? I'm sure he's been squared as number 14. A week from now, maybe 10 days, hallelujah, they've agreed on a plan! Only of course the plan was written at the White House … Oh yes, that's exactly what's going to happen," he finished bitterly.

He was right too.

CHAPTER 39

"Have you heard from Brad and Dana recently?"

Nia Henderson's elegant voice crackled through my Black-Berry as I sat in the bar at Morton's waiting for Hazen to finish his lunch with the chairman of the European Central Bank. Nia's call had interrupted me halfway through my own lunch: a 10-ounce hamburger, neatly bisected and the other half returned to the kitchen, per Valerie's instructions that morning when she'd heard my plans for the day.

Nia's question was posed in a very neutral tone, but it was impossible to miss the real message: *You owe me, buddy, and I'm calling to collect.*

"My girlfriend helped them unpack. They are very excited about the new job." Grudgingly I added, "Thank you."

"I am always so delighted to help any friend of Senator Hazen's. And how did Senator Hazen feel about the Joint Session speech?"

There was the invoice for the balance due.

"You talked to him yourself this morning," I said cautiously.

"We had a wonderful talk. He was not yet ready to take a definitive position. Which is perfectly understandable. But I was hoping you could offer some insight into his thinking process."

"He's said nothing more to me than he's said to you."

The faintest trace of irritation entered her voice.

"I'm not asking you to betray any confidences. I only want an indication of how I could be maximally helpful to the senator."

I threw myself on her mercy, I said as abjectly and (I hope) as sincerely as I could, "Nia, truly, I don't have anything for you. He's playing this very close to the vest. He's not confiding in anybody. Not me, not Daphne, nobody."

In the next breath, Nia's voice returned to normal. I'd convinced her.

"All right. Talk soon. Give my regards to Brad and Dana."

That was awkward. The next conversation was even worse. Senator Joliette was on the phone.

"It was such a pleasure to meet you at Lamont Forrest's."

"Thank you, Senator."

My half-hamburger was beckoning to me. I'd managed only one additional bite between Nia's call and Joliette's.

"As I told you at Lamont's I was a great admirer of your father's. After our dinner, I had my staff do a little research. I'm just aghast to discover that apart from the presidential citation, this country has not done anything to honor your father's heroic sacrifice. I've been thinking that Senator Hazen and I should introduce a bill to fund a suitable memorial. A statue maybe. What do you think: Should it be located here in Washington? Or maybe in Providence instead?"

This at least was not an invoice. It was payment in advance.

"That's a very touching thought, sir. Maybe you should discuss it with my grandmother?"

He chuckled. "I hear your grandmother is quite a woman. But it's your input I'm most interested in. Along with Senator Hazen's input of course, because your father and Senator Hazen were such good friends. By the way … what does Senator Hazen think of this Deficit Reduction commission idea?"

"I'm sure I know less than you do. Would you like me to arrange time for you to speak to him yourself?"

"We had a little conversation this morning on the Senate floor," Joliette said with a friendly chuckle. "But it was so busy and distracting. I thought you might have heard something that might give some insight – nothing confidential, just any kind of stray comment?"

"I wish I knew! He's playing this one pretty close."

"Ah. Too bad." I could tell that, unlike Nia, Senator Joliette did not believe me. "Well, let's talk again in a few days. And I'll be speaking to Senator Hazen about the memorial project, just as soon as we finish with this commission business. But let's get the commission behind us first."

I didn't have time for even a single bite of burger before the next call. Elmer Larsen? After our last meeting, I would have doubted he could pull me out of a police line-up. I guess those blinking eyes had retained more of an impression than I had realized.

"What is your boss doing about this God-damned deficit commission?"

I'll credit Elmer. He got straight to the point.

"He's thinking about it."

"Well tell him he'd better think straight if he knows what's good for him. This is the dividing line between Constitutionalists and Nationalists. If he does the right thing, we let bygones be bygones for all our past differences. It's a new page. We start over. If he does the wrong thing, he's on the enemies' list. Got it?"

"Got it."

Bzzz. A text. From Daphne. "C me aftr u drop sen @ airport. Want full report re deficit cmttee."

I touched my hamburger. Cold. My appetite had vanished anyway.

I texted back: "Cant return 2 office. Errands 4 Haz must do b4 COB today. Pick up prescriptions etc. Brief u Mon?"

"That was almost total fiction. Not to mention insolent. But I had a confident intuition I could get away with it.

Daphne texted back: "OK Monday."

Intuition confirmed.

Spring comes early to Washington, but with nasty relapses. The second week in March of that year qualified as one of the nastiest relapses. Gray, cold, wet.

After lunch, Mehtab and I drove Hazen to Reagan airport to put him on his Friday afternoon flight to Providence. I did have to collect a prescription, that part of my text had been accurate. But after that, I was looking forward to heading home for a hot bath and a quiet glass of Talisker before Valerie came home.

Mehtab and I returned to D.C. via I-395. Almost as soon as we entered the ramp to the bridge, the traffic slowed, then crawled, then came to a dead halt. A wall of bright-red taillights blinked back at us through the drizzle.

Living in D.C., you get used to weird traffic patterns. Motorcades, security checks, protest marches can cause jams and delays at any time of the day or night. I reached over to the back seat, and collected the Senator's discard newspaper pile to read. The front page of the *Wall Street Transcript* described another murderous day on the bond markets, dropping dollar, loss of investor confidence.

I read my way through the long piece, looked up – and noticed that the car had not moved an inch. "Traffic not going anywhere," grunted Mehtab. I called the office and asked for Jack.

"Hey, Jack. Mehtab and I just dropped the senator at the airport. We're returning northbound on I-395 and have hit a humungous jam. Can you go online, see if you can figure out what's up?"

"I don't need to go online. I can look out the window," said Jack.

The truck convoy from San Antonio had reached Washington. Jack said that more than a dozen trucks were driving around and around Capitol Hill. Cars were following the trucks, rubber-necking. Police were following the trucks and the cars, shouting through rooftop loudspeakers at the vehicles to keep moving.

"It's a zoo! Too bad you can't watch the news on your Black-Berry," Jack chortled. "You should have got the Droid, man."

"But why the police? Truckers have a right to drive around."

The trouble was, the truckers did not want to drive. They wanted to park. First they had tried to park themselves on the grass on the west front of the Capitol. The Capitol police had blocked that plan. Then they had tried to park on the streets near the Capitol. But they had been warned they would be issued parking tickets and contempt citations. So instead, they were driving round and round, backing up traffic all the way to the Virginia bridges.

"So what should I do?" I asked Jack.

"You got an umbrella?"

There was a small collapsible number on the floor. It did not look very promising, but the alternative was to spend the remainder of the afternoon in traffic. I said goodbye to Mehtab, popped the umbrella, and hoofed it home.

I arrived drenched. I changed into pajamas and switched on the local news. The police were relenting. They had negotiated a deal to allow the trucks to park in front of the Ulysses S. Grant monument at the Capitol. What would become famous worldwide as the "Trucker Protest" had arrived in Washington.

CHAPTER 40

Senator Joliette's fingers stroked and smoothed the lapel of Senator Hazen's suit jacket. It was just past 11 in the morning on the Monday following the truckers' arrival in Washington. The two senators stood deep in conversation at Hazen's desk on the Senate floor as a desultory "debate" snoozed around them.

My BlackBerry buzzed. Nia Robinson. I stepped to the back of the chamber to answer.

"Your boss should know: There's going to be news in the Durango situation later today. Some of our previous statements – well, they're going to have to be corrected. I don't know exactly how bad it'll be, but bad enough. Please tell the senator that if there's anything I can do to make things easier for him, just indicate what it is, and it'll be done. If he wants to see the president, just call."

SitRep.com posted the story only 45 minutes later, well before either the White House or DoD could organize their statements. The site reported that Montoya's bank account had received 4 wires of $9,950 each (just below the level that triggered federal reporting requirements) in the eight weeks before the ambush. Three other soldiers in the column, all Mexican-American, had also received wire transfers totaling $20,000 each over those same eight weeks.

All four soldiers remained alive in insurgent hands.

I caught Hazen's eye, and we exited the chamber together. I read him the full story on the subway back to the office. As we crossed the threshold, Vernon Mallory was speaking gravely on TV.

An email from Daphne pinged on my BlackBerry. *Come see me now* said the subject line. Could be avoided no longer. I girded myself: Which would I see? Daphne's iron fist? Or her velvet glove?

Daphne leaned forward in conspiratorial friendliness as I took a chair and faced the bleak landscape through her window. Velvet glove it was.

"It's not even two months, and the wheels are coming off this administration," she said by way of greeting.

"Things do look bad."

"It's important we keep as much daylight as possible between the senator and President Pulaski. What news do you have for me?"

"He's not sharing very much of his thinking with me. He wants to support the president if he can."

"Details! I want details! The White House is trying to exploit Senator Hazen's loyalty to manipulate him into a dreadful political mistake. It's our job to protect our senator." The tone was still lilting. The velvet glove remained in place.

"Any question I ask him, he clams up or changes the subject."

"Direct questions won't work with Hazen. But you spend so much time in his company, you must have some indication."

"I don't think I have anything more than I've already told you."

The friendly smile faded. The voice hardened.

"I can hardly believe it. You make me wonder whether I've given this mission to the right person."

I plastered a big "I'm a funny guy" grin on my face and replied, "I hope not!"

Daphne nodded gravely, accepting my guilty plea. "I hope not too," she repeated. "I'll give you another chance – but not a very long one. Take notes. Keep records. Tell me everything. Or I will remove you."

Hazen's office door remained closed as I exited Daphne's office. It was approaching 5 pm. Time for Mark Dunn.

Dunn's show opener pulsed with the retro sounds of rapid typewriting, the clatter of telex machines, the whir of the newspaper printing press, culminating in a newsboy's shout: "Ex-tree! Ex-TREE!"

Then a close-up on his soft, round face, his eyes moist with concern for the country.

"Hello America. Tonight's theme is betrayal. The betrayal of our armed forces from within – and the betrayal of our brave combat soldiers by a politically correct leadership above. Truth-tellers like my friend Dr Vernon Mallory have been warning of danger. But the PR generals in the Pentagon have had a message for truth-tellers: Shut up."

Hazen opened the door into my little vestibule. "Wagons ho." Treason or no treason, we had an event to get to: a 6 o'clock reception hosted by regional electrical power distributors for the New York-New England congressional delegation.

It took only a few minutes to reach the venue: Capitol Hill's favorite restaurant, John Henry's Steakhouse. The name was kind of a joke. John Henry's occupied the ground floor of a marble-faced building erected in the late 1970s as the head-quarters of a union, the International Brotherhood of Railway Workers. Dwindling numbers had long ago forced the union, like most unions, to abandon its palatial former headquarters. The only reminder of the building's original purpose were the carved scenes in the building's lobby of muscular men working on the railroad.

The restaurant name spoofed the old railwaymen. But the interior of John Henry's owed nothing to the age of steam. It was all aquamarine glass, shiny chrome, and butterscotch leather – very different from Washington's usual drab style.

As soon as we entered, Senator Hazen was greeted by a pleasant-faced middle-aged woman in a functional office hairdo and bright red suit jacket. "Senator Hazen! So delighted you could join us!" She hurried the senator deeper into the room.

I was distracted by a waiter carrying a tray of lamb chops. Soon followed another tray: miniature crab cakes. Senator Hazen did not like me to drink on the job, but he surely would not wish me to go hungry.

Grilled vegetables on skewers with goat cheese! I *love* goat cheese.

Duck spring rolls!

Tiny tacos stuffed with shrimp and guacamole!

Sliced marinated steak!

The steak looked too messy for a napkin, so I asked a server for a plate and a fork. She looked at me as if at an utter newbie. "No plates or forks tonight, it's a congressional function."

I did my best with the steak anyway, then headed to the bar for a sparkling water. Through the throng, I spotted Mac Kohlberg. He looked anxious and distracted.

"Hey Dr. Kohlberg."

"Hello," he grunted.

"Do you know why I can't have a plate here?"

"Ethics rules," he said to a place in space somewhere over my shoulder. "Lobbyists are not allowed to buy meals for members of Congress dinner. And dinner is defined as anything eaten with a plate and cutlery."

"But they can eat appetizers all night?"

"Oh yes, nothing corrupting about appetizers." His eyes darted around the room, looking for somebody. I didn't see her either.

"I have to go," he said abruptly. He left too early. The next waiter presented porcini-stuffed quail.

As I wiped the quail juice off my fingers, I was approached by the red-suited woman who had met us at the door. "You're with Senator Hazen, yes?"

"Yes, indeed."

"This is for him." She handed me an unsealed envelope. I couldn't help peeking inside: a stack of checks, probably thirty altogether, each in the amount of $5,000, each inscribed to Hazen's campaign fund. That pleasant smile again. "We thought it would save trouble if we gathered all the contributions in one place."

The senator had a private dinner scheduled at eight at an apartment in the Ritz Carlton on West M Street. I glanced at my watch: 7:30 already. Time to go. I pushed my way through the now almost impassable crowd of suited men and women. I found Hazen sipping mineral water abstemiously. No quail for him. I escorted him past the valet parkers to Mehtab and the car. "Shall I come with you sir?"

"No need," he answered. "That's the end of the working day. Get yourself some rest. Oh" – he glanced at my feet – "and get yourself a shoeshine. We have a meeting in the Oval Office tomorrow."

The senator closed the car door behind him.

Well, that was a surprise.

The restaurant faced the parking lot at the foot of the Capitol Hill in which the truckers had made their camp. Through the cold night sky I could see huge fields of white light for the TV cameras and small dots of orange light: the truckers' heating panels. They cast a bizarre glow on the monument to sad President Garfield, first assassinated, then forgotten. The smell of the diesel exhaust from the generator that powered the heaters tainted the air.

I'd never actually seen these truckers who had caused so much mayhem. I stepped toward the fumes.

CHAPTER 41

The trucker encampment was surrounded by a thin cordon of police. My Senate staff badge persuaded them to allow me through.

Inside the cordon, you felt the weight of the huge mass of surrounding equipment: the trucks themselves, the police cars beyond the trucks, the TV sound trucks beyond the police cars. You smelled diesel fuel and Port-a-Potties and heard the echoes of talk radio and Patriot News.

As I approached the center of the action, suspicious faces scrutinized me. The protesters, maybe three dozen of them, were sitting in clusters. I approached one of the clusters: four men, one woman. Three of the men and the woman were seated in lawn chairs. The fourth man was kneeling on the pavement fiddling with a bunch of wires leading from one of the trucks to a small TV set on a rickety little plastic table facing the chairs. Except for the unhappy expressions on their faces, they looked like they had settled in for a tailgate party. But maybe the unhappy expressions expressed a reaction to me. In my staffer's suit and badge, I must have looked like everything they had come to Washington to protest.

I introduced myself. "I'm with Senator Hazen's office." The name did not seem to mean much to them, but the title did.

"U.S. Senator?" asked one of the seated men, a man in perhaps his early sixties wearing an orange parka overtop blue jeans. The parka, obviously once expensive, now showed wear at the elbows and rips at the cuffs.

"Yes, sir."

"Which state?" queried Orange Parka.

"Rhode Island."

"Not much of a state!"

"He's one hell of a senator."

That broke the ice.

Another of the seated protesters spoke up, the group's one woman, in her early seventies maybe, little curls of a faded blond perm peeking from beneath a knit pink wooly cap. She was wearing a pink fleece stamped on its left side with the slogan, "Don't Tread on Me."

"Where's your senator on the Trucker Protest?"

The answer, "I don't know" probably would not satisfy anyone. I improvised. "He's always proud to see American citizens exercising their free-speech rights."

"That's good," she said. Beside the woman sat a man of the same vintage, wearing in khaki Dockers and a black fleece blazoned with the same "Don't Tread on Me" slogan. His hair, where he still had it, was close-cropped in military style. He nodded in agreement with the woman's words.

I asked, "Everything going OK with the police?"

"They've been sweethearts," said Mrs. Don't Tread on Me.

"Did they give you the Port-a-Potties?"

She shook her hand, "No, that was Barney's idea," pointing to the man on his hands and knees, fumbling with tangled cords. He was a tall, heavy man in his mid-fifties or so, which made him the baby of the group. A heavy golden watch on a metal link band protruded from beneath his lined windbreaker. "Barney loaded them in his truck when he heard about the protest."

"You should have brought beer," I said.

That made them all laugh. "No beer on federal property," answered Orange Parka. Mrs. Don't Tread on Me asked me my name.

"Walter."

Mrs. Don't Tread on Me nudged Mr. Don't Tread on Me. "Why don't you get Walter a chair?"

A broken-down old lawn chair was produced. I was poured a cup of sweet milky coffee from a thermos.

Introductions were done. Orange Parka was named Bob. He had been a builder up in Minnesota until his contracting business went bust two years before. Mr. and Mrs. Don't Tread on Me were a married couple from Alabama, named Mary Beth and Dale. Dale was a retired army major; Mary Beth, a retired Veterans Administration nurse. Barney, the man on his knees, owned a trucking company. The last member of the group, a slight, nervous-seeming man with a grey goatee had retired this past summer after 40 years of teaching math in a Fort Worth high school. He hesitated to give his name, but the others gave it away: "Dennis."

"There!" announced Barney triumphantly, and the TV came to life.

He stood up and turned to shake my hand.

"Is that your truck?" I asked.

"Yep. I used to have six. The bank took the others, but I kept the one with the satellite dish."

This time I was the one to laugh. "What are you watching?"

"I hope we're going to watch Mark Dunn. I DVRed his show, but we had a little trouble with the wiring. I think I've fixed everything though."

"That seems a lot of trouble for one TV show."

Dennis the retired math teacher spoke up softly. "No it isn't. You have to watch Mark Dunn every day. Otherwise you miss the connections."

"The connections?"

"Everything's connected. It's all linked up. The banks, the bailouts, the people selling us out in Mexico – you don't understand it until you watch Mark."

Mary Beth, the former nurse, caught my skeptical look. "So what are they saying about us up the Hill?"

"A lot of concern that you're taking up so many parking spaces."

"We're all sorry about that. I've never even had a speeding ticket. But some things are more important."

"Like what?"

Bob in the orange parka asked sarcastically, "Would you listen if we told you?"

"All ears."

"We talk to people from the media all day long. If it's not the media, it's pollsters. If it's not pollsters, it's some smart-ass blogger trying to provoke us to say something against blacks or gays or Mexicans. But nobody seems to listen, not really. We're not haters or crazies. We're not even really a movement exactly. Most of us met for the first time when we parked here."

"So what brought you?"

Dennis the math teacher inserted himself back into the conversation. "The US military is pretty much the only institution worth a damn in this sad country of ours. Now they're being sold out the same way the politicians have sold out everything else."

Bob added, "I'm here to do something to stop this crazy spending, all this debt. It's wrecking this country. We're going to be papering our walls with worthless dollars."

"It should mean something to be an American!" Barney said intently. "These people flood into our country. America means nothing to them, just a way to earn a few bucks. My mother's father came here from Greece. He opened a restaurant and flew the flag every day! But now? You can't recognize this country any more."

"Mark Dunn says we're losing our country piece by piece," insisted Dannis. "And our government doesn't do a damn thing about it."

I had discreetly sloshed the muck in my Styrofoam cup onto the grass. I refused a refill as politely as I could. "The government seems to be doing a lot," I said.

"Too much," said Dennis.

Bob reclaimed my attention. "When I was your age, I never believed it myself when I heard an older person say this or that used to be better. Don't older people always talk about the good old days? But the old days *were* good – better than now, anyways. My dad served in World War II. When he got out of the service, he found a job in an auto parts plant near Pittsburgh. Just like that. And him a man with an eighth-grade education! He became a supervisor, bought a nice house. He took us camping every summer. He retired to Florida and lived a comfortable life all the way to the end. He taught himself golf, even.

"Now look at me. I'm 55 and divorced. My ex-wife got the house. Who's ever going to hire me again? And my kids? Loaded up with student debt. My son is working in a Starbucks. They call him an assistant manager. He makes the same as my dad made in the plant in the 1970s! I know because my dad kept all his old pay stubs in the attic. Now my daughter's pregnant. The guy's disappeared. And she doesn't care! She says she never liked the guy that much anyway, she *wants* to raise the baby on her own!"

Dale – a man who apparently had long ago decided to let his wife do the talking – suddenly burst out: "And the drugs! God, they're everywhere. I wanted my son to go into the military, straighten him out. He flunked the drug test. They wouldn't give him a second chance. And now they're covering up for all these Mexicans? Who the hell is selling us these drugs anyway?"

"And get this government off our backs," said Bob from his orange parka.

"Wait a minute," I said. "Wasn't Dennis a government employee?" I pointed to Mary Beth. "And you?" I turned to Dale. "And you, too?"

They shook their heads at my cluelessness.

"I taught math!" said Dennis. "I'm not some bureaucrat. You think we can stand up to the Chinese without math? My ex-wife, she was a big union activist. I said to her all the time, 'You teach music, of course you need a union. But my work is the real deal.'"

"Sounds like your ex-wife needed to watch more Mark Dunn," I said.

Dennis ignored the irony, assuming he even heard it. "Without Mark Dunn, I'd never have got through my divorce."

"So, Walter," Mary Beth said, "what's this boss of yours going to do for us?"

I felt the weight of the envelope in my suit jacket pocket, stuffed with campaign checks. I thought: *Maybe if you could write us some of these* ...

"I can reassure Bob a little. Senator Hazen wants to try to balance the budget, stop us getting so deep in debt."

Barney laughed savagely. "Ha! They all say that!"

"You going to raise my taxes?" demanded Dennis.

"We'll try not to."

"Or cut my Medicare?"

"Or our veterans' benefits?" added Mary Beth.

"I don't know that we can balance the budget without any cuts to anything," I said.

"Of course you have to cut things!" Mary Beth said cheerfully. "Welfare and foreign aid. And all those people who don't pay any taxes at all – they should be paying something, even if it's only $10 a month. I see them drinking frappa-dappa-chinos, they can afford contribute something. They're riding in the wagon, they should get down out of it and help the rest of us pull the wagon. What I'm talking about are the benefits we've *earned*. Our veterans risked their lives for this country, they deserve everything they get. Dale did two tours in Vietnam. Medicare? Seniors have *paid* for it."

"We're not asking for anything we're not entitled to," said Dennis. "No handouts. We want our country back, that's all. The way it used to be."

"And we'll raise hell if we don't get it!" Barney boomed.

"I'll tell the senator," I promised.

I thanked them for the coffee and hoisted myself out of the lawn chair. I took a roundabout route home, through the Hotel Monaco. The shoeshine man was still on duty. He did a beautiful job too.

CHAPTER 42

The Oval Office was chilled to the temperature of a florist's refrigerator. I wished Hazen had warned me to wear an undershirt rather than worrying about my shoes. On the upside, when you're shivering from cold, you're not sweating with nervousness.

The nervousness started even before we entered the room. Our little group had waited to be admitted to the Oval in a large reception area right by the front door to the West Wing. The group had included not only Senator Hazen and me, but also Treasury Secretary Monckton, looking if possible more gray-faced and gray-haired than when I had seen him at the Lamont Forrest dinner.

The waiting group included Hillary Anderson, a fiscally conservative Nationalist senator from Oregon. Anderson had married two billionaires in a row. She had buried one and divorced the second. Once a legendarily beautiful woman, Senator Anderson at nearly 60 still looked tapered and slender in an elegant navy-blue suit that set off her beautifully coiffed hair. She absent-mindedly tapped the heel of one expensive pump on the toe of the other, drawing eyes to her slim calves.

Hazen and Anderson worked together so often and sponsored so many bills together that the typical cable viewer might begin to think that "Hazen-Anderson" was actually the name of a single person. Yet today, they sat side-by-side on the couch, not saying even a single word to each other.

In the middle of the group stood a man who uniquely seemed completely at his ease. He greeted passing staffers by

name with a laugh and a compliment. He chatted with Senator Anderson about her ski lodge and with Tony Monckton
about his grandchildren. The poised man's plump figure was
elegantly wrapped in a beautiful blue suit that looked as if it
had been pressed by whoever presses suits for the Prince of
Wales. Hazen murmured his name to me: David Maurice, the
uber-lobbyist married to Valerie's boss.

Our appointed time arrived. An aide stepped into the
reception room and invited us to follow her down a narrow
tall blue-carpeted corridor to another waiting area, this much
smaller, just outside the big white door to the Oval Office itself.
This door was flung open precisely on the hour.

Nia had emailed yesterday the names and images of the
White House staff expected today.

In front of one of the two long couches that ran from the
fireplace into the middle of the room stood Tommy Bemmis,
the budget director. He was a man of almost compulsive self-
effacement: thinning hair, pale face, drooping body, mumbling
voice. They told a joke about the newly elected member of Congress saying to a committee chairman, "I don't know whether
I've ever met Tommy Bemmis." The chairman answered, "Then
you *have* met Tommy Bemmis."

Beside a wooden chair at the foot of the coffee table stood
Seamus Soloveitchik, the former deputy to Iggy Hernandez
who had displaced Iggy as the president's chief political adviser.
Seamus could not have been more than three years older than
me. Yet according to SitRep.com, he'd already elected a governor of New Jersey, then helped elect a president. Quite a guy,
but not very pleasant to look at: short, round, red-haired, with
a face that communicated aggression.

And there, in the midst of them all, the president. His
wheelchair was aligned at a slight angle to the iconic fireplace,
exactly the same angle as the striped armchair to the president's right – the chair to which Nia directed Senator Hazen.

I'd never seen George Pulaski so close. I noticed that the edge of a burn mark peeked over his blue shirt collar. The president greeted the group without a smile. The time was only 10 AM, but he was already at least four hours into his working day, with nine or ten more hours to work through before his night's rest, if any. Not a piece of paper could be seen on the president's desk. Behind the desk, a row of photographs: wife, children, parents, graduation day at West Point.

In display cases on the walls there stood rows of unread leather-bound books, interspersed with neglected little ornaments. A portrait of Washington ornamented the wall over the famous Oval Office fireplace. A bust of George C. Marshall was centered on the mantle. Through the French doors, we could see the budding greenery in the Rose Garden. Sound seemed to echo off the Great Seal of the United States carved into the stark white ceiling, bouncing from end to end of the long room.

Anderson, Bemmis, Monckton, and Nia took seats on the two long couches extending away from the fireplace, flanking a long low table holding a big display of orange-red roses.

Patrick Cleland had an armchair to himself, as did Joyce Friendly, the president's top communication aide: a stout, grim-faced woman of 50 who seemed to have spent her entire life in rebellion against her name.

Maurice tossed himself into an empty space on one of the long couches, as casually as an undergraduate dumping his backpack in a lecture hall. From this seat, Maurice beamed smiles at everybody, while surveying the room with hard, watchful eyes.

Beyond the couches, at the widest space in the oval, were jumbled a half dozen hard chairs in the dead zone between the fireplace and the presidential desk. These were the seating for the junior members of the group, including me, the very least important attendee of them all.

Monckton glanced at some notes in his lap, removed his reading glasses, and passed his hands over the top of his head. The Adam's apple bobbed once or twice in his long, thin neck. Formerly a Constitutionalist stalwart, Monckton was now faced with a devil's dilemma: execute a policy that would enrage all his friends - or else resign after barely two months in office the job he had coveted all his career. As usually happens in Washington, he had opted to keep his job. He started to speak in a raspy voice.

"I don't have to tell the people in this room about the deteriorating economic and financial situation. It's bad, it's getting worse – and fast. The president believes that we must act urgently on new job-creation measures to stimulate the economy over the next 12 months, and then pivot rapidly to longerterm deficit reduction, including both spending cuts in entitlement programs and - " Monckton paused, as if frightened by what he had to say next, "revenue measures."

His little speech finished, Monckton slumped back into his chair. He'd cast his lot in the coming war.

Colonel Cleland said simply, "Nia?" He added as an afterthought: "You should all know that the personnel office will announce this afternoon that Nia has been promoted to Assistant to the President for Legislative Affairs. Armand Bragg has decided to seek opportunities in the private sector."

Nia smiled a warm but impersonal smile. "Thank you Senator Hazen and Senator Anderson for coming today, and thank you all for respecting the confidentiality of these discussions. I've already briefed the majority and minority leaders in both the House and Senate. Over the coming days, my team and I will be meeting with all members of Congress. We wanted to reach out to you early, however, as respected figures of the center in the Senate."

The aides scrutinized the faces of Hazen and Anderson the way lawyers with expensive briefs scrutinize the faces of the judges. The two senators avoided looking at each other, however. Senator Anderson spoke first, frowning a little at the gay mound of flowers in front of her elegantly dark-stockinged knees.

"Nia, you put me in a very uncomfortable position when you approach me separately from the rest of the Nationalist caucus."

Nia moved to answer Senator Anderson, but the president anticipated her.

It's a very strange thing to hear a president talk – not on TV, not across a convention hall, but right there, in front of you, almost like a normal conversation. But it's not a normal conversation at all of course – not in that awesome, reverberating space, not with the most famous man in the world scanning us all with hard, appraising eyes. In person, the voice of the president was a very different voice from the voice I'd heard so often on TV: not so clipped, not so commanding – softer, you might even say, coaxing.

"Senator Anderson, I'm not trying to put you on the spot. But you know better than me what will happen if we try to go through the leadership. Haven't we had enough of that? You and Senator Hazen have worked together so often. Won't we do better if we try to build a majority from the center outward?"

Senator Anderson shook her head impatiently. "It's one thing when Senator Hazen and I initiate legislation together in Congress. But for me to join a plan launched by a Constitutionalist president? That's very different."

"Anyway, Mr. President," Hazen added, "I don't see why you are talking to us so early. Any financial bill must originate in the House. We can't help you bypass the House leadership, even if we wanted to."

Nia and the president exchanged knowing looks. The president nodded *Go ahead.*

"Actually, Senator Hazen," Nia said, "I think we can have some comfort there. We have done some exploration. I think we will have the Nationalist leadership in the House behind us. They cannot deliver everyone, but 155 or so of the 188 Nationalists seems like a realistic tally. So we will only need to detach 63 Constitutionalists."

Hazen's eyebrows louvered up in surprise. "Detach?"

Maurice cut in with a smile. "Persuade, entice, cajole." He paused theatrically, then added with a bigger smile: "And also muscle, warn, intimidate, threaten..."

Nia fixed a disapproving eye on Maurice. "David, please – not everybody appreciates your style of humor."

He formed his hand into a fist and knuckled a mock salute to Nia. She shook her head and waved back at him with two exasperated hands.

The president ignored the Nia-David exchange. "Maybe 'detach' was a poorly chosen word. But Phil, who knows better than you how intransigent the Constitutionalist leadership can be?"

Hazen's usually imperturbable face was suddenly broadcasting visible distress. "Mr President, those intransigent people nominated you as the leader of their party. Now you want to jettison them to work with the House Nationalists?"

That irritated the president. The voice reverted from softness to the clipped military style. "I told the party in my nomination acceptance speech," the president said, "that I would govern by Constitutionalist principle in service of the best interests of the whole country. That is exactly what I propose to do now."

Seamus Soloveitchik spoke up. "This can be a big political win for you both, senators. We've polled a draft version of this plan with independent voters in each of your states. They strongly approve."

Joyce Friendly concurred. "Of course you have to do the messaging right. Really bring home the benefits to the moms and dads."

Hazen did not seem to hear these hopeful voices. "I support what you want to do," he said to the president. "Just not how you want to do it. I miss the days of the big bipartisan center even more than you, if only because I'm old enough to remember it. But that bipartisan center is as dead as the Whigs. The only people you'll find there are Senator Anderson and me, and while Senator Anderson remains as youthful as ever, I'm very nearly as dead as the Whigs myself."

Some titters were heard from the cheap seats. Nia shot us a reproving look.

"All that will happen if you pursue your plan to cut out the Constitutionalist leadership," Hazen continued, "is that you'll empower the Nationalist leadership. Maybe you can drag over just enough Constitutionalists to get your measure passed. I don't believe it myself, but maybe I'm wrong. What happens then? The Constitutionalist party will feel betrayed, outraged. Your former supporters will turn on you."

"That's if we fail," said the president. "Now let's focus on what we can gain if we succeed. Tommy?"

Bemmis mumbled his answer. "We've modeled this extensively, Senator. We expect a positive shock to both growth and employment, accumulating two points over the next seven quarters – in time to arrive before the next congressional elections."

Hazen snorted derisively. "Nothing makes me prouder to be a lawyer than listening to economists."

The president wetted his lips. He was readying himself for the big reveal. "Phil, there's one more piece to my thinking. When Tony says everybody is going to have to make difficult choices, that's exactly right. And I'm going to lead. I'm going to tell the American people that we have to wind down our commitment to Mexico. We're going to have to make the best deal we can get. I'm ready to take that heat. I'm only asking you to do what I'm doing first."

Murmurs. Senator Anderson's brown eyes widened. "Mr. President – what do you mean? We're fighting drug dealers who decapitate policeman and hang their heads from bridges. How do you deal with people like that?"

The president vibrated with sudden excitement. Clearly he'd been thinking about this a lot. "It's precisely because they are drug dealers that we can do this. They are businessmen. They make deals. They don't want to topple the Mexican government so long as they are left alone to earn their livings."

"Leave the traffickers alone to make a living!" gasped Senator Anderson. "Mr. President, have you considered what this will mean?"

The president's words tumbled from him more and more forcefully. "Yes, I have." He glanced at Tony Monckton as if to say, *Go ahead.*

"The first three years of revenues from a tax on cannabis would more than pay for the cost of our jobs bill, and then pay down the deficit without any need to raise income or corporate taxes."

Senator Anderson looked ready to jump from her seat and leave the room.

"That's" – she ransacked her vocabulary – "shocking! You'd fund the government with drug money?"

Hazen added, "You'll trigger a rebellion in our party."

David Maurice ventured to joke. "Not necessarily! We could sell that idea to Constitutionalists as a way to shift the tax burden from the wealth producers to the potheads."

Now it was Senator Anderson's turn to be exasperated with Maurice. But before she spoke, Hazen caught her attention – the first look the two senators had exchanged all morning - and somehow the interlocking of their eyes calmed her. She seemed to have the same effect on him. Her eyes sparkled. He smiled a very warm smile. Her jaw line may have softened over the years, but the old man-swaying techniques were all still working fine.

"Mr. President," Anderson said. "As you know, I've been skeptical of our commitment to Mexico myself. But what you are proposing – it will ignite a firestorm."

"I'm new to politics," the president answered with a thin little smile. "But I know what's like to come under fire. You didn't run for office in order to rename post offices did you? We're called to rescue our country. I need your help."

"Deal with those thugs in Mexico?" fumed Anderson. "Killers and torturers? And with them holding our prisoners all the time? I don't like it."

"None of us like it!" erupted Cleland.

Anderson countered, "So how can you ask us to accept it?"

"The same way we accept it," Cleland answered. "Because we don't see better options."

The presidential voice was coaxing again. "Please understand, I'm not ordering a frontal assault. I think we've developed a more … indirect … approach. We're going to reanimate the deficit reduction commission. The proposals will come from them, not the White House."

"But the commission is deadlocked and useless!" Hazen objected.

"Seamus?" said the president.

"We've discovered some interesting potential in the law creating the commission," replied Soloveitchik. "We think we've find a way to revive it and make it relevant again. "We can't reveal all the details yet. They'll emerge in the next days. And we'll bring some serious firepower in support."

Now the president motioned to Nia to speak.

"Thank you, Mr. President. I'm happy to say that David Maurice will be helping us with our outreach efforts in Congress. He represents a consortium of banks and investment firms who endorse our financial concept. They'll be investing considerable resources in educating members of Congress about the issues at stake."

Maurice chuckled richly. "I've got a commitment from my clients of up to $200 million to carry this measure through the House and Senate."

"Good God, David, what would you even do with that kind of money?" gasped Senator Anderson.

"More than campaign contributions, Senator. We can mount our own ads in the districts of every member who votes the right way. We can guarantee that any member who casts the right vote and loses his or her seat will experience a comfortable transition to private life. And with the right strategic plan, I think we can mobilize a number of influential actors without an obvious interest in the issue to align themselves our way."

"What?" said Hazen sarcastically. "You'll pay the pro-life people to endorse the measure?"

"No, no!" said Maurice with mock outrage. "We would never *pay* them. That would be unethical. But we might use money to *convince* them. The national debt does fall on the unborn, you know," he added with a self-satisfied chuckle.

Hazen tapped the back of his head, making the brain ketchup flow in his habitual thinking gesture. Then he appealed to the president, real emotion rising in him. "This is a grave, grave mistake."

The president did not want to hear it. He leaned forward to touch Hazen's arm. "Phil, don't scold. Everything I learned about how Washington works, I learned from you. Remember our first breakfast at the Regency in New York? When you told me about the fight over rural electrical cooperatives? The money they spent! The ads in every newspaper, the staffers being hired, the congressman getting retirement packages. It was you who told me how think tanks were auctioning their research agendas to the highest bidder ..."

Hazen shook his head miserably. "Mr. President, I told you those stories as examples of what has gone wrong in Washington."

The president gripped Hazen tighter. His voice was still coaxing, but it was not soft. It was urgent, intense, the voice of a commander mobilizing men to follow him on a mission from which most would not return.

"I can't fix every problem all at once. I have to use the tools I find. You think the people on the wrong side won't use every tool they can find? Why should the responsible people – the public-spirited people – people like you and Senator Anderson – surrender before the fight has even started? It was your cause long before it was mine. You can't step away at exactly the moment all your warnings are being proved right! Nobody is asking you to do anything that departs in any way from your high standards. You never have to sit in a room with David Maurice again if you don't like." Maurice shrugged good-humoredly.

"Then, after we save the U.S. economy and the global financial system, after we bring peace to Mexico – and after I lose the Constitutionalist presidential nomination and retire to private life - you can help the next president clean up this filthy town. You can tell him what an unscrupulous bastard I was, and how the great and good American people would not stand for his rough and dirty methods. I won't complain, I promise. But today the town's on fire. The clean up must wait. Don't abandon me, Phil. I need you. I can't win without you. That's not a compliment, it's simple political fact."

The president fixed his eyes on Anderson and beseeched her too.

"I need you *both*. We'll do everything we can to mitigate the negative consequences of legalization. We'll exempt drug treatment from all budget cuts. We'll direct the National Institutes for Health to invest more in addiction research. We'll do whatever you want. But sometimes a commander must sacrifice a few to save the rest. I know the pain of sacrifice. Defeat hurts even worse. Can I count on you?"

CHAPTER 43

"And what did Hazen say to *that*?" Daphne paced the room anxiously as I recapitulated the Oval Office meeting an hour later.

"Nothing – nothing much. He said he could not make any definite commitment until he had seen the deficit commission plans."

"And?"

"And Senator Anderson said the same thing. Then we all stood up and left."

"That's it? They let you go? Without more?"

"Pretty much."

"Are you being deliberately stupid? No president allows a senator to leave the room without some indication of yes or no."

"That's all I know. Sorry. If I'm stupid, it's not on purpose."

Daphne emitted a disgusted, "Oh!" She dumped herself back in her chair, rooted among the implements on her desk, found a pencil, and pitched it hard at my head. She missed. I don't think she was seriously aiming.

I can't blame her for being vexed with me. I *had* omitted an important element from my report. It just seemed ... none of her business.

Eight or ten steps out of the West Wing, before we even glimpsed our car, Hazen had asked me, "Do you like poetry, Walter?"

Weird question, right? I answered, "I'm a product of the finest educational institutions in the United States and Great Britain."

Hazen smiled. "Ah, so you know ..."

"Absolutely nothing."

Hazen whistled some unrecognized tune for a moment, then began to quote. I caught only a few words. I Googled them later, so now I have the whole thing:

And how can man die better
Than facing fearful odds,
For the ashes of his fathers,
And the temples of his gods?

After that, Hazen held silent until we were settled into the car interior. I looked into the mirror back at his face. It wore this dreamy look. He noticed me studying him, smiled, and commented: "I thought that would be a more awkward meeting than it was."

"Yes, tough to be lobbied by a president."

Wait a minute – was that a *blush* on the grizzled face of Philip Hazen?

He did not say any more until the car deposited us on the pavement outside the Senate wing of the Capitol. I walked him toward the entrance. He paused about thirty feet from the door and looked me direct in the face.

"You know Senator Anderson and I are good friends?"

"That's what the blogs say, but for most of the meeting, it sure didn't look that way."

"We've had a little rift. You see, the last time we were alone together, she suggested that we get married. I didn't handle it very well."

Boing. BOING. *BOING!!!* I stared the senator full in the face. "That's very progressive. My generation is still hung up on the idea that the man should ask the woman."

Hazen laughed aloud. "Mine, too!"

"Do you mind my asking – how does a woman say a thing like that? Especially if, I mean, you're not already …" I cut off the sentence early because I could not think of the right words.

Hazen shook his head. "No we are not 'already,'" he also had to pause to ransack his vocabulary, "intimate."

"So – how?"

"We were discussing a confirmation matter. I didn't realize it, but I had a sore on my cheek. She said to me, 'That looks as if it might be serious. Have you seen a doctor?' I said 'No.' She said, 'That's what happens to you old bachelors, you start falling apart. You really should get married again.' And I said, 'Who'd have a broken down old carcass like me?' And she said, 'I would.'"

"There's no mistaking that."

"No."

"What did you say?"

"I said, 'I have to think about this.' Which was the worst possible thing to say."

"Senator, take it from the master. That was not the worst thing you could have said. I can think of 20 worse things to say, and I'm sure if I'd been in your shoes, I'd have said every one of them."

The senator laughed again. "Yes I suppose I could have said worse. Still – well, I was taken by surprise, that's all."

"She probably surprised herself."

"Yes," he said in a meditative tone. Then he added, "I had a word with her as we exited, did you notice?"

"I was too busy peeking inside the Cabinet Room."

"Of course, yes, your first visit. Well, I did. I asked her to have dinner with me this week. She's clearing an evening."

"A date?"

He shook his head in self-amazement. "Yes. I suppose so. Imagine that."

"Why not!" I said with enthusiasm. "I'm glad to hear it! You need a higher class of company than me!"

"Senator Anderson is a higher class than either of us. Strange that when I was young and healthy I married for love, and now that I am old and decrepit I might marry for money."

"Am I supposed to believe that?"

He chuckled. "Practicing my defense for when I meet Mrs. Hazen in the world to come."

"From everything you've told me of Mrs. Hazen, I imagine she'd say you were entitled to some consolation in your later years."

"And a consolation prize for my political career?"

"Do you think it will come to that?"

Hazen shrugged and resumed walking. We pushed open the doors, he walked around the detector, and waved me good-bye. "I'll see you back at the office," he said cheerfully.

Hazen had a lunch scheduled in the Senate dining room with the Bishop of Providence. That would last at least 90 minutes. The bishop visited only when he had substantial business to discuss. I walked out to get a sandwich on Pennsylvania Avenue. My BlackBerry rang as I stood in line.

"Well, you've made a new friend." It was Valerie.

"Who?"

"My boss's husband. She just told me that he'd met you in the Oval Office and wants to get to know you."

"I didn't say one word."

"Maybe that's what impressed him?"

"Cute."

"Well, anyway, they're coming to dinner Friday night. I've been asking her for weeks, but she's always had an excuse. You're free, right?"

"Sure."

"Don't forget."

CHAPTER 44

So of course I forgot.

It was raining again on Friday, hard. I arrived home squelched and soggy. The apartment smelt of roasting oranges and other delicious things.

Valerie looked up irritably from the kitchen island. "Let me guess. You forgot."

"No, no," I insisted. "I haven't forgotten. I remember! Only – can you remind me what I'm remembering?"

"Dinner. With my boss? And her husband? David Maurice? The uber-lobbyist you met at the White House? Here? In 90 minutes? You were supposed to buy wine, and not one of your bargain Malbecs either. Don't tell me you forgot that too?" she added ominously.

"I'm on it! McPherson Wines will deliver."

That's the plus side of living through an economic apocalypse: lots of deliverymen.

I placed the call to McPherson, but Valerie wrested the BlackBerry out of my hand. "Mickey, do you have any of that consignment of the Goldeneye pinot noir left? Good. We'll have half a case, plus a couple of half bottles of the Ca' Togni. What's the charge with delivery?" She saw me flinch. "You can afford it," she said.

Valerie otherwise let me off lightly for forgetting the dinner, probably because she sensed my reluctance about the whole evening. I had not liked Melanie Maurice the few previous times I'd met her. A giddy chatterbox with a surgically improved chest, Melanie's conversational topics were limited to the parties she ran, the houses she owned, and the vacations she took. I'd heard about the 14,000 square foot mansion up River Road; about the Maurice family vacation compound on Maryland's Eastern Shore; about the twice annual trips to Europe, for which the Maurices would hire entire floors of grand hotels for themselves, their new baby, the nanny, their respective personal assistants, David's children by his previous marriage, David's grandchildren by his previous marriage, etc. etc. etc.

Despite herself, Valerie was impressed by Melanie's show. She was impressed too by David Maurice, whom she had met at various Melanie-run events. As she chopped and simmered and sizzled, she briefed me on David's story.

David Maurice was the son of psychiatrists on New York's Upper West Side. He had started life as an anti-apartheid campaigner at Columbia University in the late 1970s. He was expelled in his sophomore year for disrupting a debate with the South African ambassador. Maurice claimed he never intended to injure the man, but his charge unto the stage knocked over the elderly Afrikaaner and sent him to hospital with three broken ribs and a broken wrist.

Maurice moved to Washington, changed his name – he had been born "Moritz" – and got a job as a staff aide to the Congressional Black Caucus. By age 24, he was staff director. By age 26, he had worked as a communications director on a (losing) presidential campaign. By age 29, he was Iowa field manager for a (winning) campaign. Then White House communications director, then senior counselor, then out the door to start a lobbying firm with a former Constitutionalist Senate Majority leader. The ex-leader brought the clients; Maurice did the work.

Wow, did he work. Valerie had found online an old magazine profile of a younger and thinner David Maurice titled "Mr. Relentless." She forwarded it to my tablet computer to read as she reduced a sauce. The article quoted a congressman saying of Maurice, 'When I see him coming through my door, I just say yes straightaway. It saves time.'

I looked up from the tablet. "Hey Valerie, this piece quotes David saying he made $2 million a year. That was like, 25 years ago!"

She licked a little sauce off her fingers. "Yeah, Melanie told me a funny story about it. She said when the article appeared, David's friends thought he'd sunk himself. Lobbyists weren't supposed to make that kind of money, and they sure weren't supposed to talk about it. But people weren't shocked at all! They were awed. Three days after the story appeared, David got a call from the Kennedy Center asking for a check. He donated $100,000. They invited him onto the board, and after that he was golden. Of course today he probably makes ten times what he made then. Now you'd better go change. Please dress nicely. This is important to me."

I reappeared a few minutes later wearing the blue shirt and red tie Sylvia had bought me. "Walter, you look gorgeous! Where did you find them?"

"In New York. Bergdorf's was having a sale."

"So you *won* at poker? You do keep your secrets."

The buzzer sounded, the door flew open, and the Maurices burst in.

CHAPTER 45

"… but unfortunately that was the first time the president of Pakistan had ever visited an aircraft carrier. He tried to step out of the fighter jet, tripped over the airframe, hit the deck, and puked all over our president's shoes!"

Valerie and I convulsed with laughter. We couldn't help it. David Maurice was a very funny man. He had enthralled us over dinner with a secret political history of the past 30-plus years.

"Esther Minden was never going to run. If she'd entered the race, she couldn't have kept hush-hush her daughter's affairs with the radio preacher and the LSU running back. Don't tell me you don't know that story?"

No, *of course* we didn't know that story! And off he hurtled into another astounding anecdote.

Melanie beamed proudly at every word. Marriage to David Maurice had promoted her from party planner – AKA "the help" – to one of the grand ladies of Washington. Unlike many other Washington grand ladies, Melanie never forgot who had bestowed her position. She laughed and clapped at stories she must have heard 50 times before. She never tried to claim the spotlight for herself. She interrupted Maurice only to say things like, "But David, the king of Jordan himself said that it was all *your* idea …" or "You're leaving out the part about Angelina Jolie flirting with you all night long. I was quite worried the two of you were going to run off together!"

The seared duck breast and the costly red wine had been ingested with enthusiasm. Now David Maurice was sipping his way through a half bottle of dessert wine as he enjoyed Valerie's poached pear with lavender ice cream.

"I told President Williams, 'You have to open up this White House, get some experienced Washington hands.' We were up at Camp David, two Christmases ago, I'm sitting across from him in one of those little cabins. He was wearing this fuckawful ridiculous brown cardigan sweater.

"He asked me, 'David would you be my chief of staff?'

"I said, 'On one condition Mr. President. You have to give me authority to remove Joe Chumley from the ticket and recruit George Pulaski as your running mate.'

"He shut me down, just like that. Then nine months later, they finally followed my advice. But of course by then it was too late. Iggy Hernandez was already gearing up his Draft Pulaski movement. At the White House Christmas party after the election – the last party, the one with that stupid Caribbean-themed Christmas tree – Williams put a hand on my shoulder. 'I should have listened to you, David.' What could I say?"

"President Pulaski listens to you!" exclaimed Melanie.

"What happens to the Nationalists now?" Valerie asked.

"For the time being, they're demoralized, disorganized, and broke," David answered. "But defeated parties recover pretty fast. When they do recover, they'll have to make a strategic choice.

"They can fight President Pulaski with everything they've got. They probably lack the muscle to obstruct Pulaski the way the Constitutionalists obstructed President Williams. But they can certainly rev up their base, raise a lot of money, and position themselves for the midterms.

"Or – and here's their second choice – they can make nice with President Pulaski, try to pull him closer to their positions, and drive a wedge between him and the Constitutionalist party. The more they praise him, the more they undermine him.

"The second strategy will delight what's left of the old mainstream media. They love seeing politicians go all kissy-kissy with each other. It will tempt Pulaski too. In his mind, he's a leader above party, a unity figure, who can unite all people of goodwill blah, blah, blah. He doesn't accept that the days of country-above-party are dead and buried, if they ever existed at all, which I doubt. Good thing he has me and my coalition and our $200 million backing him up. Otherwise, he'd get very lonely, very fast."

Valerie moved us all to the living area. She vanished into the kitchen, returning with a tray of delicate cobalt blue coffee cups I'd never seen before. Melanie trilled over them. David Maurice raised one of the cups to his lips, revealing a mouthful of expert dental work.

In the brighter light of our living area, you could see that Maurice's shiny face had been tightened by the surgeon's scalpel. The tight face beamed with good cheer, but despite the wine the gray eyes still scanned us closely and carefully. As charming as David Maurice was, you could never feel at ease with him. I sure felt uneasy. Fuddled by wine myself, I'd already said more than I'd wanted to say about the visit to the Oval Office and my work with Senator Hazen.

The Maurices sat side-by-side on the sofa. I offered Valerie the big armchair. She refused, instead pulling over for herself a dining room chair that she placed between the sofa and the kitchen.

"Do you have any trips planned?" Valerie asked Melanie.

Melanie pulsed with excitement. "You know we're going to the Sedona Resort next week for four days R&R. It's been so busy! But I'm planning a big family trip for next Christmas: India."

"I've never been to India," said Valerie wistfully.

"Neither have I!" chattered Melanie. "David goes about three times a year; he has big clients in the pharmaceutical industry there. But he's never had time to see any of the historical sites. Except the Taj Mahal of course, they always take him to see that. So David has booked off the whole month of December, and we're going to take our entire group to India: the kids, everybody. We've chartered our own 737 to travel the whole country. David and I have our own bedroom and bathroom at the back of the plane. We're staying mostly in hotels - David says the new hotels are splendid - but I've rented a renovated maharajah's palace for five days in Jaipur, where we're giving a house party for all of David's Indian clients ..."

As Melanie spoke, Maurice visibly lost interest. He'd got from me everything he wanted to get, which was evidently nothing very useful to him. His eyes focused on Valerie. He abruptly broke into his wife's travelogue.

"You've never been to India, Valerie? Why don't you come join us?"

Melanie tapped Maurice on the elbow reprovingly. "Oh David, I need Valerie to run the shop for me while I'm away. She's indispensable."

Maurice pressed. Mr. Relentless.

"Come for the house party in Jaipur – just a few days."

"There really won't be room in the house," said Melanie with an audibly nervous laugh. "You've already invited nine clients, plus all the grandchildren!"

"There's room for Valerie," said Maurice, his eyes lingering appraisingly and hungrily. The wine had made him bold. "And Walter too," he added after a pause. He leaned forward to speak more exclusively to Valerie.

"India is a thrilling country," he said, "much less predictable than China, and crammed with new opportunities. One of our India-based clients is a US-Indian joint venture. They do drafting work for US architectural firms. Cuts costs by over 70 percent!"

"What happens to the Americans who used to do your clients' work?" I asked, attempting to insert myself into the conversation.

Maurice barely turned his head toward me. "They have to do something else of course."

"Or not."

"Or not," Maurice agreed, his eyes still devouring Valerie. "It's up to the particular person. It's always been that way. It's the American way."

"But there are so many people out of work in this country." I couldn't keep the annoyance out of my voice, not that I much wanted to.

That got Maurice's attention.

"You're looking at it from the wrong end of the telescope. What about the Americans who can now pay less for an apartment because we've cut the construction costs? What about the Americans who will gain new construction work because by cutting costs we have made it cheaper to build? Not to mention the Americans who make and sell the software the Indians use?"

"Have you ever tallied how it balances out?"

He shrugged. "I'm not an economist, it's not for me to say."

Valerie detected Maurice's chilling mood. She shot an imploring glance at me. *Stop it.*

Maurice raised two admonitory fingers toward my face. His voice quickening, he said, "Even if more Americans did lose, I'd tell you – and I'm speaking as an old anti-apartheid campaigner – justice is global, not local. Suppose moving a job to India does push one American worker out of our middle class, but adds three Indian workers to their middle class. Isn't that a good trade?"

"For who?"

"For the people of earth," he said expansively.

Melanie tried to redirect the conversation. "You know David won a lifetime achievement award from the Urban League?"

"Really?" Valerie said with artful enthusiasm.

"Yes! Tell Walter and Valerie about your work on credit limits." Melanie smiled soothingly at me "This is a perfect example of how David's company brings a social conscience to its client advocacy."

Maurice extended his coffee cup for a refill. Valerie gracefully leaned forward to pour. Maurice twisted his neck to enjoy the view.

"Back during the Williams administration, the Treasury department circulated a proposal to tighten up consumer-protection regulations on credit cards. I won't bore you with the details, but one of the ideas was to restrict fees on customers who exceeded their credit limit, that kind of thing.

"The credit card issuers hired me to make their case. I hired experts at the Constitutionalist Institute and the Center for National Progress. They collected some very interesting figures that proved that the new regulations would drastically reduce the availability of credit for poor people and minorities."

"Maybe it's dangerous to make credit too available to the poor?" I ventured.

Maurice snorted. "Yes, poor people can use credit irresponsibly. So do a lot of rich people. The Williams' administration's answer was to make it impossible for poor people to use credit at all, responsibly or irresponsibly. I feel good about preventing that."

Valerie nodded appreciatively. "I had never thought of it that way!"

Melanie glowed with pride. What a guy her David was. He basked in the attention of the two women.

I knew I should quit talking now. But I didn't like being lectured about global justice by a man who made his living selling access. I didn't like the mauve monogram on the cuff of his hand-made shirt. And I sure didn't like him leching after my girlfriend right in front of my face. So for once in my life … I spoke up. I poured the last of the red wine into my glass. I took a big swig and said, "Lucky for those poor credit-card holders that somebody was there to pay your fees."

"The Constitution guarantees everybody the right to petition for redress of grievances," Maurice replied, his voice a little thickened by alcohol, "even banks. I'm just as proud of my lobbying work for the financial industry as any of my pro bono work – or my work for the White House for that matter."

"But some petitions are a lot more equal than others, right? What about the people who can't afford to hire you? I was at one of those Trucker Protests the other day. They think nobody's listening to them. And you know what? Nobody *is* listening."

"They have nothing to say!"

"That's not true! Sometimes they don't know what they're saying, but that's not the same thing. They're hurting. Millions of them. Their homes are foreclosed, their pensions are cut, their health insurance is being canceled if they even have health insurance to begin with … Yeah, it's kind of stupid of them to blame everything on the Mexicans. But they have to blame somebody. Maybe they're not thinking very clearly. No wonder. There's some very high-priced talent working hard to confuse them."

"Should I take that personally?" he asked with a sly glance at Valerie. *Your boyfriend's getting agitated – that proves I'm the alpha male.*

"Of course not!" Valerie countered, looking straight at me. I took another gulp of wine.

"It's getting late," Melanie interposed.

"Maybe we all should take it personally," I said. "God, David, can't you feel it? You're up there on River Road, I'm on Capitol Hill behind guards and metal detectors – but something is rumbling out there, and the guards won't keep it away, not for long."

"People always say that," he said, standing and patting my arm. "It never comes to much. Every once in a while, there's a big 'change' election. They throw the bums out. They throw new bums in. But I don't go anywhere. What would they do without me? People like me – we make the system go."

"But the system's going to hell! People can't find work, the dollar is collapsing, and you yourself say that you have to shove hundreds of millions of bankers' money at the politicians to get anything done!"

"I had no idea Senator Hazen employed such a barn-burner. Is this what they teach at Brown these days?" Maurice chortled as he emptied the last of my Ca' Togni into his glass.

"I didn't learn much at Brown. I'm starting to regret that I didn't. But I can see what's in front of my eyes."

To my surprise, Maurice's tone suddenly altered. "Me too," he said. He scrutinized me. "And maybe there's something to you after all. Call me when this battle is over, we'll have lunch."

"What got into you?" Valerie demanded as soon as she shut the door behind the Maurices.

"I don't know. I didn't like ..." I reconsidered what I was about to say. "I didn't like him."

"Obviously!"

But there was something unexpected in the way Valerie was looking at me. She wasn't mad. She seemed impressed. "I've never heard you talk like that before."

"You're not mad at me?"

"I should be, shouldn't I? But no," she said wonderingly. "I'm not mad. I don't know where this new Walter came from, but I approve. Even if I get fired because of him."

"I didn't think of that."

"You never do, that's your charm. Now go finish the dishes and pots. I want to call my mom and tell her about the dinner. Also about this charismatic new rabble-rouser I'm dating. He's the kind of guy she's always wanted for me, somebody who can really stir the masses."

"Ha, ha," I said without laughing.

She put her arms around my neck and placed a long, lingering, and very exciting kiss on my lips. "Well, at least he stirs me."

CHAPTER 46

"Walter? It's Seamus Soloveitchik."

Seamus Soloveitchik was calling *me*? That made no sense. "Yes?"

"Do you have some kind of personal connection with Michael O'Grady?"

Soloveitchik must have misinterpreted my pause as ignorance, because he added, "The boss of Patriot News?"

My first thought in the interval had been: *No, don't be ridiculous, of course not. He's just a guy I read about in the paper.*

Second thought: *Oh, you mean the guy whose girlfriend I screwed and whose room service tab I ran up?*

Third thought: *Holy fuck – why is the White House asking me this question?*

"Why do you ask?"

"Because I've had a call into O'Grady's office for days asking to meet with him to discuss …" He paused as he remembered he was talking to an unsecured line, "future coverage of possibly pending financial events. Not very respectful of the presidency, to keep the White House waiting, right? I heard back from him just today. And you know what he said?"

"I can't guess."

"He asked if I knew you. Isn't that odd?"

"Very odd." I hesitated. "Why are you sharing this with me?"

"Because of what he said next. He invited me to come see him tomorrow in New York, and he asked me to bring you with me. Can Senator Hazen spare you for half a day? We'll take a Marine helicopter up and back. I'm asking on behalf of the president, just in case you were wondering."

"I'll ask the senator. But the whole thing sounds like some kind of weird practical joke."

"I've known Michael O'Grady for years. Not even his best friends credit him with a sense of humor."

The senator of course excused me. Then he asked the obvious question: Why did I think Michael O'Grady wanted to see me?

I spontaneously lied. "Maybe he knew my father?"

Hazen nodded. That made sense.

The next morning, the senator and I took our walk as usual. Then Mehtab drove me out to Andrews Air Force base. The helicopter's scheduled departure time was 10 o'clock. I arrived at the base about 9:15, giving me 45 minutes to clear the checkpoints and absorb the shock of a full view of Air Force One at the head of a long row of Air Force passenger craft.

Mehtab dropped me at the VIP lounge, a free-standing building facing Air Force One. Seamus arrived at 9:50, chauffeured in a battleship grey Chrysler sedan, strange antennae bristling from the roof and trunk. A Secret Service man opened the door for him. Seamus hoisted a big black litigator's briefcase from the seat beside him. The air was soft with the beginning of spring, technically still a week away.

An officer in camouflage indicated our helicopter: a small, bug-like flying contraption that looked exactly like something a local TV station would use to report on traffic. Seamus stepped in first, helped himself to a forward-facing seat. I stepped around him and found myself facing backward. Seamus reached to the side of his seat and produced two sets of headphones with accompanying microphones.

"You'll want these."

It was already noisy on the tarmac even before the rotor began to turn. Then, ignition – and suddenly the noise was overwhelming. I clamped the headphones over my ears.

The rear of the helicopter abruptly lifted up, tilting my knees toward my chest. Then the front followed, jerking upward, but not as high as the rear. My stomach lurched.

Seamus reached into a netted pouch behind his calves. He produced an airsick bag and calmly handed it to me.

I grabbed the bag, but not quickly enough for accuracy. I blew violently into the bag, but splashed some vomit onto my raincoat. I heaved and heaved. There went breakfast and coffee. Another heave, and up came last night's dinner, Thanksgiving turkey, pencils I chewed in third grade. Finally there was nothing left. I mean nothing. My stomach felt as if it had been scraped to the lining. The helicopter stabilized, and we flew flat, straight, and north.

Seamus handed me a foil packet containing a moistened paper tissue. I weakly ripped it open and dabbed at myself. He handed me a water bottle from an unnoticed side cooler.

"Feeling better?" His voice resounded in my ear.

I nodded.

"First chopper flight?"

I nodded again.

"Yeah, a lot of people have that reaction. Want another bottle?"

I shook my head. No, thanks.

A beat or two passed. "So – let me know when you're ready to talk."

"Jesus Christ, Seamus," I said. "What is this? Enhanced interrogation techniques?"

"There's no point holding back. You're not protecting yourself, you're just sending me into the meeting blind. Which is bad for the president. Which is bad for your boss. Which is bad for you."

"If it's going to be bad for me, there's nothing I can do now to stop this from being bad for me."

"No, but you can make it less bad for your friends."

"OK, let's leave it at this: O'Grady and I were once interested in the same girl. Maybe he's still annoyed at me over that."

"Are you telling me that the head of America's most powerful news organization ordered me to haul a fifth-level Senate aide to New York at taxpayer expense because of some love triangle?"

I croaked, "If you net-net what I owe the taxpayer for this trip – and what the taxpayer owes me for all the meals I've just thrown up – I think we'll come out even."

"You don't know what these rides cost."

"If it had been up to me, I would have preferred the train."

The Maryland suburbs fell away. Ninety-five minutes after we lifted from Andrews, we were lowering atop the Patriot News building in the west Forties of Manhattan. What a wonderful feeling when the chopper at last rested upon solid substance and the rotor fell quiet.

My raincoat did not look very beguiling. I slipped it off and left it inside the helicopter cabin. I followed Seamus as he strode out to greet the small rooftop reception party: three eager young Patriot News interns, two in striped ties, one in a mid-calf skirt.

We were led through a rooftop door to a flight of stairs, then down the flight of stairs to a bank of elevators. Our escorts punched "14": surprisingly, Michael O'Grady had his office just above the newsrooms not on the lofty executive floor. The elevators opened again, and we were led through a warren of corridors and surprisingly shabby offices into a small reception area. We were left alone for seven or eight minutes - just long enough to make the point.

I was still grouchy about the helicopter lift, so I did not resist jibing, "When was the last time you waited to see anybody other than the president?"

Seamus surprised me by not taking offense.

"You know how the president is always described as the most powerful man on earth? From where I sit, it's not true. The most powerful men on earth are the governor of the central bank of China, whichever asshole senator has chosen this week as the week for his latest temper tantrum, and Michael O'Grady. He knows it too, so this little show is unnecessary. It's wasting his time as much as ours, because he's only watching daytime TV until he's ready to let us in."

The moment arrived. The door flung open and O'Grady welcomed us with an affable, "Come in!"

Michael O'Grady was surprisingly tall. He was a flashy dresser in the Las Vegas style. He wore a brown tailor-made suit, pulled tight at the waist, puffy in the chest. The suit was matched to a shirt of beige silk and contrasting white collar, the white collar trimmed in a border of the same beige as the body of the shirt. The trick was repeated on the cuffs: white cuffs trimmed at the edge with beige silk. O'Grady finished his ensemble with a tie and pocket-handkerchief in a matching orange-and-brown pattern.

O'Grady's face was orangey too. He looked as if he had just returned from the Caribbean. Perhaps he had. His black hair was allowed to surprisingly long at the back; his black mustache, precisely trimmed. I knew O'Grady was 62, but only because I'd looked him upon on Wikipedia. Based upon his appearance, you would deduct at least half a decade. Valerie says that men must never dye their hair because they won't invest the time for the layering and highlights. O'Grady had evidently not begrudged the time. His hair glistened as black as a prep school boy's.

For the most powerful news executive in the country – a millionaire many dozens of times over – O'Grady had contented himself with a surprisingly unostentatious office. The room was large, but not huge. The furnishings were only hotel quality; the walls were painted rather than paneled. For decoration,

O'Grady had hung mementoes of Patriot News' rise and success: magazine covers, advertising posters, that kind of thing.
On the wall opposite his desk, he displayed a huge blowup of
the cover of a now-defunct trade magazine. The cover, dated
15 years ago, proclaimed that Patriot News had for the first
time drawn a bigger audience in the 6:30 slot than the evening
news of any of the old networks. That had once registered as a
shocking fact. Now Patriot News' #1 position was taken utterly
for granted by Constitutionalists and Nationalists alike. Patriot
News mattered. No other newscast did.

After my encounters with Sylvia, I'd started reading arti-
cles about Patriot News. One made a point that stuck with me.
"Patriot News," the article said, "was the first of the social media.
People who watched Patriot News weren't just spectators. They
joined a community as participants. That's why nobody ever
got anywhere exposing the inaccuracies and misstatements
and biases of Patriot News. The people who watch Patriot News
aren't passive consumers. They are the coauthors of the story."

O'Grady jovially commanded Seamus and me to sit at a
long conference table. We gazed out across Sixth Avenue at
another office building. A waiter arrived to serve lunch: a lettuce leaf filled with two big scoops of lobster meat mixed with
mayonnaise, the lobster still tasting of the can.

"Thank you for making this time available to us Michael,"
said Seamus in his best approximation of ingratiation.

"Seamus, it's always a pleasure to see you. And Walter,
thank you for making the trip."

O'Grady must have noticed my wan face, because he snickered unpleasantly. "You didn't enjoy the ride?"

"No," I answered and drained my ice tea.

"I won't pretend to be choked up about that. But still, I am
glad you are here. I've learned a great deal about you these past
days, and I did want to see you in person. It's only human for
me to wonder what you've got that I haven't, right?"

I didn't like where this was going. Seamus, on the other hand, seemed to have entered some state of suspended animation, awaiting events.

O'Grady wielded his knife and fork expertly. He was a man accustomed to the business lunch, adroitly able to chew and talk in rapid succession.

"Don't worry, I'm not angry. Not any more. I've closed the affair we were disputing. She's all yours if you want her, although you'll have to fly to Hong Kong. She's just signed a five-year contract with our affiliate there."

Didn't he look pleased with himself!

"But just speaking man-to-man – and after all, we have shared an intimate experience haven't we? – my advice to you is to forget her and settle down with the pretty Valerie."

I twitched with alarm. I noticed something I had not noticed before: a manila file folder at O'Grady's elbow. He opened it now, revealing a stack of documents, all face down. He grasped the first of them, turned it face up and threw it into the middle of the table for both Seamus and me to see: a high-resolution photograph of Valerie in coat and boots exiting our building. He turned over the next: a telephoto shot of Valerie in panties and brassiere, bending over to pull on her stockings, taken somehow through our bedroom window. I nearly jumped out of my chair in horror and anger. How had he done this?

"Lovely body," he said with a lascivious little smile. "Do you want to see the rest of this series? No? I'll just leave them here for now." He moved five more photos facedown from one side of the folder to the other.

Seamus stared at the images, then at me, aghast.

O'Grady next pulled from the folder and pushed in front of me what looked like transcripts of text messages. "She's loyal too. Quite a lot of girls would have their heads turned if Ruben Beloz made a move on them." Ruben Beloz was a heartthrob of the moment, a star of some romantic series that ran on Patriot News' entertainment affiliate. "Ruben met her at one of those parties she organized, got her number, took her to lunch, exchanged flirty messages, took her to dinner, made out a little in the back of a limo, but in the end," O'Grady paused for dramatic effect, "he failed to score."

I glanced through the columns of flirty banter. They extended back almost three weeks. O'Grady had set this plan in motion within five days of my good-bye to Sylvia.

"Still," O'Grady continued, "these messages might interest the people at DCGossip.com. If nothing else, they'd help to quell those ridiculous rumors that Ruben is gay.

"We're investors in DCGossip," he added. "Frankly, it's not going very well. You know Benjy Bartsein don't you, who runs it? No? You're not missing much. Personally, I think he's a psychopath. The site's not doing well. Benjy needs another infusion of cash from us if he's to survive. I told him my next investment was contingent on him generating a minimum of 25-million page-views this quarter. It looks like he'll fall short. Unless he can find himself a hot scandal to promote?"

He shoveled a mouthful of lobster and chewed thoughtfully. Seamus stared at him, his own lobster puddling in mayo in its lettuce leaf.

"Wait, wait, I think I have it," announced O'Grady. "Imagine this headline: RUBEN BELOZ'S NAUGHTY ROMP WITH GIRLFRIEND OF HEIR TO SCHOTZKE FORTUNE.

"Isn't that perfect? We might play it like this: *Tragedy runs as thick as mustard in the Schotzke family. Senate staffer Walter Schotzke might seem to have everything – but not quite enough to hold onto his live-in girlfriend, Valerie McNaughton, shown here in intimate embrace with sizzling-hot Patriot TV star Ruben Beloz.*"

O'Grady pushed forward a blurred shot of Beloz's hand half inserted inside Valerie's sweater as the dark-haired man buried his mouth into her neck. Valerie was turning away her head, not exactly saying yes, but not exactly saying no either.

If I hadn't heaved up everything I'd ever swallowed in that helicopter, I'd be heaving now. I wanted to smash O'Grady in the face. Seamus read my mind. He reached across the table and gripped my forearm with his left hand and squeezed tight. He was surprisingly strong for such a small, chubby guy.

"What do you say Seamus?" O'Grady demanded. "You know Washington media better than anybody, would that generate the traffic we need?"

Seamus looked queasy, like a young doctor watching his first amputation. Yet he uttered no protest, made no sound.

O'Grady shook his head in theatrical disappointment. "Well, maybe not. For the story really to pop, we'd need to see more of Valerie. That's the problem with these limousine spy cams – very difficult to program exactly the aperture you want. I just can't tell whether or not Ruben has his other hand up her skirt. If we could only see more thigh …" He brightened suddenly, just as theatrically. "But wait a moment! We have this!"

He dealt out more pieces of paper. These looked like redacted emails.

"I never can understand why people choose such weak passwords for their email accounts. In this day and age, actually using your birthday? Still I can't complain. One person's sloppy security protocol is another person's fascinating afternoon reading."

O'Grady patted the stack with a manicured hand.

"I read here, for example, that even a senator widely admired for his integrity has used the power of his office to get a top job at NASA for a jobseeker fired from his last job for suspected embezzlement. So disappointing!"

He formed a little pout with his mouth. "The jobseeker's main qualification seemed to be his friendship with the girlfriend of one of that senator's aides."

He fanned the papers open so that I could see the messages. They seem to have come from Dana's machine, because they included messages between Dana and Brad as well as between Dana and Valerie.

"As I try to make sense of what happened here, I think I see a larger scandal." He spoke musingly, as if testing the story in his own head. "*The failed heir to a distinguished American family was desperately trying to persuade his girlfriend not to leave him for Ruben Beloz. All that money couldn't buy him love. So he used the patronage power of his office to score a job for an unqualified friend of his girlfriend. Maybe then the girlfriend would stay with him instead of ditching him for a hunky actor?*"

For the first time in my life, I had an ambition. I would murder Michael O'Grady. I didn't know how, I didn't know when, but I would do it.

"OK, Michael, message received," intervened Seamus. "Can we get down to business?"

O'Grady ignored him.

"Question," O'Grady said with thickening sarcasm. "Did young Schotzke's boss know? I can't make up my mind about. Certainly it would be interesting to see that the respected Senator Hazen is just another patronage-dispensing politician. On the other hand, the senator is getting very old – almost senile, really, poor man – so maybe he has lost awareness of what's going on his office as his aides abuse the public trust? Or perhaps I should leave it to Benjy Barstein to decide?"

I lunged at O'Grady, but Seamus had anticipated me. He rose from his chair, placed both hands on my shoulders and used the full weight of his body to shove me back down into my chair.

"Michael," said Seamus in a voice that pleaded for mercy, "this story hardly meets the high fairness standards of Patriot News."

"Yeah," I said hoarsely. "I wonder how your wife would feel about hearing the *whole* Sylvia Tescher story. Or maybe some of the stories about your other Patriot bimbos? I hear a New York divorce can be very expensive."

O'Grady only smiled suavely. "I have no worries about Mrs. O'Grady's reaction. She's not easily shocked. But let me reassure you, we're not proceeding with any of these stories."

O'Grady gathered all the loose photos papers and shoved them back inside the manila folder. He pushed the folder toward me.

"There. You have everything. Case closed. But if anybody ever questions our commitment to shoe-leather reporting here at Patriot News – please tell them you know better."

He snickered again. He was done with me.

"I wanted you to see this," he said turning to Seamus, "so you'd understand: I'm not acting out of some kind of vendetta. I'm not mad at Walter any more. I'm not mad at Senator Hazen. I'm not mad at the president. What's going to happen between this administration and me is business, not personal. I want you to know that because – well, because a man likes to be understood, that's all."

"I do understand you!" burbled Seamus ingratiatingly. "I have huge respect for you and for Patriot News. Which is why I'm here today. You've helped elect a Constitutionalist administration. We're only asking for a fair hearing ..."

O'Grady picked up his emptied lunch plate with both hands, moved it to the side. He leaned forward and brutally interrupted Seamus.

"Seamus, now hear this.

"First, you dicked over my friend Iggy Hernandez. If Iggy were sitting in that chair, as he should have, I might listen to him. *Might*. But you? Who the fuck are you to ask me anything? Two years from now, maybe three, you'll be back in this office slobbering over my shoes begging me to hire you to comment on the news. And you know what? If you're a good boy, I'll do it too. Why not? I paid $300,000 to renovate my boathouse, I can pay $300,000 for you.

"OK, next. I know all about your so-called plan. What, you think the most powerful cable news network in the nation has to wait for a *briefing* to know what's going on? You're going to cut my viewers' Medicare and you're going to raise my investors' taxes. Why would I support that? Legalize cannabis? Are you fucking nuts? You want to balance the budget? Cut the welfare you pay to the people still watching fucking network news.

"Finally, and last: Even if you had treated Iggy with respect, which you didn't; even if I liked your plan, which I don't; I would *still* fight you. You know why? Television. I'm in the television industry. You know what's terrible television? Accountants balancing the budget. You know what's great television? An all-out fight between Americans and traitors. The Williams administration was the greatest thing ever to happen to this network. Your administration? Meh. Ratings are down. Traffic on our websites is way down. The election was great for us, no mistake, but over the past five months alone, the defeat of Monroe Williams has cost this network almost $100 million in forgone revenues.

"We need a new story line. I was hopeful that Durango could provide it. But so far, Durango has been a ratings flop, despite the best efforts of Dr. Vernon Mallory. We've just signed him to a contract by the way.

"Now, though, you've given us the story line we need. The Pulaski administration is the Sergeant Montoya of Constitutionalism. We're all in formation, ready for the fight, and – bang! – sneak attack. Betrayal. That will draw eyeballs, don't you think? And when we link that story of betrayal to how you guys have covered for the traitors in the Durango column, everything will make sense."

A little of Seamus's former bravado returned to his crushed face.

"Michael, are you seriously suggesting you'd start a political war against the president of the United States?""

"Why not?" answered O'Grady cooly. "I've already beaten one."

Seamus tried again.

"You'll find George Pulaski is no Monroe Williams. You start a war with him, you best be prepared to fight to Appomattox."

O'Grady shook his head. "You don't understand. You can't beat me. Everything you do to beat me, helps me. Take away our front row seat in the White House press briefing room? We'll make a week of news out of it. Attack us as liars and sensationalists? The audience believes us, not you. Pressure our advertisers? What can you do to them, really? Compared to what we can do to your donors?"

"You have a board of directors," Seamus was trying to sound fierce, but only managed to sound pleading. "They have interests. We have clout. But Michael, why are we having this crazy conversation? It's not good for anybody. We should be friends."

"We're not friends. We're not enemies. Like I said, it's business. You've just been cast, that's all. Let's hope the show has a nice long run. Thank you for coming, gentlemen."

O'Grady rose from his place, crumpled the napkin in his lap, and tossed it onto the table. "I wish we could visit longer, but I have a broadcast to produce. Stacy will show you out."

In stepped one of the three young interns from the roof, the young woman in the mid-calf skirt: a graduate, no doubt, of some Bible college in the South or Midwest. She must feel so proud to work for the one network that stood for God, family, and country. I wondered if O'Grady was banging her too.

Seamus and I stood up. What else could I do? I picked up the file folder.

Seamus tried one last appeal. "Michael, we want to work with you. Won't you let us?"

O'Grady's back was already turned, a telephone at his ear.

CHAPTER 47

The cabin of the helicopter smelled strongly of disinfectant when we re-entered. A sealed garbage bag shoved under my seat held my filthy raincoat. I apologized to the pilot for the mess. He shrugged. "I've seen it before, man."

Seamus had tightly compressed his lips through our elevator ride up to the roof. He remained silent until the helicopter pilot shut the cabin door upon us. Not until after we lifted off did he pass me the headset and microphone. As I tightened the chin strap, Seamus' voice suddenly erupted into my ear: "Fucking Iggy. Fucking Iggy, I see his fingerprints all over this, the fucking bastard, fuck, fuck, shit." Oh. So *now* Seamus was going to be a tough guy.

I didn't answer. I felt too sick and sore, too angry and humiliated.

"I will screw Iggy to the wall. I will ruin him. I will break him and smash him and crush him." Only after a minute or two of obscene monologue did Seamus finally wind down. "Jesus, what did you do to that guy? Fuck his daughter?"

"His mistress."

"Do you have some kind of death wish, you moron? You should have told me on the ride up. I asked and asked."

The oil refineries of New Jersey passed below us. Somehow the helicopter ride was not bothering my stomach so much this time. I guess a man gets used to anything.

"What difference would it have made?"

"At least I wouldn't have been taken by surprise. I would have had time to plan what to say."

"What could you have said? And who would have expected ..." I clenched my fists in another spasm of disgust.

Seamus slapped the back of his right hand against his left plam. "We'll show O'Grady a president has some weapons too."

"Seamus, why are you playing it this way?" His Big Man routine was grating on me. "If O'Grady's war really is driven by Iggy, why not make peace with Iggy? It's not too late. Bring Iggy back to the White House, kiss and make up."

He gave me a look that said, *Don't tell me my business.* "Obviously I thought of that. It's too late. Iggy hates me now, he'd never come back so long as I'm there."

I rubbed my temples, a tic I'd acquired from Hazen. "Then maybe you owe it to the president to take yourself out of the picture."

"You don't understand," said Seamus impatiently. "The president makes these decisions. Really. When Iggy began organizing for Pulaski, Pulaski was 100 percent focused on the war in Mexico. Iggy assumed that it would always be that way, that a President Pulaski would obsess over everything Iggy didn't care about – the outside world basically – and leave Iggy to guide policy at home."

"And maybe Pulaski encouraged that assumption just a little?"

Seamus shrugged away the cynical suggestion. "Maybe. Who knows? But whatever Pulaski had in mind at the start, by the time he'd won the nomination, he definitely had begun having ideas of his own. Iggy believes in nothing. You tell him that the deficit will destroy this country, and he'll answer that his data show that an increase in the federal tax on diesel fuel will cost us 14 points among Midwestern white married men with two years of college education."

"Is he wrong?"

"Iggy's never wrong! He's just right about irrelevant things. The president wants to solve problems, big problems. Iggy only wants to beat the Nationalists."

With that, he turned off his microphone and stared out the window, sunk in his own brooding. I leaned my head against the glass and contemplated the view of downtown Newark.

We set down at Andrews about 3:30. As we walked away from the noise of the rotor, he extended a hand. "Some day you and I should have a drink and figure out what happened today. Was I collateral damage for you? Or were you collateral damage for me?" Then he was gone, marching fast toward his Chrysler and driver.

I took a little longer to pull myself together. I reached for the garbage bag with my filthy coat, then the manila folder with its filthy contents, and backed out of the cabin. The pilot had come around to the cabin to assist me. Another officer walked forward to help.

"Are you all right?" I guess I looked worse than I felt.

"Okay, for now, thanks."

Then an idea occurred to me. "I work with Seamus Soloveitchik, the counselor to the president. We have some sensitive materials here." I showed the folder. "And we have to dispose of them. Do you have a facility for that?"

"For sure," he answered. We walked together to the VIP lounge. Mehtab was waiting for me in the adjoining lot, sitting on the hood of the trunk finishing a cigarette. Nice of Hazen to send him. I waved to Mehtab, then followed the officer inside. The officer picked up a phone and placed a call. About ten minutes later, a small SUV pulled up in front of the lounge door. We both stepped in.

The SUV zipped around and behind the lounge toward an agglomeration of low-rise brick buildings, each with a wooden numerical indicator over the door. We halted in front of one, and the driver directed inside. There stood two large metal containers. They looked exactly like the heating equipment inside my grandmother's pool house – except that on top of one of the unit squatted a wide-mouthed metal cylinder with a handle.

"These are incinerators?" I asked the bored young woman on duty.

"We don't incinerate any more. These are *disintegrators*. They pulp paper, optical devices, computer tape."

I passed her the folder of photos and papers. She inserted them inside the cylinder and turned the handle.

"Buh-bye," she joked.

"I hope," I said.

The apartment echoed empty when I flipped on the lights. No surprise there. Valerie rarely arrived home before 6 o'clock. I poured myself a heavy Talisker. Glug, glug. Then I poured myself into a chair to think.

Actually, I didn't think. I just revolved in my mind the horrible scenes of the day, feeling rage and shame, but coming no closer to any solution when … the phone. It was Valerie.

"Walter, hon, I have some bad news. I was going to have a good dinner for you after your big meeting in New York. But I just got a call from Melanie. She's sobbing hysterically. Something horrible has happened, but she won't say what. She is begging me to come out to her house to see her. I'm so sorry! Someday I'll find myself a more professional boss."

"No, no, that's OK. I'm already home. I was airsick on the helicopter. I'm exhausted and disgusting. I'll forage for something in the fridge. You do what you need to do for Melanie."

"I'll text you as soon as I can escape. I want to hear everything about your trip. Did O'Grady explain why he wanted to see you? Was it about your dad?"

"It was a spy thing."

"Yes, that makes sense. I'm really sorry about this, but I'll get home as soon as I can."

CHAPTER 48

The next thing I knew, Valerie was shaking me awake. It felt like three in the morning. I glanced at the clock: 10:22. I was sitting in an armchair, still more or less dressed.

"Are you OK?"

"Tough day," I said groggily. My head felt thick. How many whiskeys had I had anyway? I could not remember. "How's Melanie?"

"Awful." Valerie released her hold on me and dumped herself into a chair.

"What happened?"

"Can you listen? You're not too sleepy?"

"I'm sleepy, but I can listen." My mouth tasted bad. It hurt to look at Valerie's face. Did I even know this girl? I wanted to confront her, but I didn't know what to say.

"Do you want some wine?" I finally asked.

"I've had too much already." She kicked off her shoes. Her feet splayed apart from her bunched-together knees. "You won't believe this, but Melanie found a sex tape on David's computer this morning."

If I'd thought the day couldn't get weirder, I'd thought wrong.

"You mean – a sex tape *of* David? Gross."

"Yes, a sex tape of David. With another woman."

"Poor Melanie. Yeah, I can see why she'd be hitting the Chardonnay. Well, that's what she gets for snooping." I struggled to pull myself upright in my chair.

Valerie frowned. "She wasn't snooping. And even if she was, so what? She found what she found."

"So what's Melanie going to do?"

"What's she going to do? What *can* she do? She confronted David. She drove straight to his office and confronted him."

"And?"

"He brushed her off! He said it was none of her business. He said it was just his way of blowing off steam, the way some men golfed. He said he assumed she knew that. After all, he had been married to another woman when he started with her."

"Wow. He has balls."

Valerie frowned again. She didn't like my attitude. Fine. I had some dislikes of my own.

"Pigs have balls too."

"So is she leaving him?

"That's what we were talking about for the past four hours! I She can't decide. David told her not to be ridiculous. He said she had a beautiful child and a wonderful life – and that she'd be crazy to throw it all away for a woman who meant nothing to him."

"I'm guessing that didn't convince her."

"No. But then – then he reminded that she'd signed a very tough pre-nup. If she divorces him, she'll get $150,000 in child support plus a one-time payment of half a million for every year of marriage. Nothing else, not even the house."

"How long have they been married?"

"Eight years."

I rose out of the chair to pour some water for myself. Maybe it would retroactively dilute the liquor.

"So that's $4 million," I said on my way into the kitchen. "Plus $150,000 a year. Plus she has her own income from the business. So what's her problem?"

"I agree! That's what I said. But the money David is offering won't pay for chartered private jets. It won't rent a floor in a Cipriani hotel. She likes all that. She said she didn't know until now how much she likes it."

"So it's like the old joke. We know what Melanie is, now we're just arguing over price.

Valerie's gorge was rising now. She got out of her chair too and padded around the living room in her pantyhosed feet, her voice more and more upset.

"That's not fair! Melanie invested in her marriage. It's her *life*. Melanie asked me: Why should she give all that up to another woman, as a thank-you present for fucking her husband?"

"Do we know who the woman is?"

"Melanie didn't recognize her, but I did. Yes, I saw the tape - I can read your dirty mind. It's that new Patriot News girl, Heather Needham."

Heather Needham! I almost blurted out that she was Mac Kohlberg's girlfriend. Then I remembered how I knew that and bit back the blurt. "At least *that* wouldn't be gross to see. So long as he kept the camera focused on her, anyway."

"Well she's not so hot with her makeup off," Valerie said testily.

"Maybe I can judge for myself?"

Any other day, that might have amused Valerie. Not today. The angry look on her face moved into the red zone, explosion imminent. I sipped my water.

"So how did you finally escape?"

"She passed out on the sofa. I told you, we'd been drinking a lot of wine. And she had a big head start on me. I found a blanket, made sure she was comfortable. I'm lucky I made it home without wrecking the car."

"Is that the end of the story?"

"No. I saw David! He arrived home just as I was leaving. He didn't look flustered at all. He must have guessed why I was there, but he did not acknowledge anything at all. What a *pig*!"

"Pig" seemed to be the word of the day.

"But it sounds like Melanie will be staying with Mr. Pig? I guess that's a happy ending all around. He keeps making his motion pictures. She keeps her vacations in Italy."

"What the fuck is the matter with you?" The gathering storm finally erupted. "Every time I answer one of your questions, you say something jerky. Just stop it, OK?"

I knew what was the matter. And I was not stopping. Like Michael O'Grady earlier in the day, I was only getting warmed up.

"You buy the Crackerjack," I said, "and you get the whistle in the popcorn. You marry David Maurice, you get bimbonic plague along with your fancy vacations. I mean look at the way he looked at you when they were here ... Why is Melanie acting all surprised now?"

"What do you mean, 'How he looked at me?'"

"Valerie, he was totally scoping you out. That's why I got mad at him. And don't pretend you didn't notice."

"All right, he was a little flirty. I didn't think it meant anything. What was I supposed to do? And *of course* Melanie's surprised. What are you saying, that when she married a rich man she was giving him permission to fuck around on her? You seem to have a big definition of rich-guy rights. You're a rich guy. Tell me, can I look forward to seeing you in a sex tape with another woman?"

The battle lines were drawn now.

Oh, what I was burning to say. *Valerie, I saw a man with his hand in your shirt!* But her eyes were already brimming with tears. And somehow I couldn't bring myself to say the words that would crush her – and maybe end everything with her. So. I only grumbled, "I'm not making any sex tapes."

"Not that I know of at least!" The tears were flowing fast now. "But who knows what's coming? And then you'll say I deserved it because you are Walter Schotzke, and the whistle comes with the Crackerjack."

Wait a minute. How was I losing this argument? She was the one catting around behind *my* back! I mean, not counting Sylvia.

"I don't think of myself as Crackerjack," I said. I could hear how defensive I sounded.

"You damn well shouldn't! When I met you, you were getting high every weekday and getting drunk every Saturday. You were living in an apartment full of crap. You had no job, no plans, no future except to wait until your trust fund came due. Now you're helicoptering alongside a counselor to a president. How'd *that* happen, Walter?"

"I always give you credit ..."

She crashed back into the chair and covered her face with her hands. Then she recovered herself and stared boldly at me.

"I'll admit it, I'd like to be married to a rich man. *If* I loved and admired him. *If* he loved me. Why not? Who wouldn't? But I'd rather work in a Starbucks than be married to a rich man I didn't love. Or who thought that his money gave him a right to abuse me."

"I don't think my money gives me a right to abuse you."

"Well you sure are exercising it."

She jumped out of the chair and stomped out of the room into the bedroom. She emerged a few minutes later with an overnight bag, just as I was pouring myself a calming glass of Talisker. "I don't want to see you any more today. I'll spend the night at Dana's."

She glanced disapprovingly at the whisky. "I really wanted to hear about your day. Too bad you decided it was your day to be a dick."

With that, she was gone. I held the drink in my hand, then tossed the burning fluid into my throat in one long flow. I walked to the bathroom, drained a couple of glasses of water, and gargled with mouthwash. I undressed and threw myself on the bed.

I awoke before the alarm sounded. The whisky had passed through me, but the rage all remained, cold and gnawing. I looked at my phone. No text from Valerie. No Facebook message. No email. Fine. I had nothing to say to her either.

I stepped out into a grim, damp morning, the worst kind of Washington early spring day. Frigid humidity gathered on my face as I walked toward Hazen's apartment.

I arrived early for once, barely past seven. Hazen looked eager to see me. He put aside the papers immediately, pushed away from the table, and headed to the door. He tut-tutted that I had no coat. "It's a nasty day," he said. "I am surprised that your young lady let you leave the apartment like that."

"She didn't see me go out."

Hazen was right about the coat. The long walk was chillier than I expected. I was already physically uncomfortable even before I had to address the question I had dreaded since yesterday: Why had O'Grady wanted to see *me*?

The least painful way to tell that part of the story was to start with the unavoidable confession about Nia getting Brad a job.

"Why did I hear nothing about this?" Hazen demanded, adjusting his muffler more tightly around his throat.

"Well sir, I had a kind of inkling you probably wouldn't like it."

"And Daphne?"

"I imagine she was protecting me."

"She doesn't work for you."

"No, sir."

He fell silent for a while after that, thinking. Then he asked, "So that's it? O'Grady asked you to New York to confront you with the Brad story? Why in the world would he care about that?"

So there it was. The direct question. Could I lie my way out? No, not with Seamus as witness to the event. Even if Seamus agreed to cover for me – and why should he do that? – he was certain to let slip the truth sooner or later. My humiliation was too good a story to hold forever.

So I confessed. More or less. I told him about Sylvia, the whole story from beginning to end, minus only the pornographic details. It took me all the way to Washington Monument to finish.

I recognized the expression that spread across Hazen's face as I talked. He was disappointed. I recognize that expression because I know it so well. I'd seen that expression on the faces of teachers and headmasters, girlfriends and coaches. I'd seen it on the face of my grandmother almost every time she saw me. Even my mother – one of the world heavy-weight champion disappointers herself – generally looked disappointed in me, if only because it was such a chore for her always to be finding me a new school after I'd been expelled from the last.

Of all the faces in my life, only two were missing from the gallery of disappointment. One was my father's. He had vanished before my career as a disappointer began. The other was Hazen's. And now he had joined the ranks.

Yet Hazen's disappointment was different from the others. It was not even slightly angry. It was just sad.

"Does Valerie know any of this?" Hazen asked, in his cautious probing way as we began the climb from the street up to the big white obelisk.

I shook my head.

"Did O'Grady have anything to say beyond simply telling you that he was aware of your relationship with this other woman?"

I hesitated a long time.

"I think you'd do well to tell me the full story." That was said so gently that I almost felt that the worst was over.

I told him the rest. I told him about O'Grady spying on Valerie. I told him about Beloz. I told him that it all happened in front of Soloveitchik. I told him about the handing over of the documents, about destroying the documents, and then – why not? – about the fight last night. Hazen absorbed it all, in perfect calm, except for the bit about David Maurice. That visibly disturbed him.

By the time I finished, we were within eight blocks of the office. Hazen stopped in the street. I stopped alongside him. He put a thin arm around my shoulders and spoke quietly into my ear.

"You have not asked me my opinion. But as your friend – not your boss, but as your friend and as your father's friend – I'll tell you anyway."

I nodded gratefully.

"First, have you checked yourself for sexually transmitted diseases?"

I shook my head no.

"Do that right away. Today. If the test returns positive, you must inform Valerie. But if not, you must never tell her about your adventure with Sylvia. You will only cause pain. Don't confess, don't apologize, don't ask for forgiveness. Just go to work, starting now, to *deserve* forgiveness.

"As to what you have learned about Valerie – really, what did you expect? You have this girl living with you on pins and needles, never knowing when you'll decide you are finished with her. A handsome actor flatters her. Of course her head is turned for a minute. Why not? Your options are all open. Why wouldn't she keep her options open too?

"The way you are living, it's a wonder she has not already been driven completely crazy. She shares your bed, cooks your food, cares for you when you fall sick. What do you do for her? You pay the rent? There are words for this kind of arrangement, and they are not very pleasant words. I think Valerie behaved as well as can be expected under the circumstances. If you want more from her, it's up to you to change those circumstances. You want a wife's fidelity from Valerie? Then make Valerie your wife. A woman is never really herself until she is married.

"If you do decide to stay with her, you will never reveal your knowledge of this incident. Not a hint, not if you live to be 100. You will bury it in secrecy, and you will forget where you buried it. If you ever must think of it, think of it as a judgment on you – a very gentle judgment, in comparison to your own mistake. You understand that?"

I nodded again. *Got it.*

He dropped his arm and resumed walking.

"None of which subtracts from the monstrousness of O'Grady's actions. I often say that if you think the worst of people, you'll never be surprised. But this one time – yes, I am surprised. Have we ever seen anyone like O'Grady in this country? They tell me Hearst was worse, but I have trouble believing it."

"Is there anything to be done?"

"By you? Not much. By the president? Actually – not much by him either."

We toiled up Capitol Hill. The damp seeped through my jacket into my shirt and underwear.

"About Brad's job," I stumbled. "I have to say, I'm very sorry. I've exposed you to risk. Stupidly. Selfishly. Is there anything I can do to set things right?"

"It was stupid, and it was wrong," Hazen agreed. "But we cannot repair the situation. It's done. Now we live with the consequences."

"Maybe we'll get lucky?"

"Maybe. Maybe we'll be overshadowed by a bigger story." Hazen allowed himself a thin unhappy smile. "Like for example that the man leading the lobbying initiative for the president's most important domestic initiative has been caught in a sex scandal. I think that's a story that might interest Michael O'Grady, don't you?"

Holy crap, I hadn't thought of the David Maurice angle at all. Yeah, that was a bigger story than anything involving me. We began to walk the stairs to the building entrance.

"Nobody knows about that!" I protested.

"No? You do. I do. Valerie does. None of us is likely to tell. Maurice's maybe soon-to-be-ex-wife? She might tell. Or if Maurice stays with the wife, then the mistress?"

"Why would the mistress talk?"

"She's not sleeping with David Maurice for his sex appeal. She has her eye on a prize: becoming the third Mrs. Maurice. If she does not win that prize, she'll search for another prize. Michael O'Grady has many prizes to give. And now she has something to trade."

Hazen put his hand on the bronze door of the office building. Some long-ago artisan had carved the "EQUALITY" onto the bronze. Hazen's hand rested above the capital-Q. "We're playing for very big prizes. Don't expect people to play nice."

CHAPTER 49

"They think they are *soooo* smart. And they think you are *soooo* dumb." Lou Rogers' voice sneered with heavy sarcasm out of Jack Campozzo's computer.

"They don't like the cars you drive, and the cereals you feed your kids. They don't like your music, they don't like your clothes, they don't even like the way you take your vacations – *if* you get a vacation after working all year to pay the taxes that they spend. They just don't like *you*.

"They're the ruling class. They're the ones who decide that your taxes will pay for welfare and food stamps – not repave the highway that takes you to your job. They decide that some-body pissing on Jesus is art, and that Christmas is now politi-cally incorrect. They are the ruling class. And as far as they are concerned, you belong to the shmuck class."

Jack hit the stop key on the audio player.

"That's from Rogers' monologue last night attacking the president's budget plan."

"Does he know what it's in it?"

"He doesn't care what's in it. He only cares who proposes it. Williams was the enemy before. Pulaski is the enemy now. Now listen to this bit," said Jack, moving the bar to the 26-minute mark.

"President Pulaski, I know you are listening to me, or any-way that your people are listening to me." Rogers was talking low into his microphone. The sarcasm had vanished from his tone, he was now murmuring in earnest, coaxing entreaty.

"I'm talking directly to you, Mr. President. You took an oath to defend the Constitution! Let me read you something from that Constitution. Article 1, Section 7. *All Bills for raising Revenue shall originate in the House of Representatives.* Where does it say anything about a commission appointed by the president? Where? Huh – tell me that? Where?"

Rogers's voice gained volume and pitch, like a plane talking off from earth, until he was shrieking into the microphone like a crazed delicatessen owner ordering the local teenagers off his stoop.

"Where? NOWHERE, THAT'S WHERE! IT'S NOT *IN* THE CONSTITUTION! IT'S *AGAINST* THE CONSTITUTION! IT'S AGAINST YOUR OATH OF OFFICE! IT'S AGAINST YOUR CAMPAIGN PROMISES!"

Rogers's voice abruptly dropped in volume, but it still seethed with anger.

"We fought Monroe Williams when he attacked our Constitution. We broke him. I'm warning you that if you attack our Constitution, we'll fight you and break you too. You say I should respect your uniform?"

The voice erupted into another tirade.

"I SAY *YOU* SHOULD RESPECT YOUR UNIFORM! WE'VE GOT ENOUGH TRAITORS IN UNIFORM DOWN IN MEXICO!"

Jack hit pause again.

"What's wrong with that guy?" I asked.

"Nothing's wrong with him. He's early that's all. There's going to be a lot more of this, just you wait."

The speakerphone on Jack's desk beeped. "Is Walter there with you?" It was Hazen.

"Yes, senator."

"Send him to my office."

I arrived via the internal door just as the last of a delegation of Rhode Island businessmen vanished out the door to my antechamber and the external corridor. Hazen's elbows rested on his desk, fingers massaging his temples. From this angle I noticed the width of the gap between his neck and the collar of his blue shirt. He was losing weight, and there had been no weight to lose.

"A problem?"

"I'll have my buttermilk now."

I fetched the morning snack.

"Tough meeting?"

"Interest rates are rising again. These men are being squeezed. They're pleading for action fast on the deficit. They kept saying over and over again: *Just do it.*"

"So that's good news, right? They'll back the president – and they'll back you if you back the president the way you want to?" I set his plate of biscuits down in front of him on a spread-out napkin.

"Not exactly," he said wearily. "When I say, 'Just do *what*?' they can't answer me. They have a long list of things they *don't* want. Don't raise their taxes. Don't raise their customers' taxes. Don't cut the roads, they're in bad shape already. Don't stop the airport projects, we need those.

"Here's the thing," Hazen said, dipping a biscuit in his milk. "We Constitutionalists have been the stronger party for most of the past 35 years. We've shaped the whole government to suit our people, and when it comes time to shrink the government, it's our people who will feel the pain.

"But our people don't appreciate how much they benefit. They imagine the money is going somewhere else: to immigrants, or minorities, or ungrateful young people. When they say 'cut back' they mean cut *them*. Not *us*."

"If we can get out of Mexico ..." I ventured.

"If." He dipped the biscuit again. "Come get me in an hour. I'll have to be a little late to the committee hearing. I must make some phone calls."

I sat down at the computer in the antechamber and opened Facebook. Valerie was online.

Hi. I typed. A minute passed. Then:

Hi.

Lunch?

Can't.

Can't or won't?

Both.

Why not?

I have to go to NY today. I'll stop by the apartment to pack.

Whats in NY?

Your grandmother. She's coming back from Barbados. She has doctors appts in the city. She asked me to come up today to get her aptment ready.

Why doesn't the housekeeper do it?

Never does it 'right.' Plus she wants me with her at the docs. She's not feeling well. You'd know that if you ever called her. I'll return next week. If I'm invited.

Invited? It's your home.

Not exactly.

On our way to the committee, I told Hazen that I'd communicated with Valerie.

"That's good," he said. "All OK?" I shrugged. He clutched my arm just above the elbow and leaned to whisper into my ear, "I've been playing Cupid myself."

"Today? Aren't you kind of busy? Who are the love birds?"

He smiled grimly.

"I called David Maurice. I told him that word was leaking about his … personal situation. I told him that he owed it to the president to get his life in order. Choose one woman. Then find some way to mollify the other. His decision *which* woman. Then destroy that stupid tape."

"And I thought David Maurice was a hard ass. You are one cold bastard yourself – sir."

"Cold as ice," he said, and the smile was already gone.

CHAPTER 50

As the weather warmed that spring, the already dismal economy weakened further.

You could see the slump in the statistics, if you bothered with the statistics. Few did. So many people had quit looking for work that the unemployment numbers no longer meant very much. Young people moved back in with their parents and spent their days playing video games. Older people persuaded Social Security judges to qualify them as "disabled." Immigrant women went door-to-door peddling counterfeit handbags. Young men sold drugs, or waited in the parking lots of big box stores for day labor, or stole.

President Willliams had used government money to fund temporary jobs. One by one, those programs lapsed during that first spring of the new Pulaski administration. The big new Constitutionalist majority in the House of Representatives debated cuts to food stamps and housing subsidies. Senator Joliette excited the blogs by quoting on the Senate floor a century-old veto message by a forgotten president: "The people should support the government. The government should not support the people."

The trucks had departed from the parking lot near the Capitol. Yet the Trucker Protest did not end. It spread. By now, the issues animating the truckers had enlarged beyond the prisoners in Mexico. The issue was ... everything really. And Patriot News covered each gathering everywhere in the country with cheerleading enthusiasm, no matter how remote the place or how marginal the demonstrators.

Treasury Secretary Tony Monckton hit the Sunday morning talk shows on the first weekend of spring to urge shared sacrifice. "Everybody will feel the pain, but it's the price of a better tomorrow."

Here in Washington, the main pain was trying to book a restaurant table on a Saturday night.

Valerie texted Sunday night. "That was a good deed," she typed without even a hello.

I had no idea what she was taking about.

"I spoke 2 Melanie. She cried and said 2 tell you 'thank you.'"

I bluffed. "Glad to help," I texted back, glad to take credit for whatever it was. I was still mad at her. But I was missing her too.

Barely had I hit SEND when the BlackBerry rang. It was Valerie.

"David called Melanie on Saturday," she said again without a hello. "He apologized that she found out about Heather in this way. He said he never meant to hurt her. He told her he was committed to their child. And he offered her a generous settlement if she'd agree to an amicable separation. She got a lawyer's letter with all the details today. She realized that David must have heard from the White House that they didn't want a scandal. The White House must have heard the story from Hazen. And Hazen must have heard from you."

Her voice melted a little. "So you're not a total jerk after all."

"Did you really think I was?"

"I've been wondering. Anyway, now you're a hero."

"Just doing my job, ma'am," I said in an imitation western accent.

"I wish I were there with you – we could kiss and make up."

"Kiss?"

"We'd start with a kiss."

"Now you have my mind going."

"I don't think it's your mind."

"It's where I keep my mind."

"Mmm," she breathed.

And then it was Monday, and the commission's report was released, and all hell broke loose.

CHAPTER 51

I don't pretend to be any kind of budget expert. But then, you didn't need much expertise to understand the package the commission was sending Congress. SitRep summarized it in their morning round-up:

1) A huge up-front package of public works programs to create employment;

2) The public works to be paid for with spending cuts to start as soon as the unemployment numbers declined below seven percent; and

3) A package of "revenue increases" to fall mostly on upper-income people, delayed to go into effect 24 months after adoption of the plan.

One of the taxes was especially complicated to understand: a plan to end the exemption from capital gains tax on sales of homes that had been purchased after the collapse of the housing market.

The idea was that people who had bought houses at the bottom of the market might score a windfall profit.

For fairness' sake, the argument went, the profit should be taxed. The measure would not raise much money. But the commission described it as a way to share the pain of the housing crisis with people who had otherwise escaped.

Frankly, it all sounded too boring to be explosive. But then … so does nitroglycerine.

The report was released shortly past 9 o'clock on the first Monday morning of spring. A few minutes before ten,

I was serving the senator his buttermilk and biscuits. Hazen motioned me to sit down in the chair opposite his desk.

"The trouble starts now," he said gravely. "The president will make a statement at noon, endorsing the package. He wants as many Congressional leaders as possible standing with him as he makes the announcement. He has asked me – and I have agreed."

I was stunned. "But you've been so negative about this whole project!"

"I was dubious, not negative. I remain dubious. The administration has the right answer, but they are imposing that answer in completely the wrong way. It won't work, and probably it shouldn't work. Yet the crisis is real. I've been calling for a solution like this for years. I can't walk away now – especially since I helped persuade George Pulaski to run for the presidency. He needs me, and I'll stand by him."

"I understand," I said, but of course I didn't. "But you've been predicting this could end your career?"

"Probably." His face lightened. "Don't worry about me. You know I've had a better offer."

That made me laugh. "Lose a Senate seat, gain a senator wife?"

The light still shone in his face a little. "Her term ends before mine. And if I tell her yes, she won't seek another."

"But are you really ready to quit?"

The light faded. "Your father did braver things."

I hope my face showed my appreciation of the tribute.

Hazen's voice grew more serious still. "Now there's something I want to do in your father's memory. Would you get your laptop from the front office?"

I returned a minute later. The senator rose, clasped his hands behind his back.

"I want you to create an email and type exactly what I dictate."

Not normally my kind of work, but OK.

He rose from his big leather chair, clasped his hands behind his back, and paced the room. His voice assumed unusual distinctness.

"*Dear Senator Hazen,*" he began. I typed. He paused, waiting for me to catch up. "*It has been a great honor to work for you these past four months. However, I cannot accept the decision you have made today to endorse the proposals of the Deficit Reduction Commission.*" He paused again. "*With great regret, I must resign my position in your office effective immediately.*"

I ceased typing at the words "accept the decision." I lifted my eyes from the keyboard and stared at Hazen.

"Senator – I don't want to … I don't agree … I would never say …"

"Keep typing," he answered, and repeated verbatim, "*With great regret, I must resign my position in your office effective immediately.*"

"Senator! Have I let you down somehow?"

"Not for a minute. This is for your sake. Now type please: *With great regret, I must resign my position in your office effective immediately.*"

My eyes stung.

"*I have deeply appreciated the opportunity of public service you extended to me. Yet principle must come first. I entered your office as a committed Constitutionalist, and as a committed Constitutionalist I must now depart. Please accept my continuing personal respect and good wishes.*

"*Very truly yours,*

"*Walter Schotzke.*"

Among the million seething thoughts racing through my mind as I transcribed the senator's dictation: *Is there anybody on earth who is going to believe I wrote this letter myself?*

"Senator, I've got it all down. Now may I speak? I don't want to do this. I can't believe you'd make me do this."

He sat on the edge of the desk right in front of me. He placed his hand lightly on the top of my head.

"If you want a future, you *must* do it. It's a fact of politics: Sometimes the right side of the issue is not the right side of the issue to be on. Someday it may be your duty to sacrifice your career for the good of the country. But not today."

"I don't need a career," I protested. "I've got my mustard money."

He shook his head. "That's the old Walter talking. We've been making a new Walter."

"But this letter – it's just so ugly! You've got me here implying you're some kind of turncoat."

"Good," he nodded. "I worried that it was too subtle. You can't make new friends until they're convinced you've burned your boats with the old friends."

I must have looked as baffled as I felt. The senator leaned forward to explain patiently. "You send this letter to me. I forward it to – let me see – Mac Kohlberg and Freddy Catesby. I'll accuse them of turning you against me. I'll stress that this letter is private correspondence for their eyes only, totally off-the-record. They'll of course forward it all over town. If it takes as long as an hour to appear on SitRep.com, I'll be amazed. You'll be the Constitutionalists' new hero by dinnertime."

I felt something catch in my throat. "And you'll be the new villain? I want no part of this."

"It's Washington. Call it my last lesson to you: creative betrayal." He rose from his perch on the edge of the desk. "I'll miss our walks." He extended his hand.

I rose too, and took the hand, feeling overwhelmingly sad. "Goodbye?" I asked.

"Not yet. You'll accompany me to the ceremony at the White House. Send the email after we get back. About one o'clock. That'll give me time to deal with it before the Majority Leader summons me and the other pro-administration

Constitutionalists to his office for an emergency chewing out. The meeting should last at least an hour, so you'll have time to clear out your desk and slip away before I get back. I don't want any dramatics in the office."

By 1:30 in the afternoon, I was gathering my few personal items from the little foyer office. I sent Valerie a text asking her to Skype me later. She was the one person I could tell the whole story to.

What about my grandmother? This job had been her idea. I counted the months on my fingers. Barely four. Would she be disappointed in me? She'd certainly never believe the "resigned over principle" version of events.

Talking to her in person or even over the phone would lead to disaster. She always overwhelmed me, put me in the wrong. I'm not good at arguing. I'm only good at agreeing. What alternative did that leave? Email? Hah. Facebook? Double hah. I realized I'd have to write her a letter. In an envelope. With a stamp.

Problem: We didn't own a printer at home. We'd never needed one. We both printed everything at the office. And here I was at the office, with an hour to spare, and a great pile of "OFFICE OF SENATOR PHILIP B. HAZEN" stationary waiting for me in the maw of the little printer beside my desk.

I flipped open my laptop and started writing.

I'd got nearly halfway through my self-excuse when my BlackBerry buzzed.

"Walter Schotzke?"

"Yes."

"This is Frank Liu with SitRep.com. I have a copy of your letter of resignation from Senator Hazen's office. May I ask you a few questions?"

"No!" I blurted. "I have no comment!"

"Just some basic facts?"

"No comment! Wait a second, I do have one comment. Senator Hazen is the finest public servant in Washington, and it breaks my heart to leave his office. That's it. Goodbye."

"In that case, I'll have to go with the text as I have it."

"You're going to do whatever the fuck you want, no matter what I say."

I clicked END to the conversation and sat back in my chair, panicked. What had Hazen just uncorked? I got the answer within ten minutes, when the door to the foyer office flung open and Daphne burst in, glaring rage and hate. "You BAS-TARD!" she shouted at me. "You fucking treacherous shit! You scheming, deceiving, lying snake!"

She stepped into the little antechamber, grabbed both my shoulders and shook me furiously. Hard. My head snapped back, and I felt a pain twist my neck. My hands twitched to grab her back – and grabbed the edge of the desk instead. I could feel my ears burning. No controlling that.

"You listen to me, you asshole. This is a village. Everybody is connected to everybody, and every wire leads back to me, and I will follow you through your life, and I will fuck you over as you have never been fucked over, and then I will fuck you up the ass, and then I will cut your throat, and then I will mangle your carcass, and then I will piss on what's left of you. I tried to be your friend, but you stabbed me in the back, you filth, you sneak, and now you're going to see what kind of enemy I can be. Don't bother asking around, everybody who could tell you is dead and buried."

"What did I do to *you*?" I croaked.

She thrust her BlackBerry in my face. "You are dumb enough that you don't need to play dumber."

I grasped the BlackBerry. The screen read:

SITREP BREAKING NEWS. A close aide to Senator Philip Hazen has resigned to protest the senator's endorsement of the

Deficit Reduction Commission package, SITREP has learned. For more go to SitRep.com

"This must come as a great surprise to you," Daphne said with heavy sarcasm. "I assume you have absolutely no idea how your letter of resignation ended up in the hands of SitRep."

I kept quiet on that point.

Daphne's sarcasm gave way to another burst of rage. I pushed my chair back – I didn't want to be grabbed again. "I brought you into this office to help me save Senator Hazen – and all of us – from the senator's worst instincts. Instead you threw everybody under the bus to save yourself."

I got a little voice. "I just quit my job. That's all."

"Fuck you, you treacherous fuck. You can quit your job without issuing a fucking self-aggrandizing press release. *Oh look at me, I'm the man of integrity! And all my office colleagues are sell-outs.* Fuck you! Should I tell SitRep you didn't even vote in the last election?"

Long past time to exit. I pushed my chair as far away from the chair as I could, stepped out of it, while disconnecting my laptop from the printer. "Daphne, I sent that letter to Senator Hazen and nobody else."

I tucked the laptop under my arm. All I had to do was somehow step past her, out into the hallway, and I was free.

"I'll have that pass. And your BlackBerry. It's government property."

I surrendered both.

"I'll have your balls later. Now get the fuck out."

CHAPTER 52

On the way home, I stopped by the Verizon store to buy myself an iPhone. One side benefit of not working for the government any more: I could choose my own technology.

I texted Valerie the new number, then posted it on my Facebook wall.

By the time the new system had initiated, my voicemail box was already completely full and accepting no more messages. I scrolled through them: all from media. SitRep. Hill-Call. Washington *Guardian*. A bunch of Patriot News numbers. ProgTV. An array of columnists, Constitutionalist and Nationalist. ProgTV again. BBC. BBC World Service. BBC Scottish Service. BBC Welsh Service. Too many to return, too many even to read. I deleted every single one. As I finished, the new phone rang. It was Freddy Catesby. "Walter! I've been trying and trying to reach you!"

"My government phone was impounded."

"Yes so I heard – about the eighth time I called, I got our friend Daphne. She had some choice things to say about you."

"She had some choice things to say *to* me."

He chuckled. "Congratulations. You're a hero."

"For facing down Daphne?"

"That too. Can you have dinner tonight? 6:30?"

"I suppose I can slot it in. I'm unemployed."

"Not for long, Walter, not for long."

I resumed reading backward through my messages. One from Valerie carried the subject line: "OMG did u see this?" The message linked to a story in the Style section of that morning's *Washington Guardian*: "Washington Power Couple Calls it Quits."

David and Melanie Maurice will separate after eight years of marriage. The DC super lobbyist and the glamorous party planner are parting amicably, according to a statement provided to the Guardian by Melanie Maurice's lawyer.

"David and Melanie remain good friends and look forward to co-parenting their son, Zeke. They have reached an undisclosed financial settlement. The decision to separate was Melanie's. Building her company "Perfect Parties" into Washington's premier event planner has absorbed all her energies. She says she has been joking to friends, 'David needs a full-time wife. And so do I!'"

Melanie has moved into an apartment at the Ritz-Carlton. David Maurice will retain the couple's famous River Road mansion. Melanie will keep their Eastern Shore farm, "Mandela House."

Awww. How sweet. How question-settling. How Philip Hazen.

When the cab dropped me off at the address Catesby provided, I thought I had come to the wrong place. I had arrived in the middle of the George Washington University campus, students milling on their way to dining halls and fraternities. I checked the address on my phone: 1964 E Street. I looked across the sidewalk and up a flight of stairs at a big old unmarked white brick mansion wrapped by a white wood porch. Must be it.

I pushed the round brass handle in the center of the front door. The door sprang open, and I was greeted by a tuxedoed butler.

"Yes?"

"I'm a guest of Mr. Catesby's."

The door widened, and I stepped into a large reception room hung with portraits of Confederate naval officers.

I plopped myself down in an armchair, looked at the coffee table in front of me strewn with magazines and newspapers. They had Catesby's magazine too, the dead-tree version. Kind of a shock to see it, like watching an old movie and glimpsing a cameo appearance by the very young face of a now-famous actor.

The magazine was illustrated with a cover cartoon of President Pulaski in his wheelchair crushing assorted enemies of society beneath his treads: Mexican insurrectionists, shaggy lesbians, the anchor of one of those dying network news broadcasts, a black university professor who had been the target of one of Mark Dunn's angry tirades. "Pulaski Rolls On!" announced the cover. Out of date already.

Catesby arrived almost on time, as natty as ever: navy suit pinstriped in some kind of gold thread, overtop a double-breasted vest. The tie billowed in rich green silk; the tiny shoes gleamed.

"We have half an hour to ourselves," he confided. "The others won't arrive till seven." He ticked off the invitees on his fingers. "Mac Kohlberg. Bill Mihailovich. Elmer Larsen. But you'll never guess the last!"

"If I'll never guess, why are you asking me to guess?"

Catesby giggled with self-delight. "Iggy Hernandez! Walter, you have made the big time."

"Doesn't feel that way."

"It will! But we have to manage this correctly."

"Manage what?"

"Your transition."

I goggled blankly at him. He leaned forward to speak softly in my ear.

"Back in the Cold War, if a KGB defector showed up on our side of the wall, we didn't say, 'Welcome aboard, let us show you where we keep the secret CIA codebooks.' We tested him, forced him to prove himself. That's what's going to happen with you. The scrutiny will be extra severe for you because you'll have Daphne shrieking all kinds of allegations against you. I hope you never molested any children? No? Good."

"You lost me three miles back."

"You have to prove yourself a Trucker Protest kind of Constitutionalist. And I have just the way to do that. I've secured you a job with Elmer Larsen."

"I don't want a job with Elmer Larsen!"

Catesby twitched, glanced nervously around, then leaned even closer to me and lowered his voice even deeper.

"You've quit one army. If you want to survive on this battlefield, you'd better join another. This is no town for individualists, not if they want a political future. And you want a political future. Otherwise you wouldn't have leaked that resignation letter."

I flinched, and he grasped my arm. "I'm not scolding you – I admire your shrewdness. You are showing real potential. I'm just helping you to the next step. When the time comes, you'll help me."

What could I do? I nodded assent.

His eyes glittered. He leaned back away from me, smiled and resumed his old bantering talk.

"Excellent. Now all you have to do tonight is agree with everything everybody says, but especially with everything I say. Got it?"

"Got it."

"Ah, and here's Mac Kohlberg arriving right on time." But how different from the last time I saw him. Kohlberg suddenly seemed older and paler. He wore a new lapel pin, a fish wrapped around a crucifix. We shook hands.

"Hello Dr. Kohlberg," I said as warmly as I could. "How are you?"

"Not bad, praise God."

"Mac's had a rebirth," Catesby explained with mock-solemnity.

"Yes," said Kohlberg wholly solemnly. "I've committed myself to the Lord." Poor bastard. I guess with David Maurice available, Heather Needham had no more use for a mere think-tank vice president.

Freddy intoned to me with more mock-solemnity, "I can't think how you were left off the invitation list when Mac and Grace renewed their vows."

"No joking, Freddy," Kohlberg upbraided him. He looked earnestly at me, silently transmitting secret messages. I did my best to transmit back: *Don't worry. I won't tell.* "It was a private and personal ceremony. My friends know I'm not a perfect man. I've sinned and strayed. But I've found my way home."

Heather Needham had found herself a nice home too.

Elmer Larsen stepped in as a waiter took drink orders. Elmer shook my hand, blinking at me through his unearthly eyes. "Are we winning?" he asked. Was that a joke? I couldn't tell.

"I don't know. Are we?" Elmer stared at me appraisingly, left my question unanswered and turned without a further word to shake hands with Bill Mihailovich, whose big, doughy form pushed through the club's front door a half-minute after Elmer. Mihailovich greeted Elmer cordially, moved on to shake hands with Catesby and Kohlberg, and arrived at me last. He looked at me as if trying to reassemble my face out of fragments of memory.

"I mentioned you in my column for tomorrow," he said. The words were grunted grudgingly, as if it pained him to use the word "you," even if only as the direct object of a sentence that opened with the word "I."

The butler led us toward a private ground-floor dining room concealed behind a closed white door. Catesby whispered, "The main dining is upstairs. I requested this private room so Iggy can enter the club from the alley - undetected." He giggled at his own cleverness.

A round table was elaborately laid with starched napkins, shining silverware, and china stamped with the club logo. A row of wine bottles lined a sideboard. Catesby presented one of the bottles to Mihailovich for his review. Mihailovich pulled out a pair of reading glasses, studied the label, and nodded a cold approval.

"You're stepping into history," Catesby murmured as we sat. "This was the home of Commodore Lachlan Crittenden before the Civil War. He threw in with the South, became an admiral in the Confederate navy. After the war, he returned to Washington and tried to recoup his fortune by operating his old home as a supper club. The concept did not work at first, until he had the second bright idea of turning the upstairs into the city's pre-eminent brothel and gambling den. Admiral Crittenden's second wife maintained the old traditions into the 1920s. The club's become utterly respectable today. But if you ever wondered, 'So where *did* Warren G. Harding go when he wanted to bang a showgirl?' - then look around."

Unasked, the waiter ladled lobster bisque into our soup bowls. The traditions of the club did not include menus apparently. Which was too bad, because lobster bisque is one of the very few foods I do not like.

"Gentlemen!" propounded Catesby. "A toast! To Walter Schotzke, the first man to fire a shot for Constitutionalist principle!"

I blushed, God help me. Mac Kohlberg crossed himself, then raised a glass brimming with Diet Coke. Mihailovich perfunctorily raised his glass a couple of inches above the tablecloth, then promptly replaced it. Good solder Elmer lifted his glass high and blinked rapidly in my direction.

"And now tonight's question," continued Catesby. "What is to be done? How can we emulate Walter's magnificent example, and each strike our own blow for true Constitutionalist principle against this Benedict Arnold administration?"

The language seemed as ridiculous as Catesby's dandy vest, but the guests seemed to approve. Only Bill Mihailovich appeared to chafe, but I could see that Bill would have chafed at the Gettysburg Address if Lincoln had included any praise of anyone other than Bill Mihailovich.

Elmer answered first. He might be a space alien, but he was a decisive space alien.

"We have to strike this deal at the most vulnerable point. The commission plan – no, let's call it the president's plan, because that's what it is – heaps taxes on all the most productive people in our society. But productive people are not always popular people. Most of the tax increases will sound reasonable, unfortunately, even to some of our Constitutionalist voters. It's the house tax that is the vulnerable point. Attack *that*, and you have shoved the knife under the wing of the turkey. You can then easily carve up all the rest."

"Yes," agreed Mac Kohlberg. "I'm amazed that they included that silly house tax idea. It's an idea that's been kicking around the think tanks for a while, even ours. We had some dweeby economist we hired from Perdue University who got fascinated with it. He wanted to publish a Constitutionalist Institute backgrounder promoting it. I shut him right down. I told him that if he ever so much as mentioned in the lunchroom, he'd be riding the next plane back to Perdue. The Constitutionalist Institute never endorses tax increases. Period. You should have heard him squawk. '*But it's so efficient!*'"

Kohlberg mimicked a nasal, lisping voice. I couldn't tell whether Kohlberg was mimicking the actual economist or some imagined ideal of how a dweeby economist *ought* to speak.

"I agree with Elmer," Mihailovich chimed in ponderously. "However the house tax got into the package, it's the point to hit, and hit hard, and hit again and again."

The closed door of the dining room opened a surreptitious few inches, and in slipped Iggy Hernandez, huffing a little out of breath. Hernandez's pear-shaped body was not built for strenuous exertion.

Hernandez patted his suit coat with a fluttering hand, then shook all our hands cordially before easing into his chair. The waiters cleared the soup bowls, then presented the next course: pork tenderloin with scalloped potatoes. After lobster bisque, pork tenderloin is the only other food I don't like.

Once the waiters had exited, Catesby spoke directly to Hernandez.

"We are discussing two questions: how to hit this deficit plan hard – and how to deploy our brave young friend. We've been talking about the house tax as the president's greatest point of vulnerability. Do you agree?"

Hernandez cast a warm, pink-faced beaming smile at me. "You're a gutsy guy. Like father, like son! I wish we had a dozen members of Congress as principled as you." In his good humor, his Cuban accent rolled thicker. It was as if he'd moved a thermostat in the room. Until that instant, I'd been an awkward outsider, constraining the conversation in the room. Now suddenly, I was inside.

"Freddy and I have been discussing that Walter might come work for me," said Elmer with a hint of a question mark.

"Good idea!" beamed Hernandez, and he suddenly launched himself into a tuneless song:

"We got so much in common,
We strive for the same old ends,
And I just can't wait, wait
For us to become friends."

None of the other guests seemed to think this behavior strange. So, that was that. Iggy had spoken. I was welcomed aboard.

"Start tomorrow," said Elmer. It was not a question.

"OK," I answered.

Mihailovich had loftily ignored all this byplay. He resumed exactly where he had paused when Hernandez entered the room, booming in his penetrating TV fight-show voice, "I say we hit the house tax. What do you say, Iggy?"

Hernandez winced at the noise, raised a finger to his lips.

"You are exactly right. As always. I kept telling the president, 'You need to invite Bill Mihailovich to lunch and listen to him.' The president did not take that advice. If he had, we wouldn't be in this trouble now."

Mihailovich took the flattery like a man swallowing a surprisingly small oyster. Where was the second bite? Still his mood did mellow.

Hernandez continued, softly and urgently, "But we have to remember our mission. We're not trying to wreck this presidency. We're trying to save it. That's why what Walter did today is so important."

He grinned at me to make sure I had not missed the compliment. "It's Hazen and his group who are isolated. The people around this table speak for the Constitutionalist majority. And we're the people the president needs. Especially you, Bill."

"Okay. So what do you recommend?" grunted Mihailovich.

Hernandez leaned forward onto bent elbows, as if imparting a precious secret. "Bill's read the situation very astutely, as usual. The house tax is the point of vulnerability. But we gotta understand, even though we're going into battle with some good allies here – Patriot News, the *Transcript, Constitutionalist Review* – we'll be fighting the weight of the financial community. And those boys have committed major dollars. Maybe that money can't bully Patriot News. But what if the big Wall Street Houses threaten to pull their advertising from the *Transcript*? Won't your publisher panic?"

Mihailovich frowned. He disliked to be reminded of any limits to his omnipotence.

"Fine," said Mac Kohlberg. "So go back to Bill's question. What do you recommend?"

"We need to set the country on fire! We need a movement that does not look like it's been summoned up over dinner at the E Street Club."

The table fell silent thoughtfully.

Elmer slowly cracked the knuckles of one hand, then – more slowly, almost contemplatively – the knuckles of the other. "I think we can do something with these trucker protests."

Hernandez smiled, poured me another glass of wine, and passed the bottle to Catesby. "Now you're thinking."

The party broke up soon afterward. Catesby held Elmer and me back to discuss the details of my new job.

Elmer mentioned a salary that was double what I'd been earning with Senator Hazen. He ordered me to meet him at Union Station the next morning at 8:30. He would be a guest next night on the Mark Dunn show, plus he had meetings the next day with important supporters. "Bring an overnight bag," he said. He scribbled a few words on a paper cocktail napkin. "Download and read these two books. You'll be meeting the author the day after tomorrow."

CHAPTER 53

I staggered out of the club, hazy with too much wine on an empty stomach. My new iPhone was crammed with emails. One from Seamus Soloveitchik said: "You treacherous shit. You and Michael O'Grady deserve each other." There was also a text from Valerie: "OMG What hv u dun? Skype me 2nite after 10."

Which I did.

"Your grandmother is fine, in case you were worried." she said.

"Good to hear."

"You sound drunk."

"Jes' a little."

"That's a relief. I thought you might have had a stroke. Because otherwise I couldn't figure out why the hell you would quit your job, blast Senator Hazen in an email, and leak it all to SitRep without telling me?"

"Principle."

"Don't bullshit me. Who put this crazy idea in your head? Daphne? Are you such a fool you listen to that woman?"

"I'll tell. Not Daphne. Hazhen."

"*What*?!"

I narrated the full story of the day as best I could through the alcohol fog.

Valerie absorbed it, amazed. "He stabbed himself in the back?"

"Yesh."

"To protect you?"

"Yesh."

"Wow. I don't know what to say."

"You better say something, because I don't know what to do."

I told her the story of the dinner, then added, "At leasht you can tell my grandmother I've been offered another job. But I don't want to take it."

"Be quiet for a minute, I need to think."

She held silent for a long time. My Twitter account was pinging rapid-fire with mentions of my name. I closed the program.

"There's no choice," she finally said. "You must take the Elmer job."

Which is how I found myself on the Acela the next morning, working my way through the writing of Jasper Philpott.

The night before, I'd emailed one of my old pals at the Constitutionalist Institute: "What should I know about Jasper Philpott?" The answer came whizzing back in minutes:

Jasper Philpott is one of the intellectual giants of constitutionalism. His first book, Welfare and Freedom, *documented how welfare assistance perpetuated poverty. His second book,* Poverty of the Mind, *about the role of IQ in individual success, was a huge bestseller in the mid-1990s.*

My grandmother had a copy in the library in the Rhode Island house.

His last book before leaving CI was titled Lives of the Social Scientists, *a dozen short biographies of leading social thinkers. About five years ago, he was hired by a CI donor, Hugo Velkampt, to run Velkampt's personal foundation.*

I'm attaching an article that came out when Welfare and Freedom *was first published.*

I clicked the attachment. It popped open a PDF photocopy of a cover story in what had been the biggest of the defunct old newsweeklies: "Thinkers for the '80s." In the center of a group of nine men and women, white and black, stood a slim man in his middle forties. He was already bald, but the features of his face were chiseled and handsome. I read the text:

If his name is not a household word, it is about as close as a social scientist can get. Even his most bitter enemies concede his formidable intelligence. Though much of official Washington regards him as a menace, Philpott's influence is still on the rise ....

Elmer had mercifully refrained from assigning me the 656 pages of *Poverty of Mind*. The first of the two books he'd mentioned, *Welfare and Freedom*, was conveniently unavailable in downloadable format. So I bought *Lives of the Social Scientists*. A few seconds later I was reading it on my tablet computer. Three hours later, I was still reading.

If you had ever predicted that the day would come when I would stay up till one in the morning reading biographies of Thomas Malthus, Herbert Spencer, Francis Galton, and a bunch of other dead professors I'd never heard of before ... well I'd say you were on crack, that's all.

But here I was, doing just that.

The book grabbed me by the collar and wouldn't let go. It answered questions I didn't know I had. It made me want to know more. It made me want to be the kind of person who could ask these questions and know these answers. It made me ashamed of the way I'd been living till now, and it made me aspire to live a better life in the future – a life more like Jasper Philpott's.

On the northbound train, I told Elmer how much I was looking forward to meeting Philpott. "Good," he said. "He's going to be very important to us."

"I'll have a lot to learn from him."

"Yeah. You know who else you could learn from? Mark Dunn."

Elmer opened his laptop, clicked onto Dunn's site and scrolled through the video clips. He found the one he wanted, then explained the back-story. A writer had written a mocking profile of Dunn in a glossy magazine. The writer's name was Roger Thibault. Thibault inherited his name from New Brunswick lumbermen who had migrated south to take jobs in the Massachusetts textile mills. Dunn taunted Thibault by making believe that the man was filing his copy from the Sixth Arrondissement.

"I see my old friend Roh-zher Tee-BO has written a follow-up piece about me. Let's uncork a bottle of Chateau Pomme de Terre and have a toast to Roh-zher."

Pop. Glug, glug. Sniff.

"Perhaps not the best vintage, but a still a magnificent bouquet. I'll open the 1982 when they finally name Roh-zher to the Lay-john d'On-air, as is long past due."

Then he pushed the over-full glass aside, frowning defiantly. "Roh-zher may call me an ugly American, but I prefer Pabst."

At the end of the clip, I asked Elmer, "OK, you stumped me. What am I supposed to learn from this?"

"How to talk to the average Americano," he answered. "You're a rich guy. Elite. Out of touch. Dunn's rich too. He made $26 million last year! But nobody think's he's elite or out of touch. When he goes on air, he's like: *I'm just an ordinary guy trying to figure things out. I'm thinking aloud here. I don't pretend to be smarter than anybody else.* Remember that."

"I'll try."

"If you want a career in politics, you'd better."

I returned to *Lives of the Social Scientists*, but now I couldn't focus. Instead, I opened my laptop to read what Roger Thibault had done to provoke Dunn. Turns out that Thibault and his magazine had dug up some embarrassing details of Dunn's failed first business venture, online marketing of homeopathic medicines. Dunn had promised all kinds of health benefits. Sick people paid fantastic prices. The medicines were all just tap water. The customers never did get better. You could look it up, but I suppose few of Dunn's fans ever did.

CHAPTER 54

Valerie was waiting for me at Penn Station, all smiles, all hugs, all forgiven. I introduced her to Elmer, who blinked at her without interest.

"Hazen called your grandmother," she whispered excitedly in my ear. "He told her that you had done exactly the right thing, that he was proud of you, and she should be proud too."

I whispered back. "That's not exactly true."

"It's not exactly false either. She's happy. Isn't that what matters? She's invited us for dinner tonight after the Dunn show."

I grimaced. "At least we have our own hotel room, so I don't have to stay with her."

"I do. She needs me."

I grimaced again. Valerie registered my displeasure. She grasped my hand and asked Elmer, "Can you spare Walter this afternoon?"

"I suppose," he said negligently. "Till four. That's when we're due at the Patriot News studio. You know the address right?"

Oh yes, I knew the Patriot News address. My balls were still living there, in custody of Michael O'Grady.

Valerie whispered in my ear. "We'll go straight to your hotel."

Two hours later, she had drained me as thoroughly as a careful cottager preparing his pipes against the winter freeze. Two hours after that, I was standing beside Elmer in the green room of Mark Dunn's studio at Patriot News, Elmer gloomily staring down upon the scanty fruit platter offered to waiting guests.

We heard a commotion outside the room: a lot of feet and bodies moving through a narrow hall. A second later, barrel-chested older man with the shaved head of the lifelong soldier pushed through the open door of the greenroom, followed by a couple of young Patriot News greeters.

The man's head and neck seemed to have no shape at all. From the collar of his beige shirt they rose in a single, massive column of sunburn and stubble.

Elmer recognized the man immediately. He pushed through the entourage to shake hands. "General Meyer, it's an honor to meet you. I'm Elmer Larsen, head of Americans for Entrepreneurship."

They made a contrast, those two. Though thick at the waist and neck, the old soldier seemed entirely made of muscle, still ready to shoulder a pack and march twenty miles on a bottle of water and a Pop-Tart. Larsen was shorter, flaccid, and pudgy. But it's not the muscles that make a man a killer.

"Nice to meet you, Elmer," Meyer spoke with military cordiality and clutched Elmer's hand, hard. I went unintroduced.

"It's about time somebody gave you a national platform," Elmer said to the general.

"Yes," said Meyer with gusto. "And I have an article going into tomorrow's *Wall Street Transcript* too. I'm developing a deal with Patriot Books too."

"Great! *Great!*" I'd never before seen Elmer look even mildly pleased. "You'll nail Pulaski?"

"Yep. To the wall."

A rap on the door. "General Meyer? Makeup?"

He snorted. "Don't need it. I'm dyed red permanently."

"Well maybe a little powder then. We can apply it on set."

Suddenly, the hall buzzed with an even bigger commotion. Mark Dunn himself stepped into the little waiting room, followed by two rapt producers, one carrying a clipboard.

In person, Dunn was a surprisingly big man, at least three inches past six feet, carrying a lot of weight. I noticed that beneath his math-teacher outfit, he wore a pair of very expensive Italian loafers.

"General! I'm so glad you could join our show!"

"I thank you for having me. It's a real honor to meet you, I watch you every day."

"The honor is all mine. All ours. To have such a heroic soldier on this program, bringing such a powerful message at just the time we need it most – you're going to change the country, general. But you have to deliver your message right. I'm going to throw you one curveball after another. Don't be bothered by anything I say. Don't argue with me. Just tell your story as simply as you can. The viewers will believe you, don't worry about that."

Mark Dunn took Elmer aside for a very short private conversation, then turned and approached me. "So you are Walter Schotzke?" I nodded. He patted my shoulder. "You are about to become a very famous young man."

They all tumbled out, toward the set. A producer motioned me to follow. I was shown to a folding chair beside one of the cameras. The floor manager raised a finger to his lips, and I nodded that I understood the need for silence on the set.

"Good evening America." Dunn spoke seriously and soberly in his trademark Clark Kent glasses. He had not worn them in the green room.

"Sometimes we hear information so shocking, so disturbing, that we don't want to believe it. I know I don't want to believe what tonight's first guest has to say. But it's a message so potentially important to your family, to your children, to our nation that you must listen. It's a matter of duty.

"Our guest tonight knows a lot about duty. He is General Alfred Meyer, a highly decorated veteran who has served our country in three different theaters of war. He retired from the army two years ago. General Meyer has worked closely with President Pulaski. In fact as a young lieutenant, President Pulaski served in a company commanded by General Meyer. Now General Meyer is speaking out – telling America there's a lot about President Pulaski we don't know. Join us."

Music, credits, Dunn stepped back toward a pair of armchairs in the center of the set, where General Meyer sat waiting.

Dunn efficiently moved Meyer through the early part of Meyer's story: the early relationship between the two men, Pulaski's rapid promotion, Pulaski assuming command in Mexico.

Then Dunn paused dramatically. "You believe that there's a reason we're not winning the war in Mexico. You don't blame our fighting forces. You don't blame our combat officers. You don't blame our strategy. You don't condemn our mission. So why are we not winning? How have insurgents penetrated our military and taken our soldiers hostage?"

Meyer gripped the arms of his chair tightly and leaned forward into the camera: "Because our commanders in the field are playing footsie with the enemy! They are doing business with them – taking payoffs!"

Dunn pantomimed shock. "General, that's an incredible accusation."

Meyer went even redder than natural. "It's not an accusation! It's a fact!"

Dunn nodded judiciously, all fairness. "Okay, walk us through the evidence – after the break."

This was the craziest thing I'd ever seen on television, and I'd seen a lot of crazy things. Would Dunn allow this furious old man to accuse the president of the United States of bought-and-paid-for treason in front of a TV audience of two million people?

As the show returned from commercial, Dunn removed his Clark Kent glasses. He held them in one hand and tapped them against the palm of the other, the investigator in action.

Step by step, Dunn guided Meyer through his so-called evidence. To me, it seemed weak to the point of ridiculousness. A friend of Meyer's had proposed a raid on some insurgent strongpoint. Pulaski had over-ruled the proposal. Another friend of Meyer's had interrogated a detained insurgent. The detainee claimed that his superior had a secret meeting with Pulaski. And so it went: a sequence of allegations, surmises, and inferences adding up to – well it was never quite clear what it all added up to. Dunn deftly diverted the general each time he approached too near an explicit charge of treason. Instead, Dunn left the accusation poised in the air, somehow more cutting for being left unarticulated.

Throughout the half hour, Dunn elaborately enacted the part of a man whose disbelief was being worn down by an accumulating weight of overwhelming proof.

"I agree that's very disturbing."

"You raise a troubling question."

"What else don't we know?"

And then it was Elmer's turn to sit in the comfortable chair alongside Dunn.

As odd as Elmer was off-camera, he had an easy and natural presence on camera. Calm, unexcited, and very poised, he knew exactly what he had come to say.

"Mark, we need nothing short of a second American revolution. Our soldiers lost their freedom in Mexico because they were betrayed by their leaders. Now each and every one of us is threatened with a loss of freedom – and again, we are betrayed by our leaders. They want to crush this country with new taxes, starting with a new tax on every homeowner in the country."

Dunn gravely agreed.

"But what can we do Elmer? We just feel so powerless as individuals."

"We can fight back!" Elmer answered with unfamiliar passion. "The citizens of this country are not privates in General Pulaski's personal army. We do not have to salute when he gives orders. We still have our Constitution, thank God."

Dunn pushed back into his chair, relaxed. No longer the prosecutor, he now played the family therapist. "What you're telling is: We're not alone. We are not powerless. We are not worthless."

"Yes! And that's why these Trucker Protests are so important. They're something every single one of us can participate in. You don't need to get bogged down in a lot of Washington jargon. You don't have to feel intimidated by people with fancy degrees and fancy talk. Just show up and express your feelings."

Elmer offered a web address for more protest info, which Dunn helpfully posted onto the screen. Then Dunn addressed the camera directly.

"I want to tell you about a brave young man, who put his own career on the line to save our country. His name is Walter Schotzke. Yes, like the mustard. Only 28, he has more money to spend in a day than most of us will earn in a year of busting our butts. You might expect him to kick back, go yachting with the Nantucket Nationalists like Hillary Anderson."

Dunn switched abruptly into the same dowager duchess voice he used to mock Roger Thibault.

"*Shall we have luncheon on the rear deck? Hargreaves, please set the table with the lobster forks. I do fancy a Campari and soda ...*"

Equally abruptly, he switched his voice back to normal, his tonsils quavering with extra sincerity.

"Instead, young Walter decided he wanted to make a difference. He took a stand for the Constitution and our way of life. He went to Washington and went to work for one of our Constitutionalist senators, Philip Hazen of Rhode Island. Walter took the hardest job in the office, supporting the senator's work 24-hours-a-day, 7-days-a-week. By all accounts, he was an outstanding aide.

"But then Senator Hazen announced he'd be joining the president in an attack on our Constitution. So Walter resigned."

Dunn extracted a piece of paper from his pocket, and read aloud the resignation Hazen had dictated to me. He read it as if he were reading the last letter home of a slain hero of Iwo Jima. My cheeks burned. Why had I gone along with this farce? Why was I *going along* with this farce? Why couldn't I ever stand up for myself? But the farce had another minute to play. Eyes moist, Dunn again addressed the camera:

"A letter like this is usually the end of a person's career in Washington. They never forgive you for standing up. Oh, you can get away with it if you're a Nationalist. The rules are different for the other side."

Dunn was working himself into a rage. "You want to be a ski bum, a playboy who sniffs cocaine, while some bureaucrat with a Ph.D. after his name pulling a six-figure salary tells honest working people that they're too fat, that they can't have a soda on a hot day? That's fine, go right ahead, see you at the Cannes film festival." Dunn drew out the word "Cannes" for three full seconds: *Cahhhhhhhhhn.*

"But if you speak up for the Constitution? You're finished in Washington. Well, not this time. We won't let it happen. We need a thousand Walter Schotzkes in every town and city in America. We need a million Walter Schotzkes to say, 'I won't stand for it. It's not right. I'll fight.'

"Walter Schotzke, come on out here!" Suddenly the floor manager's hands grabbed me. They pulled me up and out of the folding chair and out in front of the camera. "My friends – Walter Schotzke!"

The camera crew, the producers, the interns all erupted in applause. Mark Dunn applauded. General Meyer applauded. Elmer applauded. The sound of clapping was somehow magnified through the studio. Dunn addressed me directly.

"Walter, thank you for what you've done. God bless you."

Dunn redirected his fleshy face square to the camera.

"Good night, America. See you tomorrow."

CHAPTER 55

"Mr. Hero!" Valerie teasingly greeted me in the black and white tiled foyer of the Park Avenue maisonette.

"Quit it."

She stopped laughing as she saw the look on my face.

"You're not upset?"

"I'm mortified."

"But why? The Trucker Protest needs heroes. You've been elected. It had to be somebody. Why not you?"

"Because I'm a fake?"

"Who isn't? Anyway, you've seriously impressed your grandmother."

"Sorry, that's supposed to cheer me up?"

"It makes up for the credit you didn't get for the things you did do. Consider it a little dose of cosmic justice. Now smile. She's waiting for you in the small dining room."

You might think it strange for any house, even a mustard king's, to have two dining rooms.

After my grandfather died, the dining room in my grandparents' Park Avenue maisonette had been converted into a kind of music room. My grandmother's friends ate as little as she did, so she entertained them (if that's the right word) by arranging them in rows of hard-backed chairs and hiring musicians to play the piano and sing at them. Then they all retreated into the living room (my grandmother called it a "drawing room") to eat petit-fours. I had not attended one of those lugubrious evenings in years. Like the Israelis, my motto was: "Never again."

Meals were eaten instead in a small room that had once been my grandfather's study, now redecorated in an *Arabian Nights* theme. The walls were clad in yellow silk stamped with minarets and turbaned pashas and dancing harem girls in balloon pants. The chairs were upholstered in the same yellow silk, and more of the silk flowed over the small rectangular table where Valerie and I tonight flanked my grandmother.

Like all her cronies, my grandmother had watched Patriot News for years, working herself into terrors that Monroe Williams might one night jimmy open her window, steal her money, and unionize her household help. It had been a difficult winter for her, adjusting to the change of the Patriot News editorial line from pro-Pulaski to anti-Pulaski. She satisfied herself with judicious comments like, "President Pulaski knows more about all this Mexico business than he's letting on," and "Agree with him or not, we all have to admit that Mark Dunn is sincere" – although "sincere" was not the first adjective I personally would apply to the fleshy broadcaster.

Seated in the small dining room, I contemplated the tiny tournedos that looked so isolated on its big blue-and-gold plate. For company, the tournedos had a dozen mixed green and yellow beans, a tablespoon of scalloped potatoes, and a dollop of cream-colored sauce about the size of a Hershey's kiss.

This was a menu my grandmother always reserved for her most honored guests, although the portion size had contracted since the death of my grandfather. The tournedos were prefaced by smoked salmon, garnished with a sauce seasoned made of Schotzke's mustard. As certain as Monday follows Sunday, dessert would be a flourless chocolate cake and raspberry sauce.

The wine also was the stuff poured for A-list company: champagne to start, then the decanting of a dusty bottle with a brown-flecked label.

"This is from the last case of Margaux that your grandfather bought," my grandmother announced proudly.

Valerie did most of the talking through dinner. "You would be so proud if you could see Walter in Washington. He knows all the most important people on the Constitutionalist side."

My grandmother looked genuinely impressed. "Do you entertain, Valerie? My friend Charlotte Entwhistle – her late husband was Secretary of the Treasury under ... oh now, I forget which president ... one of them back in the 1970s ... or was it the 1980s? ... well it doesn't matter. Anyway she always told me that if a man wanted to succeed in Washington, his wife had to entertain properly."

"I always remember that wonderful advice," Valerie answered. I think about it every time we have friends over – although I doubt that our parties would impress Charlotte Entwhistle."

"Everything depends on having the right house," my grandmother pronounced confidently.

"I don't want a house," I said. "I like living in apartments."

My grandmother's eyes narrowed for a moment. Then she remembered that tonight was her night not to be annoyed with me, and she brightened. "You'll feel differently when you have children."

She redirected her attention back in the more congenial direction of Valerie. "Tell me which are the best neighborhoods these days?"

And off the two of them went into a real-estate discussion, while I tried to chew my steak as slowly as possible to extend my meal.

Today had been a day of strange emotions. Shame I knew; shame was an old familiar, I'd been ashamed of myself probably most of my life. But in the past, I'd always felt shame when I'd done something the people around me disapproved of:

flunked a test, been expelled from school, wasted money, been fired from a job.

But now everybody was applauding! When had that happened last? I could not even remember when. And what were they applauding? Something I did not even really do. And something – if I *had* done it – that they ought to have hissed me for, not applauded. Senator Hazen was a good man. Hell, President Pulaski was a good man. Were they right? Don't ask me, I can't even add three numbers in my head. But they were men to respect, men to trust, men trying to do the right thing. I'd turned on them when they needed me. I'd hurt them when I should have helped them. And instead of being disgraced for life, I'd been cited on national television as the next Nathan Hale.

I wanted to say it turned my stomach. But that was not accurate. My stomach would gladly have accepted another couple of the little tournedos.

"And how much would a house like that cost?" my grandmother inquired. My attention was yanked back to the conversation.

"Oh I don't know," Valerie was saying gaily. "I just stopped by at the open house. More than we can afford."

My grandmother bit the bait. "Walter will be a rich man in just a few more years. And if he's settled in life, if he's doing something useful, if he were married to the right girl – some of that money could be released early."

Valerie continued more gaily than ever. "Maybe Walter will find the right girl someday, but for now he only has me."

"He could not do better," my grandmother pronounced. Then for once in her life she caught herself. "Of course," she added, "that's not for me to say."

The Margaux was working on me. I reached over and took my grandmother's hand. She almost jumped out of her chair she was so startled. "Who better than you, Grandma?" I said.

Startlement slowly gave way to a surprised pleasure. Maybe I had learned something from politics.

A few more conversational exchanges, and my grand-mother excused herself for the night. Valerie emptied the last of the Margaux into my glass, and then led me by the hand into the living room. She gently turned down the dimmer switch on a table lamp by the walnut door, until it pumped out only a few watts of faint light. Then she layfully pushed me into a crimson sofa at the extremest corner of the room. She dumped herself alongside me, kicked off her pumps, grasped me around the shoulders with both her arms, and nestled her head against my chest.

"Wasn't that a nicer evening than you expected?" she murmured.

"So what's this house you want?" I said, not quite managing a murmur back.

Her head lifted up and her arms drew back. She propped an elbow against one of the great overstuffed crimson back cushions, leaned her head against that instead. The shadows hid the expressions in her face. Was she embarrassed? Not Valerie.

"I don't quote-unquote *want* it. It was something I noticed when I was helping Dana shop for her apartment. A row-house on N Street. Beautifully renovated. A separate dining room, which I know you like. A little garden. Four bedrooms. I stopped by the open house just to peek inside."

Two fingers jabbed me below my ribs. "But don't worry, I'm not going to start bugging you about *our relationship*." She pronounced the phrase with heavy irony. "Besides, it was ridiculously expensive."

So while I'd been screwing Sylvia, Valerie had been house shopping. I should have felt guilty. Instead I thought, *My God, there is no stopping this woman.* I could grumble and cheat. But unless I outright rebelled – unless I looked Valerie in the face and told her everything was over – that house on N Street was my future. The life of the young married Washington couple was my future. And then? It took no genius to guess why Valerie wanted a third and fourth bedroom.

So should I break off with Valerie? I could do it right now. I could say the words, make a dash for freedom. There would be crying and yelling and drama, but only for a little while. But the what? Another woman? Wouldn't she want all the same things?

My fingers extended, coiled themselves in the sweet-smelling brown hair. It felt like mine. What about O'Grady's photograph? It still enraged me. Was I a hypocrite for being angry at her for doing less than I had done? Fine, I'm a hypocrite. That hand in that photo, that hand shoved inside Valerie's dress was invading *me*, grabbing what belonged to me. Valerie had pulled Ruben Beloz's hand away, but how had the hand ever been allowed to come so close? I knew what Senator Hazen would say to that. If I wanted her to act like mine, I had to make her feel like mine. But if I made her feel like mine – what would happen to *me*?

"I haven't got that kind of money right now. And I'm not going to ask my grandmother for it."

"No, of course ..."

Yet there were worse fates than the one being mapped out for me. And if there was a little part of me that chafed, that wanted to map my life for myself – that part had not been very creative in proposing alternatives. I'd read a book in college that opened with the question, "Whether I shall be the hero of my own life ..." For Walter Schotzke, the answer to that question had always been an emphatic, "no." Now that Senator Hazen and Mark Dunn had combined to invent me as a thoroughly bogus hero, the "no" felt more emphatic than ever.

So I said, "But if you liked the house that much, I guess it wouldn't do any harm to take a look."

The arms were tossed around my neck again. Soft lips pressed my mouth.

"Maybe you're not such a jerk after all."

I kissed her back, not so softly. At that moment, my grandmother's voice flooded the room. My heart lurched, until I realized it was only the intercom speaking.

"Valerie, are you coming up?"

"Yes, on my way." She pecked me on the cheek. "Walk back to your hotel. You could use the exercise."

CHAPTER 56

The phone rang and rang. My hand groped for it, found the receiver. "Good morning Mr. Schotzke. This is your 8 o'clock wakeup call."

"I didn't ask for a wakeup call," I croaked.

"The order was placed by the party that booked your room sir."

Not exactly a vote of confidence on the part of Elmer. Then again, his lack of confidence was well-placed.

Elmer was waiting for me in the hotel breakfast room. He'd already ordered his food, a cholesterol fiesta. I followed Valerie's edicts and ordered shredded wheat, grapefruit juice, and decaffeinated coffee. Elmer frowned at my order. He probably thought I was turning hippie on him.

"So you remember we're meeting the editorial board of the *Wall Street Transcript* at 10:30? By the way, did you see this?"

Elmer tossed the actual physical paper from his bench onto the desktop. It was open to the editorial page, almost of which was occupied by a long article under the byline Alfred R. Meyer, US Army (Ret.) The headline: "TIME TO VET THE PRESIDENT."

I glanced through the piece. Here were all the allegations that Meyer had bumbled on last night's program, well organized and plausibly written. Somebody smart had worked on this. You had to read very carefully to detect the gaps between the claims and the evidence.

Elmer dispatched his ham and eggs while I studied the op-ed. "That's well done," I said, when I had finished.

"Isn't it though?" he replied admiringly.

He lifted his coffee cup from the saucer on the tabletop. Some of the coffee and cream had sloshed into the saucer, and a drop trembled agonizingly on the underside of the cup, threatening his grey pant leg below.

"We have a lunch meeting midtown with one of my donors, then a meeting at four with somebody … interesting."

Elmer replaced the cup, redipping it in the creamy mix.

"Your job," he said to me, "is to support everything I say. Beyond that, you keep your mouth closed."

"What if I am asked a direct question? What if somebody asks me about Mark Dunn's statement about me?"

Elmer hoisted his cup again. "Words are the ordnance of political warfare. Use them sparingly, always aim. Before you say anything, ask: Why am I speaking? Will these words advance my mission? Hurt my enemy? If not, shut up."

An even larger coffee droplet now dangled from the cup. I probably should have said something. But then I remembered Elmer's advice. Why was I speaking? Words were ordnance. I was a conscript soldier in this political war, not a volunteer. I shut up. The drop plunged. It hit the tablecloth. Elmer took no notice.

As Elmer finished his breakfast, I scrolled through my email and texts, then Facebook. My God, there were hundreds of messages. I'd never read them all, much less answer them.

There was one that I did answer though. From Charlie Feltrini: "Are you high? Have you gone crazy? What the hell are you doing? Call me when you're sober again. But friends always."

I emailed back: "Not crazy, not high. I will call as soon as I understand it myself. And thanks."

Elmer signed the check, and we hailed a taxi downtown. Yesterday's chill had vanished into the balm of a brilliantly sunny late winter day. "Gorgeous!" I said as the air touched my face. Elmer looked at me quizzically. "Is it?" I might as well have talked about the weather with the guy who ran the Salem witch trials.

I'd always assumed without much thought that the *Wall Street Transcript* must be located on Wall Street. We stopped instead at a glossy lower Manhattan complex at the bottom of the West Side Highway. We rode an escalator alongside granite stairs to a grand lobby, hung with huge sheets of glass that overlooked Henry Hudson's river. We walked through the lobby to an efficient security desk. There we gave our names and received stick-on bar-code security badges.

We were greeted on the building's ninth floor by a nervous intern. With a shock, I realized that he was nervous because of me! Mark Dunn had reach.

The intern showed us to a small conference room. The room was paneled in the mahogany-stained wood that had been fashionable in the 1980s boom, now badly battered. The room was furnished with a two long rectangular couches and four big cubic armchairs, all upholstered in a caramel leather also scuffed and soiled by more than a quarter-century of ideological combat.

Carafes of coffee and tea waited on a sideboard. Elmer poured himself another of his dangerous sloppy brews. A moment later, Bill Mihailovich pushed open the conference room door, followed by three colleagues.

"Hey Bill," said Elmer. "Nice piece this morning, good job."

Mihailovich shrugged. He could not accept the compliment for himself, so it did not interest him. He jerked his hand to an older man whose plump body filled his suit like a sausage inside its casing. "Alex's work." Alex – Alex Lidell - was a neat, prim man, his long grey hair artistically barbered. A carefully folded white handkerchief protruded from the breast pocket of his carefully pressed suit. "I always turn to Alex for our toughest editing assignments."

Lidell stiffened with pride. "It's an inherited calling. My father edited William Saroyan and John O'Hara. I have a marvelous letter to my father from O'Hara framed in my office, if you'd care to see …"

That was enough for Mihailovich, but Lidell missed the non-verbal cue. "General Meyer was no John O'Hara obviously. What I had to do was provide an over-arching narrative to unite his individual incidents into a coherent indictment …"

"This is Tibor Wigierski," Mihailovich said, cutting Lidell short. "Tibor writes on tax and budget issues."

Wigierski was one of the stranger-looking people I'd ever met. Thick tufts of grey hair bulged from the sides of an otherwise bald head. A gelatinous belly overhung the belt of his pants. His face twisted in an ominously combative smile.

"Good to meet you Walter." He grabbed Elmer's hand with both of his. "You guys were great last night – great! We're going to beat these bastards."

"Thanks Tibor," said Elmer. "Good to be here in the war room with you all."

"The war room! Ha! Ha ha ha!" bellowed Wigierski in explosive laughs. "That's right, that's right!" His eyes bulged like crazy ping- pong balls. "Political war – we'll fight 'em, we'll whip 'em, we'll kill 'em." He erupted into laughter again, this time a high-pitched giggle. "War room!"

"And here's Sylvester Reggio," finished Bill, expecting me to recognize the name. I did. Reggio wrote a daily Web round-up, under the title, "We Not Amused."

"I like your blog," I said to him.

He flinched as if stung. "It's not a blog. It's an *online column.*"

Elmer shot me a cautionary look. I could not understand what I'd done wrong. Clearly though I had done something wrong, for the heavy jowls of Reggio's eggplant-shaped head now framed a ferocious frown.

Elmer soothed him. "You were hilarious on *Hair of the Dog* last night." *Hair of the Dog* was Patriot News' attempt at a comedy show.

"A Constitutionalist has be twice as funny as a Nationalist to get half the credit," said Reggio. "Not that it's hard."

Elmer, Liddell and Wigierski all laughed at that. Even Bill Mihailovich smiled a proprietary smile. *That's our Sylvester!*

As we settled into our seats, I leaned forward to ask Bill something that bothered me. "Bill, when I met you at the *Constitutional Review* dinner in December, you told Grace Kohlberg not to listen to General Meyer, that he said crazy things. What changed?"

"There are important issues here that deserve a hearing," Bill answered imperiously.

"A full editorial page of hearing!" cackled Wigierski.

Reggio grinned in agreement. "And if they still don't hear, we'll yell louder."

"Let's get to business," Elmer said. His eyes flashed me a warning against further interruptions. *Words are ordnance.* Elmer addressed the whole room but always began and ended each sentence with a look at Bill. "We've got Patriot News behind us. We've got the Washington think tanks. I'm building the grassroots movement. Let's face it, though – the big money is lining up behind the president. Big financial companies, foreign creditors of the U.S., they just want the budget balanced and the dollar to increase in value. They want the job done, they want it done fast, and they don't much care how we do it. And from everything I'm hearing, they are committing major resources to pushing the package through Congress."

"It's the people against the interests! I love it!" Wigierski cackled theatrically.

"Okay, this time we *are* amused," chortled Reggio.

"David Maurice is spearheading the lobbying campaign," Bill informed his colleagues.

Lidell whispered insinuatingly, "Maurice just split from his wife. Maybe we can do something with that?"

Bill shook his head. "I've looked into it. The ex-wife is not talking. Somebody got to her."

Elmer lowered his voice, as if suspicious the room might be bugged. "We'll need every instrument in the arsenal, and if you can deal with Maurice in an unorthodox way, that's fine. But let's be realistic here. Even if we could eliminate Maurice from the equation, they'll find another Maurice. There's no avoiding the central front in this battle. We have to split the business community, find allies against the creditors and the financial interests."

"Let's mix it up!" Wigierski exulted. "For the entrepreneurs against the bondholders! For capitalists against rentiers!"

Lidell tut-tutted. "Tibor, it's 'RON-tee-air,' not 'ren-TEERS.'"

Wigierski pivoted in his chair with a snarl. "So sorry, I didn't do graduate work at Oxford. I don't belong to the Association of Literary Scholars and Critics. My father didn't edit John O'Hara, whoever the fuck he was, and I don't collect autographs from dead authors. I'm just a shoe-leather journalist from Brooklyn College."

Lidell visibly quailed. "Tibor, no disrespect –"

Mihailovich raised his hand. "Enough, you two."

Elmer resumed as if nothing untoward had happened. "We need the *Wall Street Transcript* to speak for America's silenced wealth-creators against the bondholders, just as Tibor said. We need to remind every Member of Congress that there are millions of business owners out there who disagree with the president and David Maurice and the big international banks. And, yes, maybe Maurice can offer them a soft landing if they lose their seats – but our side can help them keep their seats! The Members may figure their voters will forget what they hear on Patriot News. But their donors read the *Transcript* – and if you can persuade the Members that you will be relentless and you will not forget and not forgive…."

"We'll have an editorial every day!" Wigierski was almost hopping in his chair with excitement. "Any Member who gets on the wrong side – we'll hammer and hammer him! And now we've got Walter, so Senator Hazen is dead, dead, dead! Sylvester, maybe you should interview Walter for your next column?"

I had assumed they had forgotten about me. I didn't like this new twist to the conversation. I groped for an excuse. "We may disagree with the senator's stance, but we have to respect his distinguished…"

"Don't be ridiculous!" shouted Wigierski. "Respect nothing! With us or against us! The whole free-enterprise system is at stake! Pulaski will wreck everything, he'll wreck the economy, he'll wreck the Constitutionalist party …"

"The economy was pretty wrecked already," I suggested.

"I've got enough on Hazen," said Reggio. "Seems he got a totally unqualified person a top job at NASA as a purely political favor. He acts so high and mighty, but I'll dirty him up."

My stomach lurched in dread.

"That sounds promising," said Bill.

Reggio grinned nastily. "It's much more than promising. I think we can really do something with this, make a running gag of it. *Snobby Senator Lost in Space.* Or something like that."

The others all laughed again. *That's Sylvester – what a guy!*

Mihailovich added smilingly, pleased at last. "I can always count on you, Sylvester."

"Just doing my job, boss," said Reggio with a nod of the eggplant head.

"You'll make it sting?"

He smiled a self-complacent smile. "I'll make it *burn.*"

"That went well," said Elmer in the taxi uptown. "And now we meet Jasper Philpott and Hugo Velkampt."

"I think I have a good handle on Jasper. Tell me about Hugo."

"I thought you'd know him. He's your kind of people, inherited rich."

"We're not a tribe."

Elmer only blinked at me. Then, as if retrieving a file from some archive, he settled into his seat to tell the story as the taxi shot up the West Side Highway.

"Grandpa Velkampt founded U.S. Greeting Cards back in the 1920s. Had like eight kids. The eight kids had like 50 grandkids. The fortune got kinda chopped up, but still the Velkampts remained pretty rich by the standards of Muncie, Indiana, where most of them lived.

"Hugo was the eldest son of the eldest grandson, so he inherited the CEO job back in the 1980s. Company did fine so long as he was in charge, nothing spectacular, nice steady business

"One of Hugo's younger cousins drops out of college in like 1980. He heads out to San Francisco, smokes a lot of drugs, hangs out with the alternative-rock crowd. He gets to know some of the early Silicon Valley guys. He ends up working for a digital design company. And he becomes convinced: the greeting card industry is doomed."

"Smart guy."

Elmer carried on with his story. "The cousin moves back to Muncie, starts lobbying the cousins that there's going to be this other thing called the Internet, and the family has to get into it. Hugo doesn't believe it, but he's overruled. Pretty soon the nice respectable family fortune has boomed into a big family fortune. Everybody's happy. Except Hugo, of course.

"The family decides to appoint the smart-aleck cousin co-CEO, responsible for the new online greeting division. He and Hugo fight all the time. Everything becomes dysfunctional. So the cousins vote to fire Hugo – and, as a consolation prize, to set up a family charitable foundation for Hugo to run."

Elmer eyed me suggestively. I must have looked to him like exactly the kind of booby who'd end up in charge of a family foundation myself.

"The CEO cousin gets interested in politics. He becomes a big Nationalist donor. That's when I meet Hugo. It's about 1998. He's moved to New York, bought himself a big apartment, got a new wife. He goes to the office every day, gives away a little money to cancer research, art museums, children's aid.

"But he's bored. You can't fill a day at the office by writing a half-dozen checks a year. And his checks aren't big enough to make him a player by New York standards."

We exited the highway in the West Fifties, and the taxi slowed to a crosstown crawl. Elmer checked his watch nervously: a black digital job he'd received as a promotional gift from some long-ago lobbying campaign.

"I showed Hugo that his money could have a much bigger impact in politics than in high-society charity. When the Constitutionalists took back the White House in 2000, Hugo gave $100,000 to the Inaugural Committee. That kind of money wouldn't get you a seat by the kitchen at a New York fundraiser. He's now the go-to man for every Constitutionalist candidate and Constitutionalist cause. Including mine.

"Of course, it's no fun getting rich when the guy you hate most is getting even richer. The CEO cousin bankrolled the Williams effort in the Iowa caucuses in 2008. When Williams won the presidency, he invited the cousin onto his transition team. Only a titular job, but it pushed Hugo into overdrive.

"Which has been great for me. Except that it means we'll face a delicate problem today. Last year, Iggy Hernandez persuaded Hugo that Pulaski was the only candidate who could beat Williams. Hugo poured millions into the Pulaski campaign. So it's not going to be easy to persuade him that he has to reverse course. He won't like it at all. It will take very delicate handling ..."

We crossed Tenth Avenue. "What do you want me to do?" I asked.

"I don't know. Keep your eyes open. Work on Jasper."

"What's Jasper's role in all this?"

"He has Hugo's confidence. Advises all his giving. He can be very helpful to us – or very unhelpful. So be sure to tell him how much you liked his book. And don't stop telling him."

I started to say that obviously Elmer did not understand the character of a scholar like Jasper Philpott. The words were interrupted because the cab came to a definitive stop. We stepped out into 54th Street and walked up the stairs to the Collegiate Club.

CHAPTER 57

I suffered a pang of post-traumatic stress as we walked into the Collegiate Club's baronial lobby. The one and only previous time I'd set foot in the club had been the spring of my senior year at Brown. A friend of my grandparents' had taken me to lunch in the magnificent dining room to discuss my future. The discussion had not gone well. The friend had reported to my grandmother that I was utterly useless and that the only thing to do was pay me a small allowance on condition that I do social work in some remote part of Africa. The club had not changed a micron in the intervening years.

Elmer and I were directed to the main dining room, one storey up: a vast room under an impossibly high wooden ceiling, carved with the coats of arms of the colleges of the Ivy League. Spring sunshine streamed through the tall windows, flecked with little spots of collegiate dust.

Hugo and Jasper were waiting for us at a round corner table, the faces of both men glowing with the sun of some recent tropical vacation.

Hugo was a tall man, red-faced, big-nosed, under a great pile of curly, wooly red hair. It had to be a toupee, I thought. But on second inspection: no, it was real. Poor guy, it must be difficult to be taken seriously with hair like that. He wore expensive clothes badly, a luxurious charcoal suit jacket crumpled over his sunken chest.

Jasper, by contrast, was much more unobtrusively dressed: a professor's blue blazer, white button-down shirt, striped rep tie, reading glasses on a cord around his neck. But the man inside the clothes? Impressive indeed. If Jasper Philpott thrust a hand inside his jacket, puffed out his chest, and threw back his head, he would have looked like the model for one of those deceased marble statesmen in Congress' Statuary Hall. The body had thickened since that long-ago magazine photograph. The tonsure of hair surrounding the huge bald cranium had silvered. The eyes, however, still shone bright, and the matinee-idol chin still thrust forward.

"Hello, Elmer," Hugo Velkampt mumbled red-faced. "This must be, um, um, Walter Schotzke? I, um, saw you on TV last night. Um, good job."

Philpott beamed benignity.

"It's a pleasure to meet you, Walter," Philpott said, clasping my hand. "And not *only* because of Mark Dunn. I see your mother in your face."

I flushed a little. "What an honor to meet you, Dr. Philpott. I just finished *Lives of the Social Scientists*. What a fantastic book! I just wanted to keep reading and reading."

"You liked it? It didn't have the sales of my previous books, but I was always very proud of it."

"Please sit," insisted Velkampt, and we all did. I kept talking.

"I more than *liked* it. I was inspired by it. I'm really excited to read the second volume you talk about at the end, about the social scientists of the 20th century. When do you think you'll finish that?"

Suddenly Philpott seemed much less pleased. "It's mostly complete already – but my duties at the Hugo Verklampt foundation – travel and lectures – you can understand…"

Elmer shot me a warning look.

I corrected my blunder. "Well, the first volume is perfect, exactly the way it is."

The compliment restored Philpott's good humor. "I'm impressed by your new protégé," he announced to Elmer, and Elmer dispensed one of his rare, carefully rationed smiles.

We all picked up the menus laid at our places. Velkampt presented a thick, vinyl-wrapped wine list to Philpott. "Choose something good."

Philpott adjusted reading glasses onto his museum-quality nose. A deferential waiter hovered over his shoulder. "We'll have the 2005 Chambertin."

The waiter's pencil hovered over his pad. "The Chapelle Chambertin?"

"No, no," said Jasper, a patient teacher explaining to a slow student. "The Charmes Chambertin."

The waiter nodded respectfully and vanished.

"Bordeaux for dinner, Burgundy for lunch," Philpott instructed the table. " Especially on a fine day like this."

The wine was produced and poured. Philpott rotated the glass, slowly spinning the red fluid. He sniffed. He sniffed again. He poured the faintest taste into his mouth. He closed his eyes. He contemplated. He judged. At last he sighed contentedly. He nodded acceptance to the waiter.

"Parker describes this Charmes Chambertin as 'sexy and feminine,'" Philpott explained, "but I think that tells us more about what *Parker* was doing after hours than it says about the wine. I'd prefer to describe this wine as elegant, supple – really, everything a Burgundy should be. And of course 2005 was the best year of that decade."

The wine was tasty, I had to agree.

We ordered food. Velkampt and Philpott both chose the steak tartare; Elmer requested a strip steak well done. I chose the same as Philpott. He seemed to know what he was doing.

"How was Fiji?" Elmer asked.

"Amazing!" enthused Philpott. "What a wonderful choice for the maiden voyage of Hugo's new yacht –"

"*Finally*," said Velkampt. "Delivery took forever. I was getting claustrophobia on the old boat."

"Sixty-five meters!" announced Philpott proudly. "I'd never scuba dived before," he continued, making his confession sound more like a boast. "But Hugo found us this amazing instructor…"

"I picked her from a photo! She looked exactly like Yasmin Bleeth in the old *Baywatch*!" Velkampt's already red face flushed even redder in his excitement.

"She certainly liked *you*," Philpott said teasingly.

Velkampt shrugged, a man of the world.

"Another bottle, sir?" the waiter asked, uncertain to whom to direct the question. Philpott looked at Velkampt, who nodded approval. The meal arrived. Yes, I thought, as I bit into the first forkful of succulent meat, Philpott certainly knew what he was doing.

"So how are things in Washington?" Velkampt asked Elmer.

"Very tense."

"Yes, I can imagine. We missed most of the Durango stuff in Fiji. The Internet onboard was very slow. But this Deficit Commission – it seems … well, what do we think?"

Elmer mimed uncertainty, pretended to ponder how much to say. "It's worrying. They're proposing to raise taxes on wealth-creators, savers, and investors. They want to spend the money on a bunch of make-work projects for the unemployed. The fun-employed, I call them. They could find work if they didn't mind getting their hands dirty."

"I call them bums!" said Philpott emphatically.

Velkampt snorted, and Elmer continued. "You know the business world better than I do, but won't a big tax hike on people like you be exactly the worst thing for business confidence?"

Velkampt nodded emphatically yes. Philpott leaned forward confidentially. "Nobody can give you better insight into the mood of the business community than Hugo."

"Where's the president in all this?" demanded Velkampt.

Elmer shook his head sorrowfully. "That's the part of this story hardest to understand. Especially after all that you and Iggy did – how hard you worked."

Glasses were refilled. Hugo and Jasper had already outpaced me by at least two drinks each. I held a lead of a drink and a half over the abstemious Elmer.

Elmer pressed ahead. "But it seems that President Pulaski is pivoting away from the supporters who elected him to reach out to Nationalist elements. It's like he's reconfiguring his own base. But you must know more than I do about this. I'm sure you've been getting updates from West Wing types?"

"I've been away in the South Pacific. I've only been back for eight days," said Velkampt apologetically. Philpott's knife deftly maneuvered the last of his meat onto a piece of grilled wheat toast. His beautiful white teeth finished the little sandwich in two carnivorous bites. He said, "George Pulaski would not be president today without Hugo's support and vision."

Velkampt demurred. "Jasper, really, that's going too far."

Philpott produced a convincing flare of temper. "Hugo, you always do that, and it makes me very angry. You never give yourself credit for the work you do and the sacrifices you make. It's wrong, and I won't tolerate it."

Velkampt placed a placating hand on Jasper's arm.

Elmer pressed ahead. "Have you spoken to Iggy?" he asked Velkampt.

"We've had so much work to catch up on …"

"Well, Iggy feels exactly as I do," said Elmer. "He has to be discreet, but if you call him at home, he'll confirm what's happening." Elmer paused and then sighed theatrically. "I was hoping you had talked to Iggy, because I didn't want to be the one to tell you this. But after all you did for Pulaski, your cousin was invited to lead a delegation of Midwestern businessfolks to the West Wing for a personal briefing by the president."

Velkampt's face went redder than his hair.

Elmer added soothingly, "He was part of a group of 15, so it's not so very much of an honor. But I thought you should know. You're such a strategic thinker – thanks for that wonderful edition of Sun Tzu, I read it over Christmas – that I knew you'd want to hear about the rebalancing of political forces."

"It's a god-damned outrage," Velkampt erupted. Heads rotated all over the dining room, but he did not care. "Rebalancing, my *balls*! We've been sold!" He turned furiously to Philpott. "What do you make of this?"

Philpott twirled his wineglass between two strong fingers, then firmly answered Velkampt in his silky orator's voice. "You put it exactly right. It's an outrage. We've been sold."

"The Velkampt Foundation donated $500,000 to make the family quarters of the White House fully handicapped-accessible," Velkampt fumed. Now they're throwing open the West Wing to all the progressives and radicals we worked so hard to drive out?"

Elmer nodded. "That's right."

Philpott opened his palms on the tabletop in earnest appeal to the judgment of a candid world. "Iggy promised that Hugo would be the first business leader to overnight at the White House. Is *this* what we fought so hard for?"

"I don't care for myself at all – but my wife …" Velkampt did not finish the thought.

Philpott's clear voice rang out so that the next three tables could hear him. "If Pulaski turns his back on the coalition Hugo built for him, he may pass a budget – but he'll be a one-term president."

Velkampt asked Elmer, "So what do we do now?"

Elmer blinked fast. "Basically you have two options. Option one is to wait and see. Maybe Pulaski will change his mind about his new friends. When that happens, you'll be waiting loyally to help him tidy up the wreckage."

"My other option?"

"Show him that you are not a man to be – excuse my French – fucked with. That you supported him for a reason. That you want your principles respected."

Velkampt rotated to Philpott. "What do you think?"

"You are not a man to be fucked with," Philpott intoned gravely.

Velkampt rotated back to Elmer. "I agree with Jasper."

Elmer almost imperceptibly relaxed. "I meet a lot of donors and activists. No disrespect to anybody, but a lot of them are motivated more by access to power and the glamour of office. It's really a privilege to feel that our movement can count on the support of someone who cares about the ideas."

Velkampt seemed to be recovering his temper. "That's what my foundation is all about – ideas!"

"But Hugo," Elmer persisted, "I don't have to tell you, not everybody is like you. The other side will be applying a lot of pressure. And spending a lot of money."

Velkampt listened gravely.

"We don't have to meet them dollar for dollar. But we have to step up our game. I need to ask you to increase your donation to Americans for Entrepreneurship. Another million for this current year."

Velkampt looked to Philpott. "What do you think?"

Philpott tented his fingers together. "I think the future of the whole movement is at stake. And I think Pulaski has disrespected you personally. Imagine inviting your cousin to the White House before you! You were planning on giving $1 million to Constitutionalist candidates and 527s this year. I think you should zero out that whole amount and give it to Elmer instead."

Velkampt drained the last of the wine from his glass. "I think you're right. Let's do it." He pushed away from the table, a man of decision. He noticed Elmer's untouched wine. "Don't leave that for the wine waiter," he joked. He reached for the glass himself and tossed it back in one grand guzzle.

Velkampt stepped uncertainly toward the lobby and elevators. Philpott moved to follow, but Elmer clutched the shoulder of his jacket and pulled the great statesmanlike head toward his lips. "You'll see the check is executed this afternoon?"

Philpott nodded silently.

"Will you please confirm with Walter when the check is sent?" Elmer scribbled my cell number on the back of a piece of paper from the club order pad and thrust it into Philpott's hand.

He nodded again.

We watched as Philpott caught Velkampt at the elevator. They descended together.

I ventured my first comment of the meal. "Jasper seemed very helpful."

I saw again that tiny smile of pure pleasure crease Elmer's lips.

"He ought to be," said Elmer. "He gets 10 percent."

CHAPTER 58

There was still a ways to go before Elmer had completed his appointed rounds. We hailed a taxi on Fifth Avenue and returned to the Times Square Westin. We took an escalator up to the lobby. Elmer looked around, spotted his man and shook hands, and then introduced me. The man evidently did not watch Mark Dunn. Or eat mustard. My name rang no bell with him at all.

Maybe the non-recognition put me in a skeptical mood, because I reacted negatively to the man from the start. I had no real basis for that dislike. Slight build, darkish skin; I'd have guessed he was Latino if Elmer had not introduced him as "Omar." His black hair had just begun to turn gray; his beard was neatly barbered. He wore the kind of clothes you'd expect on your IT guy: jeans, checked button-down shirt, running shoes. A tablet computer under his arm confirmed the techie image.

The three of us huddled over a small table in the churning ferment of the hotel lobby.

"Thanks for coming all this way," said Elmer.

"I'm always glad to have a reason to leave New Jersey." Both men chuckled. Elmer was blinking less than usual. As little as I warmed to Omar, Elmer seemed comfortable with him, almost relaxed. There followed a few minutes of pleasantry about Omar's family, a wife and four daughters out in Middletown, New Jersey. Then, business.

"I need your help," Elmer confided.

Omar waited. I suppose he'd heard these requests before.

"You're following what's happening in Washington." It was a statement, not a question. "The president's plan will run over a lot of people in my coalition. Let's face it: Rich white guys don't command much sympathy on television. So I need your help. We need to show Americans that the plan hits all kinds of people. People of color, immigrants, middle-income people."

Omar nodded. He knew such people.

"The attack on housing capital gains will especially hit people who bought homes in decaying cities and then turned their cities around."

Omar nodded again. Yes, he knew such people as well.

"We have to make these people visible. Get them in the streets. Ensure their voices are heard."

Omar spoke with only the faintest trace of a far-away accent: "Elmer, my friend, I can do all this. But you appreciate, there are always information costs, opportunity costs, overhead costs…"

"I've got a budget for this campaign. What do you need?"

"The question is, what do *you* need?"

"I need protests where they can be seen by TV crews in Ohio, Florida, New Jersey, and Minnesota. Big crowds, lots of women and children, not too white but not too foreign-looking either. Angry. Noisy. Just enough commotion to make news, but nobody getting hurt."

"Starting when?"

"As soon as possible."

"How many media markets?"

"As many as possible."

I could not believe the conversation I was hearing in the middle of a thronged lobby in the middle of New York. Then again, where better to hold a surreptitious conversation? The background roar drowned out the quiet voices of Omar and Elmer, even assuming that anybody had been interested in listening – which in New York, of course, nobody is. Two men standing on a deserted Brooklyn pier at midnight form an interesting sight to anybody who might catch a glimpse of them. Ditto if Elmer and Omar had gone for a walk down a quiet country lane. But here, they were just another human clump impeding the flow of tourists pulling roll-away luggage: not worth a second look, too familiar to eavesdrop upon.

"You said you had a budget. Not a tight budget, I trust?"

"Name the number."

"$75,000 for me, plus expenses. We're looking at maybe $300,000 altogether."

"I'll pay weekly; the money flows as long as I'm happy with the shows."

"Cash?"

"Can't do that, not with a buy this big. But I can wire the money anywhere in the world you want it to go, and to any beneficiary you designate. We'll have to be creative about generating the receipts, that's all."

Omar frowned. He liked cash. Who doesn't?

"Wires can cause trouble. So visible. So easy to misunderstand later."

"If $300,000 in cash exits my accounts, that's visible too, Omar. Raises even more questions. It will have to be this way."

Omar resigned himself. "If it must be, it must be. So – message – people of color against the house tax?"

Elmer nodded. "Yes, that's right. And also some sub-messages: These are people who have never participated in politics before. They are not Constitutionalists, not Nationalists. Just Americans – new Americans, Americans of color – frustrated with both parties. Frustrated with the Washington elites. These are people who are trying to make a better life for their kids. And now they are going to get hammered by a secret tax deal cooked up behind closed doors by the rich and powerful. It's 'we the people' against the big banks."

Omar noted these talking points on his tablet. "OK," he said. "Got it. I'll make sure all our people get the briefing."

"Drill them. No freelance messaging."

"I understand." The two men rose to shake hands.

"Don't do anything I wouldn't do," added Elmer. "And if you do – make sure nobody finds out." Elmer actually laughed. Omar only smiled an irregular yellow-toothed smile. Maybe Mrs. Omar liked that smile. I sure didn't.

On the elevator down to the street, I said, "Elmer, you're the boss – but are you sure you know what you are doing? I get very bad vibes from that guy."

Elmer was blinking again. "I've known him five years. I trust him. Iggy trusts him. Iggy credits Omar with delivering New Jersey for Pulaski."

"You and Iggy trust a guy who doesn't like to issue receipts?"

"He's got different imperatives." We stepped onto the street. "But he delivers. I've been trusting you, too. Are you telling me my judgment is wrong?"

I wanted to say, *Oh yes, Elmer, you are wrong. Oh yes.* But I didn't. Instead, we walked silently to the bell captain's station to claim our bags for the train ride home.

CHAPTER 59

At Elmer's direction, I'd begun making a regular habit of watching ProgTV, taking notes on the coverage.

Some differences jumped out at me. Where were the leggy blondes in miniskirts?

Another difference took time to notice. Patriot News told a strong, clear story. The story might change unexpectedly. The story might depart from reality in all kinds of ways. But the story always cohered. It was as if everyone at Patriot News had absorbed the joke Catesby had told me about how the British cabinet system worked: "It doesn't matter what damn lie we tell, so long as we all tell the same damn lie."

ProgTV lacked the guiding hand of Michael O'Grady. Some of the hosts and guests wanted to applaud and salute Pulaski. Some mistrusted a cunning Constitutionalist ploy. The hosts argued with each other, the guests argued with the hosts, and the audience was left to guess what to think. The Patriot News audience was never left to guess.

I had lots of time to watch the guessing, because my grandmother claimed Valerie's attention for another few days more, leaving me to toil alone as Elmer's henchman.

Elmer occupied offices on K Street, two floors of a skinny, shabby building just east of Connecticut Avenue. The upper floor was mostly given over to a huge conference room where Elmer chaired weekly meetings of activists from across the city. My new office, on the lower level, was a glass-fronted room three times the size of my old closet beside Senator Hazen. The room was placed directly across the corridor from Elmer's own. When Elmer and I happened to talk on the phone at the same time, we seemed almost to be staring into each other's eyes. In between the glass panels, the corridor was hung with old 1980s-vintage election posters, mementoes of Elmer's first political victories.

Elmer's personal office was about twice as large as mine, spare of all decoration except for one item: a disabled AK-47 carried home from some far-flung war zone. The gun was mounted on a big wooden plaque above a brass plate that read, "So many enemies. So few bullets."

Altogether, Elmer's team numbered almost two dozen. The colleague I got to know best was Elmer's in-house economist, Paul Dussman. Paul's name was almost too ridiculously apt, for he did indeed seem always to be covered with dust.

"Do you live in a construction site?" Elmer would regularly ask. Paul would only smile and shrug.Hunched, pale, bald as an egg, and crippled with shyness, Paul could perform calculations in his head that I could not perform on a calculator. He'd worked at the Congressional Budget Office for almost 20 years and knew the tricks of government the way a cop on the beat knows every local troublemaker. I could see that nobody else in the office much liked talking to him, so I made the effort to hang out in his office. It did me good: thanks to Paul, I did finally master the difference between an appropriation and an authorization.

Paul introduced me to the quirks and oddities of Elmer's organization. For example: Elmer had incorporated an auxiliary group, "Europeans for Entrepreneurship," headquartered in Slovenia. As far as I could tell, the only function of Europeans for Entrepreneurship to sponsor a lavish conference once a year at a European grand hotel to which Elmer invited members of Congress and their spouses. (Last year's conference had been at the Hotel Cipriani in Venice. I was sorry to have missed that one.)

These events cost a lot. And on top of the events' heavy actual costs, the European group superimposed a 20 percent management fee, with the result that Europeans for Entrepreneurship had built itself quite a little treasury over the past decade. How much exactly? For that information, you'd have to file a disclosure request with the Slovene government. In Slovenian.

Elmer seemed satisfied with my work. Increasingly often, he answered questions and requests by saying, "Walter will take care of that." One morning he walked into my little office. "I need you to find me a private jet. Lou Rogers has agreed to speak at a Trucker Protest in Anaheim. It's a big win for us. But Lou won't fly commercial."

"Lou Rogers, the man of the people? That Lou Rogers?"

"Lou's earned his success," said Elmer with asperity.

"What about all those out-of-touch elitists he's always attacking? Didn't they earn their success?"

"You don't get it. Lou's audience – the American people – they don't resent money. The people look at guys like Mark Dunn and Lou Rogers and say, 'Someday I'm going to make it big myself, and then I'll buy the big house, the golf vacations, the boat. And, yeah, the private plane too.' So long as a rich guy spends his money the way the people would spend it, they understand it and accept it. You know how a rich guy loses the American people?"

"How?"

"When he buys bullshit modern art. They think he's making fun of them."

"I'll try to remember that."

Trouble was, that with all the money we were paying to Omar, the Americans for Entrepreneurship budget couldn't stretch to the cost of a transcontinental jet charter as well. Elmer gave me a handwritten list of names of supporters who owned or controlled private planes and told me to call them and ask for the loan of a plane for a few days. He added, "Don't email. Call."

That caution triggered a memory, something I'd read in the news columns of the *Wall Street Transcript* a few days back.

"Aren't there legal issues with a guy lending us a corporate jet for non-corporate purposes?"

Elmer frowned, displeased. "We're not doing anything wrong by *asking*. It's up to our supporters to take the appropriate precautions. They're savvy players. Anyway, the law's not like a light switch, on or off. It's more like a dimmer switch. There's more legal. There's less legal. And there's a lot of shade in between."

Operating as he did in those uncertain zones between more legal and less legal, Elmer could never wholly trust anybody.

One day I logged into my personal Gmail account and noticed that a couple of new messages that I had not in fact read had been marked as read. I changed my password just to be on the safe side. Sometimes when I typed on my office computer, the machine would go weirdly slow, as if some secret spyware were straining capacity as I worked.

Meanwhile, David Maurice's money roared like a tsunami through Washington. TV screens were suddenly jammed with advertising from a new group, "Your America, Your Future." The ads showed bulldozers, highways, airports, lunch buckets. In one of the most frequently broadcast commercials, a white man in a military haircut spoke in a Deep South accent: "The Army taught me, if we want to win together, we have to stand together."

Elmer was demanded in more and more places. One day, he flew to Austin to address a breakfast meeting of Constitutionalist state legislators, hoping to mobilize them to pressure the Texas delegation in Congress to oppose the deficit deal. The next day, he spent six hours in his big conference room, hosting a series of delegations from state chambers of commerce.

Yet another day, he walked the corridors of the House, pleading with Members to stand fast.

The busier Elmer got, the more often I was asked to substitute for him at his lesser meetings. Which is how it happened that I found myself one lunch hour waiting in the lobby of the K Street Hilton Hotel to meet two state legislators from Wisconsin.

I spotted the Wisconsin men as soon as they entered the hotel lobby: a pudgy man and an outright fat man, both wearing yellow ties over blue shirts, the official color scheme of the American Midwest. They entered the block-long lobby through a revolving door and immediately paused, disoriented and uncertain. An outbound businessman pulling a wheeled suitcase nearly crashed into them, cursed, and then accelerated past. I approached.

"Senator Hahn? Assemblyman Jorgenson? I'm Walter Schotzke. Elmer's been called out of town; I'm here on Elmer's behalf."

If the ghost of Vince Lombardi had materialized in front of them, the two men could not have greeted me more enthusiastically.

The pudgy one, Hahn, erupted first. "*Walter Schotzke!* I knew it was you! I'm so honored to meet you. I'm a huge Mark Dunn fan. Anybody who has Mark Dunn's approval is a hero to me."

The bulkier Jorgenson got off to a slower start, but if anything he packed even more force into his handshake. "You've got guts," he said to me.

We quickly dispensed with formalities. Assemblyman Jorgenson was Bill. Senator Hahn was Carl.

As we took our seats in the hotel's informal restaurant, Carl said, "I'm only disappointed that I won't have a chance to tell Elmer thank you for all he did for the Wisconsin party in November. I hate to think where we'd be right now if it hadn't been for that final $75,000 he sent us. It's damn near impossible to raise any money from anybody when you're heading to a loss, but that's when last-minute money can make the most difference. Without Elmer, it would not have been a loss, it would have been a wipeout."

"I'll tell him."

"And you tell him," Bill added, "we don't regret a thing; we'd do it exactly the same way all over again. We busted the government unions forever. And we've still got the governor's veto pen even if the Nationalists wanted to restore union power, which they don't."

I jotted a note on my pad. "I'll tell him that too."

Bill continued, "Now I expect you want to know – what's going on with Nyman?"

They expected right. That was exactly what Elmer did want to know.

You'll need some background here to follow the story.

Jim Nyman was chairman of the Budget Committee in the federal House of Representatives – a very important man. Nyman been a key Elmer ally since he entered Congress in 2003. Now, suddenly, Nyman was "too busy" to take Elmer's calls. That boded ill, and Elmer had summoned these local power brokers to explain the lay of the land.

Carl sighed heavily. "It's that damn David Maurice. If there's a point of weakness, he'll find it."

"Where? And don't take anything for granted; I don't know anything about Wisconsin, and I must be able to answer any question Elmer asks me."

"It starts with Senator Howard." Howard was the junior U.S. Senator from Wisconsin, elected only two years before.

"Go on."

Carl went on. "State tax authorities found some irregularities in Howard's taxes. OK, *a lot* of irregularities. Maybe not enough to send Howard to jail, but enough to make his life pretty damn uncomfortable.

"We think David Maurice reached Governor Filkins, and got the governor to propose a deal. Governor Filkins would lean on the tax authorities to negotiate a quiet deal with Howard, on two conditions. Condition one: Howard had to vote for the president's deficit package. Condition two: after he cast his vote, Howard would announce his early retirement on health grounds. Howard did have that heart attack in his first year in the Senate, so the excuse would sound plausible."

"What's this got to do with Nyman?" I wondered aloud.

"Nyman wants to go to the Senate. Always has. And if he votes for the package, Filkins will appoint him to fill the balance of Howard's term. That's four years, and Nyman figures those four years give him enough time to make his peace with the Trucker Protesters and the die-hard Constitutionalists."

"It's a plan," I agreed. "What's Filkins' angle?"

"He's term-limited," said Bill. "He's thinking about his future. We hear David Maurice is arranging corporate directorships for him and fund-raising for an endowed chair at the University of Wisconsin."

"Oh, man, that Maurice is good."

"You don't know the start of it," said Carl. "Word is that Filkins had a nasty gambling problem when he was the Milwaukee county executive. He'd travel down to Biloxi, play the tables, and usually lose. Maurice represented the Mississippi gambling industry, and he persuaded them to suspend collection of Filkins' debts. Notice I said 'suspend.' It would have been an illegal gift to forgive the debt. Of course, once Filkins leaves politics, the casinos can wipe the debt away. If Maurice tells them to, that is."

"Noted, got it."

"So," said Bill, changing the subject. "What's Mark Dunn really like?"

I told them what they wanted to hear.

CHAPTER 60

Dunn opened big that night. I was watching at the office. With Valerie not returning home for two more days, there seemed no point in hurrying back to an empty apartment. Dunn opened his monologue:

"The things that are happening in this country don't make sense, unless you go behind and above the stage to see who is really controlling the show. The people on the stage – the members of Congress, the pundits – they are just the puppets. The person making the show is the puppet-master.

"His name is David Maurice. That's not his real name. He was born David Moritz, on New York's Upper West Side. He started life as a violent radical, with an arrest record to prove it. He still hates this country, hates our values, but now he attacks in a different way. Not with brute force. But with corruption …"

Lou Rogers took up the theme on his radio show at six.

"You've heard of this man David Maurice? Let's call him by his real name, David Moritz. Big lefty. Nearly went to jail as a young man for criminal assault, did you know that? But now he's super-respectable. Gives to all the charities, sits on the board of the Kennedy Center. Oh yes, he's very respectable. He has his name on a brass plaque on his own wine locker at Morton's. I've seen it. I've seen the waiters bowing and scraping and kissing his ass. Bet that doesn't happen to you at the Golden Corral. *If* you can afford to eat out at all in this economy.

"But Moritz can afford whatever he wants. I hear that he's planning to treat himself to a safari in India after he collects his bonus for raising your taxes. I hear he's rented a maharajah's palace – just so he has room to be comfortable. He's got a new fiancée too, going to be his third wife. Heather Needham, maybe you've seen her on Patriot News? Women like that don't come cheap either.

"Who's paying for all this? *You*, you fool. *You*, you pitiful sucker! Unless you speak up! Call your member of Congress, tell them to oppose the Moritz plan – and to stop Moritz's big bonus. Let him screw Heather Needham on his tab, not yours."

Who would have told Lou Rogers about the India trip? I was weighing suspects when Elmer popped his head into my office in the middle of Rogers' tirade.

"I'm glad you are still here. I need a ride."

"Sure. Where to?"

"Out the Dulles Toll Road. I'll direct you."

I took a cab home, picked up the car, and drove back to retrieve Elmer. The evening was suddenly lovely. The earliest of the Washington blossoms were bursting into intense mauve and bright yellow. I pulled up in front of the K Street office at 6:45.

Elmer hopped into the passenger seat and punched an address into my navigation system. The car computer directed me across the river, out I-66, and then to the second exit on the Toll Road, just beyond the Beltway. That exit deposited me into a strange jumble of warehouses, big box stores, and low-rise offices.

I executed a series of turns and roundabouts, to end in a parking lot in front of ... well it was hard to say what it was. The closed corrugated-steel entrances to the eight truck bays suggested a warehouse. The sign over the door – "Indulj" – and the pounding music emanating from inside suggested that the owners had converted their warehouse to a new line of business. Whatever the business was, we were early for it. The parking lot gaped empty, except for a half dozen battered vehicles in the farthest corner.

Elmer swung open the door. The space inside was dark and cavernous, lit by flashing multi-colored laser lights. A huge empty dance floor stretched toward a bar in the furthest corner of the room. The bar's front pulsed with yellow and blue neon. The noise of the music overwhelmed the ear.

Immediately behind the club entrance, a long cashier's desk barred further entry. At this apparently still early hour, the desk was untended.

Three long rows of little round tables and stools topped in red vinyl extended to the back of the club. As they neared the rear wall, the small tables gave way to big tables. Instead of stools, the big tables were wrapped by semi-circular banquettes. The banquettes were upholstered in vinyl too, but white, not red. At one of the banquettes sat a big figure of a man, only his form visible in the intermittent multi-colored beams of light. Elmer strode unhesitatingly toward him.

The man rose as we approached. The music pounded us like an assault. The man was big: as tall as me, maybe 40 pounds heavier – but burly, not fat. His wavy brown hair looked as if it had not been combed in days. His graying beard looked no fresher. He wore a blue blazer over an open-necked purple polo shirt flecked with little spots of grease or spit or maybe beer. His khaki pants were creased and crumpled.

He grabbed Elmer's outstretched hand with his two big paws. Elmer whispered something to him. He nodded, walked toward the bar – and seconds later the sound level dropped to a background beat.

The big man pointed us toward one of the banquettes. "Enjoy it," he shouted at Elmer. He'd gotten used to roaring over the loud music. "When the night gets going, it'll cost you a $300 bottle of vodka to sit here. But for now, it's my treat. What'll you have?"

"A Diet Coke."

"Same for me," I said.

He shook his burly head sadly, then turned his head to shout in the direction of the bar. "Wanda! Two Diet Cokes – and a double vodka tonic." From the red rims around his eyes, it seemed it probably was not his first vodka tonic of the evening. Or not the first something, anyway.

That shout was the first indication that the huge hall held a fourth person. She stepped out a minute later, holding a tray of drinks: a girl with Asian features in a tight white miniskirt, also made of vinyl. She wore matching white stiletto shoes, and a black sleeveless sweater, skin-tight and deep-plunging. The first effect was not too bad. The second look was deeply scary.

Don't get me wrong, I'm all in favor of breast implants. But there's a limit to everything, and this girl had overstepped it.

Having deposited the drinks, Wanda turned to go, but our host clutched her around her slim waist and pulled her tumbling back into his soiled lap. Another arm snaked around Wanda's shoulder, into the plunge of the sweater.

I expected Wanda to express annoyance, but no. She smiled a flirty little smile, made a moue at Elmer, and announced to the world, "Benjy loves my sexy body." It was not a boast, just an informational bulletin. Benjy groped the interior contents for another three or four seconds, then moved his hand beneath her seat and propelled her up and away. She blew him a kiss. "I sex you down later."

She took a step away from the table and fixed a glare upon Elmer: "You pay him good money." It could have been a question, but it sounded more like a command. Benjy sniffled and wiped his nose on the back of his knuckles.

"Benjy," said Elmer, "this is Walter. Walter, this is Benjy." Benjy sniffled again, wiped his nose again. I decided against shaking hands.

Now I recognized him. "Benjy" was Benjy Barstein. Michael O'Grady had dangled the threat of a Barstein exposé

in front of me. Here was the man himself. He looked more pitiful than intimidating.

"I know all about Walter," said Benjy, in not a very friendly
tone of voice. "I started at the *National Investigator*, don't forget. The Schotzkes are always big news. Now he's Mark Dunn's
special pet. I would have thought he was too posh for your
grubby outfit."

"Be good," said Elmer to Benjy. Then to me, in an unusual
tone of near-apology, Elmer added, "Don't get annoyed. That's
just Benjy's way. He's a major talent, but right now things are a
little tough."

Benjy interrupted. "A little tough? Michael fucking O'Grady
just put DCGossip out of business! That was my bread and
butter. I've spent 15 years fighting for Constitutionalism, and
what have I ever got out of it? I started Sludge.com. I started
Dirigible.com. I launched the *Constitutionalist Review* site. I've
made other people rich, but I'm poorer than when I started.
Now O'Grady's cutting the oxygen to the site that was finally
supposed to make me some real money."

"BigCorruption is looking good," Elmer allowed.

"Thanks, but looking good don't pay the bills."

"I've got some information for you that, if promoted right,
will send your traffic jumping. Walter, tell Benjy what you told
me about Senator Howard. But, Benjy, this is on a non-attribu-
tion basis. In fact, you and I have never spoken. This meeting
did not happen. None of us are here tonight."

Benjy nodded hungrily. He pulled a thick little spiral-
topped notepad out of the side pocket of his blazer, along with
a small chewed pencil. Strangely low-tech for a would-be web
mogul. I started telling my story, but it was not easy to do.
Benjy interrupted every couple of minutes, occasionally with
a question, but more often with just a random angry outburst.
He'd sniffle, wipe his nose, his talking would rev, and off he'd

race into a high-speed monologue: "This is so fun, you have no idea how much fun this is!"

When I finally finished, Benjy manically erupted at Elmer, "It's great, it's just what BigCorruption needs, but how can I confirm this? I want it air-tight, I want it perfect."

Elmer blinked. "I've confirmed it for you."

Elmer's words arrested Benjy for a couple of beats. Then he revved back into his manic mode. "OK, OK, if you vouch for it, that's good enough for me."

Benjy turned over his shoulder to shout over the subdued dance music, "Wanda! Another vodka tonic!" He turned to us. "You guys want anything more?" Elmer and I shook our heads. Benjy added confidentially, "I'm going to need another sponsor."

"O'Grady will sponsor this."

"Not now. When he cut off DCGossip, I told him exactly what I thought of him."

Elmer sighed. "Do you have to burn every bridge?"

"The man's a fucking cheapskate!"

"I'll find you another sponsor."

Benjy nodded. "Okay, but I need money fast. Like right-away fast."

"How much?"

"Ten grand, or I go dark."

Elmer answered unhesitatingly. "I'll find it."

"I need something *now*."

Elmer calmly reached into his jacket, pulled out a wallet, and counted out eight $100 bills. "Will this carry you through the next 18 hours?"

Benjy clutched the money. "You're a hero of the movement, Elmer!"

Wanda shimmied over with the drink. She dipped at the knees to place it before Benjy. He placed a proprietary hand on the outward curve of the white vinyl skirt.

"I have to turn up the music now," Wanda said, stepping away from him. "It's almost 8:30; the manager will be arriving any time."

"We've finished," said Elmer, rising to leave. I imitated him.

"Come on, Wanda, let's dance before the paying customers arrive!" shouted Benjy, stumbling after her. She skeetered away from him on her high heels. I couldn't help glancing backward. Wanda reached the sound system. Benjy caught her, embracing her from behind, a meaty hand on each silicone tit, the dirty khakis grinding into the plastic-wrapped buttocks. "Yeah, baby, sex me down!"

The strobe light showed the annoyance on Wanda's face – until one of Benjy's hands reached into his pocket, extracted Elmer's money, and fanned it before Wanda's eyes. Annoyance changed to a sultry smile. She raised two hands above her head, coiled her fingers, and danced backward into him, grinding and kneading with practiced skill. Elmer and I walked out toward the whoosh of the traffic on the Dulles Toll Road just in front and overhead of us.

CHAPTER 61

Valerie gave a smutty laugh over Skype as I described my evening at Club Indulj.

"I sex you down any time, Walter Schotzke!"

"Not recently."

"I'll be back the day after tomorrow. I'll see if I can find a vinyl miniskirt before I catch my train."

"I *did* like the skirt."

"I'm sure. By the way, the medical news is all positive up here."

"Tough old lady."

"Not so tough that she wouldn't appreciate a concerned word from you every once in a while."

"She's got you."

"Well, I am concerned. And one thing I'm concerned to do before I finish is to reconcile you two stubborn Schotzkes."

"I'm not stubborn."

"Stubbornly evasive."

"Don't play word games with me. I always lose."

"OK, well, then I'll tell you a secret before I say goodnight."

Oh, Valerie, I know your secrets. "Yes?"

"Your grandmother's secret. She was so tired when we came home from the eye doctor today. I made her a little soup and toast for supper, and then we got into our pajamas, and I asked her, 'How did you and Grandpa Schotzke stay married for 47 years?'"

"Let me guess. She said, 'Inertia'?"

"No! She said, 'I learned to think like a man – and he learned to think like a woman.'"

"That's helpful."

"No need to be sarcastic. I asked her to explain what she meant. She said, 'I knew perfectly well that my husband's trips to New York weren't always strictly business.'"

It took me a second to understand. Then I got it. But I still couldn't quite believe it. "My grandmother said that? Clara Schotzke? The woman who slices her corn off the cob?"

"Yes. She said, 'I had some health troubles in the middle years of our marriage. If I were too sick to cook, would I expect my husband to go without eating? Or would I send him to a restaurant?'"

"Picking up jaw from table, reinserting in mouth. Wow. Wow again. And she told you all this?"

"She seemed to think I'd find it helpful."

I recognized that remark as a huge potential trap. I side-stepped.

"Um, so what was the 'thinking like a woman' part?"

"She said that your grandfather was a busy man. But he always told her the exact hour when he'd be home. He was always on time. And when he arrived, the first thing he did was to pour a drink, sit beside her, and just *talk* to her. He might have had lunch with the governor of New York or borrowed $10 million from the Chase Manhattan Bank that day. But he always made her feel like she was the most interesting person in the world and that he'd been looking forward all day to speaking with just her."

"I never knew that."

"Obviously."

"Is this a hint?"

"No. It's just interesting to think about. But it would be nice if you put the BlackBerry away before you walked in the front door. Don't get your hopes up, though, I don't share your grandmother's views about 'home cooking.' If I'm sick, you can miss a 'meal' or two. Here's what I will do, though, when I'm home again ..." And she told me, too, down to every last lascivious detail.

CHAPTER 62

Vernon Mallory headlined the next day's morning show on Patriot News.

"General Meyer is an American hero. And if he says that our army's disloyalty problem starts at the top – well, that's an allegation that anybody serious about the truth has to take ..." Mallory searched for the right word, didn't find it "... seriously," he concluded wanly.

Endorsing the flaky Meyer allegations seemed a risky move for Vernon Mallory. But what could he do? The Deficit Commission had banished his story to second place. If he wanted to recover top spot, he had to escalate the accusations.

When I arrived at the office an hour later, Elmer frantically waved to me through the two walls of glass. I stepped across the corridor into his office. He was talking into a headset. As I entered he said, "I want Walter to hear this. I'm putting you on speaker."

"Hello, Walter." Mac Kohlberg was speaking, his voice more diminished even than the last time I had seen him.

"Hey, Dr. Kohlberg."

"I was telling Elmer, we've got a real emergency situation on our hands with one of CI's long-time supporters, Yamaha Bank. They give typically $500,000 a year. Last night, the head of Yamaha's Washington office called to say that Yamaha's contributions to CI would be halted unless we supported the Deficit Commission plan."

I was genuinely shocked. "Your donor thinks he can dictate CI policy?"

Elmer was shocked in a different way. "$500,000 is not even 1% of your budget."

"A half million is a lot more money than it used to be, Elmer. And it's not only Yamaha Bank. We're hearing that David Maurice is leaning on other corporate donors as well. Munsinger is flipping out."

"Where is Munsinger now?"

"Pacing up and down his office, calling everyone in the CI universe to ask what he should do."

"Leadership!" Elmer spat the word in sarcastic disgust. "Don't let Munsinger leave the building. I'll be there in 20 minutes."

Elmer passed the ride furiously typing on his BlackBerry. I stared out the window. The white blooms of the cherry blossoms lit up the gloom of a gray mid-March day.

Mac Kohlberg met us in the lobby, our security badges already printed. Five minutes later, we stood at the door of Munsinger's office. We heard an agitated telephone conversation from within. Kohlberg rapped on the door, then pushed it opened. Munsinger motioned for us to go away. Elmer walked into the office anyway.

Munsinger fired an astonished look at Elmer. He covered the mouthpiece and said sternly, "I'm on an important call."

Elmer blinked at him. They stared at each other for a beat or two, then Munsinger spoke again into the phone. "A delegation has just come to my office – I'll have to continue this later." He hung up.

"What the hell do you think you are doing?" demanded Munsinger fiercely.

"What the hell do you think *you* are doing?" answered Elmer, raising his voice for the first time since I'd known him. "You're jeopardizing the entire movement, throwing away everything you've worked to build. All because somebody who gives you a fraction of a point of your income has wagged a finger at you? If you can't tell an over-demanding donor to screw off, you have no business running an institution like CI."

You might expect that Munsinger would have Elmer thrown out of his office for daring to speak to him like that. You'd expect wrong.

The eyes in the pudgy face turned uncertain behind the big aviator glasses. "I'm getting pressure from other banks too," Munsinger pleaded, the defiance ebbing from his voice. "And all my defense contractors."

"You're getting pressure from David Maurice," Elmer retorted. "*One guy.*"

"That *one guy* has got the entire financial industry behind him!"

"Big deal. There are other industries."

"Easy for you to say," Munsinger mumbled.

"It's easy for me to say because it's true."

"Elmer, I'm under pressure here!"

"Oh yeah? Let me show you what pressure really looks like. Take a look at your email."

Puzzlement flickered across Munsinger's face.

"Go ahead, look."

Munsinger turned in his big leather executive chair, rotating to face the monitor that gleamed bright white atop a mahogany hutch to one side of his big pseudo-colonial desk. Elmer stepped around the desk to stand behind Munsinger's chair. As Munsinger opened his email program, puzzlement gave way to amazement. I stepped around to see what he and Elmer were seeing.

Munsinger's email inbox held 817 new messages. No, wait: 856. No, wait: 1,321. New messages crashed down upon the old, like little space invaders landing in the antique video game.

Outraged and frightened, Munsinger demanded, "What's going on?"

"Take a look at Dirigible.com."

Munsinger hit a key – and confronted a huge, unflattering image of his round face. "CI SELLS OUT?" screamed a big headline.

"Of course, things won't really get busy," said Elmer, "until the afternoon, when talk radio revs up. Then there's Mark Dunn at five, Lou Rogers at six, the Patriot News line-up in primetime. Any of your small donors watch Patriot News? And don't you raise three times as much from small individual donors as from your corporate guys?"

Munsinger turned a beseeching look up toward Elmer's face. "Surely this ought to be the kind of issue that Constitutionalists can disagree over in good faith?" His voice warbled a note or two higher, changing his weak assertion into a pleading question. "Personally, I'm totally with you. Mac Kohlberg too. But institutionally, CI should have room for all Constitutionalist points of view–"

Elmer brutally interrupted. "No. It's make or break. Life and death. In or out. This is the red line. Are you with us or against us?"

Munsinger seemed to be crumpling in front of me, as if the fat that made up half his body weight was being melted by the heat. "Our top budget guy, Kevin McManus, leans more to the president's side, and I have to respect that. The Yamaha people think very highly of McManus. He spoke at their investors' conference last year. He testified yesterday at the House Budget Committee that the plan has a lot of positive elements."

"Fire him."

"*What?!*" Munsinger looked stunned, then frightened. "I can't fire McManus! He was director of the Congressional Budget Office. He won the Tullock Award!"

"Then it will send an even clearer message. Fire him."

"He's been with us for 13 years. He has a family."

"Fire him."

Munsinger sank back into his big chair. He gazed up at Elmer with basset-hound eyes. "Be reasonable. Give me some room here."

"Have you ever considered that for some people, the purpose of ther life is to serve as a negative role model for others? Let that be McManus – not you."

Munsinger's legs splayed. His belly bulged over his lap, pushing his blue tie forward in a big arch. How old was he, anyway? 63? 67? 71? He looked lot older now than before Elmer had entered the room. He tried one last defense. "Don't you worry about making a martyr of McManus?"

"He'll be a martyr for 48 hours. He'll be an example for a long, long time. I'll take the trade."

Munsinger sighed his surrender. "You win. We do it your way."

That tight little smile of pleasure reappeared. "Our way, Gordon. The Constitutionalist way."

CHAPTER 63

"So I bet you think I'm a pretty hard guy," Elmer said as we exited the CI building.

I didn't answer.

"You think I victimized some poor SOB just trying to do the right thing?"

Not a word from me.

"Look," Elmer continued, an unusual defensiveness in his voice. "We have no choice. We have to be as tough as the people we're up against. This is a 15-round prizefight. You can't just show up in round 12 and blame me because there's a lot of blood on the floor."

I stepped into the street to hail a cab.

"You spend a lot of time with Paul," Elmer said. I was surprised he had noticed. "Has he ever told you the story of how he ended up working for me? Brilliant guy like that, you'd think he'd have a hundred better-paying offers, right?"

That caught my attention.

"Well, now that you mention it - no, he never did."

A cab halted, and we climbed in.

"Let me tell you. Paul's parents were immigrants from Eastern Europe. His dad made fur coats for a living. There were five brothers and sisters all crammed into a tiny wood-frame house in some crummy neighborhood of Chicago. Paul was the smart one, the hope of the family, the only one to go to college. He got himself a degree in math, then a Ph.D. in economics.

"He did well, too. He wrote his dissertation on some topic in monetary policy. I won't pretend to understand it. The point was that wage and price controls were absolutely the wrong way to stop inflation. So who do you think they invited to quiz Paul at his thesis defense? Henry Laird!"

I stared blankly at Elmer.

"Don't tell me you've never heard of Henry Laird?"

"Sorry."

"Maybe it's just as well. Shows how his reputation has faded. He died about ten years ago, but he used to be a huge deal, the country's most famous Nationalist economist. He advocated tight government control over the economy, including wage and price controls.

"He was quite the celebrity, too. He was always jetting around, being photographed with presidents and prime ministers. He dated Ava Gardner back in the 1960s. His books were huge bestsellers. He guested on the *Tonight Show*. He was supposed to be a great wit, if you think it's funny to ridicule businessmen as ignorant bumpkins.

"Anyway, Laird took Dussman's thesis very personally. You know how nervous Paul gets when there's any pressure on him? Laird carved him up in front of the thesis committee. But that wasn't the worst. Laird brought with him his latest girlfriend, some sexy young number in a minidress. Paul had probably never been with a woman in his life at that point, and certainly not a woman like this. He was so distracted, he couldn't focus on Laird's questions. So finally Laird picked up the jug of ice-water on the conference table – and poured it in Paul's lap! He said, 'You see, Mr. Dussman, it takes more than monetary policy to cool overheating.'

"The whole room burst into laughter. The incident became a famous joke. You can still see the line on Laird's Wikipedia page, although they don't mention Paul's name.

"Paul was totally humiliated. It's like his life took some horrible wrong turn from then on. He got the Ph.D., but he never got the big university offer. He eventually found a civil service job. He was marking time in the Congressional Budget Office when I hired him."

The cab pulled up in front of our office.

"That's a terrible story," I said as I paid the fare and collected a receipt.

"It's a totally typical story!" Elmer answered, his face mottling in anger. He planted his feet on the K Street sidewalk, not taking another step until he'd ventilated everything he had to say to me.

"You have no idea what it used to be like for us. No idea! They controlled *everything*. They controlled the media and the universities. They decided that Henry Laird was a genius and that Paul Dussman was a loser. They decided who was ridiculous and who was witty, who was cool and who was pathetic. They picked the guests for TV and the photos for the covers of magazines. Henry Laird got a full-page obituary in the *New York Herald*. Our guys were buried in unmarked graves. Until Patriot News came along, they even decided who should be our leaders – who was acceptable and who was too quote-unquote extreme. All we're doing now is what they used to do. You think their guys don't get fired if they stray from the party line? Except they call it 'insensitive' or 'sexist' or 'racist.' It amounts to the same thing."

I could not hold back. "Yeah, but do they have enforcers firing people just for *thinking*?"

"Yes!" Elmer shot back. "*They've* been doing it so long they don't even realize they're doing it. That's the real difference between us and them. They don't have to think about what they do. They're the dominant culture. All the forces of gravity pull their way."

"Today, you pulled very hard the other way."

"I have to! Every organization that isn't totally and completely Constitutionalist will sooner or later become Nationalist. The struggle between us and them is not even or fair, it's not *close* to even or fair!

"When one of ours tells a dirty joke to an intern, we get gavel-to-gavel coverage of the hearings on sexual harassment. And when one of theirs has a boyfriend who runs a male prostitution ring out of his townhouse? No biggie.

"When one of ours carries a holstered sidearm to a political rally – carrying his permit, everything completely legal – my God, you'd think we were plotting to overthrow the government. And when a hundred of theirs violently attack the cops? Oh, we all have to understand their frustrations, their student loans are too expensive for them!"

Passers-by were staring by now, but Elmer did not notice – or maybe he did not care.

"I'm not saying it's fair …"

"No, you're saying I've offended your gentlemanly sensibilities." He ventured his own version of the hoity-toity accent that Mark Dunn had mocked so much better.

"'Play up and play the game!' See, I had an education, too. Only it's *not* a game. It's war, with live ammo and dead bodies. You're willing to quit your job in a senator's office to make a statement. Good for you. Well done. Applause. But nobody wins by resigning. You win by *fighting* – and yeah, by punishing those who break ranks in the face of the enemy.

"You better realize now: If you're going to be any use to this movement, you have be as tough as the other side. Tougher. Because there really are only two choices. We win and they lose – or else, they win and we lose."

"There's a third possibility."

"What?" he demanded aggressively.

"We all lose."

He stared non-comprehendingly at me for one beat, two beats, three beats. Then suddenly he laughed. And laughed and laughed. What was he laughing at? I have no idea. For once, I intended no joke.

CHAPTER 64

Thank God for the recession. If the apartment next door had been leased, the occupants would likely have called the police when they heard Valerie's scream.

The scream ebbed into ohs and ahs, and then murmurs, and then, "You'd better let me up. These kitchen tiles are awfully cold." Valerie sat up, tossed back her hair, buttoned her blouse, and adjusted the vinyl skirt. Less than 20 minutes had elapsed since Valerie had opened the door after returning from her stay with my grandmother.

I rose to my feet and pulled up my pants, still breathing hard. "That was incredible!"

"Sorry, they only had the skirt in black."

"Black is better."

She vanished into the bathroom. When she emerged, I said, "Come sit." I pulled her into my lap in one of the living-room armchairs. "Tell me everything you did in New York."

We talked for an hour, drank wine, and then made love again – on a bed this time. Valerie cooked us omelets for a late supper. We finished the wine sitting in bed, still talking.

About 11 o'clock, I said, "I don't think I can stay awake much longer." She kissed my naked chest. "Go to sleep. That was the nicest evening in a long time." I had finally learned something from my grandmother.

The following morning, I was already showered and dressed when Valerie emerged from the bedroom in silk pajamas. I frothed a caffe latte for her, then sat down with her at our kitchen counter.

"Breakfast with Walter? I like this new job better already."

"I don't," I said flatly.

"Why not?"

"I'm on the wrong side."

Valerie stirred yogurt into muesli. She set the bowls on the kitchen counter. I made a face: I hate muesli. She tapped the back of my hand with a spoon. I swallowed a big bite.

"So who is on the right side?" she challenged me. "This president who's bribing half of Washington to ram through his big idea?"

"Hazen doesn't approve of the bribing, you know that. He disapproves of the whole scheme. He's a good man in a tragic situation."

Valerie raised her eyebrows to make a big *Can you believe this idiot?* expression. "I love Senator Hazen almost as much as you do. OK, not that much, but really quite a lot. Still – you think your hero got himself elected three times to the Senate by not knowing the score? Remember, this is the guy who broke David Maurice's kneecaps until he paid off his wife and got himself engaged to his bimbo."

"That deal may be coming unraveled. I think Melanie blabbed." I told Valerie what Lou Rogers had said.

She shook her head. "Melanie would never even have heard of such a creature as Lou Rogers. If she were leaking, she'd call the gossip magazines. He's got another source." Her eyes lit up as her brain electrons flared. "Of course. It's Daphne. It has to be."

The moment she said it, I realized she was right.

"I have to warn Hazen!"

"Nope. Too late. You switched sides. Hazen has to solve his problems without you."

"Don't be mad at him. He took care of your friend too, don't forget that."

"I agree. He brokered what was needed to keep Melanie quiet. I never denied he was a shrewd negotiator. So everybody's happy, except maybe those of us who can imagine being the discarded woman ourselves."

"It's a tough game, and Hazen didn't write the rules."

"Well, who asked him to play the game at all?" She stirred the remainder of her muesli with angry little jerks.

"He likes to quote a saying that if good men are indifferent to public affairs, we'll be ruled by evil men."

Valerie instantly fired back, "Maybe the evil men started as good men who asked that same question?"

"That's too tricky for me."

"Never mind. Just quit moaning about your new job, that's all I ask. Is it any more difficult to carry Elmer Larsen's raincoat than Senator Hazen's?"

No need to carry a raincoat on this beautiful late-March day. I walked all the way to Elmer's office to enjoy the air. The cherry trees were fully blooming now, the thick white blossoms clumping like popcorn from the tree branches. I found Elmer in a euphoric mood, flashing his tight smile at everyone in the office.

"Enjoying the cherry blossoms?" I asked, just for fun.

He blinked at me. "Are they out?"

"Never mind. What's up?"

He waved me over to his desk and proudly showed me what was on his computer. A headline covered the screen: "SENATOR HOWARD'S DIRTY DEAL."

I checked the URL: Benjy Barstein's BigCorruption site.

Below the headline there followed a detailed explanation of the Filkins-Howard deal. Curiously, though, the story made no mention of the Nyman angle. I asked Elmer about the omission.

"I'm hoping Nyman will get the message if we make an example of Howard. Nyman's important and influential. We want to lure him back to the good side of the Force. Howard is just a big zero of a businessman from Wisconsin. He's dispensable."

Alongside the story was a video box featuring Senator Howard's face with a microphone shoved in front of him. The trademark Barstein ambush interview. Elmer pressed start – and wow.

Night scene. Clatter, noise. A door to a local restaurant – couldn't catch the sign, looks suburban, not one of the big downtown joints – swings open. Out steps Howard. His face is flushed. He's obviously had a few drinks.

Behind him, customers mill about, all trying to exit at once. Following close behind the senator is a big-busted woman in a tight dress. Wanda.

As soon as she sees the camera, Wanda emits a theatrical little scream. Then she darts back inside the restaurant, pulling the door hard after her. Howard is left alone to face the interview, unprepared and half-drunk.

"Senator Howard?" It's Benjy, suddenly stepping aggressively into the picture, shoving a microphone into Howard's face.

The camera closes in upon the two men.

In the video, Benjy is wearing the same clothes I'd seen him wearing at Club Indulj. (They had got no cleaner in the interval.) Five inches taller than the senator and a lot heavier, Benjy looks like a man who could be very dangerous. Howard looks like what he is: a 62-year-old accountant whose prudent investments had earned him the second-biggest fortune in Appleton, Wisconsin.

"I am Senator Howard."

"I'm Benjy Barstein, with BigCorruption.com. I want to ask you a few questions about your deal with Govenor Filkins. I have information that you agreed to quit your office early if the governor stopped the investigation into allegations that you cheated on your taxes."

Howard staggers, as if slapped in the face. "I … I … I don't know what you're talking about, whoever the hell you are. I've always paid all my taxes. I'm not quitting office. And you have some nerve ambushing me here as I'm leaving a private dinner!"

A leer plays about Benjy's features. "Yeah, very private. But we had no choice, your office would not return our calls."

Behind the closed door of the restaurant the throng seethes, as if something were blocking the exit.

"Senator, can you confirm to us that you did not receive a notice from the Wisconsin Department of Revenue dated November 19 pertaining to possible deficiencies in the property tax dues on lands you hold near Lake Geneva?"

Howard has regained most of his composure by now. "Any revenue notices I received would have been promptly resolved. We pay all the taxes that are due, although" – stagey laugh – "as a Constitutionalist, of course, I think those taxes should be lower." He looks over his shoulder, apparently searching for someone.

Benjy moves even closer, thrusts the microphone almost into Howard's upper lip.

"But isn't it true that you promised Governor Filkins that you will vote to raise taxes as part of the budget deal – and then step down?"

"That's outrageous! And that's the end of this interview!" The senator side-steps Benjy. Benjy side-steps too and moves closer into the senator's space.

Suddenly Benjy is shouting. "I pay your salary!" He raises his big hand, and slams the restaurant's glass door with the butt of his fist. "Answer the god-damn question!" *CRACK!* The glass shatters. Blood flows from Benjy's hand. He does not seem to notice. "Answer the god-damn question!" Benjy shouts again. The senator flees.

At that moment, the restaurant door is flung open and the crowd spills onto the pavement, Wanda pushed to one side. CUT.

"Great video," Elmer chuckled. "I guess I'll be paying for a broken door." He looked up at me from his big Aeron chair, the tight smile of pleasure on his lips.

I couldn't believe what I was hearing. "Elmer, that was a total setup!"

"That's certainly what the senator will say. I wonder if anybody will believe him. Politicians don't have much credibility these days."

"You had the facts on your side with the tax story. Why add bogus details?"

"Tax stories are so complicated. Also boring. A little spicy sauce helps to hold people's attention."

I lost my temper. I couldn't help it. It was stupid, but I did. "That's unethical! It's … *lying!*"

The tight smile vanished. Elmer looked – how did he look? Angry? No. Hurt. He blinked reproachfully at me.

"Is it ethical to trade votes for immunity from prosecution, or for promotion to higher office? Is it ethical to twist this nation's institutions to advance a narrow agenda? What about piling taxes on our wealth-creators while hammering ordinary homeowners? Is *that* ethical? Let me read you something that's guided my life."

He lifted his BlackBerry, touched a button on his phone, and pulled up some kind of text that he'd bookmarked there. His voice suddenly acquired a solemn tone:

"'If a man chooses to live, a rational ethics will tell him what principles of action are required to implement his choice. If he does not choose to live, nature will take its course.' That's Ayn Rand," he added reverently.

"I'm not sure I understand that, but it sounds sort of amoral. Ethics are what get us what we want? Aren't ethics sometimes supposed to tell us 'no?'"

"I wish Pulaski's ethics told him 'no.'"

Elmer was right about at least Benjy's video. It went viral. Senator Howard retired at the end of his first term.

CHAPTER 65

Bad enough that I'd had to beg a plane for Lou Rogers' ride to California. Elmer now ordered me to take care of Rogers' trip to the plane the next day.

I booked the car service to collect Rogers at his house deep in the Virginia countryside. I called his assistant to coordinate the details, and she asked, "Who will be meeting Mr. Rogers when he arrives at the airport?"

I gave her the names and mobile phone numbers of the California-end organizers.

"I have that information already. I mean, who will be meeting him at the outbound terminal? If there's a problem with the flight, Mr. Rogers won't want to have to deal with it himself. We'll require a representative from your office to be onsite."

"I guess that would be me."

So it was. The next morning I drove the long route from downtown to the private aviation terminal at Dulles Airport, arriving 45 minutes before the scheduled arrival of Rogers' car, two hours before the jet's window for wheels up.

The private aviation terminal had a pleasant golf-clubby feel: a lot of corporate types serving themselves sodas from the bar, chatting in little groups in the comfortable sofas and armchairs. I presented myself at a long concierge table. Yes, our plane was fueled and ready to go. They'd signal me when it was time to walk onto the tarmac. Luggage could be placed right over there. That was all for passenger formalities. Otherwise, no baggage screen, no metal detectors, no pat-downs. If you traveled this way at all often, the airline experiences of the rest of America must seem like some remote bad dream.

I helped myself to a soda from the snack bar and settled in to read the news on my tablet. Minutes passed. Suddenly, a piercing dog howl grabbed my attention: *arrrrr-ROOOO!!* The sound emerged from the gullet of an old, slow-moving beagle. A long leather leash tethered the dog to a pudgy man wearing jeans, windbreaker, and baseball cap: Lou Rogers. Behind Rogers followed a limo driver, carrying a duffel bag stamped with two golf sticks and the legend "Royal Siam Golf Club."

The terminal's concierge rushed toward Rogers.

"Sir, I beg your pardon, but dogs must be kept in crates until they board their flights."

Rogers fixed the concierge with a look of instant, boiling rage. "Who the fuck are you?"

"I'm the deputy manager of guest services – "

The poor man never finished the sentence. Rogers gripped a mobile phone and shoved it in the man's face. "In like five seconds, that's going to be who you *used* to be. I'm Lou Rogers. As in, *The Lou Rogers Show*. This is Baxter. Where I go, Baxter goes. You wanna cage Baxter, you'll be shoving me into the same cage. And I wouldn't advise that, you understand me?"

The concierge nervously yielded. "Maybe we could make an exception this one time."

"Good thinking."

I interposed. "Hey, Mr. Rogers, I'm Walter." He did not react. "We sat together at the Lamont Forrest dinner?"

"I remember. You were working for that dope Hazen."

"I work for Americans for Entrepreneurship now."

"That's a start." He stared toward the big glass picture window. "Which is my plane?"

I indicated an aircraft parked between two much larger jets. He took five short-legged steps toward the window and frowned.

"What kind of plane is that?"

"A Citation."

"Obviously. What kind of Citation?"

Uh oh. "I don't have the model number. But it meets all your requirements: it can fly cross-continent without refueling, it has sufficient headroom so that you can stand upright..."

"Are you an idiot? No way can I stand upright in that plane."

"I checked it thoroughly. You're five feet, seven inches tall. That plane has five feet, nine inches of clearance. You should be fine."

"You *are* an idiot. Planes are cylinders. If it's five-nine at the center point, it's going to be a lot less on either side. Plus I'm five-eight – who told you otherwise?"

Rogers' own secretary, actually, but I thought it wiser not to mention it.

"I'm really sorry for any inconvenience, Mr. Rogers. Our whole team went all-out to get you the very best plane we could. We called every one of our friends and supporters. We looked at commercial charters too, but then there would have been issues with Baxter's travel. I know it's not a perfect solution. But Elmer always talks about how generous and supportive you are. Might I ask you just to be a little flexible this one time for a good cause? I've stocked the plane with everything you asked: I got you the two meatball subs from Agnelli's, with fried onions and hot peppers and a side of potato salad; a dozen Diet Cokes; all the movies you listed; and the treats for Baxter. You've got a Cadillac Escalade waiting for you on the other end. I found an Agnelli's franchise in Orange County, so we can stock the subs for the return flight too. Please, I hope this will be OK."

The appeasement mollified him, at least a little.

"Agnelli's has an Orange County location?"

"It's new."

"Well, that's something. All right. We all have to make sacrifices for the cause."

"Exactly," I said. "Can I walk you out to the tarmac now? Let's get you settled as comfortably as possible."

"Mmmph," he said cryptically – but he and Baxter followed without further complaint.

CHAPTER 66

Back downtown after putting Lou Rogers aboard his plane, I waited for my lunch guests: three bloggers whom Elmer wished to cultivate, but did not have time to meet himself.

The most important of the three was Juanita Bimpan, whose site drew a million visitors a month. Juanita regularly appeared on Patriot News, and no wonder. Even by the exacting standards of Michael O'Grady she was dead sexy. Her website featured a gallery of enticing photographs. In one, Juanita mimicked the famous over-the-shoulder Betty Grable pose from the 1940s - except that instead of a swimsuit, Juanita wore a National Rifle Association t-shirt over short-shorts.

But don't be deceived. Beneath the luscious packaging boiled the temper of a serial killer.

That very day, Juanita's wrath had been provoked by a Nationalist blogger who had made reference to her looks in a column attacking her. She wrote in reply:

"If you are a Constitutionalist and a minority or woman (or like me all three), you will be ceaselessly subjected to rhetorical projectile vomit. We say U-S-A, they reduce us to T-and-A. Where are the feminists when these leering goons demean and objectify us? Hypocrites!"

I noticed that she'd uploaded some new photos to her blog, including one in which she wore a cheerleader outfit blazoned with the American flag, one bare leg fetchingly lifted toward her tight, tight sweater.

The second guest was a much more mild-mannered character. Luke Clark was a few years older than me, a clean-cut and well-dressed contributor to a start-up Constitutionalist site. When I surveyed Luke's posts in advance of the lunch, I was mystified by Elmer's interest in him. I asked: "Why are you courting Luke Clark? He says exactly what everybody else says. Why bother with him?"

"Luke's important *because* he says what everybody else says. You know how frozen food companies test all their new entrees in Columbus, Ohio, because it's the most typical town in America? Luke Clark is the most typical Constitutionalist in Washington."

I frowned. "Elmer, it sounds like you are saying that the thing you like about this guy is his total mediocrity?"

Elmer heard the barb in my tone, but again he answered completely seriously. "It's taken a lot of hard work by a lot of smart people to package Constitutionalism so that it can be understood by Luke Clark."

The third guest ran an investment site, Cross-of-Gold.com. His blog fused intense Christianity with sledgehammer insistence that every American problem could be fixed if only the United States would revert to gold and silver as its sole money. Godfrey Breckenridge was the name of this blogger, and I was frankly curious to meet him. I'd never read one human being predict so many different disasters.

"Terrorism is one of the most significant threats to our way of life," Breckenridge had written just the day before. "But we need to prepare also for killer pandemics, an electro-magnetic pulse attack, martial law, race riots, and the collapse of our crippled financial system. If those disasters occur, things happen, you'll see rioting, looting, and shooting. Those who look to government to protect them will be very bitterly disappointed. You can rely only on your faith, your guns, and your gold."

By violating the speed limit, I managed to arrive from Dulles barely ten minutes before the scheduled start of the lunch. I had time to settle into my booth and review the menu. Then, one by one, the maitre d' showed them back to me: Juanita in some kind of eyeball-arresting scoop necked lycra number; the well-barbered Luke; and Godfrey last of all – an older gentleman who looked exactly like somebody you might see dozing in one of the big chairs in the New York Yacht Club, in just the same green-and-red striped rep tie. It was hard to identify the prophet of doom at Cross-of-Gold.com with this decayed remnant of WASP gentility.

"We'll have to make this fast," snapped Juanita, "I have a 3:20 hit at Patriot News."

Luke nodded. "I have to record my weekly comment for Channel 57 this afternoon myself."

"I'll get to the point. Elmer asked me to convey how much he appreciates your dedication and commitment. The fight's really going to warm up in the next days. So Elmer wanted me to ask: what can we do to be maximally helpful to you?"

"Warm up?" Juanita laughed. "It's already steaming hot. That was incredible video that Benjy got. You'd think a rich guy like Senator Howard could hire himself a higher class of hooker." She flipped her own hair with the full disdain of the naturally beautiful woman for the plasticated replica.

Luke solemnly affirmed Juanita's point. "We're definitely at the boiling point."

The waiter appeared, took orders efficiently, then vanished. Washington restaurant owners long ago discovered that Powertown lunchers will not tolerate lengthy waiter recitations about the curry with mango coulis.

I said, "Elmer wants maximum pressure on Congressman Nyman. If Nyman breaks, the president's position in the House collapses."

"It's not enough to fight the president's tax plan. We have to reconfigure the whole monetary system," asserted Godfrey. "We have to return to Constitutional money."

"Constitutional money?"

"Gold and silver are the only money mentioned in the Constitution."

"Isn't that like saying the Army and Navy are the only Constitutional armed forces, because the Air Force isn't mentioned in the Constitution?" (My studies at CI had availed me something after all!)

"They're the only money that can protect us from hyper-inflation."

"I don't want to get off topic here, but aren't we in the middle of a depression?"

"The depression is the preliminary to hyper-inflation. You'll see. And don't say I didn't warn you. Your paper symbols of wealth will become worthless. A dollar should be as real and unvarying as a kilogram or a meter. Anything else is an attack on property rights, on our Constitution, and on God's law."

"What's God got to do with it?"

"Gold and silver are the only money mentioned in the Bible."

Luke came to my rescue. "I did a blogpost on Nyman last week. A friend of mine emailed me that it was the best thing I'd ever written. Would you make sure that Elmer sees it?"

"For sure."

Luke nodded. "Of course a thorough reading of my work would paint a clearer picture of my political philosophy. But I suppose that's a challenge every writer faces."

Juanita flashed Luke an impatient look. "Yeah, right. Look, Nyman is powerful. His seat is safe. If we're going to reach him, we need to find another way."

"He's a politician," I said. "They can all be reached."

"They can all be reached by the paper-money industry," Godfrey said sorrowfully.

"How were you planning to reach Nyman?" Juanita demanded.

"He wants to be a senator. His seat may be safe, but his nomination to state-wide office can be contested."

Food was deposited before us. Luke poured about a fifth of a bottle of ketchup onto his plate, dunking his cheeseburger into the puddle before every big carnivorous bite. Godfrey suffered from some stomach condition that limited his diet to soup, which he ate with an elegance that confirmed he'd known better days. As for Juanita, she clearly shared my grandmother's food ideas. It required a visible struggle of will for her to swallow each of the individual peas that accompanied her small slice of poached salmon.

Juanita again brought us back to business. "So if Senator Howard is forced to resign, Elmer gains leverage over Nyman?"

I nodded. "With a few intervening details, yes that's right."

Her eyes gleamed. "So Howard is the first target? And his whore?"

"Go get 'em."

Godfrey shook his head. "You're mistaking the symptoms for the disease. Until we end the Federal Reserve and coin our money out of metal as the Founders intended, nothing you do is any use."

Ninety minutes later, I tuned into Patriot News at Juanita's scheduled hit-time. Juanita was not just targeting Howard and his "whore" – she was firebombing them. She would repeat every hour on the hour into prime time.

As for Luke, he did his job too, posting an article that evening: "Time for Congressman Nyman to Rejoin the Movement."

Godfrey signed me up for his distribution list. I was soon receiving dozens of items of spam a day from antique-gold vendors, survival-kit makers, and weirdo candidates for office.

CHAPTER 67

Lunch ended, I walked across the street to the office, up the elevator and found all of Elmer's staff standing silent in the conference room watching TV. I heard snatches of the broadcast as I entered the suite, more and more as I approached nearer and nearer the conference room.

"Release of the American prisoners …"

" … recuperating at an army medical center …"

" … no statement for now on allegations of collaboration with insurgent forces …"

" … president will address the nation tonight at 9 o'clock …"

The first step in the president's big war-ending scheme was being put in place. Score one for Team Pulaski. A few moments later, Elmer arrived. Staff stepped apart to open for him a view of the television set.

"What's the word, people?"

We watched TV for another ten minutes or so, but there was not much more news than the snatches I had overheard between the front door and the conference room. The prisoners had been released to US Army representatives, except for Sergeant Montoya and two others who had elected to remain with the insurgents, the apparent final proof of their treason.

Elmer frowned in concentrated thought. "That complicates things," he said at last. Then: "Walter, you know Vernon Mallory, right?"

"I've met him."

"Set up a meeting. As soon as possible."

"I'm not sure he's your kind of guy."

"The revolution takes all kinds of guys. It needs its Trotsky as well as its Lenin."

"Was Trotsky a charlatan?"

"Depends who you ask."

I poked my head into Elmer's office half an hour later. "I just had the craziest conversation."

A quizzical blink from Elmer.

"Mallory won't speak on the phone: 'security concerns.' So I spoke to someone who called himself 'chief of staff to Vernon Mallory.' They have agreed to a meeting, but they won't discuss time or location over the phone. He wants me to stand in front of our building. Sometime in the next half hour, somebody will approach me and hand me an envelope with meeting instructions. It's like they are living in some kind of spy movie."

"They may have their reasons."

"Or they may be just crazy."

"Yes, that's possible too."

I waited on K Street in front of our building. At the appointed time, a strange little person walked toward me. Before I could greet him, he put a finger to his lips. He walked past me, look back, and motioned with a crook of his neck that I was to follow.

Why not? The magnolias were blooming, it seemed a perfect afternoon for a stroll. He led me into McPherson Square, where he sat on a park bench. I sat beside him.

"Are you Quintus Kim?"

He did not answer. Instead, he reached into the right outer pocket of his suit jacket, produced an envelope, and shoved it into the left outer pocket of my suit jacket. He never once looked at me, just stared straight ahead and spoke as if addressing the pigeons.

"Do not discuss any of the details inside by any electronic means," he said.

I moved to open the envelope, but he stopped me. "Not here. After you have read it, please destroy the message. Shred, then burn."

"Whatever you say."

Back at my desk, I read the message, handwritten on a piece of cardstock. *Tonight, 2300 hours. Echo Park Exxon station. Look for a black Infiniti G Sedan with California plates.*

I showed the paper to Elmer. "I'll need a ride," he said.

Then I told him about Quintus' request about the paper. "We don't even have a shredder!" I said.

"I do," he answered. There it was behind his desk. He fed the paper into the device, collected the remains, carried them to the office kitchen, placed them upon a piece of aluminum foil, and lit a match.

"Where shall I collect you?" I still did not know where Elmer lived.

"Meet me here at 9 PM. We'll watch the president's speech first."

"OK. You don't think this is all too crazy?"

"Maybe. Or maybe just crazy enough."

CHAPTER 68

I arrived at the office few minutes before nine. Valerie had fed me a light supper, no alcohol, to ready me for the night's skullduggery.

Elmer and I watched the president's speech in the conference room. The president said that the released prisoners were heroes, and the American people were heroes too. He promised that the fight inside Mexico would end soon. A "new strategy" would secure the border and leave Mexicans to find their own future for themselves.

As soon as the president finished, that hour's Patriot News anchor announced an "exclusive interview" with Vernon Mallory. I glanced at my watch. The man sure made use of every available minute: TV interview on Capitol Hill at 9:20; clandestine meeting in the Maryland suburbs at 11 PM.

On TV tonight, Mallory wore a look of special concentration and determination as he appeared on the screen – and also a very funky new pair of black rectangular glasses. He spoke suavely, deftly.

"The president is not solving the problem. He's just moving it closer to home. The army is a microcosm of our society. We're a 70-30 nation: 70 percent of us are proud to be Americans. 30 percent owe allegiance elsewhere. That's how the army got infiltrated in the first place. Ending the war won't end the infiltration. We need a cultural revolution in this country that recommits all of us to the founding principles now upheld only by 70 percent of us."

Elmer switched off the TV as soon as Mallory's segment ended.

"Cultural revolution?" I asked.

He looked up and pursed his lips, as if weighing the words in his mouth. "Catchy phrase," he finally said.

Elmer and I reached the Glen Echo gas station with 15 minutes to spare. I filled the tank to occupy the time. At 10:55 a black Infiniti pulled into the lot. It parked in an unlit corner, far from the pumps. I started the Land Rover and rolled alongside. Mallory stepped out of his car and walked toward my driver's-side door. I said with some surprise, "You want to sit here?"

"Thanks," he said perfunctorily, as if nothing could be more a matter of routine than displacing me from the wheel of my own car.

I stepped out of the car to make room. Mallory climbed into my seat and shook Elmer's hand. Before I could close the door upon him, he turned to me and said, "I'm parched. Buy me a Diet Coke." He asked Elmer: "You want one?" Elmer nodded yes. Mallory extracted a $10 bill from his wallet and handed it to me. "Get us a couple of Cokes."

I guess it went with the henchman job.

Soft insect sounds and the pungent smell of new-laid mulch filled the quiet early springtime air. Through the glass of the garage's front window, I could see a clerk hunched over a thick book. He did not look up as I entered. I opened the refrigerator door, and took two Diet Cokes from the refrigerator. Only as I extended the money toward the cash register did the clerk lift his head and ... what do you know, it was Jeff Gillespie.

I'd met Jeff Gillespie in freshman year, when he beat me for the last spot on the Brown varsity tennis team. The coach had filled most of the roster with talent-spotted recruit, but he'd left one place for a walk-on. Twenty freshmen tried, and the coach had winnowed us in a series of sudden-death matches. I had faced Jeff in my very first match, and he'd blown me off the court 6-1.

I'd stalked off, furious with myself. But nobody could stay mad at Jeff for long, he was so good-natured. Besides, as he always said, "Be grateful I beat you. Would you have liked to spend four years as the worst player on the worst tennis team in the Ivy League?"

We had hung out together, become pretty good friends – but lost track after graduation. Now here he was.

"Jeff?"

"Walter!" he answered cheerfully, as if it were the most natural thing in the world for him to be sitting in this weird place wearing a striped Exxon uniform shirt.

"What the hell are you doing here?"

"I'm the night manager. It pays the bills while I finish my MBA. You heard I got married?"

"No, the last thing I heard was that you had scored a big job at that private equity firm in Los Angeles, what was it?"

"Merton Associates."

"Right!"

"That's where I met Madeleine."

Another man might have been embarrassed that his Brown degree had deposited him here. Not Jeff.

"Congratulations! But how …"

"We got back from the honeymoon three days before Merton went bust."

"That sucks."

"Yeah. We'd spent all our savings on the wedding and honeymoon. What can I say? We made the decision before the crash. *Derb.* So we pretty much had to start over. Madeleine found a teaching job at National Cathedral School, I got into the George Washington U. business school. We get by."

"Gee, Jeff, you make it sound almost easy."

"It's not easy. But it's not like we're the first people in history to have a tough time. You know what I bought Madeleine for an anniversary present this year?"

"What?"

"A bag of peanuts."

"Did she hit you?"

"No, it's part of a story my grandmother told me. Back in the depression, the Great Depression that is, a young guy was starting out. He had no money, so on his first wedding anniversary, he bought his wife a paper bag full of peanuts from a street vendor. He brought them home and said, 'I wish they were emeralds.' Years pass. They go through life together. They have a family. They get rich. On their fiftieth anniversary, the guy brings home to their mansion a paper bag. It's full of emeralds. He says, 'I wish they were peanuts.'"

Jeff sat smiling on his manager's stool, relishing his story.

"Very sweet. But kind of hokey."

"What's wrong with hokey? Anyway the point is, we'll be fine. We'll make it work. Do I wish I were still pulling 130k at Merton? Sure. But I'm not complaining. And I'm not quitting. I'll be richer than you before I'm through."

He said that with such a nice smile, it took the sting right off.

"But, hey, what about you? I heard Mark Dunn talk about you. Very impressive!"

"You saw it?"

"I usually watch the news in the morning, but somebody posted a clip to our class listserv."

"What did you think?"

"I'm proud of you, man, for standing up for Constitutionalist principle."

"Since when did you become a Constitutionalist?"

"When I lost my job. I finally had time to pay attention to politics."

"I thought people who lost their jobs usually went in the other direction?"

"You mean, looking for a handout? Not me."

"No, no, I wasn't suggesting anything like that. Maybe I'm just cynical because I spend a lot of time with politicians. You see a lot of bad stuff, you know."

"I'm sure. I bet it's just as true on the other side. But you can't let yourself think that way. Principles don't become less true because some bad people believe them. They don't become more true if some good people believe them. Good people can be wrong. Bad people can be right. You want me to ring up those Cokes for you?"

"You're a wonderful guy, Jeff," I said. "Can we have a drink sometime?"

"That would be great." He wrote his email address on an invoice sheet. "You can find me on Facebook too."

He glanced out into the dark lot. "What's going on out there?"

"Just a confidential late-night meeting."

"Oh, yeah. We get a lot of that. Somebody published a spy novel a couple of years ago where the characters meet at this gas station. Ever since, we get all these spook wannabes meeting here in the middle of the night. The joke is: They could not pick a worse place. Security cameras take a picture of the license plate of every car that enters the lot, whether it pulls up to a pump or not. The real spies never come here, they meet in the coffee shop of the Key Bridge Marriott."

"How do you know that?"

"The new FBI director is a regular customer. We got to chatting."

I gathered my change and the Diet Cokes. "I mean it about the drink."

"I'll look forward to it."

I carried the Cokes back to the Land Rover. I passed them through the passenger door to Elmer. Mallory fixed me a disapproving look.

"That took a long time," he said irritably.

Screw him. "The attendant thought he recognized you."

Panic creased Mallory's face. I enjoyed his distress for a moment and then made up a little story to torture him some more. "It took me a few minutes to persuade him that he was mistaken – that you were not the Patriot News guy, just a Bethesda businessman, slipping away from the wife and kids to have a quiet moment with your lover here."

I jerked my thumb at Elmer. Mallory enjoyed the joke just as little as I had hoped. Elmer blinked uncomprehendingly.

"I assured him that I was the driver, and that you'd keep everything in the car strictly PG-rated. The attendant will keep quiet. He is really a romantic at heart, especially after I slipped him $100."

"You shouldn't have done that," Mallory said anxiously.

"Don't worry," I said, deliberately missing the point. "I'll expense it."

On the return drive I asked Elmer, "So did Lenin and Trotsky come to an understanding?"

"Oh, yes," said Elmer. "Very much yes."

CHAPTER 69

And now it was full spring. The last of the sequence of blossoms opened and fell: dogwood and apple.

The nights grew long and bright and lovely. Which was convenient, since David Maurice's lobbying campaign was flooding his separated wife's firm with party business and Valerie was coming home late most evenings.

Valerie was directing seven, eight, nine events a week: receptions, lunches, dinners. Valerie alerted me to extra-lavish parties that I might gatecrash. "DeutscheBank USA is laying on a seafood buffet: grilled shrimp, crabcakes, sushi. You won't want to miss that!"

And at every event, Maurice or one of his underlings distributed campaign checks.

"Isn't that a little gross?" I asked Valerie, watching David do his business at a tasting of vintage Cabernet Sauvignons co-sponsored by a gigantic hedge fund and the Abu Dhabi sovereign wealth fund. "Why not just put the check in the mail?"

"David likes the old-fashioned method. He feels it's more personal." She gave a cynical shrug. After watching David Maurice pay off his soon-to-be-ex-wife with catering contracts, she was hardly going to be shocked at the way he wooed his lobbying targets.

Elmer's work intensified too. I'd thought the president's big speech on the POWs was fine, but it hadn't moved the polls at all. The deficit package was losing support with every passing week, drifting down from over 60 percent to barely 40 percent.

As the plan's approval faded, Elmer's strength gathered. He had meetings on the Hill all day long, every day, late into the night. Elmer did not carry envelopes. He carried threats.

The anti-administration protests were becoming bigger, angrier, and more frequent. The line between the anti-Mexican trucker events and the protests against the proposed house tax blurred. General Meyer spoke at anti-tax events; Omar's militant homeowners denounced Pulaski's Mexico deal.

Incited by Patriot News, by the talk-radio shows, and by blogs like BigCorruption and JuanitaBimpan.com, the crowds grew and grew. The crowds got rowdier too. Some of the protesters arrived with sidearms holstered to their legs and semi-automatics slung over their shoulders. The weapons were legal, but that didn't make them any less unnerving.

The Nationalist House Minority Leader, Kenya Washington, complained to reporters about a supposedly "thickening atmosphere of hate." On Patriot TV that night, Juanita Bimpan was asked about Kenya Washington's comment. Her brightly glossed lips curled in rage: "It's the Trucker Protest that is the victim of hate!"

Confrontation and shoving erupted more and more regularly at the anti-administration rallies. A camera phone operated by one of Omar's operatives captured one awful encounter:

A disabled white trucker, sporting an American flag from the back of his motorized scooter, was approached by a large black woman wearing a "Pulaski for President" sweatshirt. Angry words were exchanged. A cluster of people in Pulaski sweatshirts reinforced the black woman. Somehow the disabled white trucker was knocked from his scooter. The black woman put her foot on his head.

Within 12 hours, that two-minute clip had gained two million views. I showed it to Elmer on my phone. He studied it with his now-familiar tight smile of satisfaction. "Nice work," he said. The man, Frank Hastings, immediately became a Patriot News celebrity. Nobody ever did manage to identify or locate the black woman.

Juanita seethed on Patriot News again later that evening, her push-up bra quivering in indignation under her camisole. "This sell-out administration and its Nationalist allies are using goons and thugs to crush peaceful dissent."

In the thick of the fight, I texted Charlie Feltrini.

"R we still friends? Lunch?"

He answered: "Friends always. Tuesday. BLT Steak. You pay."

At lunch, Charlie ordered like a man who was expecting cornflakes for dinner: first oysters, then the New York strip.

"What's the news from Mexico?"

Charlie frowned.

"I appreciate the steak, but on what basis are we talking? Will you be sharing this with Elmer and" – his mouth looked like it had suddenly tasted something bad – "Vernon Mallory?"

"Not if you tell me not to."

His mouth looked like it was weighing that too. I hummed a bar of the Wellfleet Academy fight song. He laughed and hummed too. "For the school?"

"For the school."

"Even though it nearly expelled us?"

"*Because* it nearly expelled us!"

"Hell, let's have a bottle of wine and really talk. And then … I'll phone the office, tell them I'm sick, and get home for once in time to put the baby to bed."

I ordered a favorite California Cabernet.

Charlie raised his eyebrows, pleased and impressed. "Did you cash a dividend check today?"

As the wine filled our glasses, Charlie expanded. "Here's what's we know about the Durango incident, and I doubt we'll ever know much more than we know now. Bottom line: there's no there, there. Yes, Montoya was disloyal. He comes from a drug-dealing family. He was taking money from the insurgents, yes, but not for information. He was simply a crook. He was a supply sergeant, and he'd been selling the insurgents rations and gasoline out of army stores."

Charlie paused to slurp an oyster.

"But Montoya did not tip off the insurgents to the column's movement. He had no advance access to the column's planned route. He couldn't share what he didn't know. Once the column rolled, he had no way of communicating with the insurgents. We've investigated this exhaustively. The column was in motion for 14 hours through terrain with no cell coverage. Every second of use by every satellite phone in the column is accounted for. The National Security Agency has checked every single communication, voice or data, sent within 100 miles of Montoya's various locations for every second since the column got its orders to move. They've found nothing, zilch, nada."

"Maybe he spoke in person?" I countered. "Some kind of courier?"

The second and third oysters chased their colleague.

"Are you joking? An insurgent courier approaching an armored column? Impossible. He'd have been halted, captured, or killed as soon as they captured his body heat on their sensors. No, we can be definitive about this: the ambush was just good surveillance work on the insurgents' part, plus they got lucky. It happens. There was no big conspiracy, no network of informants inside our army."

"Montoya *did* shoot Mali?"

"Oh, yeah. Definitely. Mali had disciplined Montoya. Ironically, not for anything to do with Montoya's contact with the insurgents. Back at base, Montoya had been operating another illegal racket, selling bootleg liquor to enlisted personnel. Mali had caught him. As far as Mali knew it was a first offense, so instead of handing him over for prosecution, he fined Montoya and confined him to quarters. Montoya took advantage of the firefight for a sneak's revenge."

"But what about the other two soldiers who stayed with the insurgents along with Montoya? Wasn't that a sign that the whole unit was compromised?"

"This has been investigated exhaustively too. They're just ordinary deserters. We've been fighting in Mexico for ten years now. The quality of our forces is not what it was."

"So Vernon Mallory is talking bullshit?"

Charlie took a long, meditative sip of wine.

"I'd like to say yes. He exaggerates, distorts, enflames opinion – all in all, he's a nasty piece of work. But I can't say he's *wholly* wrong, much as I'd like to. We've got 30-plus million people of Mexican origin in this country. It stands to reason we're going to have some mixed loyalties. And in the army too – how could we not? Frankly, it's amazing that the problem isn't a lot worse."

The waiter cleared away Charlie's oyster shells, and the steak arrived.

"If the administration had spoken as frankly as you're speaking," I said as Charlie applied his knife and fork, "wouldn't it have more credibility now?"

"I don't know." He put a slice of steak in his mouth and chewed with pleasure. "Maybe, but probably not. You always hear these people calling for an 'honest discussion' about this or that: race, ethnicity, religion, whatever. I don't know that big, sprawling, diverse countries can afford frank discussions. Maybe we need to be the Euphemistic States of America. 'Diversity is our strength.' It had better be, or else we are well and truly fucked."

"So let me turn it around," I said. "Maybe Vernon Mallory is doing a public service by forcing us to think about things we don't want to think about. The climate-change people had to exaggerate too, before anybody believed them."

"No!" Charlie clattered his knife and fork into his plate. "No. We don't lie our way to truth, sorry. We've got a limited and fixable problem. Mallory wants to provoke a national crisis, and all so that he can terrorize dim-witted rich people into opening their wallets for him. I can almost respect Elmer. He's a fanatic. An unscrupulous fanatic, sure. But at least he's acting on the basis of some kind of principle. What's Mallory's excuse?"

He paused, as if he'd realized that maybe he'd said too much. "So – how's Valerie liking D.C.?" We caught up on personal stuff until Charlie finished the last of his steak. Then he poured himself a last glass of wine and asked, "You heard that Daphne has quit Hazen's office?"

"No, I hadn't! Does she have a new gig?"

"Nothing definite. It's tough for her: the anti-administration types don't trust her because of the Hazen connection, and the pro-administration types don't trust her because … they don't trust her."

"Who does trust her?"

"Who trusts Daphne? Let me see … Alzheimer's patients. Nursery-school pupils. People who've previously bought the Brooklyn Bridge. Unfortunately for Daphne, ultra-gullible people tend not to have attractive jobs to dispense."

"I suppose they wouldn't. So she's completely out of work?"

"No, she's got a six-month contract at the Constitutionalist Institute to write some research papers on the reform of the Senate rules."

"Daphne? Write? Words? Like – one after another?"

"Yeah, it does seem improbable. I suppose she's circulating her résumé to the lobby firms. It'll be tough for her, though, falling between two stools the way she does. She should have done what you did: split with Hazen for the ultra-Constitutionalists."

"I'll tell you that story someday, not now."

"I'd like to hear it!"

I called for the check. "It's good to see you, Charlie."

"It's good to see you too. Hey, you remember your Latin?"

"A little."

"*Forsan et haec olim meminisse juvabit?*"

"'Perhaps someday it will be pleasant to remember even these things.' God, I can't believe you got away with stamping that on the cover of the yearbook!"

"The faculty adviser was just so impressed by any Latin at all. Anyway, take it as your Washington motto. Engrave it under the Schotzke coat of arms."

"In mustard yellow."

"That's the spirit."

Nobody was targeted for anger more than my old boss, Senator Hazen. Sylvester Reggio excoriated him the *Wall Street Transcript* every day, repeating the NASA story over and over, occasionally with some new scrap of real or invented information, more often with new sarcasms.

Before the Deficit Commission fight, Hazen could have walked through any airport in America (other than Providence, *maybe*) without attracting more than a couple of hellos. Now thanks to Patriot News, Hazen had suddenly achieved the profile of a Hollywood celebrity in a shoplifting scandal.

Somebody figured out his movements, and a cluster of protesters now waited for him every morning on the Pennsylvania Avenue sidewalk. They carried signs: "Hazen Hazard." "Pulaski Pimp." "Sellout."

At first, the anti-Hazen protesters were not very numerous. Nor did they seem very dangerous. They yelled a few epithets at him as he trundled on his now-solitary walk. The first couple of days, he waved at the protesters. Then he ignored them.

Some anonymous cameraman recorded these encounters. Juanita hosted them on her site, under the header: "the Hazen

Hunt." The crowds outside Hazen's apartment grew in size and noise.

On the last Monday in April, Chairman Nyman's car exploded.

Nobody was hurt, thank goodness. The car was parked in the garage of the Nyman family home in Janesville, Wisconsin. The bomb detonated at 4:30 AM. It contained too small a charge to do damage to the family sleeping in the house 35 feet away.

Weeks later, the police investigators would determine that the bomb had been intentionally set for an hour when the car was unlikely to be used. That information did not much reassure anyone though. Whoever made the bomb knew enough about explosives to avoid harm to people – which meant that the bomb-maker knew enough to harm people if he wanted to.

Yet Nyman expressed resolve. "It takes more than a little firecracker to intimidate me." That very same day, he moved the deficit-reduction legislation out of his committee into the full House.

CHAPTER 70

Of course, we did not know any of these police details at the time. As of 7:30 AM the following morning, the explosion was an unexplained event. Which did not in any way impede the rush of punditry to explain it.

As I ate my Valerie-mandated muesli, I watched on our little kitchen TV a Patriot News interview of Juanita Bimpan.

"We're watching a media lynch mob at work. They want to hang the Trucker Protest for every crime. But I keep remembering Frank Hastings, the disabled Trucker shoved from his scooter by an anti-Trucker thug. You want to talk violence? You should read my email: hateful, hateful, graphic racist and misogynistic threats of rape, perverted, disgusting acts I cannot even mention on air."

Juanita was wearing some brown, glossy lip stuff. It suited her.

Valerie looked up from punching messages into her Black-Berry as Juanita began to speak. She watched to the end of the outburst, then asked, "Do you find her attractive?"

"I know I'm supposed to, but I don't."

Valerie looked more surprised than pleased.

I stirred the muesli. Maybe I could get lunch someplace good.

"Juanita and these other Patriot News and talk-radio people – they are so enraged all the time," Valerie wondered aloud. "I don't understand it. Look at that woman. She's beautiful. She's on TV. She dresses like they are paying her something. Yet she just seems to hate the whole world. Is it all an act?"

I shook my head.

"I've met Juanita. It's not an act. Maybe she heightens the performance for TV, but it comes from somewhere authentic inside her. Elmer might send somebody to the dungeon for an ideological crime. Juanita would do the torturing."

That caught Valerie's attention. She put aside her Black-Berry.

"And I don't mean that in a sexy way," I added.

"You sound angry yourself."

"Not angry. Just fed up. I've been trying to tell you for days – weeks. I'm *done*. I'm finished. I don't belong with these people any longer, I don't belong here any longer."

"So you're quitting?"

"No, I'm not quitting. Anyway, I can't. My grandmother and all. But it's disgusting. I just wish somebody would fix this rotten system."

"Somebody? *Who*?"

"I don't know."

"How about you?"

"*Me*? Are you crazy? I can't fix a tire. I just want to put in my time, inherit my money, and then keep a low profile somewhere warm and tropical. I liked South Africa. Or maybe Costa Rica?"

Valerie looked displeased.

"You'd enjoy Costa Rica! Beautiful beaches, rain forest, coral reefs …" I ended the thought with another mouthful of the distasteful muesli.

"If you're seriously planning to retire to some tropical villa as soon as you inherit, you'll be going without me."

"I thought you said you were a Walterist? What Walter wants is to get the hell out of this rotten town. You don't like Costa Rica? Fine. How about Rome? You did say you'd like to live in Rome."

"I want to live *here*. And I want you to make *here* better. I want *us* to make here better. I *am* a Walterist. That means I believe in what Walter can do. What we can do together. I'm not a quitter, and I won't let you be one either."

There was nothing to say to that except, "You want another coffee?"

Valerie shook her head and resumed her BlackBerrying.

CHAPTER 71

The Nyman bombing left everybody aghast, but nobody more than Elmer. The office was pulsing with the news when I arrived a little before nine o'clock on the day of the explosion. I stuck my head inside Elmer's personal office to wave hello. He was standing, pacing, a headset clamped to both ears, a delicate microphone snaking toward his mouth. Preoccupied with his conversation, he ignored my wave. I could hear only Elmer's side of the conversation.

"Omar, what the hell were you thinking?"

LONG PAUSE.

"Don't tell me that. I expect you to control everybody in your organization."

SHORT PAUSE.

"Bullshit. Of course it's your organization!"

VERY SHORT PAUSE.

"Why are you feeding me this crap, Omar? Nyman's wife and kids could have been hurt. Now there's a police investigation for you to deal with."

BARELY A PAUSE.

"Yes – *you*. Not 'us.' You. I hired you for community outreach. I have an eyewitness to our meeting, remember. He'll attest that I specifically cautioned you against any kind of illegality."

SHORT PAUSE.

"Let's hope it blows over. But Omar: no more of this. NO MORE. I want visuals, not casualties. You got that? You absolutely clear about that? By the way, has your sister resolved that immigration problem of hers? No? Too bad. I might be able to help. Or not. After this is all over. If we win. If you stay out of trouble. And if you understand that any trouble you have is *your* trouble, not my trouble."

PAUSE.

"Good. Just so that we're clear about that. Good."

CHAPTER 72

"Hey, Montoya, we're going to string you up, you traitor! And then we're coming after everyone who protects you, no matter how high up. I don't care if they're at the Pentagon. I don't care if they're in the Senate. I don't care if they're wheeling themselves around 1600 Pennyslvania Avenue. Traitors hang." – *Lou Rogers Show*, April 15.

AL MEYER'S UNANSWERED QUESTIONS – Editorial, *The Wall Street Transcript*, April 15.

"The early leaders of our country honored and cherished the military that had won the Revolution. Yet they also insisted on the principle of civilian rule. They feared that a 'military chieftain' unfitted by training or temperament for executive office could subvert our freedoms and overthrow our institutions, the way Napoleon had done in France after the French Revolution." – Professor Harold Kenyon, *Constitutionalist Review Online*, April 16.

"A study by the Constitutionalist Institute projects that the president's deficit-reduction proposals would push the unemployment rate above 11%." – Editorial, *The Wall Street Transcript*, April 16.

"The administration's plan would take from those who ride the bus to give to those who ride the hammock." – Sen. Dick Joliette, addressing a Trucker Protest rally, San Bernardino, California, April 16.

"Phil Hazen's friends compare him to Daniel Webster. Of course, Daniel Webster was on the take, too." – Sylvester Reggio, "We Are Not Amused," April 16.

"We face today a pervasive problem of disloyalty in our military graver than anything this country has known since the spring of 1861." – Vernon Mallory, interviewed on Patriot News evening program, April 16.

HOW HILLARY ANDERSON SLEPT HER WAY TO THE U.S. SENATE – BigCorruption.com, April 17.

Is the Deficit Reduction Commission constitutional? - Constitutionalist Institute invitation, April 17.

"I have never feared for my country as I do today. But I know that the patriotic officers of our armed forces would never obey an anti-constitutional order from this lawless president." – Mark Dunn, April 17.

"What David Maurice is doing in the halls of Congress is the most flagrant, grossest corruption in all my years covering Washington. It's like something you'd see in Latin America or Africa." – Bill Mihailovich on the Patriot News evening panel, April 17.

"PRESIDENT GEORGE MONTOYA" – Editorial headline, *The Wall Street Transcript*, April 18.

"66% of Constitutionalists disapprove of president's deficit plan." – Headline, Dirigible.com, April 18.

"Hey Hazen, you jerk, you raise my taxes, you better take away my gun first!" – Lou Rogers, April 18.

"A nine-year-old boy was injured today after an unknown man opened fire with a semi-automatic weapon at a Mexican refugee camp just outside of El Paso. Police are searching for a male suspect in his early forties." – Channel 57 Morning News, Washington DC, April 19.

"Those who would blame this tragic incident on the Trucker Protests commit a blood libel against this country's most patriotic citizens." – Press statement by former governor Esther Minden, April 19.

"You accuse us? We accuse you! You're the thugs! You're the wreckers of the Constitution! You're the assassins!" – Lou Rogers, April 19.

"The apprehended shooting suspect has no prior history of political involvement, but was said by police to have stored a large cache of recordings of Lou Rogers on his home computer." – Channel 57 Evening News, April 19.

"Ramdam Sessnip has inked a $600,000 deal with Patriot Press for a new book to be titled *Treason on the Border*." – SitRep.com, April 19.

"I would not be surprised if David Maurice had planned the attack in order to discredit the Trucker Protests." – Juanita Bimpan, Patriot News Sunday, April 22.

"This president is tearing the country apart." – Mark Dunn, April 23.

CHAPTER 73

I don't know what a tenterhook is, but whatever it is, Elmer was on it.

The before the El Paso shooting was Tax Day, always a black-letter day on the calendar of Americans for Entrepreneurship. Yet for once, Elmer had virtually no activities on his calendar. After wrapping up a couple of radio interviews in the morning, he spent the rest of the afternoon fretting and pacing. Waiting for something.

And then, at about three in the afternoon, it happened.

Elmer poked his head into my office. "Whatever else you do today, be here at 4:30 this afternoon. I'm going to need you."

"OK, Elmer."

"For serious. Don't even hit the john."

"*Oh-kay!*"

At 4:30 exactly, Elmer again poked in his head. "We're confirmed. Are you ready to leave?" He was too nervous even to blink.

"For God's sake, what's going on?"

"We have a five o'clock appointment."

"Where?"

"Across the street. The Carlton House hotel."

"We don't need half an hour's lead time for that!"

"You don't know who we're meeting."

"So tell me."

"Felix Horvath."

Felix Horvath? Yes, I could definitely understand why Elmer was jumpy.

The Carlton House is a handsome old pile, redecorated just before the financial crisis on a lavish scale. Elmer, Paul Dussman, and I checked in with the front desk, then rode the elevator to the top floor. Directly opposite the elevators gleamed a double set of doors. We knocked. The doors were opened by a startlingly handsome, dark-haired man about my own age, wearing a superbly tailored suit and a $200 haircut.

"Good afternoon. I'm Meldwin FitzHugh, Mr. Horvath's personal aide."

I'm a pretty robustly heterosexual guy, but Meldwin's beauty made its impression even on me. It was like standing beside a hugely valuable porcelain vase. You worried that it might topple over and smash.

Springtime sun streamed through the tall windows directly opposite the door. Meldwin led us into a large, handsome living room through a foyer wallpapered with scenes of ancient China. Two yellow couches faced each other in front of a white fireplace. Elmer and Paul seated themselves on one. I took the other.

"Would you care for anything to drink?" Meldwin asked. "Espresso? Sparkling water?" We all requested sparkling water. Meldwin vanished into a kitchen somewhere in the suite to pour. He returned with a tray laden with hotel glassware, a crystal bowl filled with cracked ice, sliced lemons and limes, and three individual bottles of some bespoke water. It was not so long since I'd had the same job, although the suit, shirt, tie, and shoes Meldwin was wearing would have cost almost two months of my old Senate office salary, after tax.

As I waited for my drink, I reviewed Horvath's Wikipedia entry on my iPhone. My thumbs kept hitting the wrong spots on the screen, so I read in snatches.

> Felix Laszlo Horvath is a banker and financier, born in Budapest, Hungary in 1949 …

Horvath's father played an important role in the military leadership of the Hungarian uprising of 1956. He was tried for treason and executed in 1958 …

Horvath's holdings are currently valued at $17 billion …

Horvath provided over $20 million in support to the Polish Solidarity movement after the communist coup of December 1981 …

Horvath paid an estimated total of $40 million to senior figures in the secret police forces of Poland, Hungary, Bulgaria, and East Germany to induce them to relinquish power peacefully …

Horvath has donated generously to causes in this country as well, including classical music performance, autism research, and gay rights …

He has been an active supporter of Constitutionalist political campaigns …

I heard the opening of a door and shoved my phone into my pocket. From the bedroom wing of the vast suite walked a man of maybe 65, wearing jeans, white shirt, powder-blue cashmere pullover, alligator loafers, and socks exactly the same color as the pullover. His white hair was elegantly cut; his pink skin shined and buffed.

Here, obviously, was Felix Horvath.

"Hello, Elmer. Hello, Paul. How nice of you to come by."

"It was nice of you to make the time, Felix."

"I'm sincerely sorry we could not confirm the appointment time earlier. The meeting with the president went longer than scheduled. And this must be the famous Walter Schotzke?"

He extended a hand.

"It's a famous name, sir," I answered, "not a famous person."

"You underestimate yourself. Mark Dunn has made you a celebrity in your own right."

"Not for long, I hope."

Horvath smiled benignly. "Probably not. But for now, why not enjoy it?"

We made an odd grouping. In this opulent hotel suite, the drab Elmer and the rumpled Paul seemed lifted up out of their element. These rooms belonged to the rulers of the earth who came to Washington to call on the president, equal to equal: the prime ministers and emirs; the CEOs and the bankers. The three of us, even Elmer, were selected, supported, and discarded by these rulers. All our scheming and scurrying was done in their service. And how little of the proceeds of that service were retained by the Pauls or even by the Elmers! Washington may be corrupt. Yet relative to what it offers for sale, the American political system sets its prices surprisingly low.

But then maybe I was losing the point. I once read a story about tiny birds that can safely sit in the mouths of crocodiles to eat the tartar on the crocodiles' teeth. From the point of view of the birds, the crocodiles are working for them, not the other way around.

Horvath had resettled himself into the couch, one sharply creased denim knee folded over the other. Meldwin found himself a straight-backed chair on the wall near the window, and pulled it forward, within range of the group, but not quite joining it.

"You'll be pleased to hear that your name recurred often during the meeting with the president," said Horvath to Elmer, speaking with only the faintest trace of a melodious accent.

Paul Dussman looked excruciatingly ill at ease in the opulent suite. Not Elmer. He answered deadpan, "It's only fair. I talk about the president all the time myself."

"Don't be conceited; it was not the president *himself* who spoke about you. The president left that to Seamus Soloveitchik." Horvath's tone became gently teasing. "Seamus warns me that you are a very dangerous character. He said that you were irresponsible. He said you maintained embarrassing associations. And he said that you would lose."

Elmer did not react, not even with blinks. "And what did you say?"

"Meldwin took notes on our conversation. Meldwin, why don't you read them back?"

Meldwin produced an elegant little red-leather notebook and read aloud in a trained actor's voice, alternating slightly to make clear when it was the president speaking and when Felix Horvath.

"They tell me you've visited this office 17 times under five different presidents, Mr. Horvath. I think that's right, Mr. President. *It never loses its thrill, does it?* No, Mr. President. *I feel the same way, and I work here every day. I should probably begin by thanking you for your support of my campaign. But as I read my briefing notes, I am overwhelmed by how much more you have done for so many causes more important than any political campaign."*

"Ah, Meldwin, you are embarrassing me! Stop, stop!" laughed Horvath. "Let's skip the exchange of compliments and cut to the business part. The president's team laid out for me a series of charts that modeled the benefits of his plan to the American economy."

"They were selling you," said Elmer. Not even the need to flatter a billionaire could soothe his truculence at any mention of the president's wiles.

"Of course they were selling me!" Felix replied with another, shorter laugh. "Why else would they invite me? But don't you want to hear the sales pitch?"

"Sure."

Meldwin resumed reading.

"The president said: *I can't deny the package will cost you some money. A lot of money. But still only a small percentage of the money you freely give away. Taxes would be rising for every-one; you are only being asked to share in the sacrifices made by all."*

Elmer snorted as the story was told. "'Share the sacrifices!' That's code for plunder. If this president cannot understand the difference between voluntary charity and compulsion ..."

"Elmer," said Horvath, a slight touch of impatience souring his geniality, "please do not school me. Do you not want to hear the rest?"

Elmer nodded and fell silent. Paul glanced nervously at Elmer and kept silent too.

"We were sitting in front of the fireplace," resumed Horvath. "Almost knee to knee. Me in the visitor's chair. The president in his wheelchair. He touched my elbow and said, 'This country sometimes does ask things of us. But not more than the country is worth.'"

Elmer couldn't stand it. He interrupted again. "He uses that chair as a prop!"

"Yes, but it is certainly a very effective prop. I said – and I was thinking of you as I said it – 'My friends say you are putting the country on the road to socialism.'"

Elmer and Paul both lit up. "Good!" exclaimed Elmer. "It's about time he heard that from somebody."

"Then I said, 'My friends also say you are splitting the Constitutionalist party.'"

"Right!" "Exactly!" This time, Paul and Elmer spoke at once.

Horvath did not seem even to have heard them. "Meldwin, I won't do it justice. Please read them back what the president said to that."

Meldwin consulted his red leather book again and resumed his reading.

"The president said: *I hope I am not splitting the party. But if so, why don't you help me to unite the party? Let's work together. You saw what happened during the agitation over the Durango prisoners. Now they're repeating the trick with the deficit-reduction package. Inciting Americans to fear and hate their neigh-*

bors! Warning that their freedom is being extinguished because the government they freely elected raises a few extra pennies in the dollar to pay our debts – and when they are free to replace that government if they don't like it. Would your father call that socialism? Would he call that tyranny?"

"Pennies!" sputtered Elmer. "It's trillions!"

Meldwin continued reading, undistracted by Elmer's interruption.

"The president said: *I will jump-start this economy. Then I will shrink this government. I will end the war in Mexico, you can hold me to that. That's almost $200 billion a year right there. I'm selling government assets, I'll be cutting all kinds of benefits. If you think I'm asking a lot of you, wait till you see what we ask of the people who get assistance from the government. But yes, I am sending a portion of the bill to people like you. Who else can I send it to? Think of what this country has done for you. And then tell me I'm asking too much of you.*"

"That's enough," said Horvath. "A very remarkable man, our president."

Disgust flitted across Elmer's face, mixed with a large quantity of apprehension and worry. "So how did the meeting end?"

"Well that's when we talked about you for a bit. Then we talked about the economy and about some of my philanthropic projects. I told the president that I would consider what he said seriously, and that before I made any major decision I would inform Seamus."

Elmer's cheek muscles twitched just perceptibly. Horvath's answer dissatisfied him, but he said only, "Remember when we used to travel together to Eastern Europe?"

"Central Europe," corrected Horvath. "I remember."

"And how we talked then about how the world could be transformed by a real freedom movement? Freedom to live how you want, love anyone you want."

"Yes, I remember." Horvath fiddled with his hands, the motions of the ex-smoker who has beaten the addiction, but not the habit of reaching for the packet. He grasped a soda-water glass instead.

"That freedom movement is gathering around us right now! The Trucker Protests – the homeowners' protests – you can see it all on Patriot News! They're the people you've been waiting for. Will you not support them? If they find out that you are aligned with the president, it will dishearten them. You'll destroy the movement you've worked so hard to build."

Horvath smiled an ironic smile. "Elmer, if this is a spontaneous citizens' movement, why does it need my support?"

Elmer took the question as a challenge. He answered in a passionate rush. "They need your support to be effective! On their own, they make amateurish mistakes. They need media coaching so they communicate effectively on TV, they need handlers to review that nobody has made a sign mocking the president's wheelchair, they need buses to get them to the right place at the same time. You didn't question why Solidarity needed your support!"

"Solidarity was facing a police state," answered Horvath, still ironic.

"If we don't stop Pulaski now, we'll be facing a police state soon enough."

"Elmer, please – you know what a real police state is like."

"I know how freedom is lost! Step by step, gradually but irreversibly. Liberals become socialists, socialists become fascists, fascists turn totalitarian. At first nobody will believe it, because nobody wants to believe it. By the time the truth is undeniable, it's too late."

"You really believe that?"

"Do you *not* believe that?"

"Not now. Not here."

"It *can* happen here." Elmer stood up and began to pace. His face flushed, and he was speaking with an intensity I'd never seen before. "But we can stop it! The freedom movement can stop it. *You* can stop it! This is the chance of a lifetime. If we win this fight, everyone will understand: the budget cannot be balanced on the backs of this nation's wealth creators. If the people want their precious Medicare so badly, let them pay for it themselves. But they don't. They only want it if you pay for it. Their welfare state only works if they can enslave you. But they are weak, and you are strong. They can only enslave you if you submit. Screw that! You are a generous man, but you will give what *you* want to give, not what they want to grab!"

Elmer's eloquence seemed only to irritate Horvath.

"Why must you be so melodramatic about this straight-forward business calculation? What do I pay? What do I get? That was the question I asked the president at the end. His staff presented me with a statistical model of the effect of his plan on my enterprises."

Horvath held up a shining compact disk. "It projects all kinds of good things for me over the medium term, in return for higher taxes in the short term."

"We've got models that say just the opposite," said Paul earnestly, finally emboldened now that the conversation had turned to his subject.

Horvath waved a dismissive hand.

"As you say. Let's look only at what can be estimated with some certainty. My economists tell me that the budget plan will cost us $20 million in the current year – and then at least $40 million the year after. It will bite even harder after that. What does the money buy? Who will remember that I gave it? Nobody. And as you say, it won't be received as a gift, it will – it would – be received as an entitlement and expectation. I don't care for that." Felix's tone had chilled to ice. I could hear the voice of the man who had made the vast Horvath fortune.

"No!" shouted Elmer.

"No," agreed Paul grimly.

"So what are you asking of me, Elmer?"

Elmer's eyes glistened. The marlin of a lifetime had just bitten at his bait.

"With $7 million of that $70 million – only $7 million – I could set this country on fire for freedom. We'd launch a freedom movement that would never be turned back! We'd transform the politics of this country forever!"

"You should see these Trucker Protests," inserted Paul. "It's a true people's movement – ordinary moms and dads – people who have never been involved in politics before!"

"$7 million?" remarked Horvath, the irony back in his voice. "Well, they do say that freedom isn't free."

Elmer only blinked at that.

"Still, spend $7 million to save $70 million? A very attractive return on investment." Horvath's voice dwindled away into a musing quaver.

"It's not a transaction," said Elmer. "It's a commitment. To freedom."

"Right," smiled Horvath, moving beyond irony to outright sarcasm. "To freedom. Of course. But will you answer a question for me? What do you truly think of these crowds you've conjured up? Do you believe in the reality you have constructed? Or maybe you don't ponder the question anymore. Probably I should not ponder it either. $7 million. is too much. See what you can do with $3 million. So long, Elmer. We did good work in Europe, you and I."

Felix rose. The meeting was over. He extended his hand first to Elmer, then to Paul, then to me.

Meldwin escorted us out of the luxurious suite. Elmer said nothing until the elevator closed. Then he smiled a tighter smile of purer pleasure than any I had yet seen. "I'd planned to ask only for $1 million."

CHAPTER 74

The morning after our meeting in Horvath's suite, Elmer followed up with a call to Horvath's CFO. The CFO promised a next-day check. The next day arrived, but the check did not. Elmer called again. The CFO apologized: a missed communication, so very sorry, the matter would be sorted out in short order. But there was no money the next day, or the day after that, or the week following.

"Maybe he's broke?" I suggested.

"Don't be an idiot," Elmer frowned.

"Or changed his mind?"

No answer to that.

If the check were the only difficulty, Elmer might have felt less anxious. But he was receiving other signals of trouble and danger. Meetings on Capitol Hill were becoming more difficult to schedule – or were canceled at the last minute. When the meetings proceeded, the congresspeople seemed distracted, vague, noncommittal.

One meeting with a member of the House of Representations, scheduled for half an hour, was cut short when the Representative abruptly said, "It's a very complex matter," got to his feet, and walked out of the meeting room.

As we exited the Representative's office, I turned Elmer's favorite question back on him. "So: Is David Maurice winning?"

He grunted. "We're fighting something bigger than David Maurice."

A few days later, I got a phone call from Bill Mihailovich. "What the hell is going on down there?"

"What do you mean?

"My CEO is looking green at the gills. He keeps asking me to tone down the attacks on the president's package.'"

"It's just talk, Bill."

Mihailovich snorted in disgust. "I can't take that risk! My contract is up for renewal next year. You guys have to win this thing faster."

"We'll do our best."

"Yeah. Do that. Don't forget: You guys got me into this."

The more resistance Elmer encountered, the harder he worked. He spent an hour a day on the phone with Omar. He found sponsors for Benjy. He summoned bloggers and reporters. He walked the halls of Congress, sticking his head into office suites, buttonholing whomever he happened to find: the member himself or herself, the chief of staff if the member were unavailable, the legislative director if the chief were absent.

Yet the gears still did not quite engage. Some invisible force restrained Elmer's progress.

April ended. May arrived, my first May in Washington. Man, was it sweet: everything green and lush and rich. And on the second day of the month, we finally discovered who and what it was that Elmer had been grappling with over the past frustrating days.

At about four in the afternoon of May 2, I was sitting in Elmer's office reviewing the schedule for the next day. The intercom buzzed, and the receptionist's voice announced, "I've got Ignatius Hernandez for you on line two."

Elmer shoved his headphones over his ears and jabbed the button beside the flashing light on his desk unit. I probably should have stepped out. I didn't. I was too curious – and Elmer was too immediately absorbed in the call to notice.

"Hey, Iggy, what's up?"

Hernandez must have told him what was up, for Elmer did not speak for a long while. As he listened, the tips of his ears slowy turned from pink to red. He finally said, "You're kidding me." After a short interval, Elmer barked "Well, what the hell are we supposed to do now?"

Pause.

"I can't."

Pause.

"I'm telling you I can't. Even if I wanted to. But I can't. And anyway: I don't want to. This was never about you. It was about our whole movement."

Long pause.

"Yes, if you could do that, it would be different. But you have to do it *first*. Take out the tax increases first, then we stop the protests later. Not the other way around. Otherwise I'm selling out everything we believe in and everybody I've worked with."

Short pause.

"Yes, it goes a long way back with me too. But you have your role, and I have mine."

Pause. Elmer's ears pulsed even redder.

"Is that a threat?"

Very short pause.

"It better not be. I never want to be on the opposite side of you. But you had better not want to be on the opposite side of me."

Pause.

"Of course, I'll think about it. But it won't change anything."

Elmer's voice ceased. Conversation over. He tore off the headset and hurled it at his desk. He bent over the desk, cradled his head in his hands, and massaged his temples.

I gave him a long moment. Although I think I had guessed everything that had been said, I asked anyway, "What was that about?"

Elmer slowly raised his head and stared at me. Blink, blink, blink. As if he could not remember me, as if he could not understand what I was saying. Then, through a fog of confusion, he slowly focused his eyes on me:

"That was Iggy. The president has asked him to serve as White House chief of staff. Iggy has accepted. He wants the campaign against the deficit-reduction package ended. He wants Vernon Mallory off the air. He wants the attacks on Senator Hazen stopped. He said, 'It's over.'"

"Wow. Like that?"

"Yeah." More of Elmer's mind seemed to be rejoining the conversation. "Yeah, *just* like that. I'm supposed to tell people, 'Sorry, folks, it was all just a Washington power-play. Our leader got the job he wanted, campaign over. All those principles we said we had? Forget them.'"

"Does that mean you'll refuse to do what Iggy says?" I could hardly wrap my brain around it. I thought Iggy was the bigger boss!

"It doesn't matter what I do. You don't manage an avalanche. One person – a few people – can start it. But that's not how it ends. It ends when the rocks stop rolling."

"So does this mean we have to fight Iggy now, too?"

"I think we've been fighting Iggy for a while, without knowing it. But no, we can't fight him for very long. He can turn off our money. He can cut us off from our key supporters, one by one. We could mess him up pretty good, but in the end he'd win. So we'll have to wind down. Slowly. *After* he gives us something we can call a victory."

He reflected a moment, then exploded: "But he should not have taken the White House job! Not now, not yet." He slammed his hand hard on the surface of his desk. "What the hell am I supposed to say when people ask, 'Doesn't anybody in this town believe in anything?'"

You could say: Only the suckers. That's what I thought - but didn't say. Elmer had already dropped his head back upon desk, cradling his skull with his hands. His thick, pudgy body slumped into a shape of utterly forlorn misery. He didn't need my sarcasm heaped on top of him. By his lights, he had been nothing but good to me. And after all, there were worse people.

His pasty face lifted itself up again. He perceived I was still there, still looking at him. He smiled cheerlessly. "I always thought we'd get more done before we became completely corrupt."

Then he stood, straightened his tie, and walked out the door.

I wandered back over to my own desk. I looked at SitRep.com, then at Twitter. No mention yet of the Hernandez hire. Elmer must have been one of Iggy's very first calls.

Within five minutes of Elmer's unusually early departure, a general stampede erupted for the doorway. Mindy left last. "G'night, Walter!" she said cheerfully.

I was left alone.

So this was how the story finished. Had Hazen guessed wrong and sent me to the losing side after all? No, he was right. He had played a very complicated game. He had played to win, and despite the odds, he had won. But the Constitutionalists would draw their next generation of leaders from the losers of this fight, not the winners. Hazen had given me a future, if I wanted one.

I walked over to my little window and stared out into the loading dock behind our narrow, shabby building. A vagrant sifted through a big blue dumpster. A parasite. Every system needs them – and who was I to look down on him?

I sat at my computer and started drafting a letter of resignation. I'd be losing not only my pay, but also probably my allowance too. I'd have to find another job, a real one this time. Good luck with that.

I struggled for a while with my letter. Nothing sounded right. I got frustrated and opened Twitter. Chirrup, chirrup, chirrup, the messages whizzed by. Then, from @benjybarstein: "I'm on Mark Dunn at 5 with shocker new video. Watch!"

Almost 5 o'clock now.

I settled myself in the conference room and switched on the television. I texted Valerie that I'd be staying at the office for another hour.

I thought I was ready for anything. I was wrong.

CHAPTER 75

"Good evening, America. Senator Philip Hazen. Maybe you've heard of him?" Dunn gestured toward a table strewn with magazines and newspapers. "They call him, 'The conscience of the Senate.' The 'great negotiator.' The 'voice of moderation.'"

All this was said with great sarcasm.

Dunn fixed his eye upon the camera. His voice went hard with indignation. "And also, as we'll show you tonight, a-state-of-the-art sleazeball. We'll be right back."

Evidently, Mark Dunn had not received a courtesy warning call from Hernandez. Or maybe he had got one and did not care. Or maybe, as Elmer said, it was all too late.

After the break, the camera opened on a two-shot: Dunn and Benjy in face-to-face armchairs. Dunn introduced Benjy.

"Benjy Barstein is one of Washington's most daring, most unstoppable investigative journalists. A few days ago, a confidential source provided him with shocking documentary evidence of corrupt deal making by Senator Philip Hazen. Benjy, tell us what you found."

Benjy had got himself a clean suit for the occasion. But the little sniffs still punctuated his speech, and the eyes still glinted bloodshot.

"Mark, these documents show Senator Philip Hazen's office negotiating a lucrative government job offer for Brad 'Commodore' Chauncey."

Oh, no. I'd almost forgotten about my little secret. And now it was about to be spilled all over national television. Damn,

damn, damn, damn. I texted Valerie: *Mark Dunn on attack re Brad's job. Better watch.*

Benjy was still talking.

"Brad Chauncey is Hazen's kind of people: entitled. That nickname? It's a prep school joke about an ancestor of his who commanded a squadron in the War of 1812. Brad's connections got him a big job at CreditZurich's New York office. But Brad's brains were never as good as his connections. Credit-Zurich fired him. And there are rumors that it was not just incompetence that cost Brad his job."

"Stop right there, Benjy," interjected Dunn with a chuckle. "Don't say anything that the Patriot News defamation lawyers haven't approved!"

Both men laughed.

"I won't," agreed Benjy. "But Chauncey was out of work for almost eight months. He applied for dozens of jobs. No company on Wall Street would hire him. But guess who did?"

"Who?" asked Dunn, the perfect straight man.

"You did, Mark. Your viewers. All of us. Senator Hazen lobbied NASA to hire Brad Chauncey to oversee all U.S. programs for the commercialization of space. At a salary of $165,000 a year."

Dunn emitted an awestruck whistle. Then he removed his tortoise-shell glasses, folded them, and leaned forward for the decisive moment. Screw you too, you populist phony in your Italian loafers.

"But can you really prove that Senator Hazen was responsible?"

"Can I?" gloated Benjy. He opened a folder on the coffee table and extracted some sheets of paper.

"Here's an email from Nia Robinson, the White House congressional liaison: 'Please tell my dear friend Senator Hazen that we've secured the NASA job for Brad Chauncey.'"

Dunn cut him off. "Anybody can compose an email and read it on the airwaves, Benjy. That's no kind of proof."

Benjy closed his folder. "Mark, you are absolutely right. So I did something better: I asked the senator himself. Can we show the video?"

Mark shouted over his shoulder, "Play!"

The studio lights dimmed. The TV screen filled with HD video: Senator Hazen, walking alone across the Mall, the Washington Monument rising above him. From the look of the trees, this must have been shot a while ago. The camera focused on Benjy, walking toward Hazen, north of Fifteenth Street. Wanda must have pre-positioned herself, pretending to be a tourist filming the sights.

When Benjy had reached within four feet of Hazen, he accosted the senator in a loud voice. "Senator Hazen! May I ask you a question? Why did you press NASA to hire an obviously unqualified friend of yours, Brad Chauncey?"

Hazen did not even break stride.

"Never heard of him. And this is my walking time. I do interviews at the office."

Benjy reversed direction, striding alongside Hazen. He pushed into the old man's personal space. Wanda's camera kept pace. Hazen must have felt like some grazing beast, cut off from the herd, suddenly attacked by a pack of wild dogs.

"It's strange that you say that. I'm holding here over 30 emails between your office and the White House discussing your request that a job be found for Brad Chauncey."

Barstein's menacing intrusion did not crack Hazen's cool.

"Forward the correspondence to my communications director. We'll take a look at it and offer a comment if any comment seems called for."

In a sudden tirade of rage, Barstein yelled in Hazen's face, "Answer the question!"

Gruffer than ever, Hazen growled, "Go play Allen Funt with somebody else, sonny."

"So you won't answer the question?"

"My office gets thousands of emails a day," Hazen replied.

He accelerated his pace. Benjy let him escape, and the video showed Hazen dwindling into the distance.

The television screen returned to the image of a concerned Mark Dunn and a satisfied Benjy. Dunn said, "He didn't deny it."

"Right. And when I asked Senator Hazens' former chief of staff, Daphne Peltzman, about the emails, she confirmed that Senator Hazen specifically directed her to find work for Brad Chauncey."

That was a damnable lie!

Dunn faced the camera square on. "We have Daphne here with us tonight. Coming up, right after the break."

Would Daphne dare repeat the lie on national TV? You know those horrible dreams where you cannot seem to move? I sat just like that in the conference-room chair for the next three minutes, frozen until the show resumed.

Daphne had dressed for the show as she had never dressed once in all the time I'd known her: conservative suit, subdued makeup, and a functional hairdo. She looked the very model of a respectable, middle-aged government employee.

Dunn offered a short biographical sketch of Daphne, then proceeded to the questioning.

"Ms. Peltzman, you say that Senator Hazen specifically directed you to find work for Brad Chauncey."

"That's correct."

I raged. *You liar! You did it all. You did it to manipulate me, so I'd help you manipulate Hazen.*

But my negative thoughts did not penetrate the box. Daphne continued her fable.

"And of course the White House was eager to oblige the senator, who has been so crucial to their congressional strategy."

Dunn pressed ahead. "So it looks like we have a deal: the White House finds a big government job to pay off an important administration supporter. Isn't that illegal?"

Daphne hesitated, not because she did not know what to say, but to better play-act the role of the reluctant truth-teller. "That would depend on whether the senator's support was somehow contingent on the job offer. Probably the only way to reach the bottom of the matter would be to question Senator Hazen and Nia Robinson under oath."

"Nia Robinson being the White House aide who arranged the job?"

"That's correct."

"Why was Senator Hazen so interested in Brad Chauncey?"

Daphne drew a tiny breath.

"In this country, the elite looks after itself. Brad Chauncey is the 'right kind' of person: right family, right schools. Philip Hazen has devoted his whole life to getting in with the 'right kind' of people: the people who listen to public radio, who sit on the boards of the fancy universities, the big money, the old money. He filled his office with people like that. It didn't matter how stupid they were."

OK that wasn't acting. That was genuine, authentic hatred. How she wanted to take a shot at me! But she did not dare. Mark Dunn had praised me on air. To attack me now would imply that Dunn had erred. Unthinkable. Walter Schotzke was a hero of movement Constitutionalism. And if Daphne wished to re-ingratiate herself with the Constitutionalist movement, she would have to pretend to regard me as a hero too. She was trapped. Heh.

Mark Dunn creased his forehead at the injustice of it all.

"I think a lot of the folks out there are asking themselves, 'Would my senator lift a finger to find a job for me?'"

"Not unless you quote-unquote belong," answered Daphne.

Dunn shook his head mournfully. "It's a good thing we have Patriot News looking out for the folks. Thank you, Ms. Peltzman. We appreciate your willingness to speak out. What's next for you?"

"I've just joined Vernon Mallory's Center for Military Readiness as a senior fellow."

"That's terrific news. And I'm sure we'll hear a lot more from you right here on Patriot News."

"I hope so, Mark," said Daphne with a wheedling smile.

"Folks, after the break, we'll get Juanita Bimpan's take."

Dunn allotted Juanita two segments.

"Mark, you can't say this, but as a minority and a woman I can. Between special favors for the over-privileged and welfare for the so-called underprivileged, it's everyday Christian white folks who are the most discriminated-against people in this country. And when has Philip Baruch Hazen ever stood up for those everyday Americans?" She hit the middle-name hard.

Enough! I clicked off the TV and called Valerie.

"Did you *see* that?"

"Horrible. Wait a second, it's Dana calling, I'd better take it."

I did wait a second, and then another, and then about 500 seconds more. This was obviously going to be a long talk. I suddenly felt I needed a drink. I hung up the phone, pulled on my suit jacket, and walked across the street to the Carlton House hotel. I turned left into the dark bar. Unusually crowded, all the stools taken. I surveyed the tables and –

"Walter!" The voice of Freddy Catesby rang out. Catesby was sharing a table with two women, one blonde, one East Asian. Not exactly beauties, but they must have been less than half his age. "Come join us!"

I didn't want company, but there was nowhere else to sit and no obvious way to escape. I took the chair Freddy extended.

"I want you to meet my new friends, Ellen and Vivian," Freddy intoned with elaborate courtesy. "Or is it Vivian and Ellen?" he added with a wink. "They just started today in editorial assistant positions at the *Constitutionalist Review*. I personally selected them for their abundant ... talents."

One – the blonde one – tittered. The other looked glum.

"And what better way to celebrate a triumphant first day at work in the Constitutionalist cause than by going out to become better acquainted with one of the heroic figures of Constitutionalism himself? I refer, of course, to your humble servant, Frederick Catesby, editor and publisher of the nation's leading journal of Constitutionalist ideas. Ellen and Vivian, please meet Walter Schotzke, a Constitutionalist hero himself. Have a drink, Walter!"

Catesby was two-thirds of the way through a martini, and obviously not his first.

"I'll have what you are having, Freddy."

"An excellent principle to follow in life," he chortled.

Catesby bellowed across the bar at a waiter loitering with his back to the room.

"Hernando! Another of the same for my friend, *por favor*." The waiter glowered at Freddy's tourist Spanish.

"Schotzke? As in the mustard?" asked the glum girl, now looking a little less glum. She crossed one of her short legs over the other and twisted her whole body in my direction, thereby exposing the whole of her right thigh to my personal view. I'd seen better.

I started to answer, "No–" but Freddy interrupted. "The very same! You are looking at the heir to the Schotzke-mustard millions!"

Without moving her chair, the girl infiltrated herself much closer to me. Her knee touched my knee. Cleavage was presented for view. Her lips leaned into my ear. "That must be very interesting."

Oh, was I not in the mood for this. The martini arrived, and I sipped a searing mouthful.

I leaned across the table, bypassing Ellen and Vivian – or Vivian and Ellen – to talk to Catesby.

"Freddy, I assume you did not watch the *Mark Dunn Show* today?"

"Just the very top of the show, while waiting for Ellen and Vivian to complete their *toilettes*. He and Benjy Barstein certainly nailed the senator!"

"They framed him. Hazen never knew anything about the Chauncey hiring. It's all my fault. Tell me: What can I do?"

"Why do you want to do anything?"

"Because it's all false!"

"So? It won't be the first time somebody has said something false about a politician on TV. Have another drink."

My martini glass had somehow emptied itself.

"Should I call the show and ask if I can go on to set the record straight?"

Freddy laughed and laughed.

"Walter, do you think Mark Dunn or Patriot News or anybody cares about getting the record straight? This is a war. A bullet just clipped Hazen. Don't worry, it won't kill him. Do you suppose there's a single person in Washington actually honest-to-goodness shocked at the idea of a senator leaning on the White House to deliver a job to a friend? Hernando! Another round! Ladies – another glass of wine?"

My phone buzzed with an arriving text. From Valerie: *Tried 2 call u bk, cdnt reach you. Dana hysterical. Going to her apt now. Meet me there? 4 of us can go 2 dinner 2 discuss.*

Dinner with Brad? No way. Absolutely no way. I texted back. *I have situ of my own here. U go 2 Dana's, I'll c u @ apt later.*

The ex-glum girl was leaning ever further forward to offer a deeper cleavage show. Freddy's hand hospitably clutched the knee of the blond girl. The hand did not release. The room was roaring now. Catesby and and I had to almost shout across the table to be heard.

"Freddy, I can't live this way. I want to leave Washington."

Catesby's face registered shock. "Leave Washington? To do what?"

"I don't know. Make some money, I guess. My own money. It's the one thing everybody in this city seems to respect."

"Don't you already have money?" cooed my friend with the thighs.

"Not as much as I want."

My rudeness seemed only to heighten her interest.

"How much *do* you want?" she asked flirtatiously.

"Millions. Billions. Trillions. Whatever they're printing these days."

"Me, too!"

She and her friend excused themselves to freshen up. Good riddance. Catesby gallantly saluted the two girls, then leaned into my ear. "I've always been a man of ideas myself. But an idea backed by money does usually get a better hearing than an idea that arrives alone. Have you told Elmer?"

The next round of drinks materialized in front of us.

"Not yet."

Freddy lifted his martini glass in salute. "He has been very good to you. A lot of us have been good to you. We've recognized your potential."

"My potential for what?"

"Well, that's an interesting question. Let's think about it. But what do you say we have a real party? When the girls return, let's get out of this old-age home. Let's go to the Thomas Crawford Lounge!"

The Thomas Crawford Lounge was a low-grade saloon near the Capitol, very popular with interns and young staffers. I'd only gone once before. Somebody vomited on my shoes, and I swore I'd never return. Then I thought about returning home – and the risk of encountering Brad and Dana.

"OK."

"Good!" said Catesby, leaning toward me confidentially. "That gives us time to talk frankly."

Did Catesby control some intoxication switch that allowed him to turn off the alcohol when he wanted to? Ten minutes ago, he'd sounded at least half-drunk. Now he seemed to have recovered himself. He talked as lucidly as if he were stone sober. Or at least that's the way it seemed to me. Not that I was a good judge. The booze did not release its hold on me so easily.

"I think there's a lot of merit to your plans," he said. "But I have to warn you. People who leave Washington can disappear very quickly. You don't want that. Your friends don't want that for you. So let me suggest something. The *Constitutionalist Review* ends its fiscal year June 30. It seems that we may face a small deficit. Nothing very shocking, maybe $200,000. Now if a Schotzke family foundation – or any of your family and friends – or even you personally – were to help us close that gap, I think I could persuade Elmer and all your other friends that you remain a very, very important person in our movement. We'd keep your chair warm until you were ready to return D.C. – as a real leader, too."

"$200,000?"

"Let's say $250,000, just to be safe."

My ears buzzed. My face felt warm. Somehow my glass had emptied itself again.

"I don't know about that, Freddy. Remember, I haven't made any money yet."

Catesby's face twisted into a hard expression. "I feel sure you could get it, if you tried. I do feel sure of that. There have always been a lot of questions about you, Walter. Whose side are you really on? Think of this as a way to settle the question. It might be dangerous to leave the question open."

The girls returned from the restroom. Catesby rose, patted at the sides of his brown tweed suit. "Goodness! I've forgotten my wallet!" He looked at me expectantly.

At the front door, we hailed a taxi. Even by Washington cab standards, the car looked battered and filthy. Catesby and the two girls piled into the back, I opened the front door to confront a seat full of junk: crumpled McDonald's wrappers, a grease-stained street map. The driver hastily shifted the filth closer to himself.

"Capitol Hill! The Thomas Crawford Lounge!" shouted Catesby, and off we zoomed.

I checked my phone en route. Text from Valerie: *Dana and Brad v upset. Please call!*

Call Brad and Dana? Nuts to them. I needed to talk to Senator Hazen. And then it hit me: That would be very difficult to do.

Hazen's office would be on full red alert. Any call – even to a cellphone – would be screened by a handler. He did not use email, much less text. Facebook was something he'd seen a movie about. There was only one way to find him, the way I'd found him every morning for three months. I'd have to visit his apartment. I could explain in person, apologize, set things right.

So long as the gin pulsed through my blood, it seemed a good enough plan.

I texted back: *Nothing 2 say. Must talk to Hazen 1st.*

As I stepped out of the taxi onto Pennsylvania Avenue, the evening air sobered me a little. I turned to open the rear door, and the other three stepped out. Ellen (or Vivian) clutched my arm and pressed her breast against my tricep. It felt as plump as the rest of her. Freddy reached for the blonde's arm, but the arm eluded him.

The lounge was dark, noisy, crammed with young staffers. We shouldered our way through the throng in the front room to find a table at the back. Catesby expansively ordered two bottles of the lounge's most expensive red wine. Luckily for me, the menu topped out at $33. Catesby poured the contents of the first bottle into four big glasses, placed the second at his elbow to play host.

"Freddy, I've been thinking over your proposition. Maybe you are right. Everybody needs friends."

"Exactly!"

"And it's a capitalist society. Who expects friends to work for free?"

"Exactly again!"

Vivian – or was it Ellen? – was getting more aggressive, her stockinged foot roaming up my calf. Her friend was flashing semaphore eyelash messages: *Have you sealed the deal yet? May I go now?*

I wondered: Was this how Valerie had felt when Beloz hit on her? If somebody snapped a photo right now, wouldn't I look every bit as guilty as Valerie had done? And all I wanted was to get away from the woman pawing me. The last flickers of anger at Valerie died away. That wound had healed.

I put an arm around Vivian/Ellen and murmured to her, "Hey, sexy, if you keep doing that, I'm going to explode. But you gotta understand, I've already found my right girl. And I can't use two. Maybe somebody can. Not me."

The girl's foot snapped away from my calf. She jumped to her feet, her eyes flashing furious. A glassful of red wine hit my face and splashed onto my shirt and suitcoat. The two girls stomped out of the restaurant together, leaving me sodden and Catesby howling in drunken delight. Incredibly, nobody else in the bar seemed to notice. The lounge was so jammed and noisy that only those immediately around us even saw the wine tossed, and they were too drunk to care. No waiter rushed over with mop and pail. The stickiness of the floor even before the wine tossing suggested that mop and pail visited this corner of the establishment only on the most special occasions.

"You threw away your chance. Serves you right!" Catesby gasped in hysterical hilarity, pounding the vinyl-topped little table.

"More for you, Freddy."

"You're right!" shouted Catesby, still laughing. "That's the best part! They liked you – but they're going to have to fuck me! Both of them! The hot-to-trot one *and* the hot-to-not one! Come on, let's finish the wine and make a bet as to which of them gives me the best ride."

"That's a very vulgar way to speak," I said with thickening dignity. The room was moving, and Catesby was moving with it.

"Don't be so pompous," retorted Catesby. "If there's one thing I can't stand, it's pomposity. But, of course, you're young; the young are always moralistic."

"When I'm rich," I declared, "I'll be as pompous as I want."

"Better wipe the wine off your chin first," Catesby wheezed joyfully.

The room was moving faster. Soon the second bottle of wine was gone too. "Freddy, I feel sick."

"Pay the bill, and let's get some fresh air."

I stood up, tripped over the table, and knocked over all the glassware. An explosion of shattering glass spilled more wine over my trouser legs. A waitress rushed over. "Don't worry," slurred Catesby. "This is Walter Schotzke. Schotzke mustard. He can pay for all the damage."

A credit-card slip was presented. I signed it, and we staggered to the street. "Give me $50 for a taxi," said Catesby. I fumbled for my wallet, peeled out the bills.

"Good night, Freddy."

"Good night, Walter. You are a great American."

It was past midnight. I thought to call Valerie, but somewhere along the way I'd lost my phone. I thought to walk home, but my feet weighed too much. I thought to hail a taxi, but the thought made me car-sick.

Above Pennsylvania Avenue shone the bright white of the Capitol dome. Beautiful, always, no matter what it contained. I walked and stared. I stared and walked. At first slowly, and then faster, all the evening's alcohol began to move inside me. The soft evening air seemed to open all my passages. I placed both hands on my upper legs, bent over, and vomited all my insides into the gutter.

And then some more.

Then some more after that.

Cars roared past without stopping. Pedestrians on the sidewalk opposite looked away. Just another young Capitol Hill staffer who had over-indulged – they had seen it before.

Flecks of vomit landed on my shirt and pants. My mouth and throat felt disgusting. I thought about returning to the Thomas Crawford Lounge for a glass of water. But when I looked backward, I realized that the lounge was impossibly far away: at least four or five blocks. I sat on the curb to recover my strength. A lot of time must have elapsed, because when I finally stood up to make the walk, the door of the Lounge place was closed and locked. The street was very silent. I no longer felt sick, but I was still very drunk. More even than water, I needed sleep. I weaved and lurched across the street, toward the bright white dome. I saw a park, trees, grass. It was a lovely evening. Here was a bench. The bench seemed to sing my name. I sat upon it. Then I extended my body and rested my head. Then I passed out.

CHAPTER 76

I woke with a jolt. My throat was parched with thirst, my tongue still tasted of vomit, and my clothes stank. I twisted my wrist to see the time through the pre-dawn gloom. To my surprise, my watch was still there. It showed the time: a little past 6 AM.

The wooden slats of the park bench pressed uncomfortably against my stiff body. I lifted my head. That worked. I rotated my feet. Systems go. I sat upright. Yes. Most of the alcohol seemed to have evaporated from my body: most, but not all. The world felt distant and impersonal. Time to stand up.

Nearby, a fountain splashed enticingly. I creaked myself toward the sound. A vast square basin built of black was receiving water from more than a dozen spigots. The basin was shallow, but deep enough for me to wash my face and take a long, long drink. The water did not taste good - but it was an improvement over the taste inside my mouth.

I realized I was not alone. I yanked my face out of the water. A policeman's flashlight beam focused on my head. "Bath time?" asked the cop. I blinked up at him, water streaming from my hair.

"Sorry, officer, I had a bad night."

"I can see that. You got any ID?"

"Wait a minute." I looked around. My wine-soaked suit jacket was bunched up on the bench, where I must have used it as a pillow. "I'll see."

I reached into the jacket pocket. Miraculously, the wallet had not been stolen either. I fumbled for it and produced a driver's license.

"Walter Schotzke? Like the mustard?" the cop snickered.

"That's me. I mean, yes, I am the mustard."

The cop stepped back for a minute, shined the flashlight for a better look. Something he saw changed his mind, I don't know what.

"If you are, what the hell are you doing sleeping in the park?"

"It's sort of a long story."

"Let me guess. You work in a congressman's office."

"Actually, yeah. Or I did."

"They always do. OK, go home."

I grabbed my ruined clothes and started to walk … but not home, not yet. I needed to do something else first. As the sun rose over the Capitol, it lit up the monument above the fountain I'd bathed in. I'd been sleeping just a few steps away from a lofty white stone shaft, a kind of bell tower. In front of the shaft stood a bronze statue of a long-ago leader of the Constitutionalist party. Into the shaft was carved a tribute to the "honesty, indomitable courage, and high principles of free government" of the man to whom the statue had been raised. The good old days? Nah. If those qualities had ever been abundant, people wouldn't bother to memorialize them when they showed up, then or now.

It took a few tries to hail a cab, but eventually a less discriminating driver accepted me. I gave the address of Senator Hazen's apartment.

The night doorman recognized me. A tall, salt-and-pepper military retiree, who looked and sounded like Muddy Waters in his last years, he asked sympathetically, "What happened to you? You look terrible!"

"I got shit-faced drunk last night. I threw up all over myself. But I promised the senator I'd be here very early today."

"Well, you got more than an hour for a bath before it's time to walk! Good idea to arrive early, before those protester creeps show up."

"When do they usually start?"

"Usually about seven. Should I buzz the senator?"

"No thanks. I'll go straight up. He's expecting me. I don't want to bother him unnecessarily."

I rapped softly at the senator's door. The housekeeper opened. She opened her mouth in amazement at my appearance.

"I have to talk to the senator, Gabriella. It's important. He'll want to see me."

She opened the door uncertainly, and I stepped into the apartment's little foyer. A few moments later, the senator was standing in front of me, a burgundy silk robe over his pajamas.

"I'm very sorry to show up like this, sir. I had to see you, and, yes, I was drinking a little–"

He grinned and then laughed out loud.

"I raised two boys. I've seen it before. Now you go into the guest room and take a shower. We keep spare toiletries under the sink. My son Jonathan is about the same build as you. He leaves his clothes in the left-hand drawers of the bureau. You should find something to wear, a pair of chinos or something like that."

"Thank you sir. But I wanted to say, I'm sorry – it's all my fault – Brad – Nia – that asshole Benjy – Patriot News …"

He waved me silent. "Apologies sound better from a tooth-brushed mouth."

"Yes, sir." I reappeared in his dining room fifteen minutes later, scrubbed and clean, wearing nothing of my own except my shoes. The senator was also scrubbed and nearly fully dressed, waiting to hear my story. On the table awaited the toast, the egg, and – hallelujah! – a carafe of coffee.

"I told Gabriella you might prefer something stronger than tea this morning."

I poured myself a cup, added sugar, and gulped it down, black and sweet. I drink a second cup. Then a third. The senator watched the fluid disappear.

I recovered myself a little and gathered my words. "Senator, I don't know what to say. I am so very sorry – I know that's useless – but I'll do anything to make it right! I'll write a statement, go on TV. I wanted to talk to you first so I didn't do anything stupid. It seems everything I do is stupid. And I wanted you to know, too: I'm quitting my job with Elmer. I'm done with politics. I hate politics. I'm leaving Washington. You are the finest man I've met here, and I've done you nothing but harm."

Hazen shook his head over his tea and toast, over the white tablecloth and the heavy silverware and the Marie Antoinette china. "Don't flagellate yourself, Walter. And don't flatter yourself either. If they had not found the Chauncey story, they'd have found something else. There is always something. You think I've been in politics all these years without making compromises?"

"I don't know. I only know I'm sorry."

"I appreciate that. I don't appreciate that you are quitting politics altogether."

"It's a dirty business!"

"Yes, it is. Always was. Do you think it will be better without you?"

"*I'll* be better without politics."

"Really? You already seem a wiser man than the aimless young person I hired five months ago out of respect to his father's memory."

He offered me the rack of toast.

"More of a wise guy, you mean."

"Yes, that too."

"Maybe the problem is, I don't want to be part of a party that contains Elmers and Mallorys."

"You think it's any better on the other side? You think it's ever been better in any political party anywhere? Read about the party that saved the Union. The details will make you sick to your stomach."

"Is that the best justification? Everybody does it? Senator, I've *seen* it. I've seen Elmer scrounging for money, Daphne lying for hire, and Vernon Mallory inventing his so-called data. I saw Benjy Barstein falsify his videos and Juanita Bimpan spew hate on the airwaves. I saw Mark Dunn make a hero out of me when I didn't deserve it – and a monster out of you when you didn't deserve it either."

The very old get wrinkles in places you never imagined a wrinkle could go. Hazen's eyes folded into elephant flaps of thoughtfulness. After a long pause he said, "I always felt that if I waited long enough, I'd have one more chance to cast a good vote before I retired. Now here it is. Too bad we're going to lose."

"You're not going to lose," I exclaimed. "The White House is calling back Iggy Hernandez! I overheard that at Elmer's yesterday."

"I know."

"*How?* It's a super-secret!"

"Seamus told me last night. He's leaving the White House to clear out of Iggy's way. Iggy found Seamus a job as a vice president at the Port Authority of New York and New Jersey."

"Wow, that's harsh." I took another medicinal swallow of coffee.

"It easily could have been worse. Iggy's appointment will be announced in the East Room at 11 this morning. They have asked me to stand with the president, and of course I will. But it's too late. Iggy cannot turn this around, not now."

"Elmer said the same thing."

"Whatever else he is, Elmer is no fool."

"So what's the point of it all, senator? Why shouldn't I just head home to – wherever home is?"

As if repeating a formula he'd used many times before, he intoned, "If the best people don't govern the country, who will?"

"But maybe that's what the bad people said to themselves, back before they became bad."

The senator did not react to this restatement of Valerie's counter-wisdom. He glanced at his watch. "I have to finish dressing."

He returned to the dining room fully assembled. His tie throbbed bright-orange-and-blue.

"A bold choice in neckwear, sir," I joked in an imitation of a British butler's accent.

"Why should Iggy have the spotlight all to himself?" Then he turned serious. "Listen: I want to talk more about all this, but I have to start my walk now if I'm to be on time for the day. You should not be seen with me. Leave now. Exit the building through the rear door. I'll give you a ten-minute head start. Write to me at my Rhode Island home address and tell me what you have decided to do."

"Maybe it's time you got yourself a personal email account."

"Too old."

"Not you."

We shook hands. I descended the elevator, exited, waved goodbye to the morning doorman, and slipped out the rear door. I could hear the demonstrators jostling and yelling in front of the building. The crowd sounded extra militant today. Patriot News had done its work. I wanted one last peek at history before I headed home to tell Valerie it was time to plan our move out of Washington.

I turned the corner and walked around the building to join the throng. There must have been at least 80 of them, perhaps more, filling the grassy walkway leading toward the Navy Memorial and the Archives to the south, the Portrait Gallery to the north: legacies from the time when Americans hoped that if only they designed magnificently enough, the people might live up to their buildings.

This crowd lived up to nothing. Mostly older, mostly kind of seedy, they looked like the hardest core of the Trucker Protest: retirees who had lost their savings; men in late middle-age who would never work again. You'd feel very sorry for them, if they weren't so obnoxious.

I finessed my way forward, stalling at the third row, where I was blocked by a solid mass of a man in a light windbreaker. What an odd thing to wear on a warm morning in May. I tried to edge my way around his left side for a better view.

He turned an angry face to me. He was young, my age – the only other young person among all the gray and bald heads. "Stand back, bro," he snarled and jabbed his elbow at me. It hit me hard in the chest. I staggered and sputtered, now angry myself.

"Stand back yourself, *bro*," I snarled, both my hands shoving with all my force the arm and shoulder that had hit me.

A huge explosion. A shriek of pain. And the man I'd shoved collapsed onto the sidewalk in front of me, his left pant leg staining itself crimson. As he dropped, I could see a gun in his right hand. It all happened too fast for thought.

I stepped onto the man's gun arm. Screams all around me, people running away from the terrifying noise. I bent to grab the weapon from the hand. I met no resistance. The bleeding man had fainted or died, I couldn't tell which. Police replaced the protesters around me. I handed the gun to one of them.

The world seemed even more strange and remote than when I'd awoken on my park bench 90 minutes before.

"That took guts," said the cop who took the gun. And now here was Senator Hazen eye-to-eye with me on the broad emptied sidewalk, his face full of worry and … maybe … pride?

"Are you all right?" he demanded, inserting himself between the cops and grabbing hold of my hand, the hand that had just surrendered the gun.

"I think so. Yes. Yes, I am. But you know what? I'm still a little drunk."

"Then drinking suits you." He put his arm around my shoulder and led me to a seat inside one of the police cars and its flashing red-and-blue light.

CHAPTER 77

I need to stress something: I never told anybody I'd seen a gun in the shooter's hand. Never!

But every time I tried to explain that I had *not* seen the gun, somebody interrupted me. When I first gave my statement to the police, Senator Hazen stood beside me, improving the story as I talked. No D.C. policeman will contradict a U.S. Senator, especially not one who has just survived an assassination attempt.

By the time the media converged on the scene, Valerie had arrived. Dazed as I was, I still noticed that she looked extra good in an eye-catching turquoise spring dress – almost as if she had anticipated that today would be a day with a lot of photography. She made an elegant contrast to me; I was still wearing Jonathan Hazen's ill-fitting clothes, now spattered with big splashes of the shooter's blood.

The police allowed Valerie to cross the security lines. She raced to me, kissed me, and told me how worried she'd been for the past 12 hours. Then she clutched my left arm in both of her hands and jerked hard every time I tried to correct the Hazen-dictated mistakes in the original police report.

"I didn't actually see the – OW!"

So the narrative that took form that first morning went more or less this:

Mustard heir Walter Schotzke had resigned his job in Senator Hazen's office to protest the senator's support for the deficit reduction package. On the morning of the shooting, he had joined the crowd of anti-Hazen protesters. He glimpsed a gun in the hand of one of the protesters. True to his commitment to peaceful dissent, Schotzke heroically pounced on the gunman at risk to his own life, saving the senator and who knows how many other fellow protesters and passers-by from the 31-shot clip in the gunman's magazine.

Patriot News especially loved this version of events. It conveniently refuted any suggestion that the network's anti-Hazen broadcasts might possibly have motivated the shooter.

One of the nation's top radio talkers declaimed in his noon broadcaster that very first day:

"All the drive-by media lined up to blame Patriot News, the Trucker Protesters, and Mark Dunn for the attempt on Hazen's life. Then it turns out that the guy who saved up to 31 lives on that sidewalk, including Senator Hazen's life, was a Trucker Protester himself. The guy who grabbed the shooter's gun was Walter Schotzke – who quit Hazen's office over the housing tax-grab! He was a guest on the Mark Dunn program. Yet the Nationalists want to blame *us*! They are unscrupulous, amoral, vicious, lying …"

The would-be shooter survived, although his leg had to be amputated where the bullet had shattered the bone. He turned out to be a unemployed community-college dropout who had taken a bus down from New Jersey. As far as anybody could tell, he had never watched an hour of Patriot News. True, the shooter's father had worked for a while for Elmer's friend, Omar – but that association was years old and dismissed by all as coincidence.

The Nationalist media had no appetite for investigating murky associations in immigrant communities. The Constitutionalist media liked the story the way it was first told. As for the remains of the mainstream media, they were too depleted and harassed by budget cuts and shrinking audiences to re-investigate a settled story. Prosecutors would eventually send the would-be shooter to prison for 17 years on charges of violating gun laws and recklessly endangering human life.

Those charges conveniently avoided the issues of intent, plan, and associations that might have been raised by a trial for attempted murder. Sometimes I'd make noises about doing something to set the record straight. Valerie always cast her veto: "Everybody likes the story the way it is."

Meanwhile, the Hernandez announcement event in the East Room proceeded on schedule. The press corps gave Senator Hazen a standing ovation as he entered the room. The blue-and-orange tie looked great on TV.

As both Hazen and Elmer had predicted, not even Hernandez could rescue the jobs and deficit package. The plan was rejected by the full House by a 58-vote margin.

The president had wanted to help the unemployed. He'd discovered that the unemployed counted for nothing. He'd wanted to vindicate some personal notion of fairness. He'd been defeated by the ferocious resistance of those who did count. President Pulaski had aspired to transcend the party system. Instead, that system overwhelmed him, as it had overwhelmed his predecessors.

Like the military professional he was, Pulaski quickly recovered from his repulse. He adapted his plans and reorganized his forces. Step 1 was to recall Hernandez. Step 2 was to assent as Hernandez commenced organizing an amended version of the economic package.

The revised economic package delighted Constitutionalists. Hernandez proposed to relax environmental regulations, promising to create new jobs in the oil and gas industries. He proposed an array of tax cuts for the upper-income brackets. He proposed to balance the budget with spending cuts, especially to food stamps and health subsidies for lower-income Americans. He dropped Pulaski's marijuana-legalization scheme as too controversial.

The Nationalists who had nearly welcomed Pulaski as one of their own now recoiled from him. The streets filled with new protesters, younger than the Trucker Protesters and carrying placards with edgy, ironic slogans. "What About Us?" they called their movement.

However, the balance of power now tilted decisively in favor of the Pulaski administration. Hernandez brought with him indispensable reinforcements to the cause. Patriot News executed an about-face with military smartness. The *Wall Street Transcript* fell into line. Elmer saluted and obeyed, whatever he may have felt on the inside. Benjy Barstein, Juanita Bimpan, and all the others like them followed. Of course, David Maurice adjusted easily to the new regime. If anything, his clients preferred the revised version of the president's scheme to the original. The revision paid them even more and cost them even less.

If the polls were believed, the voting public did not much like the 2.0 version of the Pulaski plan. At the next election, the Nationalists won enough seats to deprive the Constitutionalists of their majority in the House of Representatives. But the Constitutionalists clung to a slim majority in the Senate. From that stronghold, they successfully beat back the Nationalist attempts to impose extra taxes on affluent America. And frankly, the Nationalists did not really try very hard.

Hernandez's new plan did not deliver quite as promised. Yet the war in Mexico did wind down. Housing prices did recover. Hiring did improve. The stock market did begin a gratifying upward climb. Most folks would not see again the kind of prosperity they had enjoyed in years gone by. On the other hand, the typical voter was certainly better off on re-election day than at the end of President Williams' single term in office. That might not sound like much, but it was enough to re-elect Pulaski at the end of his four years.

In the new Hernandez-led era, Elmer Larsen suddenly became "the man to see" (as he was proclaimed in a big feature in the *Financial Times*). Elmer expanded into a sideline lobbying venture and soon gained a small fortune. Eighteen months later, David Maurice's firm bought Elmer's – and the two men became partners in a super-firm, Maurice+Larsen LLP. Valerie and I flew down for the party celebrating the merger.

Mallory flourished too. About the time that the first deficit reduction plan failed in the House, Gordon Munsinger suffered a near-fatal heart attack. The Constitutionalist Institute board voted to hire Vernon Mallory to succeed him. Mallory forced Kohlberg into early retirement and hired Daphne Peltzman as his new number two. Soon afterward, the CI Founders' Floor was emptied out to accommodate Mallory's expanded new personal publicity and communications staff. The Founders themselves were instructed henceforward to work from home.

All of these dramatic political events came to me as news from far away. On the morning of the attempted shooting, I finished my letter of resignation to Elmer. I filled it with compliments, emphasized my respect, and expressed my hopes that we could keep in touch if my return to the business world prospered.

And prosper it did.

As my grandmother had predicted, General Brands always had a job for a Schotzke, especially one who had just risked his life to save 31 people, including a U.S. senator.

Three years and three promotions later, I reached the presidency of the Schotzke mustard division of General Brands. It's not as important a job as it sounds. Finance, marketing - really everything important – is run from corporate headquarters in Manhattan. My job is mostly to star in TV commercials. You've probably seen them:

Sepia images of workers in cloth caps and coveralls mixing mustard in wooden barrels.

Cue Walter: "Since 1872, my family has made Schotzke mustard according to the same traditional recipe…"

In fact, as division CEO, I've made only one important decision: to retain division headquarters in Providence. The decision provoked a short struggle with the corporate over-lords, but I own enough General Brands shares that it's tough to overrule me when I really want something.

The shares are mine now. My grandmother died during my second year at General Brands. Her will generously dissolved all the family trusts, and I inherited my father's and grand-father's estates directly. Did I mention that Iggy Hernandez's second deficit deal had permanently repealed the estate tax?

Valerie is renovating the house in Little Compton. While we wait for the contractor to complete his work, we spend most of our time in a condo I bought in downtown Providence. I sold my grandmother's Barbados house, ditto the Park Avenue maisonette. With a baby on the way, Valerie says she can't be responsible for twenty-six bathrooms.

Valerie and I are married, of course. Don't pretend to be surprised. And yes, *I* asked *her*. Late on the night of the shoot-ing (actually, in the early hours of the next morning) – after the police were done with me and the phones had stopped ringing, after the last of the booze had left my system – I sat in a chair in my dark bedroom, contemplating the curve of Valerie's sleep-ing cheek on the pillow. I decided: no more running and hid-ing for Walter. As Hazen would say, the important thing about love isn't how it starts. It's how it lasts.

Charlie Feltrini finally got the appointment he deserved. He's serving now as our ambassador in Guatemala, a very important observation post on the continuing unstable situ-ation in Mexico.

I found Jeff Gillespie, my friend from the Exxon station, a job in the accounting department at General Brands. He'll be CFO someday.

I heard a little while ago from another old friend: Samir. About a year and a half after my return to Providence, my assistant said, "I got an email request today from somebody who said he was an old friend of yours, asking me to schedule a telephone meeting."

I was surprised – very surprised – but very glad.

When Samir and I connected, it was instantly like old times.

"I wanted to say how sorry I was that we ended our last talk on such bad terms." He sounded truly sincere. "I wanted you to know how much I admire your courage."

"Thank you," I said, and meant it. "I am truly touched."

"It comes from the heart," he answered

"What are you doing these days, anyway?" I asked, enjoying the rekindling of the old friendship.

That question launched the old self-confident voice into action.

"I just finished a year's visiting professorship at Stanford. I taught political science and mass communication. I loved teaching, and I think it will be my ultimate vocation. But I'm back in Washington now."

"That's great!"

"Yes, I've signed on with Maurice+Larsen. Actually, that's part of the reason for my call. I've noticed that General Brands has scattered its government-relations work around half a dozen different firms, as if your divisions were all still independent companies. That makes no sense. I think we can show you that you could achieve some very powerful synergies – and save GB a lot of money – if you concentrated all your business with us. I'd oversee the account personally, of course. With the new Nationalist majority in the House, you need a firm that can talk to both sides of the aisle. I'd like to schedule an appointment to fly up to Providence to run the numbers past you ..."

Being Samir, he was very convincing.

Hazen and I talk every week by phone. He never did get that private email account. But he's happier and looking a lot less frail since he married Senator Anderson. The wedding took place at her Montana ski lodge, attended only by immediate family and a dozen of the couple's close friends, including Valerie and me. As we settled that night into our private cabin on the grounds, Valerie twinkled at me, "So that's how the really rich do it."

Our own wedding occurred on a larger scale: more than 300 guests at the Newport Country Club. After the ceremony, Valerie's dad clutched my hand.

"We all underestimated you. You are a good and brave man."

"Thank you," I said. Then I thought: Valerie was right. People really do prefer the story as it is.

I get to Washington maybe four or five times a year. Freddy Catesby got his money from me. Soon afterward, I was elected the chairman of the board of the *Constitutional Review*. A few weeks later, Vernon Mallory requested an appointment with me. Now I'm a patron of the Constitutionalist Institute as well. At this past year's annual dinner at the Washington Hilton, Daphne greeted me rhapsodically. Vernon insisted on having his photograph taken with me. Vernon and Daphne had offered me a chair at Table #1, beside Vice President Pappas, but I declined. I'd bought my own table so I could host Celestine, my French-economist mentor from my own CI days, as well as my new chum Vladimir Stankovich, recently returned from the archives in Moscow on a travel grant courtesy of the Schotzke Family Foundation.

All these donations were made on Senator Hazen's advice. "Sooner or later," he said, "you will unavoidably make some enemies. You want to maximize the number of your friendships when you can."

"I don't know that I want to be friends with all these people."

"Not friends. Washington friends. The important thing about a Washington friendship is that there's nothing personal about it."

"OK, so do I also make a donation to the Center for National Progress? I'd have even more Washington friends then."

"No. You have to pick a side and stick to it. Nobody trusts anyone who tries to be on both sides."

"But isn't this whole idea of 'sides' kind of stupid?"

"Yes, it is. That's exactly why it must be enforced so strictly!"

It's tempting to work hard at the mustard business and see if I can get as rich as one of Senator Anderson's ex-husbands. But Senator Hazen has another idea for me.

Rhode Island will not likely soon again elect a Constitutionalist in an open-seat election. But Senator Anderson has already retired, and Hazen has been getting fidgety too. It's still 14 months until his term expires. If he retires now, the state's governor will appoint a replacement to hold the seat. The governor's a Nationalist, but as Hazen points out, the governor owes me big-time for keeping Schotzke headquarters in Providence through the recession. And besides, the Nationalist governor (as usual) hates the most obvious Nationalist candidate for the Senate seat.

Hence Hazen's plan:

Hazen retires early. The governor appoints me to fill the seat on an interim basis. When the balance of Hazen's term expires, I then run as an incumbent. And not just any incumbent, but an incumbent who rebuilt Providence's hockey arena, now Schotzke Arena. An incumbent who added a Schotzke Children's Wing to the Rhode Island Hospital. An incumbent who risked his own life to save 31 people from an assassin on Pennsylvania Avenue. Hazen insists: "If we can get you into the seat first, your re-election will go down as smooth as Schotzke's honey mustard."

Personally, I'm not totally enthusiastic about the idea. But Valerie loves it. So I suppose we all know what the final answer will be.

If I do take the Senate seat, I know what I want to do with it. I learned some important lessons from my first Washington experience. Don't try to change everything at once. Don't look for some grand bargain that will transform the political system on one glad day of redemption. Above all, don't wait for the people to rise up in righteous indignation. You could wait a long time for the rising, and if and when the people do at last rise up, you'll most likely find the equivalents of Hernandez and O'Grady working the controls on behalf of the equivalents of Velkampt and Horvath.

But suppose just a few of us – people with a little more security than most, people who have less to lose than most – suppose *we* decided to work together to fix one of our country's problems? And then another? Maybe a third after that? We might work a substantial change for the better, not all at once, but gradually over time – until it's our turn to leave the work to younger hands and fresher faces. As Senator Hazen did.

You are not required to finish the work, Hazen wrote to me in a letter. (On paper, with a stamp.) *But neither are you permitted to shirk it.*

I had the feeling he was probably quoting somebody. With Hazen you never can tell.

Enclosed in the envelope was an unmistakable quotation, a print-out from one of the books Hazen is always recommending me to read:

"Many who before regarded legislation on the subject as chimerical, will now fancy that it is only dangerous, or perhaps not more than difficult. And so in time it will come to be looked on as among the things possible, then among the things probable; and so at last it will be

ranged in the list of those few measures which the coun-
try requires as being absolutely needed. That is the way
in which public opinion is made."
"It is no loss of time," said Phineas, "to have taken the first*
great step in making it."

"The first great step was taken long ago," said Mr.*
Monk, "taken by men who were looked upon as revo-
lutionary demagogues, almost as traitors, because they
took it. But it is a great thing to take any step that leads
us onwards."

A few days ago, I stopped by Hazen's dad's former store.
I introduced myself to the new owner, the Peruvian chicken
roaster. We had a long talk. And you know what? I think
maybe I can help him a little after all. The chicken was pretty
good too: crispy skin, lightly seasoned, juicy inside. Thinking
of Valerie, I skipped the sauce.

END

ACKNOWLEDGMENTS

This novel has benefited from the comments and criticisms of many friends. It's probably most tactful for me not to name specific names, but rather to say to each: I am intensely and eternally grateful for your generous help as I learned in midlife to write in a way I'd never written before.

Some names, however, can be singled out:

Arianna Huffington, who with her unvarying elan and flair backed this project to the utmost;

Tina Brown, who gave me the liberty and space to complete it;

Jay Mandel, who transformed vague hopes of a new approach to publishing into a working reality;

Britton Schey, who did the work;

John Montorio, who midwifed this book's public debut;

Tim O'Brien and Andrew Lowsowsky, who supported every step;

Hannah Todd, who solved production problems infallibly;

Elizabeth Shreve, for bringing the book to the public eye;

And above all, my wife Danielle Crittenden Frum, who lives in every line of these pages, and who was at once editor, critic, agent, psychiatrist, publisher, and muse. May Walter be as happy and grateful in his choice as I have been in mine, over a quarter century of love and joy.

Made in the USA
Lexington, KY
17 August 2012